Ryan's legacy comes from generations of plumbers and mechanical tradesmen. Growing up in a small business, and surrounded by colorful people has shaped Ryan into the person he is today. Discovering his love of writing while in college, Ryan used any and all spare time to develop his creative works, which would one day become more than just a dream.

For my brother, Jarrod. If only we could go back to '89 and listen to gangster rap in your empty work van (with those massive subwoofers) again. RIP.

Ryan Rex

AMERICAN DYSFUNCTION

The Ballad of Alex Walker

AUSTIN MACAULEY PUBLISHERS™

LONDON • CAMBRIDGE • NEW YORK • SHARJAH

Copyright © Ryan Rex 2023

Ordering Information
Quantity sales: Special discounts are available on quantity purchases by corporations, associations, and others. For details, contact the publisher at the address below.

Publisher's Cataloging-in-Publication data
Rex, Ryan
American Dysfunction

ISBN 9781649799722 (Paperback)
ISBN 9781649799739 (Hardback)
ISBN 9781649799746 (ePub e-book)

Library of Congress Control Number: 2021923476

www.austinmacauley.com/us

First Published 2023
Austin Macauley Publishers LLC
40 Wall Street,33rd Floor, Suite 3302
New York, NY 10005
USA

mailto:mail-usa@austinmacauley.com
+1 (646) 5125767

I would like to thank Amy Gill Yanofsky, Penny Fried, and Gina Farabelli Meyer. Thank you for pushing me to find direction in my life.

Chapter 1
Alex

The party starts at 7:30. The early start means pregame for those invited. Zilla's parties kick off that way each and every week. Especially on Thursday nights. By the weekend, the college in Williamsport's basically a ghost town. Tuesday through Thursday is a different story.

Alex gets out of the shower and wipes off the mirror. The landlord hadn't fixed the exhaust fan since he moved. The only heater sits in the living room of their two-bedroom shit box. It's a gas-fired wall unit with a small fan. If Alex or Chad slept with their doors closed, they'd shiver all night. Blankets help. Lots of blankets. Or good sex with Gina. Whichever. His roommate frequently sleeps out, so Alex basically lives alone.

Most of the apartments in the Ulman Manor are like that. The place is an old converted Victorian home from a different era in the town's history. Back to its glory days. When men were men. Woodsmen culling trees, sending the partially milled trunks down the river where they'd be turned into lumber. The logging industry in Pennsylvania turned common men into millionaires back then. That was a long time ago. All that's left are the old mansions. If you can still look at them that way.

Alex takes out a can of shaving cream to hack away at the budding stubble on his chin and corners of his mouth. His beard isn't close to coming in, but Gina says it gives her a rash when they kiss. So Alex shaves it. No big deal. Worst that can happen is it grows in thicker, and he'll finally look old enough to get a fake ID.

Alex gets halfway through the white Barbasol cream beard with his orange Bic razor, but can't finish. It's too quiet. Alex doesn't care much for silence.

He puts the razor down, making his way across the kitchenette to the bedroom. Some shaving cream drips off his half-shaven chin on the carpet. He stops to rub it in with his toe before finding the phone in his room.

Walking past the posters in his room, Alex feels the inspiration wash over him. His drawings on the walls. Dr. Dre's "The Chronic" and Snoop Dogg's "Doggystyle." Two classic album covers that Alex had put on poster board after seeing his favorite cover band in Williamsport perform last semester. Chad's their drummer and their lead singer; Adam became Alex's best friend. They thought it was cool that Alex could draw so well.

Before selecting music, Alex gazes at the other poster. His favorite superhero: Moon Knight. The Marvel Comics' version of Batman. Moon Knight has a special place in Alex's heart.

He picks up the phone and hits the side button to kick it on. Punches in his code: 4552. The last four digits to his dad's number back home. Alex hits the *ON* button for the pill-shaped speaker box on his dresser. The music queues up on his phone. Save the old school rap for later. Right now, it's No Doubt's "Don't Speak." Gwen Stefani's voice gives him the chills. It's one of Gina's favorites.

Alex and Gina discovered the beauty of '90s music when they'd go see Adam and the rest of the misfits in Polyester Anarchy at the Rainbow Room over on 4th Street. It's the only bar that lets them in without an ID. Drinking's off limits because the owner got hit with a hefty fine the year before when the cops busted him for underage drinking. It doesn't matter much to Alex. He goes for the atmosphere.

After feeling the music for a few seconds, Alex makes his way back to the bathroom. He loves the way his skin feels after a clean shave. The mint scented aftershave with a hint of patchouli works to calm his nerves. The fact that Alex is going back to Zilla's house freaks him out. He can feel beads of sweat running from his armpits. Alex reaches for the Old Spice antiperspirant. Three rolls under each pit. Any more and his undershirts get a nasty yellow color. Alex's dad once figured out how to get rid of those in the wash, but it was once and done. His dad was a little too drunk that afternoon to remember how exactly the feat was accomplished.

The weather in April had gotten warmer. Once the sun goes down, it would cool off by party time. Zilla's frat house gets real hot inside though.

Alex needs to prepare himself for multiple climate changes throughout the night

He opens a dresser drawer. The faint sound of wood on wood grinds as the drawer opens toward his waist. Shirts. Neatly folded. Arranged by color and type. Tees to the left and hoodies to the right. A black long-sleeved tee and his favorite green hoodie would do it. Alex gently presses down the piles of clothes before closing the drawer. Never leaving it open. Like nobody was ever there. Everything in its place.

Last is the hair. Alex keeps it high and tight. Something passed down from his grandfather who served in Vietnam. Alex frequently thinks of his war stories as he'd sit in the barber chair. He opens the closet to get something to style it. Alex thinks of how his grandfather swore by using Vaseline. Too old school. Alex reaches for the lotion. He squirts exactly two pumps into his palm then massages it into his scalp to shape his dirty blonde hair. Not quite spiked, not quite parted. Somewhere comfortably in the middle. The lotion is a trick he learned from Zilla last semester.

Alex got too drunk to walk home one Wednesday night so Gina asked if he could crash in Zilla's "lair." The guy's kind of a human freak. Juiced up, and seemingly ready to fight or fuck at any time. So it's natural for an animal like Zilla to call his bedroom as such. Gina still hangs out there, probably getting high, but whatever—Alex doesn't really care. She's the only reason Alex still goes. When you hang in the Sigma Beta Delta Frat house, it goes with the territory.

***

After Alex woke up that morning, he found Zilla standing in his private bathroom, stark naked. Shaving his balls. Alex shivered.

"Sup, Dudeman!" Zilla shouted. It's his nickname for Alex. Frat boys need nicknames for everyone.

Alex couldn't have been more annoyed. "Hey man." He sat up. "Can you cover that thing?"

Zilla stopped shaving long enough to shoot Alex a look of disbelief with his big hog wagging back and forth like a pendulum.

"What's a matta, you got a problem with the braciole?" He pointed at his package with the DX *Suck It* motion. Zilla referred to his manhood like an Italian delicacy. He's a handsome Italian guy from Jersey and never lets anyone forget it.

"Dude." Alex averted his eyes. "I feel like you're about to whip me with that."

11

"I could if I wanted." Zilla put on a towel. He reached for the body lotion. Pumped a liberal amount in his hand, then without thinking twice, massaged into his hair.

Zilla saw Alex looking. "It's better than hair gel plus it doesn't flake up. Want to try?"

After that fateful morning with Zilla, Alex never used hair gel again.

***

Alex shuffles around his bathroom putting his toiletries away.

Chumbawumba sings "Tubthumping" in the background. Alex loves this tune.

He finishes getting ready. 6:30. Time to roll.

At the Quickstop, Alex grabs a hotdog while he waits for the party to start.

He's supposed to meet Chad and Gina there. Zilla has strict rules about who he lets in first. Gina and Chad are on the "A List." The frat boy minions enforce who gets in early. Alex doesn't need to have that fight.

The hotdog's overcooked by about half a day. Alex eats it regardless. The Quickstop has good spicy mustard and warm sauerkraut. It reminds Alex of a recipe from the German side of the family. Mom's side.

The Davies were from a small town nearby in the mountains. Coal town, USA. Her family had been in those mountains since the Revolutionary War. Their original ancestor was a man named Hansel Boner. His granddaughter would eventually marry into the Davies family.

Alex would quake in his sneakers when mom told that story at Thanksgiving dinner. Alex wanted to pronounce the name with a long *A* sound like Bonner, but it wasn't. It was Boner. Like the morning wood.

Boner was a Hessian soldier. A mercenary hired by the British to fight the war over the Colonies. The deal was for each Hessian to get half their money upfront then the rest upon his return. If the Hessian was captured or killed, the second half would not be paid. Boner gave the first half to his wife before departing.

Surrounded by the Colonial Army, Boner's fellow mercenaries were killed one by one until he was all who remained. Boner was given the option to die or join the cause. Capturing only went so far in those days so Alex's ancestor did some quick thinking. First, he wouldn't get the rest of his money, and second, he could never go home because of dishonor. Ultimately, he chose not to die. Lucky for Boner, his wife never spent the first portion. After the war, his family could afford safe passage overseas. His lineage leading directly to Alex and his day-old hot dog with kraut.

Alex finishes his meal over by the ATM. He watches as crackheads enter and exit the store. So shady. He knows they're crackheads because of how they come in pretending to look at the glass pipes in the case, but really want the straw-shaped ones behind the counter. There's lots of drugs in Williamsport. All over the place. People like to pretend the worst drugs and crime happens in cities. It doesn't. Could arguably happen more in the sticks where there's nothing else to do besides drink, get stoned, or screw.

7:00. Still too early. Alex needs some entertainment. He leaves for the six-pack shop where the high school kids try to score beer from people walking by. Alex likes to give himself an over under to see if any kids actually get any beer while he watches.

On the way, he walks past the gigantic brick house where Zilla and his fellow Sigma Beta Delta douche boys live. The beauty of the yellow rose bushes climbing the decrepit front porch looks out of place compared to the dead grass and messy front yard. Alex sees people going in the side door to pre-game. No line on the front porch yet. Feeling that familiar twinge of rejection, he keeps moving toward the beer store for some light entertainment while he waits.

7:30. Alex walks back to Zilla's house. The beer store was a dud. Only two high school kids, and no homeless people to buy them forties. A complete and utter disappointment. The sun drops below the houses on the west. It's getting dark.

Alex steps on the messy front yard. As he gets closer, the line for the party becomes visible. It's not too long tonight. Alex can barely make out the faces in the purple color of the blacklight above them. Once he steps on the porch, Alex hears a familiar voice call his name.

It's Adam. Alex sidesteps some people to cut in line to stand with him, Jesse, and Rick. Three of the four members of Polyester Anarchy.

"Sup, gentlemen." Alex slaps hands with Adam and moves in for a quick hug without letting go. He does the same for the other two guys.

Alex notices Adam's Yamaka and pants match. All black. Part of his

13

religious beliefs. Adam only owns three colors of shirts—black, white, and occasionally maroon. Variations in fabrics, but all very similar. Tonight, he went with the maroon button down. Rick and Jesse dressed casual in jeans and hoodies.

Adam's the only actual believer in the group. Once selected as lead singer of Polyester Anarchy, Adam convinced the guys that a shtick was needed to draw the crowds. Their gimmick became dressing like members of the Hasidic Jewish Community, or Hasidic Jews as they refer to themselves, and they owned it. Alex loves watching them rock out to old school '90s jams. It's unfortunate they can only get gigs at one bar in town, but Alex feels lucky. It's within walking distance to the Ulman Manor. He and Gina could make it there in about ten minutes. Alex feels bad about all the old heads and rednecks in town giving the guys crap about playing a gay bar. *People need to get woke*, Alex thinks to himself.

Adam looks at Alex with a perturbed expression. "You're missing the usual plus one."

Adam's tone annoys Alex. He and Gina do not get a long at all. "She goes early for pre-game."

"Following the 'path of illumination' one would assume," states Adam.

Not a question or an answer. More of a dig.

Rick turns around, seriously wanting to change the subject. "Zilla changed the name of the early party?"

Jesse chimes in too, "What's the path of illumination?"

Adam rolls his eyes. "It's a Dan Brown reference. You wouldn't get it."

If it wasn't for their sick music skills, Adam probably wouldn't be friends with either Rick or Jesse. He enjoys their talent, but the shared level of intelligence leaves a lot to be desired.

Dan Brown is Alex's favorite writer. It was the first conversation he and Adam had when they met. Chad introduced them at lunch one day. It was nice to find out Adam's from a school district close by Alex's hometown. They bonded immediately over of their collective love or art, books, and pop culture. That night they went to one of Zilla's parties. It was early last semester. Alex would never forget it.

In the Sigma Beta Delta basement, Alex and Adam dominated the competition at beer pong. They celebrated after winning for a third time by chugging their beers, but the fun wouldn't last. One of the frat boy minions, being a total jerk, walked past to flick off Adam's Yamaka. The fraternity referred to all their pledges as minions and typically seen being herded around by Unicorn, Zilla's second in command.

Adam being of a slight build and gentle disposition, politely picked the beanie off the dirty floor. He calmly brushed off a cobweb and put it back on. Before resuming the game, he gave the minion a solid middle finger right to his face. Alex was impressed.

Alex remembered Unicorn standing nearby scowling at the minion. His face and words sounding like typical white supremacist. "You just gone take that from a little Jew boy like him?"

"'Course not, I got this," said the minion before shoving Adam into the pong table. Beer splashing as he did. Adam recoiled to wipe the foamy yellow droplets from his shirt.

The minion closed in for smack talk. Face to face.

Alex thought of Adam's body language. Shoulders slumped, eyes to the floor. As the minion rambled on, his words were drowned out by the music. Alex couldn't remember much of what was said, just the bad vides. The minion's eyes and facial expressions reminded Alex of hard times growing up. As harsher sounds came out of the minion, Alex's insides pinched with empathy toward his new friend.

Adam was scared. His shoulders said it all. It was probably clear to everyone there. Alex felt fear like that himself as a lonely child when he lived in Philly. Being bullied was part of the deal for him. Alex learned to fight as a matter of survival, and for what he lacked in size, he made up for with heart.

Alex wasn't sure about stepping in right away. He never really took the minions seriously. It was when the bully grabbed Adam by the shirt Alex changed his mind.

Alex moved without thinking. Quickly dropping his left shoulder, then unwinding with a right hook to the minion's jaw. The fight was broken up quickly. He and Adam were bounced out.

On the walk home, Alex found a homeless guy to buy them forties at the six-pack shop. They each had three bucks, which bought two forties of Hurricane. Hangover in a bottle.

When they got to the Ulman Manor, Adam and Alex celebrated with a game of Edward Forty Hands. They wrapped the forty-ounce bottles to each other's palms with duct tape and drank till dawn. It was tough turning the TV on, so Alex nudged the remote with a toe. They got stuck on one channel all night. It was cool though. Watching old episodes of Anthony Bourdain's travel show "No Reservations" gave them lots to see. Such a big world. They talked about how great it would be to travel together, all the places they could visit.

It was a bonding experience for the ages.

Alex waits patiently with his friends on Zilla's porch. Five people walk out the door. They're next in line. Each produces ten bucks at the door, and in they go.

In the kitchen, they wait in another line for the keg. Alex looks at his phone. 7:50. He's late. No sign of Gina. She's around. The night is young.

Jesse and Rick get offered beer bongs by one of the minions. They huddle in the corner for the ritual.

Adam and Chad bump into each other. They decide to move toward the basement for a smoking session.

Alex doesn't want any part of either. Beer bongs make him too full, and he doesn't want anything to do with that hellhole basement. The stories that people tell. Like the night Zilla turned the fraternity's yearly hazing ritual into an actual fight club.

Zilla almost flunked out his first semester. He couldn't keep up with his school work during Hell Week, which is a huge no-no in frat boy land. Part of the hazing includes an older frat brother following around a "pledge" or in this case, a minion, to make sure he gets up for school on time, attends all his classes, and doesn't screw up. This act takes place each day of Hell Week after the potential minions drink and get high until the sun comes up. Zilla's brilliant idea was to take micro naps whenever he got a free moment. Apparently, it was an idea that came from a social media meme.

Taking the meme a little too seriously, Zilla ended up taking a micro nap in his brand-new Toyota Supra. However, when you take a micro nap at stop light then bump the Dean's car directly in front of you, it's not such a bright idea.

That night, the sitting President, Unicorn, told Zilla if he didn't win the drinking contest, he was out. It was the last day of Hell Week, and Zilla had only one shot at redemption. That night changed their fraternity in a big way.

It was the Beer Olympics. Six hours of straight drinking as fast as you can. The perfect combination of chugging, speed, strength, and endurance. One of the events was a chicken fight. Tigger was on Zilla's back. Those two were boys straight from the word go. Zilla on one end of the social spectrum and Tigger on the other. They must've balanced each other out. The guy on the opposing team clotheslines Tigger off Zilla's back. The minions cheered, but what they weren't expecting was Zilla to catch him by the leg and whip Tigger around to club his opponents to the floor. A feat of strength that resembled a sort of brutish poetry in motion causing a bench-clearing brawl. All the other competing minions rushed in to fight Zilla at once.

Unicorn saw an opportunity. Before the fight started, he declared if anyone could knock Zilla off his feet, they'd be king of Hell Week and get their pick of frat house positions the following month. Another thing they didn't expect was Zilla's professional wrestling experience or his Jiu Jitsu training. The guy's a psychotic monster to begin with, but his raw ability allows Zilla to reach the pinnacle of douchebaggery at will.

There were twelve pledges. All were flat on the ground within minutes. The stories ranged from Zilla using suplexes, pile drivers, hip tosses, dropkicks, clotheslines, you name it. Supposedly Zilla even climbed up on the pong table to frog splash Tigger at one point. No one was safe. Once Zilla's eyes rolled back in his head, the bodies hit the floor. One after the other.

Apparently, he was so jacked up on Speedballs (coke and Ritalin), it would've taken a truck to knock him down. Zilla cleaned house that night. It could've been bullshit. Or maybe Zilla is exactly who he pretends to be: one badass motherfucker.

After the fight, Zilla had his moment in the sun. Unicorn, being a man of his word, granted Zilla the opportunity to pick the position he'd run for during the next election.

Zilla replied with one word, "President."

The guys are off doing their thing in the basement and Gina's nowhere to be found. Alex finishes his beer alone. He walks to middle of the room to toss the empty cup.

From a distance, Alex sees a familiar face walking toward him. It's Moat, the campus drug dealer. Flanked by a couple of his crackhead followers. A female and a male this time. Moat's crackheads never really speak without laughing. Kind of like the weasels from "Who Framed Roger Rabbit." Not that Moat is Judge Doom, but the people who followed him around are so odd and greasy looking.

Moat slinks closer to talk. Sporting a tie-dye shirt with a bright green pot leaf smack in the center of his fat-ass upper torso. The shirt clashes terribly. Moat smiles. Looking greasier and more clever than both his crackheads put together. Alex wonders if smashing their heads together could create someone slightly greasier than Moat.

Moat closes in. Alex gets in bro-hug formation. Moat receives it graciously while leaning in to reciprocate the quick chest bump and back tap. The hug is cold. The smile on Moat's face is hollow. Alex knows why. He doesn't buy drugs, which means Moat basically has no respect for him. Alex can feel the tension.

Moat speaks first, "Whatchu' doin', Dudeman? Getting fucked up tonight or what?"

Moat's one of four guys who calls Alex, Dudeman. The other three are members of the frat.

Alex decides to ignore the attitude brewing inside himself. "Not much, bro. Just doing whatever. I'm looking for Gina. You seen her?"

Moat makes a face like he smelled shit. "Have I seen her? Dude, you must be jokin', man?"

The attitude surfaces. Alex scowls. "It was a direct question, Moat.
Wanna tell me where she is?"

Moat's attitude bubbles to the surface too. "Check this out. You're, ahem, girlfriend, if that's even what you can call her…"

Alex cuts him off. "I don't know, you greasy motherfucker. What else would I call her?"

Moat slaps his fist in the other palm in a thinking gesture. Then decides to break it down properly. "Alex, me and you are cool. I respect you because you ain't a total bitch. So I'll pretend this conversation's going to be civil while I drop some knowledge on you. Ya dig?"

Alex feels a cold chill run down his spin. Moat's body language changed in a way that Alex couldn't quite describe. "Yeah, I dig."

Moat looks Alex dead in the face. "I sell Gina liquid roofies so her and Zilla can drop 'em in each other's eye balls. That way she won't remember a thing when they're fuckin'. No alibi necessary." Alex feels his soul fly out from his body. Moat leans in to get the last word. "You're her backup plan, Dudeman."

Time stops as Alex's soul flies around the room. Alex knows it's true.

Deep down inside. He always knew.

Moat sees blood in the water. His attitude goes full throttle. Moat's not finished with Alex yet. "Oh and by the way, that night you passed out here in Zilla's room. Wanna know why you didn't wake up next to her?"

Alex doesn't want to know, but Moat's mouth was running too fast for him to stop it.

"It's because Zilla and Unicorn were doin' the Eiffel Tower to her downstairs." The blood drains from Alex's face. "Yeah, that's right. They tag teamed her in the bathroom where Unicorn makes his mescaline." Feeling justified, Moat bows a little when he stops speaking.

It's a gut punch. More than that. Alex wants to cry, scream, and kick Moat in the nuts all at the same time. His heart broke in ways that he never imagined possible. Not the first time a girl hurt Alex. Just so much worse than before.

Alex floats in space and time to chase his fleeting soul. He could faintly hear Moat speaking in the background.

Moat leans over to the crackhead on his left. "Yo, I think I broke him."

Alex wanders through the house like a ghost. After forcing his way through large crowds of people, he eventually reaches the hallway leading to Unicorn's room.

Once Alex reaches the second floor, he almost has a meltdown by Unicorn's dark bathroom. When he approaches it, the emotions begin flooding out. He fights back tears. Then he looks up and almost shit his pants. Alex sees what appeared to be a person floating over the bathtub. His natural reaction is to do what any red-blooded guy would do. He punches it. The plastic feeling of pleather on his knuckles, makes Alex stop himself.

Something's not right. Alex thinks to himself as he flicks on the light. What he saw makes him flinch again. The Gimp costume. Just like the guy wore in "Pulp Fiction." Hanging there right over dead cactuses in the tub.

"Man, this place is weird," Alex says out loud.

Alex shakes his head before turning the light off. "The Unicorn Experience" they call it. Body shots and mescaline.

Alex continues through the halls. *This house is like walking through a labyrinth.* He thinks as he imagines himself in ancient Greece. On a mission to fight the Minotaur. At the moment, Alex couldn't remember how that journey turned out for Theseus. Maybe he could find a magical weapon somewhere on the way for an edge over Zilla. Maybe not.

19

When he reaches the steps for Zilla's lair, Alex finds it hard not to stare at all the wacky pictures of Zilla. Of him and only him. Doing insane things. Seems to be fifty of them. Littering the walls on each side. Flanking Alex as he walks up the staircase. Zilla's psyching him out already.

Music coming from the top of the steps sounds like an old school Jodeci song "Come and Talk to Me." Same one Polyester Anarchy played late night when he and Gina got it on in the bathroom of the Rainbow Room.

Alex didn't know of the song until that night. Gina had it cued up on her phone afterward for an encore back at her place. He could still hear the words in his head…or is the song still playing upstairs?

Jodeci croons on.

Zilla's Lair. The music. What may or may not be happening upstairs. He's already inside Alex's head. And the pictures. *Wow*, Alex thinks to himself. Walls full of conceited behavior and genuine overindulgence.

One picture shows him playing football, appearing to be a running back.

Hand out in a stiff-arm. Scoring many touchdowns, Alex imagines.

In the next picture, Alex sees Zilla as a professional wrestler. On the top turnbuckle like Jimmy "The Superfly" Snuka. Getting ready to splash an opponent.

Another picture of him bodybuilding, showing all his muscles. Stark naked. Juiced up and bulging from every angle of his greasy body, including his bare ass. *Not surprising, but somehow tastefully done*, Alex thought. Zilla couldn't resist the urge to expose himself whenever the opportunity, ahem, arose.

Alex thinks of that morning he woke up in Zilla's room. It all makes sense now. Gina set Alex up to pass out then disappeared for the night. Did she roofie him too? Alex shudders at the thought.

Another of Zilla skydiving. Apparently, selfies in freefall are completely acceptable by modern standards.

Alex gets closer to the top. Over the music he could hear sounds. Not the kind Zilla usually made with his face while raving about himself. Another kind. Familiar. A sound Alex had grown to love. A sound he couldn't imagine being made with another person.

It couldn't be. Alex has to see for himself.

The doorknob within reach now. He feels a cold chill run up his spine again. Like the one Alex got the morning when he was nine.

It was fall. Saturday morning. Alex woke up early. He wanted a bowl of cereal and cartoons. Instead, when Alex came downstairs with a blanket and stuffed Ninja Turtle in hand, what he got was much more than most children can handle.

Alex remembered the fight dragging on. The violence. The screaming.

Both of them crying. Back and forth all day. Then going into the night.

Tony had fallen off the wagon again. He and Alex's mom were fighting over Tony's drug abuse. He made a comment about Sue's looks. How she would never be beautiful like his ex. That's when she slapped him. Tony tackled her, picked Sue up and slammed her on the couch. Wrapping his hands around Sue's neck, Tony strangled her until she turned purple. Alex woke up and came downstairs at this point. When he saw his mom in need, Alex jumped on Tony's back. He flicked Alex off like a little bug. Alex landed on the corner of the slate fireplace, which cut him. Eventually leaving a scar on his shoulder. Something Alex can feel to this day.

Sue's adrenaline hit high gear. She jumped up and kicked Tony in the balls, dropping the man to his knees. As he cried in pain, Sue ran young Alex up to his room for safety then back down to continue the fight with her angry, doped up, second husband.

Fear overwhelmed Alex. He needed to be strong like the superheroes in his cartoons. Then he remembered the ninja costume in his closet. The one he kept from Halloween. Alex put it on, grabbed the plastic sword and crept down the stairs.

He peered into the living room from a crack between the black cotton fabrics wrapped around his face. There was Tony. Their eyes locked. Alex froze. A nine-year-old trying to fight for his mother's honor with a plastic sword against a man experiencing a full-on cocaine rage.

Alex knew for the first time in his life what it meant to feel powerless.

Alex swore to himself one day he'd be strong enough to fight back. "Never again," Alex said aloud as he reaches for the knob.

From behind, Alex can hear Adam and Chad race up the steps to stop him. Moat must've told them everything.

Adam reaches passed Chad. He grabs a piece of Alex's shirt, but the door swings open. They're too late.

Chad gasps.

It was worse than they had imagined.

Alex flinches at the sight. He feels like Captain Jack Sparrow after meeting an old flame. His face pinching and his body jerking backward at the same time nearly falling into Adam.

The song changes on Zilla's radio to LL Cool J's "Around the Way Girl." Life moves in slow motion.

LL fills the air with lyrics.

Adam speaks with remorse, "I told you to stay away from her. Now look what she's done to you."

Alex barely hears Adam. The scene is exactly what he didn't want, but the same he imagined in the back of his head for months. Alex couldn't deny it anymore. Almost like his subconscious wished for it by accident.

Alex takes the scene in fully. It's the both of them. In bed. Gina on the bottom with Zilla jackhammering from above. The air's sticky with the smell of sex. The haze of the room reminds him of a sauna. Disgusting. Gina's too messed up for eye contact. Her head bobs from side to side. The roofies. Zilla, on the other hand, has the pain tolerance of a buffalo. He didn't even blink when Alex opened the door.

"Gina! What the fuck are you doing?" No response. "Zilla! Get off her!" Alex lunges, but is caught by his friends who are finally able to get into the mix to hold him back. "Let me go!"

Gina's head rolls toward the noise with a sign of life.

Alex gets a good look at her face. The lights are on, but nobody's home.

Yet, in spite of the intoxication, she's clearly enjoying herself.

Chad gets in front of Alex. "Alex, stop! She's not worth it!"

Zilla peels himself off Gina. Never shy about being naked, letting his big coke bottle dick wag back and forth. He lumbers toward them.

Adam holds Alex from behind. "He's coming. Let's get out of here!"

Alex thinks about Adam's unintentional pun, but shrugs it off. No time for jokes.

Alex focuses on the monster approaching. Zilla may be twice his size, but Alex has more heart. It's what got him through life so far. He'd squared off with much worse people than "Dickzilla" in the past.

Zilla is on them now. He grabs Chad by the shoulder and tosses him aside like a ragdoll. Next, he clutches Alex by the shirt with both hands to pull him in close. Alex is scared shitless, but refuses to let fear stop him now. Not tonight. He swore it to himself when he turned that doorknob.

Alex notices his legs dangling, barely supporting his weight. Zilla's massive arms hold Alex slightly off the ground. Alex tries searching for more courage, but can't stop paralysis from creeping up his spin. Giving in, Alex's arms fall limp to his sides.

Zilla speaks first. His eyes hollow like Gina's, yet his body completely functional somehow. "How goes it, little man?" Zilla moves his head to the side looking Alex up and down. "Gonna do something or what, Dudeman?" Zilla waits for a response. He gets nothing from Alex. "Your girl's right over there on the bed. I mean shit, since you're here, you want a turn or what? Unicorn says she's pretty good. Thought I'd take a turn first. Know what I mean?"

Alex summons all the strength he can, picking up his arms, raising them to Zilla's face. Zilla's grip like a vice. Alex realizes no matter how much he struggles or fights back, Zilla would just squeeze him until the lights go out.

Alex thinks of home. The letter opener. Dad never used a letter opener. Only an extra-long and sharp thumbnail on his right hand. One so strong it could be used as a screwdriver. Alex keeps his thumbnail long too. Maybe to be like his dad, or maybe it was a premonition. At this moment, he knew exactly why he kept it so long.

Alex grabs Zilla's face with his left hand, the old iron claw maneuver. As Zilla's head cocks in that direction, the skin on the right side of his forehead shimmers from the overhead lighting. Alex runs his long, sharp thumbnail over Zilla's right eyebrow slowly with all the force he could. Alex transfers his desperation to Zilla's eyebrow.

The vice eases up a bit.

The white upper layer of Zilla's forehead skin splits, exposing the purple under-flesh. As the deep cut opens, blood runs into Zilla's eye. Slowly at first, just a slight drip, but as Alex keeps his thumb moving, the trickle becomes a stream.

Zilla lets up to the point where Alex can push away.

Zilla stumbles back. He instinctively puts the base of his palm to his eyebrow to stop the bleeding.

Alex gets mad now. His fear replaced with rage. The thrill of having a slight advantage takes over. The Philly boy comes out. "What's up, Ric Flair? Can't deal with a little blood in the eye? Not so tough when you can't see, huh?"

A toilet flushes in the bathroom. Zilla, still holding his eye together, motions for them to wait. "Oh, this is the best part. You faggots got here just in time."

Chad's on his feet now. Alex hates it when people use that word around his friend. The three of them stand together in the doorway for a moment, watching Zilla manically laugh as the bathroom door opens.

A woman walks out in the filthiest lingerie Alex has ever seen. He recognizes her. It's Jamie, Gina's roommate. Black straps cover all her nasty bits, but could easily be moved for access. She stands in the doorway with a sexiness to her that Alex never thought possible. Jamie had always been Gina's average-looking friend, quiet and sort of mousy, but currently looking like something out of a horny guy's wet dream.

"Soo, we gonna do this or…" She looks at Zilla puzzled, too doped up to notice the guys in the doorway. "Hey, what's going on?"

Zilla points to the guys, "Look, babe, we got company."

Jamie turns to the doorway like a deer in headlights. She screams before retreating to the bathroom with a slam of the door.

Zilla can't control his laughter. He slaps his leg with the bloody hand. It makes a wet thud. "You can't buy entertainment like this. The look on her face! Your faces! Fuckin' priceless!"

No one laughs besides him.

Out of nowhere, Zilla's face goes flat. He stops laughing as if it were never funny at all. He looks at Alex with those cold dead eyes. "You really want a piece, little boy?"

Alex peers past Zilla with a last hope of Gina regaining consciousness. Sadly, there's nothing. She looks like a dead fish lying flat on the bed. Breasts out, eyes rolled, completely still. Hopelessly fucked up.

Zilla catches on. "Oh, she's not gonna help you. You on your own tonight, bro."

LL Cool J stops rapping. Once again, the music in the background resembles art imitating life.

Alex focuses on Zilla. Straightening up. Courage taking over instead of good sense. "Yeah, Zilla. I've had enough of you for one lifetime. Let's get this done."

"We'll do it properly. Outside. Fifteen minutes," Zilla declared as he wipes blood off his face with a towel. He reaches for some Vaseline to fill the cut.

There's nothing to do now but move forward. Alex knows it, yet nearly craps his pants when the words come out. "I'll be waiting."

The party inside all but ceased when word spread about the fight.

Outside, the crowd gathers. Alex waits alone in the middle of the front yard. One of the minions instructs him to remove his shirt and shoes. They were "gonna do it Fight Club style." Alex feels the familiar cold sting of the sweat beads rolling down his back muscles. His armpits sweat badly when he's nervous, and boy is he nervous right now. He paces back and forth.

Alex takes a break from his nerves to evaluate the scene. He recognizes most of the faces in the crowd. Some supportive, but Zilla's way more popular. As it turns out, people have been teasing Alex behind his back for being a lovesick puppy. Absolutely pathetic.

Alex looks at the faces in the crowd. They look back with disapproval. Mob mentality. Once word spreads, you can forget going back. Nothing would ever be the same again. Alex knows it. A loud sound distracts him from the new wave of rejection. Music blares from the windows.

The song transforms into a hardcore baseline accompanied by a voice that shaped the minds of a psychotic micro generation filled with self-indulgent young men.

"More Human than Human" by White Zombie. Straight from old school ECW. Hardcore at its finest. Alex remembers hearing stories about his dad and Uncle Scott cruising down to the wrestling arena in South Philly back in the day. All the greats were there.

The thought of Alex being in a similar situation gives him the chills. At that moment, Alex realizes he's the bad guy in Zilla's story.

The music rages on.

The blacklight on the porch blinks rapidly. One of the minions must be flicking it on and off for effect. Tigger runs the smoke machine from the porch. Alex thinks it looks like a haunted house.

The bass from White Zombie rattles the rickety windows in the old mansion. *It's amazing there's no cops around or even anyone who'd want to call them*, Alex thinks.

Zilla walks out on the porch. The black straps on his arms looking like an accessory the Ultimate Warrior had strapped on to keep his massive biceps from exploding. Wearing only bright red banana hammock trunks. His hair slicked back, muscles greased up, presumably from the same vat of Vaseline he kept next to his bed.

The music gets louder.

Zilla seems to grow from the pump of the music. He lifts his head to stare at Alex from the porch without blinking.

Alex's heart stops, "Aw, shit."

Zilla reads his lips. The psych-out worked perfectly. He runs off the porch stopping a few feet from Alex. The fight begins. Zilla holds out his hand to bump fists.

Alex isn't feeling it. "Come on, dude!"

"Bump it, fag!" Alex takes his eyes off Zilla's face to bump it. It's a trick.

Zilla swings first and hits Alex square in the face.

Sometimes during a fight, mob mentality moves with the punches. In this case, everyone leaned to one side then recoiled when the wet thud made an echo through the darkness.

Alex instinctively reaches for his eye. Zilla seizes the opportunity to shoot on Alex's legs. Taking him down hard. Alex's shoulder blades absorb the impact. He yelps with pain.

The sound makes Zilla happy. He pulls Alex's left arm and wraps his tree trunk legs around Alex's neck. Leg scissors with an arm bar. Alex knows it.

He fell right in. Zilla squeezes. The air stops flowing to Alex's head. His eyeballs bulge from the pressure. No rules here. Alex hopes someone would break it up before he dies.

Realizing a fate worse than death, Alex sees how close in proximity his face is to Zilla's cock. Close isn't the word. At this point, his boss hog rests right on Alex's cheek. Too much to handle. Alex goes into survival mode. This is it.

Alex reviews his options: Die with Zilla's dick on his face or take life by the hog. Alex knows what must be done.

He turns his head. Zilla's dick now on his lips. Alex opens his mouth and bites him right on the shaft.

Zilla howls with pain!

The crowd shifts again. Muted sounds of disgust file through their ranks. The only familiar voice Alex can hear is Jesse egging Alex on, "Get 'em,

Alex. Get 'em! Bite that dick!"

Alex feels the uncooked sausage wiggle between his teeth. Like chewing on a rubber change purse that a realtor gives to children during a block party.

Another life-changing event from a night that would scar Alex for the rest of his days. He internally justifies the heinous act because no one came to his rescue. No one ever comes to his rescue. He's alone. Fighting a fucking nightmare of a human being. Alex had no one to rely on but himself. The move was ugly, maybe. Effective, hell yeah.

When Alex lets go, Zilla recoils to hold his damaged goods. Alex pumps with adrenaline. He goes Cobra Kai on Zilla. *No mercy,* he decides.

As Zilla rolls on the ground in pain, Alex dropkicks him in the face. Zilla falls to his stomach. Holding his face now.

Alex falls back. Gets a running start and Superman punches Zilla. Alex feels something crack in his hand. It was like punching steel. The adrenaline would hide the pain for now.

Zilla sees the punch coming, but can't stop it. He rolls with the blow, tumbling to the porch near the yellow roses. The prickers dig in his skin. Drawing blood. Zilla takes a labored breath while trying to get to his feet.

Alex sees the gap and moves in with a flying knee to the head. Zilla's eyes roll back then he's out.

Alex wins. Miraculously. The flying knee did it. The sweet taste of justice fills Alex with pride. Exhilarating.

This bully. This shitty human being. Taking Alex's pride. Taking his girl.

Blatantly disrespecting him over and over again.

Finally, tonight Alex got it back. He got it all back.

Alex reaches down to pull Zilla up by the straps on his arms. Same as Zilla did to him upstairs. Alex can't resist sliding Zilla across the face one more time with a right hook. His hand cracked again from the blow.

A trickle of blood falls from Zilla's mouth. Splashing lightly on a rose petal.

Alex brings him in close by the armbands. Feeling cocky. "Got somethin' to say now, big man?"

There's a stirring on the dark porch above their heads. The blacklight on the porch blinks rapidly. Alex only hears the sound of shuffling feet. Zilla barely responsive, rolls his head back for a look.

Alex rants, "Let me explain something…Dickzilla…if you ever touch her again, I'll…" Alex gets distracted by something on the porch. He stops speaking. The shuffling gets louder. Alex looks up. No time to move.

Bong! Alex gets *his* bell rung this time. Only it's not from a flying knee.

It's from Tigger. Running at him with an empty keg from the darkness. Ramming it into Alex's face. The sound more than just a bong. It's a hollow thud with the clank of metal on flesh and bone. Kind of like a hammer hitting an anvil covered with a wet towel. Solid yet slick. Alex slumps over to one side. The keg rolls off into the bushes. Tigger jumps off the porch giving Alex an elbow drop to the chest.

The crowd rushes in. Zilla regains enough consciousness to run away.

While Tigger pounds on Alex's face with a rapid fist, Unicorn kicks him in the ribs.

Chad and Adam regrouped with Rick and Jesse by this point. They come to Alex's rescue. Pulling Tigger and Unicorn off their defeated friend.

Chad and Unicorn get into it with open fists pretending to fight hard. Rick dives in with a punch to Tigger's jaw.

Jesse and Adam try to pick Alex up while the others fight.

Blue and red lights flash from the street. Everyone knows what that means. The cops.

A squad car hops the curb, landing on the dead grass with a metallic thud. The siren cuts through the air like a red-hot knife. The onlookers scatter like cockroaches from an exterminator.

Jesse drops Alex on the spot and dives into the bushes.

Adam can't carry Alex alone. "Sorry, buddy. I'll have to owe you one." He disappears into the darkness.

Rick sees them bolt and quickly follows.

Unicorn and Tigger dart to the side of the house, out of sight.

Alex is all who remains. Lying there alone. Next to the bloody roses.

One of the cops gets out of the squad car. He walks to where Alex is lying. He nudges Alex's arm with a booted foot.

Lights out.

Chapter 2
Gina

Gina wakes up on Zilla's bed. Jamie lay next to her. Gina fumbles for her phone. It's on the table next to Jamie. Her bare chest lay on Jamie's face while she grabs it to check the time. Not like it's uncomfortable. Last night, they shared each other and Richard. At the moment, he's nowhere to be found. Typical.

She and Jamie must've made their way back to his room after the fight. Gina remembered all the commotion. Seeing Alex's angry face was like a nightmare. The feeling of disgrace began creeping up into her belly, but it wasn't her fault. It was the drugs. It always came back to the drugs. She just couldn't resist. Last night was different, though. Last night was life-changing. She would have to quit for a while if Alex would come back. Not like he actually caught her and Richard before. Yet, it didn't play out like she had expected.

The anticipation of being caught was like a drug itself. Heart racing, butterflies in the belly, the coke, the sex, the hiding. So hot. She puts on a song as she gathers her clothes. Gina queues up an oldie that reminds her of Alex. Jodeci. "Lately."

Gina's eyes tear up as she wipes the make-up off her face to get herself in presentable shape before the Sigma guys shout at her and Jamie for doing *the walk of shame*. She puts some toothpaste on her finger to brush the stink from her face.

Jamie stirs in the bed. Gina spits then goes to wake her friend. Jamie's bare breasts show. Gina remembers more from last night. She and Jamie weren't a regular thing, just on special nights. Like last night. Gina knew it was coming. She wanted to go out raging. Now comes the balance. Now comes the hangover.

Jodeci reinforces her depressed mood.

On the walk home, they encounter exactly two minions. Each kind enough to point out the *walk of shame*, as predicted. In turn, each is ignored. Ugly dorks. Not like they have a chance.

She holds onto Jamie, who could barely stand up. After a night like that, Richard would be at the gym just after sunrise. He would expect the partygoers to be gone when he got home. Including the *hoes*. Gina hates being called that. She really hates it. There has to be a reason she does this. It's the drugs, she tells herself again.

In their building, Gina struggles to get Jamie up the stairs. Luckily, Alex and Chad weren't outside. Those two had a habit of doing early morning laundry when everyone else was hung over. Who does that after a night of partying?

Jamie heaved a little at the top of the steps. Gina quickly opens the door and rushes her to the bathroom. Jamie lets it all out. Gina holds back her hair. What are girlfriends for?

After the purge, Gina helps Jamie to her bed. Gina thinks Jamie smells horrible. Then realizes they shared the same bodily fluids. Not a pleasant thought. Gina desperately wants a shower.

She turns on the water to let the shower steam up the bathroom. While she's waiting, Gina empties her purse. The imitation Gucci one she got from her mother at Christmas. The only time they see each other. She headed back to Pittsburgh after visiting Alex's family. *What a holiday*, Gina thinks. Seeing Alex and his semi-hot dad in the same room, then getting pole-dancing lessons from her mother less than 48 hours later. It's like Alex once said, "You live a wonderfully strange life, Lady Gina." Lady Gina had a nice ring to it. Much better than being called a ho. Her wallet opens. The polaroid of her and Alex. The night they met playing beer pong. Arms around each other. Smiling. She kisses her fingers. Touches the photo. Snaps the wallet together.

Steam enters the hallway. Gina snaps back into reality. She rummages through the contents of her purse. Transferring the items into her top dresser drawer. Birth control pills. Check. Leftover condoms. Check. Shit, the same amount she had yesterday. Ah, that sucks. Moving on.

She finds what's left. The drugs. They have a special location in the drawer.

She moves around the lacy bits to find *the box*. The wooden box her Daddy made for her when they lived in Kentucky. The one he fashioned from the old rosewood tree that fell down in the backyard. He was really sorry for getting too drunk that Saturday night after Mom moved out. It wasn't his fault. Sometimes men just need a certain kind of attention. Thinking back, it was nothing really. Only happened once. Daddy made up for everything when she opened the present.

The box was similar in shape to a cigar box, but ornate in a way that only an artisan woodworker could create. Daddy had the artistic gift. Kind of the same as Alex with his drawings, but this gift came out in the way of carving wood.

She ran her fingers over the familiar whimsical texture of the box's perimeter sections. The feeling reminded her of something Frodo Baggins would've gotten from his Uncle Bilbo after one of his great journeys. Another reason Gina loved Alex. He sometimes reminded her of Sean Astin. "The Goonies" was her favorite movie growing up, not to mention "The Lord of the Rings." Watching those movies with her Daddy as a teenager were some of her favorite memories. Especially after Mom left.

Gina flipped open the top carefully, not to damage the antique silver hinges in the back. Her eyes light up when she feels the rush of contentment that comes with the security of the box. How it creates secrecy for the items within.

She fills the box with bags of drugs and pill bottles. She grabs one of the orange containers and pushes down on the white lid to get it off before closing the lid. Gina pops some Perks to calm her nerves. The shower waits.

After getting clean, Gina wraps herself in dry towels before wiping the steam from the mirror. The eyeliner dripped badly down her face. She'd need a fuckin' chisel to get it off. Under the sink, she finds a chisel in a bag. Hot damn, make-up remover!

She cues up a song on her phone while she works on her face. Thinking of Alex, she picks one of her favorites from Cyndi Lauper, "The Goonie 'R' Good Enough."

Then there's Richard. He and Gina started school the year before Alex showed up. They had something for a minute during first semester. Since then, it was just here and there.

When it happens, she has trouble resisting. Richard is everything Alex isn't. Tall, dark, well built, and hot! Alex, on the other hand, brings out the princess in his *Lady Gina*. Making her feel like the damsel in distress when he'd comfort her after a nightmare. She'd feel rescued by the handsome,

31

dashing prince. However, during these nightmares, Richard brought out the woman in her, having her do things she would never do with Alex. Was it the drugs or a real nightmare she'd wake up from in Alex's arms? Thanks to the roofies, who could tell the difference?

She remembers the night Alex and her truly connected.

At Zilla's house. In that dank basement. It was the first time they talked since the incident with Mr. Walker. Those shorts. Gina saw Alex wear them to school one day. It made her feel uncomfortable. She had never been paid for sex before that day. It was like crossing a line of sorts. Something she never thought possible.

Alex nuzzled up next to her at the beer pong table.

Unicorn made a comment about Alex being one of the biggest dorks in school. Alex got angry. His face. The same one he made at Richard last night. So much pain.

Gina wanted so badly to make a difference in someone's life. In his life. She threw her arms around Alex and kissed him in front of everybody. It made Alex beam. She felt happy for him.

Unicorn made an ugly face after the kiss. He remarked about the disgusting public display of affection. She saw Unicorn as a poser. Maybe his dad was a big-time contractor, but if they had real money, he wouldn't be going to school in a hellhole like Williamsport. He'd be at a big-time university. Or maybe Unicorn's just a failure in life. Another lost soul, not living up to the expectations of his overbearing father. A trait Alex and Richard shared for sure.

Tired of the predictability of the frat boy attitude, Gina turned to Alex. Getting close enough that her curly hair engulfed his high and tight head. She whispered to him lovingly, "Take me home or lose me forever." Just like Kelly McGillis in "Top Gun."

That night, and many after that, Alex relived his first night in Williamsport. Gina made sure of it.

The rhythm of Cyndi Lauper's voice made the make-up come off easier.

As she reached for her lotion, Gina felt the song ending.

Gina looked at herself in the mirror. Good enough will never do. She needed to clear the air with Alex once and for all.

Her phone rings in the next room. She rushes to nswer. It's Richard. She picks up. Alex can wait.

Chapter 3
John

John Walker sits at his desk doing paperwork. It's sundown. After work. Time for billing. He looks out the office window into the alley below. His house on Church Street was the only one built with an office over the garage. The stone homes in this part of town hark back to another time in history. A simpler time. When immigrants were brought overseas. Some worked in the Asbestos plant. Others built the stone houses surrounding it. The town of Ambler, Pennsylvania grew exponentially in those days.

John thought back to when Alex was beat up as a kid. Less fortunate kids from the row homes over on Park Avenue. Alex called them poor white trash. John scolded him for saying those things. Alex was wrong for that. Didn't deserve to get jumped, but still wrong. Those were hardworking people from good families. John knows who fed Alex that information. Thankfully, his mother Sue left when Alex was twelve. Just slightly too late. She left alright, but not before damaging the boy at his core.

Leaving John. Marrying Tony Mangle. John's former best friend, whose resume included failed actor, formerly abusive stepfather, and current drug addict.

Sue was no better. She dragged Alex through the mud. Moving him to nine different schools before the 7th grade. Poor kid was a pawn. Her own son. Using child support as a living wage. Her ploy to drive a sports car. She and Tony would show up at the bar bragging about how they only shop at Bloomingdale's. Then there was poor Alex. Getting teased at school. He wouldn't even have clean socks to wear. Giving him hand-me-downs from his brother.

Tony eventually influenced Joseph too. Convincing him to follow in his stepdad's footsteps. Moving to New York, pursuing a career in stand-up comedy. John should've known Joseph would fall into "the life." Something

Tony had done himself after a run of bad luck.

Joseph lasted a full two years before getting hooked on cocaine and gambling himself into debt. Just like Tony, only Joseph wasn't Italian. He didn't have the same clout Tony did. Who knows what Tony had to do to earn his way into that life.

It all came to a climax one Easter morning when Joseph overdosed at Sue's house. Right in front of his little brother and twin sister. Joseph had been invited to spend the holiday with Diane and Alex for old times' sake. Little did anyone know that he would show up in the middle of the night on a coke binge. The seizure is what woke everyone in the morning. That's when John stepped in. Man, was it ugly. Trying to put the pieces back together of his oldest son's life was tough. Bailing Joseph out of debt from the bookies in New York put John back a few bucks alright. Twenty thousand to the mob for betting on college football games. *What a waste*, John thought to himself.

It was after a stint in rehab, Joe came home and found Jesus. That's also when he asked to officially be called Joseph. Going through the twelve-step program at Narcotics Anonymous. It helped put Joe back on track. Becoming Joseph wasn't such a bad thing for the kid. It is his given name anyhow.

John turns around to see Joseph working quietly on a plumbing quotation. Their desks sit across the room from each other. A job for a new customer. One Joseph found himself. A huge pit would have to be dug in order to change out the sewage pipe from the house to the curb. They'd done it hundreds of times over the years, but John never let Joseph or Alex in those holes. Not until this time. Up until now, it was John's job. He being the boss and father would be the one to get buried if the ditch collapsed. These days, things are different. John's not moving as fast as he used to. Getting older.

For the job, Joseph is to use Murray's Excavation. John refused to hire anyone except Ed Murray. He's the best in town. Besides, Ed and John go way back.

Ed had a certain way of doing things though. He'd use the bucket of the backhoe to hold up the dirt while John worked in the ditch. Shoring was too expensive and time-consuming. John convinced Ed to bring plywood on this one. It was too deep and would be Joseph's first time in the hole. His job from bid till check. John wasn't going to let it be Joseph's last.

A Harley pulls into the alley just beyond the window. It burns out, leaving a trail of dust. John rises to his feet getting a better look. The dust clears. A

Chopper with a red, white, and blue gas tank. Scott. John's favorite drinking buddy. Showing up for their weekly Thirsty Thursday brouhaha.

Joseph would be leaving for his addiction meeting soon and had plans to eat out with the guys after. John and Scott would have beer for dinner. John tells Joseph to wrap it up for tonight and take off.

Scott was John's friend from childhood also. Tony and Scott never got along. They fought like cats and dogs. Tony was Italian and Scott was Irish. Scott's family moved to Ambler back in middle school from Oreland, a small town only a few miles down the tracks. Different school district. High school rivals. Back in those days, the Italians in Ambler didn't like newcomers, especially of the Irish kind. John was exempt from that form of cultural rage. His family had been of Quaker descent. Peaceful, hardworking people. The Walkers were ancestors of the original settlers of Ambler. Been here since the time of Billy Penn.

John walks down the office steps to the alley. Scott sees him and starts doing another burnout. John waves away the dust. Scott stops long enough for John to get a few words in, "Better ease up, Scott. Cops'll get ya like it's Mischief Night."

Scott looked annoyed by the memory. "Bullshit! You know I did you a favor. It's the only reason Joe escaped from the car."

John needs to bring Scott back to reality. "You punched out the window of a squad car, Scott. You know how much free plumbing work I gave out to clear your names?"

Scott let that sink in for a minute. "Huh. Yeah, I guess punching out a cop's window wasn't the best idea. Did I ever say thank you for that?"

"No, and I don't see you with a case of Pabst for tonight either."

Scott looks around like he dropped something. "Must've fell off on the way over here."

"Yeah, sure it did." John is playing. There's always a cold case of Pabst around for Thursday. "Come on, dick. We have a date with an old man for a Phillies game."

John opens the garage and starts up his Harley. They speed off.

Riding through Ambler in mid spring is beautiful. The trees blooming. Thick humid air. Slightly cool, and still sunny. Spring training is over and baseball season's underway. Passing the little league fields on the ride makes John feel nostalgic. Growing up in Ambler. Remembering playing ball with

Tony and Scott as kids. Their bus stop was there too. Then going to Ambler High. Such great memories. John and Scott were the stars of the wrestling team. Tony was the starting quarterback. They ruled.

The sun goes down as they ride up Park Ave. Passing the row homes before turning on Euclid Ave. The only street in town with the big Victorian homes. It was the street John and Tony grew up on. They park the bikes in the alley behind John's childhood home.

John sees his dad, William, pop his head out from the backdoor. "Hey, it's bottom of the ninth. The Phils got two men on base!" William sees Scott came empty-handed. "No beer again, Scott? Gotta check that saddlebag. Looks like another case got lost on the way over. Better hope your wallet didn't fall out too."

Scott instinctively checks for his wallet. He turns to John. "Everybody's a god damn comedian round here. It was a rough week." Scott is half serious.

John heard through the grapevine that Scott was laid off from the Union again. Cement work is seasonal, but Scott also developed a bad back, which had been slowing him down over the years. Everybody's getting old. Humping around hundreds of bags of cement daily had taken its toll. Scott couldn't keep up with the younger guys plus he lacked the office skills necessary to get himself a better job. John should talk. After doing plumbing work since the late '80s, his body is feeling decades beyond its age.

John slaps his buddy on the back. "Dad's just kidding, man. You know that. He's got some cold ones waiting for us in the fridge. Come on, the Phils are winnin'."

John lived only a few blocks from the house where he grew up. Tony's father, Luke, bought the house right next door about a year after William moved the family in. He and John were best friends since kindergarten. It stayed that way for a while. All the way until Tony and Sue fell for each other. 15 years ago. Early 2000s. When Alex was young. It broke John's heart. He'd never fully recovered.

Sue and Tony recently divorced, which meant she's back in town. Sue calls John periodically to have drinks. To catch up. John can't resist. Even after all she put him through.

In the house, William instructs a nurse on what Karen needs for the evening. He'd been caring for John's mother by himself up until recently. John knew Thursdays mean a lot to him. Last year, she lost her ability to speak.

Alzheimer's. Having the full-time nurses help William get enough time to sleep. They also give him a chance to sneak off to the shore. William needs a break to fight off old age. The family shore house helps him stay young at heart.

John sits with William and Scott. The game ended with a homerun over the wall in left field. Phillies close it out. Another win for the home team. Phillies, Flyers, Sixers, Eagles. Doesn't matter. Hell, they'd even watch a Wings or Union game if nothing else was on. Thursdays are their time together. Just the guys. Pound some brews and shoot the breeze.

Time passed as it did each week. The sun went down over an hour ago. It's getting late. Before they part ways, William needs to get something off his chest. "John, I know you don't like hearing about it, but we need to begin planning for your mother."

Scott politely excuses himself to sit on the front porch with his beer. John and William tend to forget he's there sometimes when they talk money. Scott understands. It's because they consider him a member of the family. Doesn't change the fact that none of it was Scott's business. John opens the fridge and tosses Scott a fresh one on his way out.

John stands for the conversation, wishing he could escape to the front porch with Scott.

William continues, "This house. Once she passes, I want it to be yours. Now, for the children. You worked hard to get the twins set up in their places, but can't leave out Alex."

John rolls his eyes.

William ignores John's immaturity. "Your mother had a very specific request for him. Your place on Church Street. As you know, it was her sister's house and she'd want it kept in the family."

John shrugs. "Dad, I know what Mom requested for the house."

"Then why haven't you signed the documents? I told you when the kid started college that he was a good boy. Maybe he got into some trouble back in high school. Maybe he was a social disappointment to you, but that doesn't change the fact that he is your son. The boy needs your love and support," pleads William.

John fires back, "The kid's mother screwed him up to the point that he had a psychiatric breakdown when he was 16. It practically happened right in front of his entire class. And his conduct when I took him to work. I mean, my god,

I had phone calls from customers complaining about him crying on the job."

John had such frustration with his son, he barely knew were to begin. Alex's delicate psyche as a child was severely damaged from all the uprooting by his mother. Nine moves before the kid was 12. The abuse from Tony didn't help either.

It was William's insinuation of neglect that pissed John off. In John's mind, there was no neglect. He paid equal attention to Joseph, Diane, and Alex. It was the mother's job to care for the children and the father's job to make the money. It's the natural order of things. John never blamed himself for what happened. That was on her. John had no choice. Working 70 plus hours a week to pay for things. He had nowhere to drop Alex. The twins were off on their own. William and Karen had to watch him. What other options did he have? Sue was nowhere to be found until recently.

William felt frustrated. "John, you're my son. I love you very much, but sometimes you can be a real ass when it comes to that plumbing business. Yes, you made great sacrifices to become successful, but you left people behind along the way."

"That plumbing business has given my family everything they could ever need. Luke Mangle taught me all he knew about the industry. After he died, I picked up where he left off. When Tony decided he wanted nothing to do with the business, yeah, I stepped in and bought it. Just like Joseph will step in for me one day." John feels the conversation taking a turn for the worst.

"That business, and your obsession with it, has left one of your children alone and uncared for…"

John cuts him off, "Uncared for? Alex had to walk three blocks to your house. It was good exercise for him. Mom was there to cook and help with his homework whenever Alex needed her."

William scratches the inside of his thumb with his middle finger. John doesn't get it. "A child needs his parents. Diane and Joseph were different. They grew up with a mother and father at home. They were teenagers during your divorce. Alex had it much worse. He needs more love. Your mother and I gave him all the love we could, but it will never be the same thing. I mean, hell, John, we're even paying his college tuition. He's studying plumbing and heating for crying out loud. The kid wants to work for you when he gets out. Now all you can say is 'Joseph will be taking over.' You can't even give Alex a shot?"

John had enough. "Dad, you know the deal. Maybe I didn't foot the bill for his school, but if he survives one full year, I'll eat my words. I mean, yeah, I called the kid a loser and said he'd never make it. Not even two semesters. The fact is, he called plumbers white trash when he was 17. The only reason he went to that school is because no one else wanted him." John feels triumphant.

William sits speechless, looking at his son with disbelief. The phone rings. John picks up his cell, "Hello?"

On the other end, a serious voice responds, *"Mr. Walker, this is Officer Fletcher of the Franklin Tech Police Department. We have your son here. We'll need a family member to pick him up."*

John rolls his eyes.

William could hear the officer speaking through the phone from the other end of the small table.

John sighs before answering. "Do I need to come now?"

"No, sir. We'll keep him here overnight, but suggest you pick him up first thing in the morning."

John slinks back in his chair. "Will do, officer." *Click.*

John holds his face up with both hands. Tomorrow morning. Who's that officer kidding? Williamsport was a solid three-hour drive. He'd have to leave tonight and get a room.

John isn't riding alone. He turns his head to yell toward the porch, "Scott, get on your bike, it's road trippin' time!"

William chimes in, "I hear you and his mother have been speaking again. Would it be wise to include her?"

John may disagree with his dad on parenting matters, but has to respect the wisdom. It's time to begin including her. Sue was asking to have Alex back in her life for some time now.

He picks up his cell to make the call.

She answers almost immediately, *"Hey, John."*

His heart skips a beat. There's something so beautiful about the sound of her voice. It reminds him of when they first kissed back in the fifth grade. He loved her every day since. "Hey, Sue. You free tonight?"

"Sure, what's up?"

"Alex got in some trouble up at school. Scott and I'll be over on our bikes."

"Oh, Alex. Can't seem to keep it straight, huh? I'll be ready in a half hour. See you then, John."

Click.

***

Since leaving Tony, Sue's been living in West Ambler with Diane. A few years back, before Luke died, he and John decided to invest in real estate. Business had been good that year. Instead of taking Christmas bonuses, they went to the County Courthouse and purchased two properties in foreclosure. Sheriff sales are technically a cheap way to buy property, however, you need one hundred percent of the money in two weeks. Luckily, they each had plenty left over at year end to cover the cost of the property plus most of the expenses needed to build the houses. John offered both twins a house in exchange for some of their inheritance.

Diane took one, but not Joseph. He couldn't live next to her and Gabe. Diane's baby-daddy is just like Tony, and his first cousin. Joseph didn't want to be around Gabe due to his bad habits. Back in the day though, things were much different between them. Joseph and Gabe ran together in high school. Knew each other well. Rumor has it they'd fight back to back when the kids from Oreland would roll into town. All that's behind Joseph now. The boy grew up and moved on. Got himself a starter house near the mall. Away from the drama of Ambler.

When John built those houses, Alex was vocal about feeling left out. Got so mad, he called his father white trash. John remembered the conversation vividly. It wasn't exactly like John was leaving Alex out. Not true. The kid was only seventeen at the time. Besides, there were other plans on the table for Alex's future. William and Karen made sure of it.

John and Scott pull up to Diane's house with their bikes. One of four twin homes. *A twin for a twin*, he'd say to her.

Diane and the baby greet them at the end of the driveway. John lights up when he sees his granddaughter. More of a toddler at this point, but she will always be a baby to him. He leans over to give them a kiss. Looks around for Gabe, not surprised he's missing. "Where's Gabe?"

Diane looks at the ground before speaking, "Working again. Downtown in Philly. Meetings with the crew."

Lies. John knows exactly what that means. Hanging at the rat hole bar around the corner. Waiting for people to call in bets for the games. Gabe runs

40

numbers for a local bookie.

He's not in Philly, nor was he going to be. Not unless he's meeting his side chick at the club. John became suspicious when Gabe showed up to a family party smelling like a woman. The next day, he called in a favor to a private investigator who followed Gabe. The pictures were discretely placed where he knew Diane would find them. Nothing came out of it. A week later, he noticed some new diamonds in her ears. Typical.

"Sure he is," John answers. "Now, where's that mother of yours? We need to go bail your little brother out of the clink up at school."

Diane looks worried. "What'd he do now?"

"I didn't bother asking. I'd put money on it being a fight. The kid can't get along with anybody…"

Diane cuts him off. "Dad, go easy on him. He's a good kid, just been through a lot."

"Ah, he's a pussy," says John with a smug look on his face.

"Jesus, Dad. If I didn't know any better, I'd say Pop is right. You're way harder on Alex than the rest of us."

Scott sits on his bike silently, finding himself in the middle of a family conversation, yet again. He revs the chopper as a distraction, hollering over the screaming bike, "Hey, John, where's that ex of yours? We're burnin' moonlight here!"

Diane struggles to cover the baby's ears. She looks around to see if the neighbors are watching. "Hey, Uncle Scott! Do you mind not waking the whole neighborhood with that thing?"

Scott stops. Still feeling a little drunk, he nearly forgot the time. Sue pops out of the house with a tiny bag.

"Well, look who decided to roll out of bed," remarks Scott.

"Shut up, Scott." She tosses John her bag. He puts it in the sidesaddle. Sue was riding with John recently and knows exactly how much luggage he can carry. The bag size is a perfect fit.

John reaches out a hand. "Hop on, baby."

Sue gracefully mounts the bike, wrapping her hands around John's waist. "Don't mind if I do."

John leans over to kiss Diane and the baby good-bye. "Don't wait up."

"Oh, I don't plan to," said Diane before rushing her baby inside.

They ride off in the moonlight. The sound of the bikes rips through the air like wet hot beer farts. Echoing off the trees. A few dogs bark. The mechanical sound of flatulence fades into the night. They're off.

***

12:00 AM. The Genetti Hotel, Williamsport, PA. They park the bikes in a lot. After checking in, Sue decides the night is young. They bar-hop on 4th Street until last call. There's more spots to hit than John remembers. The other time he bar-hopped up here was last summer when he brought Alex up for Freshman Orientation. John chuckles to himself a bit while thinking about that weekend.

***

It wasn't the first time he visited Franklin Tech with Alex, but definitely the most memorable. After moving Alex in, one of the girls in the building hit on John. It freaked him out slightly, but he saw an opportunity to hook his son up with the night of the kid's life.

Her name was Gina. A pretty girl. Curly reddish hair, curvy, and seductive.

When she asked John up to her room, he politely declined. The age difference between the two of them made John feel queasy, but Alex could possibly benefit from the awkward encounter.

"I'll tell you what," said John, "I'm old enough to be your father, but if you wanna make two hundred bucks tonight, you need to show my son the night of his life and if you bring me back the shorts he's wearing right now, I'll pay you in full tomorrow morning."

John wasn't really surprised when she accepted money to sleep with Alex that night and had no doubt she would follow through.

Gina accepted, but not without an advance. John took the wad of money he kept in his front pocket, blew off the dust, and peeled away a fifty. "Take this. Buy some beer, do whatever you guys do, but don't get him in any trouble."

Gina takes the fifty. "That's too bad, because trouble's my middle name."

John almost believed it. This girl seemed damaged beyond repair. It was obvious to him now.

That night, he bar-hopped on his own. Had a good time too. Found a crazy

42

person who introduced himself as Jerry Garcia. God rest his soul. Close resemblance though.

The next morning, John was pleasantly surprised to find Gina waiting on the steps outside their building with shorts in hand. Gina briefly explained the night, leaving out the gory details, and that was it. Alex had his first experience with a woman. Not exactly the woman he would choose for his son, but she was experienced in life well beyond her years. That much was certain.

Months later, John cringed when she showed up to the house at Christmas time. He never in a million years thought they'd hit it off. John prayed for them to break up. He knew it would tear Alex apart, but the girl was bound for a life of trailer parks, strip clubs, and crystal meth. It was only a matter of time.

***

Bar-hopping for the three of them was like old times back in Ambler. Forever ago.

John cues up "Poison" by Bell Biv DeVoe on the jukebox.

He watches Scott and Sue dance together. This song reminds John of Senior Prom, dancing all night long. Dancing was great with Sue. She was a cheerleader. Built like a dancer from "The Grind." That was John's favorite show back when MTV actually played music. The show was hosted by Eric Neis, one of the first members of the "Real World." Arguably the first reality TV show, which inevitably led to the likes of "Survivor," "The Osbournes," "Kardashians," etc. Fuckin' outrageous. John could feel himself brooding.

Sue waves him over to dance. John feels Sue pull him closer. John grinds on her front. Scott in the back. John feels his stomach drop when he sees the bulge in Scott's pants. He fights off the jealousy. Not like he and Sue were together these days. John decides to play it cool.

Sue pulls their heads in closer. Uncomfortably close. He can smell Scott's nasty dragon breath.

"Let's get some six packs to go," she whispers with a wink. Bell Biv DeVoe say their good-byes.

***

4:30 AM. John wakes in a panic. He can't breathe. His chest's caving in.

John looks around. Clothes tossed on the floor. He's naked. Sue's asleep next to him, also naked. Then there's Scott. Not on the other bed. Not on the floor. Crammed in next to her. John picks up the blanket for a look. Scott's naked too.

"God dammit," John says out loud.

John's face falls in his hands feeling a combination of sadness and hangover. The familiar effects of double-hopped beer had dried out his sinuses to the point where he could melt if some drinking water didn't materialize soon.

He stumbles to the bathroom and drinks from the faucet. The water tastes like old pipes. John tolerates it enough to partially hydrate for the time being. He turns off the water and leans on the counter for a second. Option 1: Face what's in that room. Option 2: Get some air instead. He picks Option 2.

Right before walking out, he remembers clothes are necessary to avoid receiving a special driver's license. John works through the escape plan in his head. The gears stopped turning. He musters up some courage to walk toward the bed. On the ground are his jeans and a tee shirt. John trips and falls into the TV. It doesn't knock over, but makes a loud enough bang to wake Sue.

She talks from the darkness, "John, what are you doing?"

Exactly what John didn't want. His wrestling coach in high school was right, he did have surprisingly shitty balance. "I'm going to the roof deck for a smoke. Go back to bed."

The door shuts. It wakes Scott. He's annoyed. "Where's John?" "He went to the roof to have a smoke."

"Sue, John doesn't smoke…" "So what? Go back to sleep."

***

On the roof, John shivers in his tee shirt. He tightly closes his arms across his chest. He's freezing on the cold spring night, but anything is better than going back inside. Anything is better than reliving that. How could she continue to do this? How could he be so stupid to let her back in? All he wants is the family back that he once had. Things were great, or so he thought. That was John's problem. Always had the blinders on when it came to her. His plan for the Nuclear Family didn't quite fit Sue's life goals.

He knew it was Slim Davies who talked Sue into marrying John. Tony said it once when they argued over child support money from a payphone. "It was Sue's father who wanted her to marry you, John. She wanted the quarterback, not the B-list wrestler."

Tony never understood Sue. She was John's one. His Achilles' heel. Anytime she'd come back around, there was John, hopelessly in love. He just couldn't get her out of his head. Even after all these years. It drove him mad.

He walked toward the edge of the roof. There was no roof deck up here. The door was locked at the top of the stairwell. John picked the lock with his penknife. There was nothing besides the parapet wall. Less than knee high. John leaned on it to look over.

Tears began forming in his eyes. The drunken stupor, the threesome, his greatest love, his best friend, his children. Everyone's so messed up. He blames himself. Maybe if he wasn't around anymore they could collect the insurance money and get on with their lives. Maybe they'd be better off without him. He steps up on the parapet wall looking over the edge of the ten-story building. It was now or never. He thinks about how much he loves his children, especially Alex. The cold wind blows his tee shirt.

The boy couldn't be more like him. All William ever wanted was John to go to college and work finance at the canned soup plant just like his father. Sales. That was never for John. He didn't have the grades. William went to Penn. Hit it big early and retired young. At this rate, John would work until he's eighty to get ahead.

Alex, the artist. Wanting nothing to do with plumbing and heating. Drawing pictures and watching movies all the time. The kid's lucky he got into college. Lucky to find a good tech school to teach him a trade. Art schools or big universities wanted nothing to do with a kid who lost his mind, nearly flunking out of high school.

John remembered calling his son a loser when Alex brought home the Franklin Tech application from his guidance counselor. "Too bad you couldn't get an art scholarship like the other faggots in your grade," John remembered saying coldly. He could still see Alex's shoulder's slump.

The tears well up in his eyes again. This time harder. John doesn't want to be a bad father, he just has an image of the perfect life and the further away it gets, the more miserable and resentful he becomes toward the people he loves.

The ground gets closer. Tears stream down John's face. *It's now or never*, he thinks to himself.

45

His back spasms. He levitates off his feet. His head jerking, smashing his brain into the front of his skull. He looks up. Still alive? Still on the roof? Scott leans over and gets in his face. "What the fuck are you doing?! Trying to kill yourself?! Are you an idiot?"

John loses it. Face in hands again. This time filling with puddles of warm tears. "I ruined them, Scott, I did this. It's all my fault. I want to love them. All I want is my family back. Why does this keep happening to me? Why?" Tears stream down his face. John ugly cries from past emotions hidden deep beneath the gruff exterior.

Scott can't help but tear up himself. He loves John. Their friendship means more than anything Sue could ever offer. He sits down next to his buddy and holds him close. Ignoring the cold, they both cry themselves to sleep.

***

6:30. John stirs.

"Wake up, dummy," Scott shakes John, "you got someone else to bail out this time."

John wipes the sleep from his eyes, the morning sunlight making him squint. He blocks the light with a hand. "I don't want to go back down there, man. I don't think I can do this anymore."

Scott pulls him close again with a light headlock. "You got me, pal. We all we got, we all we need. Now, let's go bail an awesome kid out the clink."

***

The Franklin Tech Police Station looks like a rundown house with a fancy garage door. The college must've snapped up all the little properties close by, and converted them to makeshift municipal buildings. The Police Station was one of them, evidently.

John makes Sue wait outside. He gave her a ride to the police station, but asked her to stay with Scott until he was done. John became Alex's sole guardian when Sue disappeared with Tony for a year-long bender. That was back when Alex was thirteen or so.

There would be no bailing Alex out. A misdemeanor. Slap on the wrist. He got into a fight, was knocked out by some idiot holding a keg, and bit another kid on the pecker. John felt repulsed at the thought until he came face to face

46

with Richard Zilla. They were taking him to another room to wait for his father, who is coming all the way from North Jersey. John thinks the kid is massive and looks rather psychotic. There is no way Alex could've taken him in a fair fight. There would be no punishment for this. Only a fair scolding. Alex was clearly standing up to a bully. John feels a new sense of pride in his son. Community service would do him good too. The black eye and bloody knuckles would heal. John is just happy Richard Zilla didn't get the chance to beat his son to death.

When John finally brings Alex outside, Sue hugs and kisses him like they're seeing each other for a holiday dinner. She doesn't even comment on his injuries or ask Alex what happened. Only says, "Can we leave now?" Her apathy makes John's stomach turn.

John decides to take control. "Hey, Alex, catch a ride with Scott back to your place and wait for me there. Your mom and I need to talk for a minute."

"Sure, Dad. How much trouble am I in?" "We'll talk when I get back. Now go."

Scott pats his hand on the sleek chrome bars next to the seat, "Time to get on, kid. Let's boogie!"

John waits until they pull off to begin with Sue. "Can't you ask the kid if he's feeling, OK? Did you even notice his eye?"

"What? Of course I noticed his black eye and the cuts. Do you want me to baby him or something? He's almost nineteen years old?"

John can't believe her. "Sue, Alex turned nineteen last fall. You can't remember how old he is anymore? Are you serious? Aren't you even upset that you couldn't go in with me to get your son? As far as the law's concerned, you're not even his mother anymore."

"Oh, really, what about when he stayed with me and Tony when he was a teenager? Hmm? It was fine then, wasn't it?"

A beautiful pearl white Mercedes sports car pulls into the parking lot while they argue. It distracts both of them. After it parks, a tall, well-dressed man gets out and checks his phone.

John ignores him. "Yes, it was fine, Sue, because I allowed it. I gave that kid a path in life. Maybe it's a path he doesn't want, but art hardly pays the bills. Now, at least he has a shot to learn a trade. The same trade I'll continue to teach him after he gets out of college. Then he'll work for a business that I built."

Sue cuts him off, "Yeah, and he'll be a loser just like you. A filthy piece of white trash working with other people's shit for the rest of his life."

That hurt. John's heard enough. "You know what, between what happened last night and this situation right here, this is the last straw." John takes the wad of cash from his front pocket and peels off a twenty. "Take this. Catch a bus home. We're done. You broke my heart for the last time." He holds the twenty out for her. She slaps it from his hand.

The twenty blows away in the light spring breeze. John turns the other cheek. He walks away quietly. Starts his bike and rides off.

***

John pulls up to the front of Alex's building. He parks behind Scott's chopper. The dogwood in the flowerbed running along the curb shades parts of the street and broken slate sidewalk. The pretty pink and white flowers began falling. They're John's favorite. He loves their smell. Fragrant and beautiful.

He takes in a deep breath. The cool air feels good when breathed in through his nostrils. The hangover from the hoppy beer dried out his sinuses something fierce. The humid mountain air rolling off the Susquehanna River provides some relief.

He walks up the high steps. The building's pretty huge. Split into four vertical sections. Alex lived in the section second to the left.

As he walks through the common hallway just inside the building, he looks at all the mail stacking up. One pile for Alex. As John picks it up, he remembers his paperwork at the office. The dig up job is today. He needs to rush back. Joseph and Ed Murray would have to begin without him. He sends Joseph a quick text to confirm everything's on target. After the panic of missing work subsides, he takes Alex's mail and moves on.

John knocks softly before opening the door to Alex's apartment. Just a formality. He has no intentions of waiting for someone to answer. John's only hope was the faggot roommate wouldn't be home. That kid Chad makes John's skin crawl. The last thing he needs is to catch him in the act with one of his man-friends. He opens the door. No sign of Chad.

Alex and Scott sit alone at the table just across the open room. He tosses the mail on the table before sitting down. Mostly bills, which he'll be paying anyway.

"Hey, Dad," Alex says nervously.

Scott leans in. "Go easy. I'll be outside." Scott pats his little buddy Alex on the shoulder and leaves them to it.

John straightens himself for the talk. Alex can't make eye contact.

"Look up, kid. Never look at the ground. You'll miss out on life that way."

Alex takes the advice well and meets John's eye dead on. This makes John ease up. If the boy takes responsibility, then he's on the right path.

"Alex, you did a bad thing. You're lucky they let you off so easy. Five weeks of community service is barely a slap on the wrist. Not to mention, it's all over a girl. This…Gina. The one you brought home at Christmas. Alex, she's hurt inside. Bad things happened to her growing up. That's why she behaves the way she does. I don't want you to see her anymore. Do you understand me?"

"I'm sorry, Dad," Alex pleads. "Please don't make me leave school." John feels terrible. He has no intentions of making Alex drop out.

William was right. School is the best thing that ever happened to the kid. Despite the weirdness of the friends and the queer roommate, Alex's grades had been up. He nearly flunked out his 1st semester, but pulled it together. John couldn't be happier with Alex's performance. Maybe the kid isn't an honors student, but he's doing more than just getting by. That's what matters most.

"I'm happy you didn't get kicked out of school, Alex. It's upsetting to me and Joseph that you won't be home to help us for the first month or so of summer. We really could've used you. Things are picking up and it's tough finding good help."

"That's the other thing I wanted to say, Dad. I want to stay here for the summer. With my friends. I have a job lined up. I can make enough to support myself. To pay my own bills."

Alex didn't need to continue. John already knows what the job is. He decided to go through the motions of typical human dialog anyway. "What's the job?"

"Adam wants me to be a roadie and help manage the band." "No."

Alex pleads again, "But Dad, I'm not even allowed to drink in these places. They put a special stamp on my hand so I can't get served at the bar."

"You can't start hanging in bars already. You're too young. Especially the fag bars. Do you know what goes on in those places?"

"Dad, I'm nineteen, and don't pretend I'm not surrounded by these things already. It's not hard for me to say *no*. I just...I need this. It's important to me. After the whole thing with Gina, the fight with Zilla, no one's going to invite me to parties anymore. I need something else to occupy my time. I'm going to go crazy again. I need to hang out with my friends, Dad. It's fun, and I can work hard doing it."

The fight with Richard Zilla wasn't the problem. John remembered being his age. Being scared to fight. He melted in his chair. Alex was a good boy and deserved to be happy. However that happiness would come.

"All right. You can stay, but you need to make enough to pay for food and utilities over the summer. I'll take care of the rent...but...if you get in

one more fight or get in trouble with the cops one more time, I will pull you out of school permanently. Understood?"

Alex beams. He lunges at his father to hug him. John doesn't know how to react. The emotional retardation that comes with being the descendant of Quakers, prevents him from being an outwardly warm person. In this moment though, John finds the strength to hug the boy back.

Chapter 4
Joseph

8:00 AM. Joseph and Ed Murray begin their daily planning. Robert showed up late again. He'd been out drinking with Alex's old posse in Ambler the night before. Probably sneaking whiskey at the new BBQ joint that opened up. Robert's too young to drink, but slick as hell. Joseph couldn't remember what cooking show the owner had been on, but they did have the most dynamite comfort food in town. That was for sure. If Joseph had fallen off the wagon, it would also be the place he'd go for a good whiskey drink. The bar is stocked from floor to ceiling. Joseph was secretly jealous he couldn't be out with Robert last night.

Robert had basically been John's ward since he was fifteen. Joseph regularly thought his father to be a saint. Taking in Tony's boy like that. Even after all that Tony had done to their family over the years. Stealing their mother, beating her in front of Alex, milking John for all the child support he could, and now turning into a full-blown drug addict. Ditching Robert for the mean streets of North Philly.

Tony and Joseph's mom had divorced a year ago. She was OK, staying with Diane, but you could tell she felt lost. A grown woman leaning on her daughter for support. No education, no drive in life other than to sponge off another human being. Joseph resents his mother. Alex does too. She only really speaks to Diane. They'd see her on birthdays and holidays, but that had been the extent of it for years. Sad thing is, she lives in Ambler right near them. Maybe Joseph moved out of town by the mall, but it's not like they couldn't meet for lunch. Even if it's just once a week.

Robert fumbles around with his coffee and phone for a few minutes before getting motivated. Joseph isn't having it. "Robert! Drop that phone and get your ass in the ditch! All I want to see is assholes and elbows, kid!"

Robert walks over to get a shovel out of the truck. Ed sits in the backhoe drinking his coffee, warming the diesel engine. They tease him, but Robert works hard. He'd flunked out of high school recently. Got hooked on cocaine with the speedball heads from the rich neighborhood. Once Alex got back into school, and straightened himself out, Robert took on the mantle of family druggie. Not that there needed to be one necessarily, but it seemed to be the order of all things.

Joseph reminded himself of the way Allen Iverson once described Baltimore. Kind of like a bucket of crabs. One crab tries to climb out, catches a glimmer of sunlight and hope, then gets pulled back in by his homies. *Ambler isn't much different*, Joseph thinks to himself. Just smaller.

Joseph found God and the twelve-step program. Alex found his salvation in being educated. Robert is another story. He has other stresses. More complicated. The Mangle family is heavily connected. There were some serious people that expected Robert to start pitching in soon. The life. Each of the Mangles were expected to pull their weight. The Walker influence kept the wolves at bay. Mostly. On the surface that is, but rumor is Robert doesn't have it in him.

Since Alex had gone to school, their father had extra time to focus on getting Robert clean. Sent him to rehab twice in two years! At first, it seemed to work. He stopped hanging with the brats from across town. Started running with Alex's booze crew instead. The merry band of douchebags those kids are. Alex likes to bitch and complain about that Zilla kid from Jersey, but Alex is no better. All they do is drink and screw. Bunch of sinners.

Joseph grabs some more shovels. He looks at his phone. 11:30. His father wouldn't be back for a couple hours. He'd love to get the job completed and make the full ten grand before day's end. By himself. That would be perfect. He signaled for Ed to begin digging the main trench.

***

1:00. Joseph and Robert are more than nine feet down. The pipe begins showing itself. They trench under to expose more. The dirt cracks above. Ed pushes the bucket from his machine up against the dangerous side. The plywood sheets still in the back of the truck. No shoring again. No time to waste. No money to be lost.

They'd uncovered the pipe in record time. Joseph beamed. He found the break. It was a six-foot section. "Yo, Robert!" he shouts over the hum of the backhoe, "Get the saw cutter. We're gonna do this quick!"

Robert climbs out the sloping side of the ditch. Joseph takes his shovel to expose the cast iron joint so he can begin repairing the pipe. Good practice told him to cut it off there. It's what his Dad would do. He takes his shovel and tunnels a bit further into the dirt. He can see the joint, but just not enough room for the saw. He could use a chain cutter on the cast iron pipe, but the saw would be much better. Less of a chance making a mistake. If he caused another break in the line, the ditch may be twice the size and the people would be without their toilets for another day. That could damage his reputation plus blow the budget. Joseph didn't plan for that when he bid the job. The saw cutter would have to do it. He tunnels a bit further.

Back at the truck, Robert yanks the saw cutter from a side bin and fills it with gas. Ed peers at him from the cab of the machine. He cracks a window, "Come on, Robert, get the lead out of your ass. Where's that saw? Time is money, you little shit!"

Robert picks up the saw and hustles back. "Alright, I'm comin'. Had to fill it up." He stopped for a second to look in the ditch. Joseph had been tunneling too far. It felt wrong. Robert had to say something. "Joseph! You're in too far!"

Joseph pops his head out from the cave. "What? I need room for the saw! I'm at the joint!"

Robert sees something change in the dirt he doesn't like. "Get the hell out of there! The dirt! It's cracking…" Then there's the quick rumble.

Joseph looks up just in time for the dirt boulder to hit him square in the face. His body disappears under the mound of dirt. Just like that he is gone.

Robert panics. He drops the saw and lunges for the shovel. "Robert, get the fuck away, I'll use the bucket!" Ed shrieks. "Dig around me. I'll help with the shovel!"

Ed uses the bucket to peel away the dirt as delicately as possible. It seems like an eternity. Robert moves a shovel-full then he sees it. The blood. It was on the teeth of the bucket. "Stop!" Robert shouts at the top of his lungs.

Ed sees it too. He leaps out of the backhoe and grabs the other shovel. He trips on his way into the ditch to help Robert, twisting his ankle.

They dig toward the blood, then see the detached arm. They frantically dig faster and find Joseph's twisted, contorted back, then the shoulder. Robert gets down on his knees and hand digs for his adopted brother's head. He finds it. No blood there. He uncovers the face. Intact. "Call an ambulance!"

Ed is frozen. The blood leaving his face. Ed's hand shakes as he dials.

Chapter 5
John

John and Scott buzz back to Ambler on their bikes. The trees look beautiful along Route 80. John likes to watch the leaves turn in fall better, but the spring drive's still very nice. The highway was carved into the large hills that make up the Pocono Mountains, part of the Appalachian range. John has an issue calling them mountains. Large hills would be a more accurate description. After riding through the Rockies and parts of Vermont on his bike, John feels the Poconos are living a lie.

He forgot his watch. The clock on his bike. 1:00. Joseph started the dig up job hours ago. They should be half finished by now. John instinctively reaches for his phone, leaving one hand on the throttle. He stops himself.

Scott buzzes past him on the chopper.

John and Scott are famished. Being hung over, the fight with Sue, traveling. They almost forgot to eat. Halfway home. A sandwich would get them by. The only thing around is a Wawa convenience store at the Turnpike entrance. The familiar brown and yellow sign reminds John of Thanksgiving decorations even though the year is exactly halfway in the other direction. Funny how seeing colors can do that to a person's mood.

John's phone rings. It's Ed. He sends it to voicemail. Couldn't be that important. He and Scott eat in the parking lot. The phone rings again.

Scott looks annoyed. "Who keeps calling you?"

"It's Ed. I'd better see how the job's going." He answers, "Ed. What's up?"

"John, where are you?"

"We're at Wawa. Getting on the Turnpike at Mount Pocono. What's the problem?"

"There was an accident. Joseph. On the job."

"Where are you now?"

"In Philly. At Chestnut Hill Hospital."

55

The air leaves John's lungs. He can barely speak. "How bad is it?" "*He's in the intensive care unit. You need to get home right away.*" Click.

John drops his sandwich and buzzes off on his bike without saying another word to Scott.

John went in a zone. His son. His little man. The throttle on the bike pinned. Damn bike. Never goes fast enough.

The engine screams. He goes deeper in thought. How could this be? John needs a fuckin' teleporter. Shitty scientists can't create anything useful.

Scott races up. John could see his friend in the side view. They race down the highway.

3:30. Chestnut Hill Hospital, Philadelphia. Ed and Robert were waiting for John when he got there. Sue is nowhere in sight. No one's looking for her anyway. John is the only one allowed to see him, but not yet. Joseph wouldn't be out of surgery for another few hours at best.

John walks up to Ed. "Was the shoring in the ditch?"

"John, there we were trying to finish in an eight-hour day. Joseph wouldn't…"

John cuts him off, "Was the shoring in the ditch?" "No, it wasn't."

John cold-cocks Ed in the eye with a right hook. "You blame my son! You weak fuck! He's just a kid. I told you to use the shoring. How could you?"

"I'm sorry, John. We were trying to make a few extra bucks so the kid could get ahead."

"Yeah, Ed. That sounds great. Know what else sounds great?" "No, John. I have no idea. What sounds great?"

"The fact that my son won't have to worry about money anymore and he can thank your insurance company for that."

"John. Please. We can work this out. A hit like that will ruin me."

"My son is sitting in the ICU and all you can think about is yourself?" John stops himself to get a grip. "Ed, you've been a good friend over the years, but it's time for you to fuck off. You'll be hearing from my lawyers."

"Don't do this, John."

"Oh yeah, Ed?" John reaches in his pocket. "Hey look, I got something here for ya." He pulls out a middle finger and shoves it in Ed's face.

Scott steps in. "Time to go." Ed leaves quietly.

7:30 PM. Surgery's over. John's the only one allowed to see Joseph.

The doctor approaches. "Mr. Walker, I'm Dr. Gimple. The replantation specialist here at Chestnut Hill."

"Replantation? Can you tell me how bad it is?"

"That's why I wanted to talk before you see him. Joseph will need you to be strong for him. The trauma caused to his arm by the backhoe operator was…serious."

"How serious, please?"

"My team was able to reattach his arm. It was severed at the shoulder, but the nerves, and most tendons, were not beyond repair. We had tremendous luck with the surgery."

"That's terrific, can I see him now?"

"Well, the arm was only half of it. When the dirt fell, his body absorbed the total impact. More especially his spine."

"His spine? Is he OK?"

"He experienced a fracture. Two of his vertebrae have been damaged. Our doctors will do everything they can, but it looks like you may want to make preparations for wheelchair access to his home."

"Wheelchair access? How long will he need for a full recovery?"

"Mr. Walker, I'd like you consider that Joseph may not be able to walk for the rest of his life."

"But the business. He was supposed to take over. What am I going to do?"

"Mr. Walker, Joseph will receive the best care we can provide. I'll make sure he has every resource available to help him recover."

"This can't be happening. Oh god. Please no." Tears begin running from John's eyes.

John falls against the wall. His body slides to the floor. His face falls in his hands for the umpteenth time. Scott rushes over to comfort his friend. He holds John close. Robert rushes over. All of them sit on the floor. Sobbing together.

Man down.

Chapter 6
Alex

Gina shows up at Alex's apartment after the hearing. Five weeks of community service at the public library. Thankfully, Alex had negotiated with his dad a few weeks prior to stay the summer. That made the transition that much smoother for the time he'd spend serving hard labor at the Williamsport Public Library. Sentenced to stock the dusty bookshelves within day in and day out until it's over.

She looked hot as usual when Alex opened the door. Wearing a low-cut top. Cleavage bulging out. Tiny jean shorts cut so high you could see her bathing suit bottom through the weave of strings connecting the front to the back. A part of the shorts Alex knew formerly as a structural portion of the garment. After Gina went at those shorts with a pair of scissors, it was anybody's guess what continued holding them together.

He invites her in to talk. They sit down on the couch.

She begins, "Alex, I have a problem. There's a lot I haven't told you about myself."

Alex cuts her off, "You mean, like the part about you screwing my worst enemy behind my back?"

"Yeah, that's one of the things. Let me explain." "No, I'm going to do the talking here."

"Ok, go ahead," says Gina sheepishly.

"You hurt me so bad. I watched Zilla have sex with you. Then he tried to beat me to death. Then I won. Then I got knocked out by a keg. Now, I'm in trouble with the cops. All because of you."

"I know. I really wish I hadn't done any of this to you. Alex, I was damaged at a young age. Since your fight with Richard, I've been talking to a doctor. He's been trying to help me figure out why I do drugs and why I hurt you so badly. Alex, I'm here to apologize and to tell you that we don't ever have to see each other again if you don't want."

Alex doesn't want that. Even after all this, he still has a special place in his heart for Gina.

"Please don't go." Alex could feel the tears welling up in his eyes. "Please stay."

Gina moves closer. She kissed him gently. He kissed her back. Her hands fall to his waist. His hands to her chest. She unbuttoned his pants. He moves in for a quickie. Just like before. Whenever Gina wore those shorts, it made things so easy.

Their bodies move to the sound of their own music. Alex feels the ecstatic rush.

Gina whispers gently in his ear, "If you cum in me, you can keep me forever."

Alex feels panic. She means kids! Gina tried this crap before one night during a black-out. Alex remembers her rambling about being off the pill and wanting five kids. With him no less!

He tries desperately to pull out. She forcefully holds him there, attempting to make him finish inside her. Alex overpowers her and moves away before sealing the deal.

He leaps up to button his pants. "You're trying to force me to get you pregnant? What the hell is wrong with you?"

"Come on. I know you want me. If we have a baby, then you can keep me around forever." She smiles. Her eyes looked hollow.

Alex sees through her lies. Gina's not going to a doctor nor is she in recovery.

"Gina, this was a big mistake. I can't believe you want to have a baby with me. I don't want to spend the rest of my life with you. Sorry, but I regret opening my door and letting you in."

Gina brushes off the rejection with anger. "Ha. Like the night we met. Well, guess what, Dick Biter? When you opened up the door and you saw me. I only fucked you because your creepy dad paid me 200 bucks. Did you know that?"

A shot went through Alex's heart. Not sure if he could bear any more pain this season, he pointed toward the door. "You gotta go. We're done here."

Gina reaches for her knockoff Gucci purse. Slinging it over her shoulder with a mild effort to hit Alex in the face. It misses by a few feet.

Alex thinks she looked ridiculous. "Nice, Gina. Why don't you snort some Ritalin with your coke next time? Maybe the speedballs will help you focus on aiming better."

She stops at the door needing to get the last word in. "Maybe you should focus on being less of a fucking loser. That way you might have prayer in life."

"Just get out."

She pretends to leave before making things worse. "Oh, by the way. Wanna know why I cheated on you with Zilla? Because he's everything you'll never be!"

The door slams.

Alex sits. His face falls in his hands.

Chad's door creaks open. He sits down next to Alex. They hug. Alex cries into his shoulder before letting go.

Chad gets up and comes back with a paper towel for Alex to dry his face.

Alex graciously takes the paper towel. They sit there for a minute in silence. The wet salty smell of Alex's tears fills the room, overpowering the smell of Gina's cheap corner store perfume. Alex appreciates having the moment with his friend. Feeling the tears finally running down his face. It's been too long since he last let his guard down with a friend. Probably since first semester the night he met Adam.

Chad breaks the silence. "This stays here, bud. Time to move on for good now."

Alex agrees before wiping his face. "No more Gina."

Chapter 7
Alex

The Rainbow Room. Friday night. 1:00 AM. The place smells like yesterday's hangover. It's a dank bar with a tiny stage. Neon lights litter the walls in a failed attempt to make it seem more inviting for any patrons willing to overpay for watered-down well drinks. Beyond that, the Rainbow Room's the only friendly place in town for the LGBT community.

The Fairfax Pub across town was something similar at one time. $20 cover charge on Friday nights. Alex heard it was mostly a place where college girls would go to avoid being drooled on by drunken douchebags. After a while, word caught on. Then any frat boy, hipster or lonely dude on the prowl was ready to pay the hefty cover charge to get in. That was when all the self-respecting gay people skipped out and headed to the Rainbow Room.

Alex watches Polyester Anarchy perform on stage. They sold the place out. Men in the crowd dance closely while Adam serenades them with "Linger" by the Cranberries. It's the band's favorite ballad. Their closer for the night. Adam channels Dolores O'Riordan to give the best performance possible.

People move closer. More rhythmic now. Feeling the love. Polyester Anarchy's doing their job. Adam seizes the opportunity. He climbs up on the bar. Getting up close and personal with fans. The crowd becomes electric.

Adam carefully steps over their drinks. They reach for his hand. Adam reaches out to them one by one. *"Linger" tends to bring out the best in people*, Alex thinks to himself.

Alex becomes distracted. He sees someone looking at him from behind the bar. A woman. Checking him out? It couldn't be.

He walks over to get a closer look. When he sits down, the pleasant shape of a woman bends over in front of him. Counting money at the register. She turns and looks into the mirror behind the bottles of booze. Their eyes meet in the reflection. The butterflies flutter in Alex's stomach. The same feeling he gets every time. Going back to when he first kissed a girl. That familiar feeling. That lovely feeling. He smiles bashfully. She winks and smiles back at him. The pink and green neon lights overhead make her smile look radiant. After giving the person next to him their change, she leaned on the bar.

As she bends over to say hello, Alex sees lots of cleavage. "Hey, you. We haven't met before. You're the new roadie, right?" After speaking she smiles again. This time a wider smile. Alex notices her perfect teeth. Brown hair falling straight down over her shoulders. Absolutely beautiful.

Don't panic, Alex thinks to himself. Think fast. Gina's gone. Move on. Trust the butterflies. "Hey. Yeah. Setting up and breaking down. I guess you could call me their roadie. It's fun hanging out with the guys. Being here."

"Hmm, nice. If you have a fake ID, I'd consider buying you a drink."

He looks down at the back of his hand. The black streak of the permanent marker by the Macho Man Randy Savage impersonator at the front door made bullshitting impossible at this moment.

"I'm Julie, by the way." She extends a thin dainty hand to shake. Silver rings on random fingers.

Alex returns the gesture. Shaking with slight pressure. "Alex. And that's a big *no* for the fake ID, but I'll take a rain check on that drink." His hand wraps around hers like mid-sized meat hook. Padded and calloused from long, hard days helping his dad with plumbing jobs growing up.

"The night is young, Alex. Looks like Adam's getting to the end. You're gonna stay and help them break down tonight?"

Alex smiles and nods.

"Good, when I kick everyone out after last call, come have one with me." "You sure it's cool?" Alex asks.

"Yup, late night's always cool for whoever sticks around. Best of all it's on the house." Julie smiles and winks before moving away to take a drink order.

When she turns around to pour, a very nice gentleman in make-up leans in with a lisp, "I think she likes you."

Alex feels comfort. The customers. Julie. There's a magic to this place. Everyone's so nice to each other. Never any fights. No beers being thrown in faces. So cool.

On stage, Adam wraps it up.

Alex gets lost in the music. He tears up a bit watching his friends play.

Chad on the drums, Jesse on the guitar, Rick on the bass, and Adam up front. Maybe they are just a cover band, but what's happening here is a thing of beauty. All of it. This place. The people. The love and joy that spreads when Polyester Anarchy rocks the house. *There's nothing like it*, Alex thinks to himself.

Adam spots Alex twisting with emotion. He points at his friend while closing the song.

Alex laughs to himself. Adam has a way of making him feel more comfortable in his own skin. Even when it means being awkwardly serenaded. From one straight guy to another.

"They got something special together. Don't they?" The sweet sound of Julie's voice brings Alex to the real world. Her words like the pleasant spectral hand of hunger from a Tom and Jerry cartoon. Lifting him off the ground. Pulling him toward a freshly-baked pie, cooling on an old lady's window sill. The heat from her face next to his. Giving him goosebumps down the back of his neck. The natural smell of her essential oil playing Alex's nose hairs like a piano.

What a night, Alex says to himself.

He cocks his head toward hers. Alex didn't realize how close she really was to him. When he turned to talk, they almost kissed for the first time. The feeling makes his heart skip a beat. He breathes in slowly to be cool about it. Julie could see his heart skipped a beat.

Alex summons the courage to speak, hoping his breath doesn't smell. "It's the four of them together. This place. These people. It brings out the best in everybody. It's never like this for them. Anywhere else."

He could feel Julie looking deep into his eyes. The lights flicker. Their gaze broken. Last call.

***

Last call came and went.

Alex places the instruments in their cases, wraps the cords, and packs up the van.

Back at the bar, the band sits together having a drink. Julie has a beer waiting for him. Silvio counts the money in the register while Julie cleans the glasses.

"Hey, Alex. You done workin'? I got you a Bud Light. Hope that's OK?"

Alex sits down and takes a long pull from the bottle. "Thanks. It's perfect. Just got everything loaded up."

He turns to his friends then raises the beer. "Guys, here's to an amazing summer."

They raise their bottles in unison.

Adam chimes in, "Alex, we didn't ask you to come with us this summer just to be our roadie."

Alex flinches a little. "Damn. Am I being fired already?" He looks to Julie, who unknowingly shrugs.

Adam smirks. "We want you to make us some concert posters. This could be your summer of self-expression."

Oh, man. Alex loves this idea. He feels the creative juices flowing already.

Chad stands up to speak next. "Hey bud, they've all been over to our place and saw the old '90s posters you made. The inspiration you felt after seeing us play. The guys really appreciated hearing that."

Rick and Jesse share a brain. They both talk at the same time trying to get a word in. Rick has the louder voice this time. "Alex, that Doggystyle poster in your room. Gave me the idea to mix in 'Doggy Dogg World' as one of our newest tunes."

Jesse thought of one too, "Yeah, then there's that Chronic poster hanging right next to it. That's why we do 'Let Me Ride' now too. I mean, who woulda thought about doing gangster rap during our gigs? Absolutely brilliant. It kills!"

Rick had a question, "So tell me. You're lookin' at community service over next few weeks because of the fight?"

Alex frowns. "Yeah, it's basically the rest of the semester plus a few weeks into summer."

"That should work out great." The guys look at Rick funny. His mouth continues to move in an effort to talk himself out of the awkward moment. "To have extra time for the posters, I mean."

Adam leans in to put an arm around Alex. "There's something else. Silvio's going to set you up with a contact list to get our gigs locked in for the next few months. His cousin owns a few bars in Philly and Allentown. You can do this while you make the posters."

Jesse smiles. "Alex, you're an uplifting soul, and we don't care what any of the haters say about you. What are they calling you these days, Dick Biter?"

Alex wishes Jesse didn't have to bring that up. One of the minions spray-painted the phrase on Alex's front door. The story had spread around campus way too quickly. The Sigma guys are merciless when it comes to smack talk.

Jesse continues, "Fuck those guys. You're one of us, bro. We want you to help us get out of this shithole and earn some real money."

Silvio didn't like that dig one bit. "Yo homie, this shithole's paying your bills." He drops a pile of cash on the bar and points at the band. "And don't you forget who made you little bitches either."

Chad jumps in quickly to change the subject. "Yeah, but anyway. I love you, buddy. We all do. Let's get this thing going together. Wanna be our manager or what?"

Alex thinks about it. He feels the butterflies again. Not the ones from Julie this time. More like the anxiety when he found Zilla and Gina together.

He can feel Julie looking at him. She leans in. "Do it."

"Sure. I could do it," Alex unconvincingly mumbles. He looks back at Julie for moral support. Her hair flicks forward as she moves in for a hug across the bar. It's the first time they touch. Alex experiences sensory overload.

Chad nudges Adam. "Hey guys, let's roll a blunt out back while Silvio counts the door money."

"Alex, why don't you stay here and start making some sketches on napkins," says Adam.

Alex agrees before they shuffle out.

Silvio picks up the cash. "I'll finish up in the office, guys. Don't get too drunk."

Alex finishes his beer. Julie pops him open another. "Fuck him. Want to play some darts?"

They move over to the dartboard. She goes first. Julie's brown hair falls over her shoulders gracefully when she walks. Her back arching ever so slightly when she picks up the darts. Alex tries not to stare at her boobs, which did jiggle a little when she threw the first dart. Her ass looks round and firm. She turns in time to catch him looking. "I saw you lookin' at my ass."

"Who, me? Nah, I didn't mean to do that." Alex is a terrible liar.

"Don't be embarrassed." She hands him the darts. "Want to know how I knew you weren't gay earlier?"

Alex was game. He reached for the darts. Their hands touch. "Yeah, how?"

"Because I saw you shine. Gay guys don't shine to straight girls like me." Julie bows in a way that made her look mysteriously dignified. It was almost like she graciously accepted him for acting like a jerk. Getting a little cocky now, she yanks the darts from his hand. "Now see if you can hit the twenty on the first try."

Alex took the darts back and hit it dead on. "How 'bout that?" Alex wasn't sure if he'd be on or off tonight. Looks like the former showed up. "Your turn."

"Beginner's luck. Let me try now." She snatches a dart from his hand and misses. "You're up again."

Alex wants the chance to get closer. "Can I show you a trick?" "Sure." She welcomes him into her aura.

Alex nuzzles in gently. He takes Julie's forearm in his hand, leaning in to teach her a little something. When he put his other arm around her shoulder to steady her balance, she meets him with a kiss.

It's a surprise for Alex, albeit a pleasant one. He opens his eyes to make sure he isn't hallucinating. There she is. Eyes closed, looking radiant. She extends her face to him a full fifty percent. He returns favor, leaning in with the other fifty.

They kiss lightly at first. Then he feels her lick his upper lip. He responds gently, not getting hot too early. She turns and puts her arms around his neck. He drops the darts on the floor.

The world fades away.

***

The phone rings. Alex wakes. He sees the clock. 6:30. It could only be one person this early.

"Hey, Dad."

"Hey bud. Got some bad news." "What's up?"

"Your grandmother passed."

***

The funeral was terrible. Alex had to see his dad cry again. His grandfather, Joseph, Diane. Everyone crying. His mom didn't show. She hated his grandmother. They didn't get along at all. Sue routinely said bad things about her each and every time Alex would return from weekends with his dad as a child. She would sit on his bed while he unpacked his Pokémon suitcase. The grilling would last forever.

"Do you love her more than me?" "Do you wish I was her?"

"You'd rather live with her, right?" "Do you think she's prettier than me?" "Why do you hate me so much?

Do you visit them because you hate me?"

Alex shivers thinking back. He felt so cold and alone. His grandmother was a beacon of hope in his life. She would spend more time with him than anyone. Alex spent the first 12 years of his life with Sue, and somehow has more memories with his grandmother. Good memories too. Memories of Avalon. Going to the beach. Swimming in the bay. She would take him to nature preserves to look at birds. There were lots of museum trips to Philadelphia. Alex could remember the city would hang all the flags of the world along the Ben Franklin Parkway on Memorial Day Weekend. That's how he knew it was shore season. They'd go to the Franklin Institute or the Academy of Natural Sciences. Alex's favorite were the T-Rex bones at the Academy and the planetarium at the Institute. She'd buy him educational books on dinosaurs, plants, and animals.

There were also the times when Dad had to work late. She'd make Alex dinner, put him to bed. Watch over him while he slept. There was always paper in the house for Alex to draw. Markers, colored pencils, pens, whatever he wanted in that regard. Alex's grandmother was the only source of enrichment he had throughout childhood. Then there was his mother. Mentally abusing him for wanting to spend time with someone who actually cared how he did in school. Who his friends were or if he had clean clothes in the morning. *Life's a bitch*, Alex thinks to himself.

Alex didn't get invited to the lawyer's office, but waits for his dad back at the house on Euclid.

Alex looks out the window. The sun's going down. He hears the truck pull up in the alley behind the kitchen. He walks out. His dad waves.

"Hey, bud."

"Hey, Dad. How's everything?"

67

"Well, your grandmother's dead. Other than that, things are peachy."

Dad's wicked sense of humor's relentless. He does that to hide his feelings. Alex gets it, but thinks it's a useless waste of energy. If you're sad, just be sad. If you're happy, just be happy. He thinks back to some Karate classes his grandmother enrolled him in the first week he lived with Dad in 7th grade. His sensei gave him a book on Buddha. The point was for him to learn to live in the moment. Not the past or the future, but the now. He never forgot it.

"I got some news for ya. Let's go sit down in the kitchen." Alex's dad hugs him quick and walks inside. Alex follows.

Alex's dad cracks a beer and sits down. He takes a long pull of the can of Busch before speaking. Alex dry heaves a little thinking about drinking Busch. He used to steal a couple each week to get used to the taste. It didn't work. Alex still hates the flavor. He wonders if his dad lost his sense of taste somehow.

"Your grandfather's moving to Avalon." "Cool. What happens with this place?"

"I'm moving here. I'd like to talk to you about your inheritance." "What inheritance?"

"So, there's the house on Church Street."

"What about it?"

"The deal is, if you graduate college next year, it's yours. No mortgage, no strings. You move in, come to work with me, and make a life for yourself."

Alex's dad sticks out his hand to shake. "Deal?" Alex leaps over the table to hug him. "Deal!"

Chapter 8
Alex

Six weeks of community service starts this morning. Alex is to report to Mrs. Smith at the Williamsport Public Library downtown on 4th Street, which is only about six blocks from Alex's building. In a city of 50,000 people, downtown may only be a few blocks away.

Alex walks methodically on the broken sidewalk to avoid rolling his ankle. The old concrete walkways along the streets had been pushed upward over time by the maple trees. When city officials plan to do something good, like plant more trees on Earth Day for example, they sometimes overlook things. In this case, the thin stretch of grass between the sidewalk and curbs may not be the best place to plant trees. Not only do the sidewalks need to be repaired, but they also have to consider how to correct the giant roots that are blocking all the sewers. Cutting them down is probably the only solution if they want to protect the delicate ankles of all pedestrians with lousy balance.

Passing through the bad tree area lasts for a few blocks until he reaches what's considered downtown. A string of old bars mixed with real estate offices and second-hand stores. A pretty cool Masonic Lodge sticks out as one of Alex's favorite spots along the walk downtown. He stops to take it in. The shapes. Square and compasses. The level and plumb. All leading back to Sacred Geometry. If you connect the dots on the square and compasses, it makes the Star of David. Alex has an idea for the poster. He'll flesh out the details later.

He passes the big catholic church. St. Alphonso's parish. The one where Jesse went growing up. He's the only local in the group. Apparently, Jesse had a difficult time. There was a priest who paid special attention to Jesse back when he received his first Holy Communion. Jesse ended up with a bit of a rap sheet from his more mischievous days as a Williamsport youth. One of which involved him mooning everyone in Sunday service after the priest in question asked Jesse if he needed assistance taking the collection plate to the office. Jesse may or may not have ball-tapped the priest before telling the crowd how beautiful his butthole looked. Jesse thought if it was good enough for the priest, it was good enough for the parish. He didn't take into account that the Catholic School would toss him out afterward. Alex thought it was a good move. He was better off without those people in his life anyway. The move to Williamsport High put Jesse on a path toward Franklin Tech. If not for all that, Alex and Jesse's lives probably wouldn't have crossed.

After shuffling his feet long enough to feed his procrastinating spirit, Alex finally makes it to the library. The mid-1930s limestone building looks somewhat out of place with the dilapidated three-story rental properties surrounding it. Alex thinks of the Masonic Lodge and the Church. Those could've been some of the original buildings. All the other crap holes intermittently rose from the ground since Williamsport's heyday during the Great Depression. Back when the city was known to have more millionaires per square mile than any other place in America. Logging. Who knew?

Alex opens the door to the library for his new adventure as a statistical hash mark in the Central Pennsylvania Criminal Justice System.

***

Alex pushes a cart of books to the non-fiction section. *There must be thousand god damn books behind the counter that need to be put away*, Alex thinks to himself on the way. A never-ending stream of dusty aisles surrounds Alex as he attempts to check for the *Aa* through *An* section.

Thinking about Mrs. Smith, she seems like an OK boss. All he has to do is shuffle books in order for the next five weeks to pass. As long as there's no screw-ups, she'll sit back and eat her tuna salad sandwiches and leave Alex in peace. *Who eats tuna sandwiches for breakfast*, Alex asked no one. Alex can't seem to figure out her odd accent. Like a southerner from the hood, but she appears to be a local. Then there's her really tan Caucasian skin that closely resembles moldy beef jerky.

The stranger part was the unfolded paper napkin tucked into the collar of her moo-moo, which seems to stop nothing from saturating the upper portion of her clothing with sandwich juice. For some reason, overweight, elderly women prefer moo-moos over regular clothes. Alex thinks the color scheme of said garment looks like a red tablecloth wrapped around a wet sack of potatoes that was beaten with a shovel multiple times a day. She could cut back on the baby powder infused perfume too. *Christ*. It makes Alex's eyes water. He can smell the JC Penny brand, Jessica Simpson labeled, odoriferous concoction from halfway across the musty library. Oh, the humanity.

Alex finds the *Aa* section after stewing about his new boss and trying not to breathe through his nose for what seemed like an hour.

He stacks the books one by one. Easy mindless work. Eyes find author's name. Hand meets book. Book shifts to other hand. Eyes find book's alphabetical home. Book meets other books on shelf.

His thoughts drift as the rhythm of the movements become second nature. As an Ayn Rand book finds its way to the shelf, he zeros in on the spine. "Atlas Shrugged." Just then, something that had previously occupied the back of his mind shoves its way to the front.

Ayn Rand's Jewish. The poster!

The poster should be something related to Judaism. The Yamakas need to be incorporated. Sacred Geometry as well.

Walking back, he thinks about the fiction books. He'd go there next. Alex could get lost for a bit to get more ideas for the poster. He makes way behind the counter to stack another round of books on his cart.

He looks to the office. Mrs. Smith's finished eating. She brushes the crumbs from her desk into a swollen leather hand. What the hell did she even have the napkin for if it served no other purpose than to signal a white flag entry into a life of obesity? She could do that with a white moo-moo pretty easily. No napkin necessary and Mrs. Smith could save some trees while she's at it. The irony of Mrs. Smith potentially giving a crap about saving trees while managing a library was not lost on Alex.

Alex's face gets pimp slapped by a green fart cloud that could have been caused by nothing other than Mrs. Smith's face hole. He tries to breathe through his mouth again to avoid fainting from the smell. After the tuna sandwich, the odor resembled something like fresh tire rubber scented mothballs.

He finishes stacking the books on his cart and makes a pact with himself to not brush his teeth and to drink plenty of coffee before coming to work. Close talking with Mrs. Smith would be a priority tomorrow morning.

Following another wave of nausea, Alex finds himself standing in the fiction aisle. At last, he was struck with full inspiration for the poster. "The DaVinci Code" shone from the humidity-damaged particleboard shelving like the Burning Bush.

That's it!

He quickly takes the book from the shelf. The one with the pictures! He opens it and flips through to find an image of the Mona Lisa.

Now, it's clear to him. The poster. The one to kick things off. He's got it.

From behind, an arm wraps around his waist. A familiar warmth on his neck and ear.

"Hey you," Julie's whisper voice rings out like a bell. He melts a little. The book in his hand drops to the floor.

She moves halfway. He moves halfway. Their faces meet to sneak a good kiss before the hug. When they stop, Julie peers over to the desk and giggles.

Alex pulls her in close again to whisper in her ear. "Hey you. Didn't think you were out of bed yet."

"Oh, come on. I was up before you were." She was right. Alex just had nothing else to tease her about. "So, where's Mrs. Doubtfire?"

Alex wonders for a second if Mrs. Smith is a man dressed in drag. Maybe Robin Williams is alive after all. Faking his death for a life of tuna salad sandwiches and red tablecloth colored moo-moos in America's armpit. Stranger things have happened.

Alex peeks around the corner. "She must be somewhere on break."

Julie pulls him in closer for a kiss. "Want to get kinky in the library?" She smiles and winks before kissing him deeper.

An idea springs in his mind. "Yeah, follow me."

***

They get comfortable in the empty room Alex found while dusting earlier. Julie sets herself on the table. Alex pulls up her shirt and unsnaps her bra in one fluid motion. Julie opens his pants.

They go at it for a few minutes before the lights flick on. Alex and Julie instinctively jump away from each other to cover themselves. Alex smells baby powder. Once their eyes adjust, all they see is a red moo-moo. All at once he understood why Bull Fighters use the color red.

"Girl, you best get yo filthy ass out my mafuckin' library." Mrs. Smith points to the door.

Julie finishes buttoning up. "See you later," she whispers before scampering off.

"And you. Put that thing away and get yo punk ass in my office. Pronto!" Mrs. Smith makes a face like she's the one who smelled shit before letting the door slam closed.

There must be an automatic arm on the door, Alex thinks to himself. *Either that or half the building is sinking into the ground.* Alex thinks more about other possible reasons to make the door slam on its own. Nearly convincing himself that Mrs. Smith's arm might pop off or deflate from that much physical exertion.

It had to be the building.

***

Mrs. Smith's office is horrific. She made sure there was minimal airflow to maximize the impact of the smell on Alex's acute senses. Feeling a lot like Wolverine from the X-Men, Alex is confident about tracking someone like her in the wilderness. On top of the tuna and the baby powder, Mrs. Smith's breath smelled like she brushed her teeth with a lump of wet dog shit. Not even like the picturesque dog shit that you want to put in a bag and light on fire on your buddy's porch, but the gross mushy kind that happens when pet owners are too lazy to venture out to buy the good dry dog food and feed the animal dollar store canned food instead.

"Boy, you done fucked up this time. Being here on community service. Now dis. Did you know we had a Kindergarten book reading scheduled over lunchtime? They should be here any minute." Alex second-guessed the dog shit toothpaste. Maybe she's really old and needs a diaper, but instead of throwing it out to get a fresh one, she eats the contents instead.

"Ah, no, Mrs. Smith. I just figured my girlfriend and I could find some quality time whenever possible. It's been a rough month for me. I want to feel something good in my life. You know?"

"Mmm, hmmm. I know what you was feelin' alright and it wasn't nothing good, but I'll tell you what."

Her fat hands drop in her lap. Alex resists thinking about what other smells may be contained within the adult diaper. He chooses to respond verbally instead of projectile vomiting in her face. "Ok, go ahead."

"Here's the deal. I saw you without that shirt on. You quite the specimen. Young, tight, blonde. This is what's gonna happen. You gonna pose for the next five Saturdays in our paintin' class here at the library. And you know what? It's gonna be in that same room you and your lady friend was shacked up in. Now, ain't that some shit?"

Alex flinches. "Yes, ma'am that is some shit."

"So, Imma forget about the crude act I found you and your lady friend engaged in only moments ago and look forward to seeing you naked in a different context a few days from now. You got that?"

Alex's mind plays catch-up. "Wait. I'm sorry," he wipes sweat from his brow, "you want me to be a nude model?"

"See. I knew you were a smart boy the moment I laid eyes on you. Now get your punk ass back to work before I call the courthouse and get you one of them Megan's Law driver's licenses."

Alex's stomach churned. Could've been the child molester joke, the body odors or the prospect of old ladies painting his dangle. Either way, Alex aspired to never be in a small room with Mrs. Smith. Ever again.

***

Saturday morning. Alex reflects on the last few days while on his way to work wearing nothing but a trench coat, boxer briefs, and sandals.

The week flew by. The first rendering of the poster was done. Alex stayed up all night after the sexcapade in the library. Willing to believe it was the inspiration he needed to finish.

The poster turned out great. He used Photoshop on this one. There was too much to draw. It was the Mona Lisa, only with bigger tits. Her iconic dress rolled down. Arms and chest covered in tattoos of Sacred Geometric shapes. Masonic tools, the Star of David. Her eye make-up more punk rock with green and pink hues. Her hair subtly streaked with rainbow colors. Her bare, tatted arms crossed with hands facing upward gently holding a baby version of Adam, Yamaka and all, suckling from her right tit while his tiny hand covered the nipple of the left.

Alex rushed over to the Rainbow Room to show the guys the next morning. After the initial shock of seeing DaVinci's great work turn streetwalker, they stood to give Alex a round of applause. It felt great to be appreciated.

They even agreed to perform at a fundraiser for Joseph. Since the accident, Alex had only been home once to see his brother, but had been texting him a lot. Dad needed forty grand to retrofit Joseph's house and his office to accommodate the wheelchair. When Alex floated the idea for the fundraiser to them, it was a slam-dunk.

He and Julie had dinner at the Triangle Tavern on Friday night. That's the pink triangular shaped Italian restaurant Gina used to take him to occasionally. It wasn't weird. Alex's favorite is their veal piccata. Julie ordered the chicken parm. One of the waiters was a regular at the Rainbow. He brought complimentary wine with their meal and shots of Limoncello for dessert. They both blacked out. It was anyone's guess if the sex after was good or not.

Alex finds himself inside the library suddenly, which is buzzing with half dead old people from all walks of life. Every color of the human spectrum. Word must've gotten out that there was new blood in the form of a naked muse. Mrs. Smith herds him into the sex room for the viewing. She changed her perfume for the occasion to cat piss and baking chocolate. Even spackled some make-up over her eye sockets looking like a darker skinned version of Mimi from the "Drew Carey Show." Alex arches his back as he's ushered in to the unusually cold room.

The tables in the room are set up in a U shape. He finds a step stool leading to a lone table in the center, which is where his crucifixion will take place. He stands by the step stool and wonders if this is rock bottom. He looks over to see Mrs. Smith giving him the clown eyes.

Fuck it, he says to himself before dropping the trench coat with a cape-swoosh. He begins stepping up when Mrs. Smith chimes in.

"Uh, ah. The deal was fully nude. Now disrobe, Mr. Muse."

Alex rolls his eyes. Then drops his drawers. So cold. He shivers, stepping out of the underpants. Stepping up to the table, he feels his middle thumb shake a bit from the motion. Then he hears a sound. Kind of like a child's laugh, but throatier. The Asian woman to his left. She's laughing and pointing. Not cool at all.

"He's not Mr. Muse. He's Mr. Rice Dick!" The laughing and pointing continued.

Alex wonders if Zilla had beat him to death in that fight and this is the punishment losers face in Hell?

***

The end of the semester came and went for Alex. Mrs. Smith laid off the Saturday painting sessions and his community service was ending in the next few days. Things were looking up.

He'd gone home for a week to help his dad build Joseph a ramp to make the office handicapped accessible. Alex thought about his brother selling his house by the mall and buying a row home in Ambler so he wouldn't need to climb steps. Joseph could wheel in right from the street.

They hired a company to put in chair rails, but a small elevator from the garage off the alley all the way to the 2nd floor was the real expensive part. Plus, he needed the car to be fitted for hand controls. Price came out to 48 grand. Way more than they had planned for.

When Alex came back, he met with the band at his shit box apartment. While he was home, the family talked about a fundraiser. Alex felt pessimistic about raising that much cash in one shot. The guys now offered to come and play for free. Alex almost began crying.

Shrugging off the tears, Alex exclaims, "Next topic, gig posters!"

He had more posters to share. New ones. The previous week, Adam took the Mona Lisa to the Rainbow to get Silvio's opinion. He liked it, but asked for some less racy ones just in case. Silvio's family back in Philly is Puerto Rican and may not be as liberal with their taste.

Alex took the advice and modeled the new posters after iconic album covers from the '90s. Adam sits still with sweaty palms.

He pulls out the first from a protective cover. Another image of baby Adam, with Yamaka, underwater in his birthday suit, chasing a one-dollar bill. Alex felt queasy about making this one. People sometimes stereotype Jewish people with having money. Adam told him to stop worrying so much. Nirvana's "Nevermind" was the defining album of the Grunge era. It could also be considered one of the most memorable images of the decade. Maybe their biggest hit had only three chords, but man did Adam and the guys rock out to "Come As You Are." The crowd ate it up.

The next was after N.W.A.'s "Straight Out of Compton."

"Oh dude!" Rick took it from Alex's hands, an instant favorite.

The image, like the original album cover, is of all the guys in Hasidic garb, looking down at someone on the receiving end of a beatdown. Pre-nineties

76

maybe, but badass, no doubt! Their version of "Dopeman" is great. Chad moves to the turntables for a Dre impression. Rick, Jesse, and Adam would take three mics and light up the stage. Rick's Eazy E impression is spot on. Rapping is when he'd take the spotlight from Adam. He's got the flow for it.

Then there's Alex's take on the Beastie Boys' "Check Your Head." The white font above and below their image perfectly replicated. The guys wearing signature garb, sitting on a curb looking off in different directions at nothing. It's Chad's favorite. He has all their albums and searched endlessly for bootleg performance of "So What'cha Want" the day after MCA died. God rest his soul.

Lastly, and Alex's personal favorite, of Jesse in a wig and nurses uniform putting on a blue rubber glove. Modeled after the famous porn star Janine. "Enema of the State" was Blink 182's 3rd album and had some fun tunes. The guys sometimes threw in "Adam's Song" with their act. For obvious reasons. Alex leaned toward this one because Jesse had the hardest time working at the gay bar. Being a local from St. Alphonso's parish, where homosexuality is terribly frowned upon, made it tough for Jesse to sit at family dinners. Alex thought Jesse had it rough considering what the *male* priest did to him growing up. Jesse wasn't shy about his experience. In fact, it was what he led with when meeting new friends. Jesse's an open funny guy though. He felt the Blink 182 reference. It worked for him after the shock of seeing himself in drag wore off.

Chapter 9
Adam

Dresher, PA. Adam takes a trip home to see his parents before the block party tomorrow. Alex and the guys were still sleeping at the house on Church Street, which apparently belongs to him now. Turns out Mr. Walker isn't such a dick after all. The old man just gave it to him. Much to Adam's surprise, Alex's dad didn't request an arm or the soul of his first-born child. Adam doesn't know why he's so surprised. Stranger things have happened.

Adam pulls up the long driveway of his parent's house with Rick's rape van. He feels a sense of pride when the engine cuts off. Home with his parents, about to do a charity gig. Life couldn't be better.

The Steinberg residence never changes. The freshly manicured lawn surrounding the 5000 square foot McMansion shimmers in the morning light. The Japanese maple trees look terrific with the newly mulched beds. Adam regrets not coming home for Tulip season. His mother routinely had tulips of every color planted when the weather changed for the better. Same as the cherry blossom trees that line the driveway. Spring is Adam's favorite season. Summer begins in a few days, which meant it would be lily season. Asian lilies smelled the best. Also meaning that golf season is in full swing— pun intended. Adam looked forward to an early game with his dad this morning after breakfast.

Adam walks into the garage. The overhead door's left open for him. Adam could smell the old grass from the yard tools. Adam's dad wasn't the type to do much yard work, but liked to request the landscapers use their things to keep the garage smelling like a hardware store. It feels important to keep things that way.

He opens the house door to the mudroom and kicks off his Chuck Taylor's. The smell of toasting bagels fills his nostrils taking him back to that warm place in childhood that felt both safe and timeless. Williamsport had no decent bagel place. There's an OK grocery store near the college that baked their bagels fresh, but there's no Jews there. The ones mom gets from the deli in Dresher are extraordinary. There's a love that's put into food of the Tribesmen that cannot be duplicated by anyone else.

His mom and dad greet Adam with hugs and kisses. They fuss over him like the parents of an only child would. Breakfast is ready. Adam looks at the spread with famishment. Just realizing he hadn't eaten since a day and a half ago. Everyone in the band rode in Rick's rape van on the way down. The vehicle is so massive that Alex was able to pack it solid with their gear, instruments, the band members, himself, Julie, and their luggage. Comfortably no less. The trip is about three and a half hours. Plenty of time to get their shroom on. Not interested in getting high, Alex drove. Everyone else chilled in the back for a jam session. Rick strummed the guitar while Adam sang some Marley for everyone. His version of "Three Little Birds" set Jesse at ease during his flashback. Poor Julie had no idea starting a conversation about the division of church and state would send Jesse on a tear like that. She figured out Jesse's weakness the hard way. Adam thought it scared Julie a bit to see Jesse lose his mind. The pain from the molestation goes so deep. She understood.

Their high lasted into the night. After that, it was 40s of Olde English 800 from the corner store at the end of Alex's street. It's that very place the block party stage will be set. Alex described it as a five points intersection of sorts, but it's more like two alleys intersecting with a couple of streets that dead end into the train tracks.

Growing up, Adam and Alex went to rival high schools. Ambler High and Dresher are very close together. Side by side on a map. Alex and Adam had no knowledge of one another until college. Adam has some friends from Ambler, but never brought them up to Alex. When they came home for Thanksgiving, Adam was tipped off that Alex Walker was a loser and a psycho. Adam didn't get it. Not until he saw Alex bite Zilla's dick. He heard other stories since then. From other people they knew mutually. Still, Adam just couldn't see it. He knows when a person is bullied for being different. His people suffered for it since the time of Ancient Egypt.

Adam's mom smeared cream cheese on his well-done Everything bagel and gave him a plate of Lox, onions, and capers to top it off. Accompanied by strong coffee, OJ, and turkey bacon. There would be no pork in this house.

Ever. Adam's mom would have cardiac if she knew he ate scrapple most mornings for breakfast at school. He, Rick, and Jesse would slice the scrapple about an inch thick. Then pan fry until crisp. Cut it in half longways like bread, and stuff it with bacon and eggs. Delish! *Some things Mom can live without knowing*, Adam thinks to himself.

"So my lil Mensch," Adam takes a bite of his breakfast and braces himself. Dad typically led his lectures with a compliment. "You've finally graced us with your presence, and to think, all it took was a crippled schmuck to get you back here."

Adam winces with emotional pain. "Ok, so Dad, it's Alex's brother. The guy's a reborn Christian. He's not a schmuck. He's in trouble and he needs our help."

Adam's father digs deeper. "Couldn't even come back for Passover? You should think about your mother more during your disappearing act. What about her feelings?"

Adam's mom pitches in, "My heart and my soul. It's missing when you don't come home. I think about your empty room and my eyes roll."

She turns to her husband, "Larry, see what his absence does to me? I'm speaking lyrically again."

"Adam, see what you do? She's rhyming. They're not even good lyrics this time. Do you want her to start writing songs again? What that would do for our family?"

Adam remembered back to childhood. Mom's famous friends. She first wrote a song back in the early 2000s. There were others after that. The first one made their family a bundle, but Mom was gone for months at a time. Long stretches back and forth from LA to New York. On tour then back home. Lasting for years. It was difficult for Dad to juggle the Insurance Company and fatherhood. Adam was raised by a nanny. Monique was her name. Adam thought of her as his Russian stewardess. Monique watched Adam before and after his pubescent years. There to steer him into manhood. Dad was present at nights and weekends. They went to lots of games together. Season tickets, courtside seats for the Sixers. The team was a laughing stock in those days. Tickets were cheap. Real cheap. Dad locked them in thinking they'd be worth more than double later. He was right. They started winning again around 2017. Dad's a great businessman like that. Terrific insight.

"Mom, I'm very sorry I wasn't here for Passover dinner. I had a paper due and couldn't make it back. You know this. I called."

Adam's Mom throws her head back. "Oh, you called. Because that's ever enough to satisfy a mother's love."

"Oy vey. You called." Larry butts in. "That school of yours taking you away from me. The insurance company. Supposed to be our family legacy. And you take off for the Poconos to study Robotics. I see the importance of the trade, but are you going to be working in a factory?"

Adam's mom cuts him off. "Larry, our cousin Jacob. He owns a factory. Adam will work with him."

"That putz! Adam's supposed to sell him insurance, not work in his sweatshop. Oh, the humanity."

Adam put his hands up for mercy. "Guys, I'm here now. Let's stop with the Passover talk already. I've called like a hundred times since then. And college. You both agreed to send me there. I mean, you're paying for it. Now you act like you don't remember?"

Adam's mom touches his arm lovingly. "Honey, it's called selective memory. Did you really think we wouldn't bring up Passover?" She squeezes his cheek and miles. "Now eat. You look famished."

"Yes. Tee time is in 40 minutes. Eat up. We need to be ready."

Adam reflects on the conversation as he finishes up his breakfast. They never talk about the band. Just give him guilt trips about his selection of vocation or his non-Jewish friends. You'd think they'd be pissed about the gentiles wearing Yamakas, but no. Mom and Dad were something of a mystery to Adam still. Maybe one day he'd understand. But until then, he has a life to live.

***

On the course, Adam and Larry spoke nothing about Passover or the feelings of an overbearing mother. They swung at the tiny white balls with the finesse of two people who golfed for the better part of their lives. Drinking light beer and smoking cigars together was an added bonus.

As Adam drives the cart to the back nine. There's a wait for the next hole. He wonders if his dad would make it to the block party tomorrow. *There's really no telling without asking*, Adam thinks to himself.

"Hey, Dad, will you and Mom be making an appearance at our gig tomorrow?"

"Of course we will. I made sure there was no work scheduled. We wouldn't miss your big day. Graduating from the homosexual taverns to the slums of Ambler. We wouldn't miss it for the world." He's joking about Ambler. Dad was a big fan of Dresher High School football and takes any chance to poke fun at their high school rivals. To people who didn't know Adam's dad, they'd think he was a prick because of the way he talks. His sense of humor never takes a break.

"Dad, I'm so happy to hear you say that. The band really means a lot to me. To have your support is…" Adam feels choked up. He really wasn't sure if his family would show.

Larry saw Adam's expression and melted. "Ah! Has my lil mensch become verklempt? Aw, come here for hug time."

Adam stops the cart for a hug and a happy cry on his dad's shoulder.

Their day is complete. No more golf necessary. They could go home now.

Adam let go first. He sees the people in front of them have moved on to the next hole. "How 'bout that back nine?"

"Good show, boy." Larry grabs his driver. "Let's see if your old man still has it."

Adam watches his hero take a good whack at the ball. *Nothing like a game of golf to bring out the best in people*, he thinks to himself before taking a swig of warm beer.

Chapter 10
Robert

The morning of the block party. Robert was instructed by John to wake Alex and build the stage. John would have the materials delivered to the front of the corner store by 10:00 sharp. The stage was the same one that Diane's baby performed her first dance routine with the pee-wee ballerinas on Memorial Day at the VFW in West Ambler. Robert already set that up and broke it down once, and it was just a couple weeks ago. He didn't really need Alex's help, but John didn't like letting Alex sleep in if he could help it. Even if the guy hasn't been on payroll for a while now.

Robert looks at his watch. 9:30. He walks into Alex's new place, which is really John's old place, and finds the two band members sleeping on the wrap around couch. The dark skinned one, Rick, lays next to a glass bowl filled with last night's blackened pot. He wishes for a second to trade places with one of them.

Block that from the mind, Robert thinks to himself. There's too much to lose. John stuck his neck out for Robert too many times. He's a good man.

Robert looks around for Chad. No sign of him. Must be crashed in one of the spare rooms on the third floor.

He makes his way for Alex's room on the second floor. Alex didn't bother to move bedrooms. John's master suite at the end of the hall had a walk-in closet and a full bath. Alex seems to be using the hall bath still. Strange.

Robert walks into Alex's room without knocking. They're asleep. Robert looks around. He sees Alex's favorite superhero, Moon Knight, staring down at him from a poster on the wall. Then Robert looks at the bed and notices something that makes his heart skip a beat. Julie's bare breast hanging out from under the covers. Robert admires how much bigger her breasts are out from her shirt. How nice and round it sits on top of her chest. Something starts to move inside his pants. *Block that out too, Robert*, he commands himself to close the door gently and knock. So he does.

"What?" Alex moans from inside.

"Your dad wants us at the corner store by 10:00 to set up the stage." "Come back later. We're busy."

"I can't. Have strict orders to throw cold water on you if we're late."

From inside, Julie pushes Alex out of bed. "Get up, sleepy head. Your little brother's waiting."

Robert hears Alex walk into a wall, while looking for his clothes. After a minute of rummaging through bags and the sound of friction, Alex materializes in the hall. Alex opens and closes the door too quickly for Robert to see Julie again.

"Sup, bro. Daddy sent you to roll me out of bed, huh?"

Robert could smell the stale party odors on Alex from last night. Robert thought of when they were young. Stealing beer and cigarettes. Hiding in their fort to smoke and drink. Robert was only twelve at the time. Alex and his friends were two years older. That was the year of Mischief Night. It's when he and Alex became brothers. Not officially, but it was when their group of friends came together.

Robert responds without flinching, "You have exactly five minutes to brush that stink from your face and follow me down the street."

Alex mumbles something unintelligible and did as instructed.

***

10:00. John's late. Alex offers to buy Robert a coffee inside the corner store while they wait. It's a place they both enjoy walking into. No matter how many times they do, it always feels like they could find something new even though the place or the contents within haven't changed since 1989, or at least that's how far back John says anyway. The décor consisting of orange counter tops with stainless steel accents, the old news clippings, phone numbers pinned to the wall of people who've been dead for ten years, the Snowball cupcakes, the dusty cans Dinty Moore beef stew.

The place is essentially a time warp, but also something beloved by many. Hence the longevity. There aren't many corner stores still in business.

The one thing that appeals to both Alex and Robert are the stacks of penny candy containers. Five cents for a strawberry flavored sour straw, 25 cents for

84

a Blow Pop, and a penny for a Swedish Fish. Robert feels there's no place like the corner store on Earth. Makes him feel at home. It's the little things like this place that make Robert happy.

Mrs. Flocco behind the counter did her thing when they ordered their food like substances that stood in for breakfast. She even picked her nose and wiped it on her apron for old times' sake. Thankfully, her sausage finger hands didn't touch anything of importance this morning. Robert wonders for a second if she's a vampire. Her face and build hadn't changed since he arrived in town five years back. Her accent kind of reminded him of something eastern European even though he knows for a fact she's Italian. *Vampires could be from Italy too*, Robert thinks to himself. It would be unfair to exclude an entire country from the option of eternal damnation.

Robert's half Italian, just not as much as the Floccos. It's not the same thing. The American born people aren't taken as seriously in those circles. It's not like the people around here don't run shit. That's not true at all. The difference is more of a cultural thing. Like how Robert refuses to hit women and children when he's older like he's seen his dad and cousin Gabe do to their women. Robert and Alex experienced that with his dad and Sue many times over. Then there's Gabe, who beat Diane in the bathroom of the VFW for letting their baby get spaghetti sauce on her dress before the recital. Robert knows it's their heritage that made his family members act that way. Or it's the drugs. Either way, he aspires for more.

Robert ponders the issue of his own. The coke. So good. Who needs coffee when you can have that? If he could do a bump right now, that stage would get built within minutes. Guaranteed. Too bad he couldn't do it again. Too much, too fast, at too young of an age. He and Joseph both. It's almost like each person has a health meter and if a person uses too much of that health meter too early in life, then they can't hang with the cool people anymore and have to submit to god like Joseph did. Yuk, Robert couldn't hack it. He tried a few times to speak at those meetings. It was awful. Like a bunch of sad old people bragging about their former conquests then lecturing people not to be like them. Fucking hypocrites.

Outside, they finish the coffee. Alex remarks about it tasting like three-day old moldy diarrhea.

Robert responds by saying, "So what, the caffeine portion does the trick. How do you know what moldy diarrhea tastes like anyway?"

Alex shrugs then tosses out the last few sips. Robert feels a ping of regret watching the cup go into the trashcan. He could've had more caffeine if Alex wasn't so wasteful. Whatever. Alex bought the coffee. Not like Robert had any say about how much of Alex's coffee actually hit his stomach.

***

John shows up exactly thirty minutes late. It took Alex precisely sixty minutes to begin dry heaving and a half hour after that to sweat out his remaining hangover.

Robert had been taking it easy since he dropped out of high school last year. It was his option. After Sue and his dad divorced, John found him sleeping on a park bench. His Grandfather Luke had been long gone, their family house sold, Tony skipped town with whatever bit of money he had left, and Robert was alone for the second time in his life.

He could remember looking up at the morning sun, and seeing John's face looking down at him. It was like a dream. John reached out his hand to help Robert off the bench, but not before uttering something very Walker first. "Get up, kid. The cops'll pick you up for alcohol poisoning." It was a reference to when Alex and Robert got caught puking in John's front yard late one night after drinking large quantities of Vodka and Hawaiian punch. It was a disaster. Alex shit himself in the bathtub and Robert pissed himself on the carpet. John grounded Alex for a month and sentenced Robert to six Saturday's hard labor in exchange for not telling Tony. It was worth it. That was Robert's first load ever. Alex's friends are the best when it comes to drinking.

Alex and those guys dabbled with drugs. Lots of pot, shrooms, sometimes acid, there was rumors of peyote, but nothing more than that. It was his time with Joseph and the much older crew from Ambler, that gave Robert his nasty coke addiction.

What Alex didn't know, and could never understand, is that Robert had been watching Joseph, Tony, and Gabe sell dope for years. It actually started way before that, when he was really little. Back when he could remember his mom and dad together. When his dad used to be in commercials. There were always lots of basketball games on, and Robert remembers telling the bill collectors at the door to come back next week. Except they weren't bill collectors. Robert was grown enough now for Joseph to share. They were actually sharks coming to collect his dad's gambling debt. The tradeoff was selling coke and ecstasy to rich kids in Manhattan.

Yeah, great times, Robert says to himself as he snaps out of his self-imposed rut.

The stage went together within a couple hours. John hired an electrician to help Alex hook up the mics and speakers while the cops blocked off the streets funneling into the corner store. There's a whole bunch of other stuff Robert can't comprehend about what Alex is doing, but it all worked well enough for Alex to call the band for the sound check.

The electrician disappeared once it was time to fire up the sound system. He took a fist full of cash from John then murmured something about not having insurance before vanishing into thin air.

A little later, Robert looks up and sees Rick, Jesse and Chad up on stage. It must've took them less than ten minutes to get ready and shuffle down to the corner store.

Robert notices Rick grab only one mic.

Alex leans in. "They going to warm up. They like to pass the mic back and forth to get it going."

Robert has no idea what the hell that means, but OK.

"You guys ready?" Rick's mechanical voice asks a crowd of three people.

Alex cheers from the street below.

Robert imagines himself clapping, but doesn't follow through. John looks like a deer in headlights.

"Jesse. Chad. You guys ready for this?" "Yeah, buddy. Goin' with the Beasties?"

They warm up to "Pass the Mic" by the Beastie Boys.

Jesse aggressively takes the mic from Rick to kick his lyrics.

Jesse tosses the mic to Chad, who catches it then breaks into a full verse without missing a beat.

From his peripheral vision, Robert sees Adam materialize next to the stage.

Adam crosses his arms, head bopping a few times before the rest of the guys on stage notice him.

Chad stops rapping and tosses Adam the mic. Adam races up the steps for a quick verse.

Adam cuts it short. "Alright! We gonna do this tonight or what?" They slap hands to celebrate.

Adam looks for his stuff, but can't find it. "Alex, we need you up here, buddy."

Alex leaves Robert and John's side to help the band.

John looks to Robert. "They're gonna get up there and rap?"

Robert responds without confidence, "Yup. Rap rockin' like it's '98."

John grimaces. "Hope this thing pans out. If not, Joseph will need a genie lamp and a flying carpet to get out of the house."

Robert flinches. "Dude, that's mean. You really think that?"

John smiles and pats Robert's shoulder before walking away. "Nah, not really. Wasn't sure if you were paying attention though. Now I know you were."

Robert stands still to scan the situation. First, he watches the guys set up for a second. Then turns to see John fiddle around in his work truck. Feeling completely out of place and utterly alone, he wanders off to Joseph's house for some spiritual company.

Robert walks from the corner store into one of the alleys. He kicks the gravel and wonders if any of the guys knew he'd left. He looks back at the people buzzing about. No one notices him or calls his name. Robert aims back toward Joseph's direction. He cuts between a couple driveways in the alley to walk up the old concrete stairway leading from the alley to Park Avenue. Driveways are really too much of a compliment for what they actually are, which is a car sized piece of concrete between the alley and the garage.

The top of the stairway opens up into a breezeway between two long sets of row homes. Probably twenty on each side, nearly joining perpendicularly at the bend of the road. Had it not been for the breezeway, that is.

Robert looks around for a second thinking about Mischief Night. That Mischief Night. It was his first school year with Alex. Before John took him in. Around the time his biological dad finally went off the deep end, and sold all Robert's stuff for dope.

As he nears the sidewalk on Park Ave, he turns around to survey the rooftops. Clear as usual, but he can still picture the black sheet being drawn by the old heads. Joseph and Tyrone carrying boxes of Campbell's chicken noodle soup to the extension ladder a few houses down. Robert turns to look down the street where Uncle Scott, fought the cops. *What an epic night*, Robert thinks to himself.

He waves on a car, before crossing the street and making way to Joseph's place a block over on Southern Ave. He turns the corner from Park to Southern. Across the street, Tyrone meets with a couple who are looking at a place he's trying to flip. He shouts across the street to his big homie.

"What's up, Ty! You got the place lookin' good!"

Ty smiles back trying to get the couple away from Robert's shouting. "Thanks, bro! Let me show these nice people around then I'll holler back at you later."

Joseph and Tyrone were best friends growing up. Robert's big cousin, Gabe was also part of their crew at one point, before spinning off to do his own thing a couple years back when he began keeping book for the local gangsters after knocking up Diane. Robert learned to stay away from that side of the family, which is really his only side of the family excluding the Walkers, who aren't blood. Robert learned that blood doesn't always count for love.

After high school, Joseph and Ty went their separate ways too. Joe turned into Joseph after his bout with addiction, and Ty built a successful real estate business by flipping houses. Robert thinks it's nice seeing one of the guys doing good. The house Ty's flipping right now is directly across from the house Joseph bought. They barely say more than a few words to each other. Robert wasn't told exactly what happened, but thinks Diane has something to do with it.

***

Inside the house, Robert smells cologne. He can hear Joseph making his way down the stair rail. The squealing of the chair is accompanied by the thudding of the folded wheel chair being dragged behind as it bounces from one stair to the next.

"Who's that?" shouts Joseph.

"You know exactly who that is," Robert shouts back.

The stair rail skids into place at the bottom of the steps. Robert takes a shot at Joseph. "Damn, boy. I can't tell if I'm looking at Captain Hook or an old lady takin' her rascal to Walmart."

Joseph fires back, "Hey look, it's Oliver Twist. If you're hungry, there's some bread and water in the kitchen."

"I'm more interested in that stash of porn my dad got you after the accident. I hear you've been giving yourself the stranger lately. Being a lefty now has its perks, huh?"

Joseph waves his good fist at Robert. "I'll give you a stranger. Remember, I still got one good arm, and if I lose that then you'd better stay clear cause I'll head butt you."

"Just like the Black Knight from Monty Python?"

"You know it. Now help me throw this thing together." He hands Robert the orange and black wheelchair. Robert takes it thinking it reminds him of going to a Flyers game. The colors and all.

He helps his big bro from the steps.

"I'm good. Why don't you head downstairs? There's something you gotta see. I'll be here when you get back."

***

As Robert headed down the basement steps, he could hear the Phillies game from a TV. Strange thing is Joseph never set up anything down here. It was totally empty last time they hung out, which was only a few days back.

Robert's teenage hand glides across ridges of the faux wood paneling as he moves closer to the sound of the ballgame.

At the bottom of the steps, a familiar voice booms from an easy chair. "Sup, kid? Been too long. Glad to see me?" Tony rises from the chair.

His chest out, shoulders back, arms extended for a hug. Black hair slicked back, dark 5 o'clock shadow reminding Robert of how handsome his dad could be even still after all the drugs and alcohol he'd consumed over half a lifetime.

"Hey, dad. Glad to see you back." Robert lies to his dad as he forces a hug.

Chapter 11
Sue

The house smells like bleach, hairspray, and nail polish remover. Sue and Diane spent the morning cleaning. Now they're getting ready for the party. No babysitting for Diane today. She and the baby would need to be together. The whole family needs to show their support for Joseph. Not to mention, Sue's new man will be attending. Heading all the way in from Jersey.

She bends down to look into her makeup table mirror to fix her lipstick and put in her new diamond earrings. Real ones. From Tiffany's. Not the Mall Store crap Tony would snatch up after a big fight. Certainly not the Estate sale garbage John would bring home. No, no. Not this time. Sue found the right guy, with exquisite taste, and the funds to back it.

The doorbell rings. He's here. The baby's crying. Shit. Where's Diane?

Sue panics as she struggles to pick up the baby and find Diane.

In the kitchen, Diane packs a bag for the baby. Sue rushes in. "Take Maria. He's here!"

The doorbell rings a second time. Sue checks herself in the hallway mirror one more time to push up her tits and check her teeth. Everything's in order.

Her heart skips a beat when she opens the door. Peter Zilla looks down at her from his 6'2" stature. Clean and neat. Wearing Polo gear. Looking like he's going to play tennis or go to a beach bar in Avalon. She notices his Louis Vuitton belt. Burberry cologne. Dead sexy.

She cocks her head and smiles. "Hi." Peter flashes perfect teeth. "Hey." "Come on in."

"Don't mind if I do."

"Want some wine or something?"

"Sure."

"Red or white?" "Red, please." "You're alone?"

"Yes, Richard made other arrangements."

"Ok, no problem. I just thought he and Alex could. Well, you know." "We discussed it. He will do exactly as I say."

Sue throws her arms around Peter to kiss him. "Thank you, baby. These last few weeks have really been magical. This helps a lot."

"Least I could do for my favorite girl. Now where's that sweet baby you keep telling me about?"

Diane rushes in on cue. "Here's our little princess. Want to say hi?"

Peter extends his arms. "Sure, I love babies. So cute!" Maria doesn't mind the new hands holding her. She's a happy baby for the most part. Nearly fatherless, but happy. Very social for a toddler.

Sue watches Peter gently bounce Maria. She thinks about the day they met.

***

Williamsport. The day after Alex and Richard fought over that southern girl with the red hair. Sue watched John pull off on his bike. She hated that bike. Before they divorced, John had a Corvette. A nice one with a newer body style. He eventually sold it and got the bike. A Harley. Yuk. Say hello to a life of gaudy t-shirts and gasoline smelling beards. No thanks.

Peter on the other hand, looked angelic. Getting out of his Pearl Mercedes. In his business attire. Closing a deal on the phone before grabbing his hulking son from the jaws of the justice system. Well, of course Alex didn't fare well after that encounter, but Alex made his own bed by spending time with that girl. Richard was just doing what he was taught. Growing up in North Jersey came with its social standards. Certain things were more socially acceptable growing up that much closer to New York. It's just the way kids from money express themselves. Alex should've known better than to fight a kid like Richard. She never understood why Alex didn't just run. He's not a big kid. Alex had that issue growing up. He refused to run when the bullies lined up to hurt him. Not like Sue didn't want Alex to learn how to stand up for himself, but sometimes it's just the smart thing to do.

Peter spoke first, "Hey. You alright? Need any help?"

Sue felt like a damsel in distress. The tears began flowing as soon as the words formed. "No, my ex-husband just left me here after getting me drunk last night and trying to pass me around with his best friend. My son got into a fight, and I'm sitting here with no money and no way home. I don't know what to do." She wiped the tears without smearing her make-up. She could see Peter softening.

"Hey listen, I need to pick up my kid too. Also getting into a fight. More than a coincidence I'm sure, but hey, maybe you could meet me at the diner a few blocks from here. Give me an hour then I'll help you figure something out."

The thought of this handsome man giving her the ol' Ted Bundy was a little more of an afterthought. The whole package screamed of opportunity not horror.

She played it off. "Sure. Yeah. The diner. See you in an hour."

On the way home, Peter and Sue kissed for the first time at a stop light. Then again when they stopped to pee. Then again at the toll booth. After their fourth kiss, she moved onto his lap for other business. Completely understanding where the family nickname of Dickzilla came from, Sue sealed the deal in front of Diane's house in the darkness of Peter's Mercedes.

She had since made an effort to visit him at the house in North Jersey and the one in Avalon. Coincidentally, the same town where William and Karen had their family home. Only Peter's wasn't a rundown bungalow from the 50s. It was a majestic beachfront home with a spiral staircase in the living room, with a foyer that had a crystal chandelier…and the bedrooms. So many bedrooms. Bedrooms and bathrooms for days. Sue made a goal to christen each room with Peter. It would be his reward for being awesome.

***

The phone rings. John's calling Diane. The show's about to begin soon. They'd better be off.

Chapter 12
Gina

The ride with Richard is taking forever. All he wants is to listen to Mumble Rap, which is just not her style at all. Gina decided that if the two of them couldn't decide on what music to play, she'd put on her headphones and nod off for a while.

The headphones went on. Music playing. Destiny's Child. The good Beyoncé days. Back before her Bootylicious gimmick become common. "Survivor." An excellent way to kick off the personal listening phase of the trip.

Just as the song gets good, she feels a tug at her nipple. A rough tug.

Making her feel kinda pissed, actually. The headphones come off. "What?"

A joint gets put in her face. "Want a hit?"

"Of course I want a hit. Did you have to pinch my nipple? I'm on my period right now and my tits hurt."

"Yeah, I meant to talk to you about that. When's it gonna be ova?"

She takes a hit and rolls her eyes at the same time feeling equally satisfied and annoyed somehow. "It'll be over when my ovaries say it's over."

"Pha!" Now Richard gets annoyed. "Gimme back da joint. Such an old maid these days."

She hands it to him, not wanting it anymore. "Here. Take it, jerk." An oddly familiar sign passes them on the highway for Ambler, PA. Panic sets in. "Richard, I thought you said we're going to the shore for the weekend. This is not the way. Where are we going?"

"I was gonna make it a surprise, but we're going to visit some old acquaintances in Ambler with my dad."

Gina stiffens her back. "You wouldn't."

"Sorry, babe. Dad has spoken and it's a stop for a fundraiser to support his new squeeze's invalid son. Oh, and not the one who used to bang you."

Gina senses Richard's sadistic sense of humor as she begins to crawl out of her skin. "Richard, I can't go there. After what happened? This is wrong."

"Pshht. Are you kiddin' me? After what you and me used to do behind Dudeman's back? You're feeling bad now? The old man's gonna put five gees up for the brother's retard lift. They should feel lucky we're gracing them with our presence."

Gina hates life at the moment. Part of her feels that Mr. Zilla is being very generous and the other part feels like she's taking a one-way trip to hell and Richard is driving her there quickly.

The pain in her stomach could be cramps or terror. She put her headphones back on for support.

Gina curls up in her bucket seat and wallows in her sorrows. Destiny's Child is of no help to her right now.

Chapter 13
Joseph

Joseph could hear them talking in the basement through the ductwork. The return duct goes straight from the top of the house to the bottom. Joseph's favorite spot in the living room is on the edge of the couch right by the return air grille. He can hear everything.

Tony and Robert got through with their differences quickly. He smoothed Robert over in less than ten minutes, which is terrific because without Tony, Joseph wouldn't have the strength today to make his own fundraiser. *Best god damn dope in town*, Joseph says to himself as he pops a couple of strong perks and washes them back with a grape soda.

The basement door opens. As they come out Joseph looks up contently.

He's happy to see them together again. "You punks ready or what?"

Tony responds first, "You know it, kid. Let's get your wheels and speed on over. It's show time, baby!"

Robert pushes the chair over to get his sort-of brother. Joseph uses his good arm to hop in. Joseph almost felt his toes wiggle a bit when his butt hit the chair. Then there's the slight tingling. *Strange*, Joseph says to himself. "Stop wiggling around so much. You're gonna fall on your face again.

You should worry about getting uglier you know." "That's not what your mother said last night?"

Tony spoke up with some aggression, "Oh! Enough with the mother jokes in this family. People are gonna think we're brother-cousins. What's wrong with you?"

"Someone didn't get his candy today. What's the matter, Tony? Run out of babies to steal lollypops from?"

"Yeah, OK. I'll give you a lollypop." Tony waves Robert out. "Let's get this jokester to the party before he loses another arm."

"All I need is one good arm, Tony. You remember that?"

"You still wishin' for that Black Knight fantasy to come true? Why would a person want to fight until they had nothing left to do, but head butt a person? Besides, Knight is Alex's nickname."

Alex's nickname. Sure it is. Alex got all the good nicknames growing up.

Robert wheels Joseph out. Tony lights a smoke then follows not far behind.

Chapter 14
Alex

The block party's starting. The band got warmed up ahead of time. Adam has two hours of material set for the concert. They're planning to bring the house down. Alex is real excited for the double set.

People began setting up food and tents around the five-point intersection at the bottom of Alex's street. The cops shut down all the streets surrounding the area. Church St., Bannockburn, Ambler Road. Even the alleys.

Members of the VFW Post brought over their smoker and set it up across from the corner store in Knights Park. Over on Bannockburn, the Floccos set up their mobile pizza oven to make fresh pies. Next to them is a giant beer tent selling the newest drafts of the local breweries. On Ambler Road, the police set up a tent with a table for donations and another for concert posters. Julie hung the merch, including Polyester Anarchy's concert poster version of the Mona Lisa. 100% of the proceeds going toward helping Joseph.

People start rolling in. Alex sees familiar faces from Dresher like Adam's parents, and some others Alex recognized from his lacrosse days. Alex was the goalie for Ambler's team. He only played for a few years. Got cut from the team for being the only goalie in the history of school who was ejected over fighting. If you could call breaking his stick over a Dresher player's head fighting, that is. Alex had to admit there may have been some anger issues he dealt with back then.

Alex looks around more, and sees people from Ambler High that he hadn't come face to face with since graduation. Two faces in particular stood out from the crowd. Jasper Rodgers and Heather Craft. Alex can hardly believe they showed up. They were Alex's best friends back when he was younger. Things changed when he and Heather broke up. Then the fiasco happened at Knights Park. Things were never the same between them again.

Nor were things good between Alex and most people back then.

Williamsport allowed Alex to put some distance between himself and the rejection he felt growing up. Alex hoped it would be enough space to begin again. After the fight with Zilla and his breakup with Gina, maybe his troubles followed him.

Robert calls Alex's attention from the alley. Alex squints to see through the afternoon sunlight. Someone else pushing Joseph's wheelchair.

"Holy shit, it's Tony," Alex says aloud.

Wow, thinks Alex. He hadn't seen Tony since Robert overdosed. Alex didn't know whether to run and hide or hug the guy. He didn't have to do anything. Tony saw Alex and made a b-line.

Tony let go of the wheelchair and leaned in with an emotional hug. Kind of an apologetic embrace. Alex feels himself rock back and forth in Tony's hard noodle like arms. Alex couldn't tell if Tony had been lifting or if he was emaciated from drug abuse. Either way, a very nice hug.

Tony lets go and holds Alex's face in his hands. "How have you been, my Bad Little Knight?"

"You are the only person on the planet who still calls me that," admits Alex.

"Everyone should call you Knight where ever you go, kid. It's the best nickname you will ever get," says Tony before lightly gut punching Alex.

Bad feelings flood back to Alex. "Besides the bad memories and abuse, I'm good, Tony."

Alex sees Tony wince from the dig. Tony reaches his bony hands out for Alex's shoulders, and scowls, "So what bad memories and abuse are we talkin' about here?" Tony raises an eyebrow like The Gringe. "Hmmm, little Knight?"

A cold chill runs up his spine. The same one he felt when Tony was beating on his mom. The feeling made Alex want to speak, but he couldn't find the strength. Alex could feel Tony looking into his soul. Wanting vengeance for the dig. Tony doesn't respond well to embarrassment. He lightly massages Alex's shoulders looking for a reaction. Alex has nothing but static going on upstairs. From behind, an angel speaks.

"Who is this Knight character, and when can I meet him?" says Adam joyfully.

Alex could see the scowl disappear from Tony's forehead. Replaced with a more pleasant, handsome one. Absent of pity, but full of raw childish joy.

"You must be the songbird." "I am. Name's Adam." "Tony."

99

Adam and Tony shake hands.

"Well, Mr. Songbird. If you want to hear some stories later about our friend Knight, I mean Alex, I'm your man."

Alex pipes in, "Nope. Nope. He's not interested in those stories." Tony smiles genuinely. "Oh, yes he is."

"Oh, yes I am," adds Adam.

Alex cuts them off, "Yeah well, I'm not interested in those stories." "Nothin' you can do about it, kid. Train's left the station." Tony winked. Familiar soft, warm hands place themselves on Alex's tense shoulders.

Followed immediately with the scent of his favorite person. Lavender and patchouli essential oils.

"Maybe Alex would like to get the number of that train," says Julie as she wraps her arms around Alex tightly.

Alex could see Tony's eyes light up. Wasn't sure if Tony's proud of Julie's looks or if he was going to try to snort coke off her tits later.

Tony pushes toward Julie to make her acquaintance. "Well, hello pretty. And who might you be?" stretching out his Crypt Keeper hand to wrap it around hers.

"I'm Alex's girl. The name's Julie."

"Oh, do I hear a bit of New York in your voice, Julie?" "Yup. Born and raised."

"I like this one, Knight. She's a keeper. Treat her good or else I'm gonna take her off your hands."

The squeal of the mic caught everyone by surprise. Chad taps on it for on last check. "Yo, everybody. We need your attention. It's time to get funky!" He tosses Rick the mic.

Rick grabs it and starts to jam. Jesse jumps on the turntables and kicks an old school beat from the Godfather of Rap. The sounds of Dr. Dre fill the air with "Is it Funky Enough."

The sly groove rips through the crowd, catching everyone by surprise. Rick nails the D.O.C.'s flow with a spot on cover of the old school song. It takes a second, but people begin bobbing their heads. For a group consisting mostly of white middle class people, that's saying a lot.

Alex feels another tap on his back. He turns around to find his mom and new beau staring back at him. Mr. Zilla, or as his dad calls him, *Peter Peter Pecker Eater.*

Sue leans in to talk, giving Alex a cold hug and an awkward kiss on the lips. She shouts over the music, "Sorry, we're late. Peter helped Diane with the baby while we were getting ready. Isn't that nice?"

"Sure, Mom. Really nice." Alex turns to Peter. "Hello, Mr. Zilla. Nice to see you again."

Peter extends his hand in a token of friendship. He leans in to shout next. "Hello, Alex. It's great your friends can do this for Joseph. I'm sure whatever money gets raised will be a big help until the lawsuit settles."

Alex feels tired of shouting and wants out of the conversation. "Yup, it's going to be a while. Thanks for coming."

Peter waves to someone from behind that Alex couldn't see. "I brought some guests. Hopefully, you guys can make nice today."

A familiar face lumbers in Alex's direction. Richard Zilla slithered into Ambler. *No fuckin' way*, Alex says to himself. He even clubbed Gina and dragged her along by the hair for good measure.

Alex looks at them for a second with disbelief before the obligatory handshake occurs. Zilla forcefully takes Alex's hand and twists his arm. This works so the top of Zilla's hand faces upward. It's his super aggressive move for showing dominance over another. Alex feels the resistance in his elbow and wrist.

Rick pops off lyrics in the background. Alex tries to hold himself together while the handshake is still happening.

Zilla's eyes widen slightly for a second before he relaxes to force a smile. "Hey, Dudema…er, Alex. Good to be here."

Alex's adrenaline spikes. He flexes his hand to break Zilla's death grip once and for all.

Zilla pretends not to notice. "Yeah, so, I brought an old acquaintance of yours. She and I are kind of a ting now."

Gina speaks from beneath her trembling red locks. "Hey, Alex. Hope your brother makes the goal today."

Alex can see his dad charging in from across the street. Angry as could be.

John gets in between his son and the Zillas. Shouting at Sue and Peter, "Are you guys for real? What the fuck are you all doing here?"

Sue looks angry now. Peter interrupts before she can speak, "John, it's a real pleasure. I've heard a lot about you." He extends his hand to John.

John looks at Peter's hand with disgust. "Bet you have, Zilla. Brought your son here did you?"

"Yes, see where I'm from, people communicate in effective ways to resolve their differences."

"Oh yeah, where's that?" "New Jersey."

"Well, here in Ambler we have a saying, 'The apple don't fall far from the tree.'"

"Same could be said for you."

John sniffs. He motions toward Richard. "So if you're anything like that son of yours, all I see coming from your way is a whole bunch of complicity and evasion."

Peter chuckles to himself. "Complicity and evasion. That's good, John. That's good. How about arrogance and hostility? Those seem to be words of which you may have an intimate understanding."

John squares off with Peter.

Richard bounces in his Yeezy sneakers. "Yeah, get 'em, Dad."

Alex steps in. "That's it! Zillas, thanks for coming out. The donation booth is over there. Dad, let's go!"

Sue decides to get in a last word, "Alex, if you don't play nice with Richard, I'll…"

Alex stops abruptly in his Adidas. He turns around. "You'll what, Mom?"

Sue shows her teeth. "This is the last stop for us, kid. You be there or I won't be."

"Just another day for us. Right, Mom?"

"I mean it this time. You'll look back one day and know you made a mistake if you don't respect me."

John leans in to Alex. "The song's changing, bud. We gotta to go." They wrap their arms around each other's shoulder and walk back to their safe zone.

On stage, Jesse spins a new record. Moving from '89 to '93. The warm bump of Snoop's "Doggy Dogg World" blasts through the crowd. Alex remembers this song well from back when they lived in Kensington. Tony would turn it on late night when his friends came back from the bar.

Rick does Snoop's part.

By the stage, Alex and his dad find Joseph, Robert, Tony, and Julie.

Julie hugs Alex. She presses her finger against the flap of cartilage on Alex's ear and leans in to shout. "Trouble back there?" She let go, motioning Alex to do the same.

102

Tony leans in to eavesdrop.

He presses hers and responds. Her brown hair falling on his face. Alex catching a breath before speaking, "I need to get the out of here."

"Nope. You can't leave," she says without moving an inch. "Mom invited Zilla."

"Oh, she did, did she?"

"Yeah, and he brought Gina just to mess with me. Now all my bad memories are at the same place at the same time."

"Even me?" She looks at him tearfully.

"You're the only one who makes me feel warm and fuzzy," he shouts.

She looks at him face to face. "Then focus on me, and only me for now on. Fuck these people and their bullshit." She stops to think for a sec. "What do they say here in Philly? Oh yeah, 'All we got, all we need.' That's us now."

"You are the best."

"I know. Now shut up and feel Rick's flow!"

Alex turns around. He sees Gina and Zilla a few rows behind. Passing an eyedropper back and forth.

As Alex turns to the stage, he notices how intently Tony pays attention to the whole crew. Alex didn't know what to make of the situation, but Tony manages to have a sympathetic look on his face.

Alex looks around. The crowd digs the old school vibe. The song selection worked perfectly.

Rick hums on.

Jesse and Chad kick in for the bridge.

Rick tosses the mic over his head and ducks off to the side. Adam snatches it from the air before adding his flavor to the mood.

Alex laughs at the old-school lyrics. Filthy, hilarious, and somewhat violent. Gangster rap harks back to a different time in American history. A time when crack ravaged inner cities. When cops beat the crap out of old men for fun. A time when the government pushed for cleaner streets, then let the CIA fill back alleys with guns and dope. The language used reflects the anger of African Americans, who can arguably fill up half of American history books with their plight.

Gangster rap is hard and gritty. Alex has never been to LA, nor had he ever spoken to any gangster rappers in person, but feels Philly has something in common with LA in that regard.

Alex's dad tosses a rolled-up poster and a shirt to the guys on stage. They unroll each to show the crowd the images of the Mona Lisa breastfeeding a baby with a Yamaka. Her shirt folded down. The baby covering her breasts. Tattoos all over her body and her face.

Adam points to Alex and smiles.

"Oh shit," Alex says aloud. Heart beating from his chest.

Adam addresses the crowd, "Everyone. In life, there are people who you meet and instantly know they're special. In these moments, it's up to you to identify these individuals, and make sure they stick around. One of these people is standing here in the crowd today. Now without further ado, I'd like to welcome up on stage, Ambler's very own, Alex Walker!"

Alex can't hear anything on his walk up, but a few people clapping.

Maybe some others cheered.

He leans into Adam, "Can't believe you're doing this to me." Adam claps back. "Go with it, dummy."

Alex waves nervously to the crowd.

Julie claps and calls his name with pride. "Go Alex. Whooo!"

Adam goes on, "This gentleman right here, is the reason why we got out of Williamsport. It was his artistic ability that put our ugly mugs on this merch for all of you. He's also the reason we're here today. When Alex told us of his brother, Joseph Walker, I immediately knew we had to get our lazy asses out of Williamsport and give back." He takes Alex by the shoulder. "Alex, thank you for showing us nothing but kindness and enthusiasm since we met. Our hearts go out to your family, and this one's for you, buddy."

Jesse plays the next song. Adam starts with his awkward impression of a nerdy German, "Gunter Glieben Glauten Globen." It's the beginning of "Pretty Fly for a White Guy" by the Offspring.

Alex snatches the mic from Adam who pretends to be surprised.

Alex puts the mic to his face. His nerves busting from his skin suit. From the side, he sees Adam putting on his guitar.

Alex opens his mouth to let out the first line. He knows the lyrics. The flow takes over.

Adam goes crazy on the guitar. Alex jumps in the air getting into character. The guitar music rips through the crowd. They love it. The tone changes from somber to electric in a matter of seconds.

Alex rocks out on the mic.

Alex looks over the crowd as the lyrics force themselves from his mouth. He sees everyone. Their expressions. Dad looking shocked. Julie looking sexy. Gina and Zilla with their hollow eyes. Jasper and Heather shaking their heads with disbelief. Joseph and Robert laughing and high-fiving. Tony and Sue arguing. Peter standing safely over by the cops. Diane and Tyrone nuzzled up together by the telephone pole, and the hundreds of others.

Adam points to Alex. Then on cue, Alex does some old-school Vanilla Ice moves while Rick and Jesse provide backup vocals.

Alex counts the beats till the next verse.

Alex finishes up the song facing Adam while he rocks out on guitar. The crowd claps. More people cheer. Alex equates the experience to when he tried wrestling in high school. He was terrified up till the whistle blew then all the fear went away. Once Adam hit that first note, it was on. Alex is so glad he went through with it.

As he walks off stage, he can hear Adam transition to "Ice Ice Baby." A smooth segway from rock back to rap.

He immediately falls into Julie's arms.

She speaks first, "You can be my fly white guy any day."

"How 'bout them moves? Took 'em straight from Vanilla himself."

Julie points to the stage. Rick and Adam do the same moves in sequence. "Looks like they took the moves from you."

Alex thinks to himself how awesome they look. The guys remind him of a batshit crazy Jewish boy band, even if there is only one real Jewish guy in the group. Jesse and Chad are definitely WASPs much like Alex. Rick's something else. Alex can't be sure if he has black in him, Puerto Rican, Middle Eastern. Nobody really knows for sure and never cared to ask. Either way, Polyester Anarchy is a perfect mess of pop culture, religious parody, and dysfunction à la Americana. Absolutely beautiful to watch. Poetry in motion.

***

Alex throws an after party at his place on the top of Church Street. He took the liberty of inviting everyone he knew, including the people he hadn't spoken to since high school. After a few beers, Alex gets into character.

Julie jokes that, "*Everybody's friend* Alex showed up tonight."

It's true. Once his happy drunk kicks in, nothing penetrates Alex, which allows him to be free of all the hang-ups for a little while. Relieving his forehead of the perma scowl.

Alex walks around enjoying his buzz. He sees everyone having a good time. Joseph with his non-alcoholic beer. Robert spinning him around in the kitchen. Julie and Heather playing old records in the dining room. Dad and Pop Walker watching the baseball game together. Adam and his parents having drinks in the family room.

The money hadn't been completely tallied, but Alex thinks it might be close to the goal. The crowd was impressive. It was almost like the whole town had shown up.

After seeing the volume of people, all his dad could say was, "Man, this is gonna be good for business."

Alex smiled to himself. Dad couldn't help it. Despite the fact that Joseph needed help, Dad still thought about the business first. It's in his nature. The guy dedicated his life to building the plumbing business. Alex couldn't blame him for wanting to be more successful.

A knock at the front door distracts Alex from his thoughts. He walks to the living room to answer. When he opens it, his gaze is met with two sets of hollow eyes. Alex can't figure out if he's stuck in a reoccurring dream.

"Your motha sent us to make nice." Zilla produces something from his pocket. "Want to smoke a peace blunt?"

Alex again feels distraction. He smells cigarette smoke, but doesn't see anyone smoking. Too weird. He directs his attention back to the twig in his face.

Gina places her hand over Zilla's. She doesn't make eye contact with Alex. "Richard, Alex doesn't smoke, but maybe he'd like to have a beer instead?"

Alex doesn't want a beer. He wants to crawl out of his skin. "Hey Gina, I'm standing right in front of you. Do you mind?"

She shakes her hair in front of her eyes to avoid looking directly at him. "Ah, yeah sorry."

Alex wants both of them gone. "You know what your problem is?" Gina winces.

"I'm not sure if Daddy taught you to have respect for others *before or after* he beat the shit out of you?"

Zilla recoils. "Oh, burn. Tapping into the daddy issues. Good one, bro!"

The cigarette smoke comes back. Possibly in the alley on the other side of the bushes. Alex can't tell.

Gina gets emotional. "Yeah, this was a bad idea." She storms off to lean on Zilla's car.

Zilla shrugs. "Looks like it's just you and me. Want to do some coke?" Tony emerges from what could only be a portal to another dimension.

Alex realizes he was he was the one smoking somewhere close.

Tony steps to Zilla. "The kid doesn't do any drugs," Tony takes a drag of his smoke and blows it in Zilla's face, "but I do."

Alex tries to jump in. "Tony, I wouldn't…"

Tony holds up his hand. "I got this. Go back inside."

Zilla fires a shot. "Later, Dudeman. Good luck with the Motley Crew you got up in there."

Tony pulls out a tiny baggie and waves it in Zilla's face. "Now, you're talkin' my language."

They walk to Zilla's car. Alex eavesdrops from the porch.

Tony puts his arm around Zilla while they walk. "Ever bet on baseball while snorting coke off your girlfriend's tits?"

"Can't say I have, Mr. Grinch."

"Well, young Zilla, tonight's your lucky night."

***

As the moon rose, people passed out or left. Sitting at the dining room table, only the night owls remain. The band members, Alex, and Julie. Playing Asshole and joking about the people in the crowd. Especially Alex's crazy family.

The cards are dealt to the six players. Chad goes out first, thus becoming President so he calls for a waterfall before the next game. This is where each player is required to stand, extend their beers toward the center of the human circle and wait for the cue to drink from the President. Once the President stops drinking, the next person can stop, and so forth. Chad being the vacuum cleaner that he is, chugs his entire can of Pabst. Alex goes out next, followed by Julie, Jesse, then after a strange spitting sound, Rick attempts to rush to the kitchen sink to puke. Looking down at the table, Rick's projectile vomiting spewed all over the deck of cards. Asshole would have to resume another evening.

Followed by a thorough cleaning and a round of lemon drops in the kitchen, Rick gets back to normal. No more drinking. Adam calls for a smoking session at the picnic table out back.

Alex, not being a smoker, grabs his old goalie stick to toss some balls at the back of the stone garages that separate his yard from the alley. The row of garages forms an "L" shape meeting with his dad's office at the back. Closer to the house is the climbing tree Alex and Robert would use to sneak out when they were younger. Alex backs up to the neighbor's fence to toss the ball.

The guys light up at the table in the middle of the yard. Julie joins Alex instead. "Got a stick for me?"

"Oh, I got a stick for you alright."

"Not the little one, I mean a big lacrosse stick."

Alex ignores her sarcasm. "On the ledge in the basement stairwell."

She comes back with a white and silver lacrosse stick. Alex tosses the ball without looking at anyone. He can see her watching. Alex shows off for a sec.

His old moves come back to him. Alex stands back near the neighbor's fence tossing the ball at the stone. The ridges of the wall make the ball bounce back at unpredictable angles. Each time he catches or stops it, Alex steps forward to throw it harder and faster. When he gets too close to the wall, Alex steps back and does it again.

From a distance, he hears Rick moan through the pot smoke, "Dude, you're freaking us out."

Alex rolls his eyes. "Careful not to choke on that joint, buddy. Wouldn't want you to puke on Jesse's lap this time."

"I'm not into that," Jesse claps back. "You must be talking about Chad and his weird fetishes."

Chad takes the joint from Rick. "They're not fetishes if you don't have any hang-ups in life, Jesse. And let's not forget about the only male here with a feminine name, shall we?" Chad casually takes a hit.

Jesse looks offended. "Hang-ups? How about that gimp costume you hung up in Unicorn's bathroom?"

"I'm not the one who dresses in it, sweety," says Chad as he blows out a big puff of smoke.

Rick looks nauseated again. "Come on, Chad."

Jesse claps back, "Yeah, that's what we're afraid of."

"You're only afraid because you were molested as a child," says Chad. "I can sympathize. However, unlike you, I shed my skin as a teenager, my closeted *Jeanine in drag* friend."

Jesse becomes standoffish. "First of all, no jokes about diddling children. Second of all, that poster was Alex's idea. I never dressed like the Porn Queen on Blink 182's album cover. Not once!"

Chad drives it home. "Alex's gaydar went off just like mine. Only he prefers the inverted kind of sexual organ. You and I prefer the appendage type."

"Thanks, Chad...I think," says Alex. Catching the rubber ball from Julie.

"No problem, homie." Chad's voice sounds raspy from exhaling the

smoke. He lightly rolls the joint between his thumb and fingertips as the buzz rushes in.

Jesse can't let it go. "There's no gaydar. I don't even look like Jeanine. I never dressed like that. I would make a terrible drag queen. Everyone knows it."

"The only people who can prove it are the secretly gay friends we all pretend not to notice," says Chad with a sly grin.

Jesse looks desperate. "I'm not afraid to hit a gay dude, you know. I'll just pretend you're my old priest. Get ready for a major beatdown coming your way, pal."

"Oh, you'll be coming my way alright. When you decide to walk toward the light, I'll be in Daddy Walker's old room waitin' for ya." He and Adam high five. "You'll be callin' me big daddy by sunrise."

Jesse tries for a resolution. "You know what, no more Beastie Boys during our sets. Find someone else to spin your shitty records. How 'bout that?"

"Beastie Boys forever, muthafucka," Chad says before blowing out another big puff.

Jesse puts his head down on the table.

Adam reaches over to hit the joint next. He takes a long drag. As he exhales, a look crosses Adam's face. Like a lightbulb going off over his head. "He guys, it's Dysfunctional Family Round Table time. Alex Walker edition."

Jesse lifts his head from the table. "Oh yeah, the creepy step daddy said his name was Michael Knight."

Chad looks at Jesse with disappointment. "You better not be that dumb when you climb into bed later."

"What?" Jesse doesn't get it.

Chad slaps him across the hair like a mischievously idiot. "No, dummy.

Remember the poster in his room?" Jesse still doesn't know.

Chad gives up. "His stepdad nicknamed him Knight. Then Moon Knight became his favorite guy."

Rick perks up. "Like you're Jesse's favorite guy?"

Jesse flexes his beer muscles. "That's it! Who wants some?" Rick looks at Jesse stone cold. "Chad probably does."

Chad leans in to Jesse. "Oh, you know it, buddy."

Jesse wants to stop everything. "That's it. No more gay shit!"

Adam joins in. "Ooh, nice rhyme. Wish my mom was here. We could write some music."

Julie catches the ball. "So can we bully Alex into telling the story or what?"

Alex rolls his eyes. "Tony had to show up today. Of all days!" He raises his hands and the giant goalie stick up to the heavens to ask, "Why?"

"Just tell the story, you faggot," says Jesse.

Chad looks at Jesse with bedroom eyes. "You say the sexiest things when you're impatient."

Rick moves in for his best impression of a gay prisoner. "Mmm, boy. Why don' chu get ova here with them tight jeans on."

Julie cuts them off, "That's enough. Alex has the talk stick now." She trades his goalie stick for her normal sized one.

Jesse feels the urge to speak. "Hey man, I told you about my experience with the church. Which wasn't easy considering how I was thrown out of the parish for mooning hundreds of people at once. Now it's your turn to embarrass yourself."

Alex doesn't want to play. "Nah, I did enough of that earlier."

Julie nudges him further. "Well, you kind of embarrass yourself all the time, so at this point it should come naturally to you."

Alex snaps back, "You're not talking about in the sack right?"

She nuzzles in close like a cat. "No, retard. I'm saying you're like a Charlie Brown type guy, and I adore that about you." She backs up to sit on the table with the guys. "Now tell us your story, the suspense is killing me."

Alex submits.

***

It was the summer Alex moved to Kensington with his mom and Tony.

Alex could remember Sue and John fighting over the phone. Alex was supposed to go to Avalon with Pop Walker. Instead, Sue planned a vacation for Alex to see her father in coal town. She threatened John with the lawyer again. After the tricks Tony pulled to max out the child support payments over the previous winter, John backed off.

The town where Pop Davies lived wasn't really considered the Poconos, more like Upstate Pennsylvania. Shamokin is the actual town. A little trailer not too far from where his ancestor, Boner, had settled after the Revolutionary War. Alex remembered feeling depressed about missing a trip with his brother and sister to the beach. He felt lonely all the way up there by himself. Sure his mom, Tony, and grandfather were present, but the company's too different for a kid to understand. They felt his anguish and decided to take him to Knoebles for the day.

Alex had heard all his mom's stories about Knoebles' Amusement Park over the years. The giant wooden roller coaster called the Phoenix. Not the oldest wooden coaster in the country, but it was the first to be dismantled and relocated. From San Antonio, Texas to Shamokin, PA.

At the park, there was a special event for kids under ten. Alex being seven at the time fit the bill. The only catch was he had to get on stage to participate. From a distance, Alex could see other kids moving to the costume area. Putting on princess dresses and valiant knight costumes. Sue and Pop Davies were in the bathroom. Alex waited impatiently while Tony smoked a cigarette. From that distance, it looked like all the good costumes were gone.

After what felt like an hour, Alex finally got his costume. The only one remaining. The Black Knight. All the other boys were dressed like heroes. Alex instantly became the villain for no reason other than the bad luck of having family members with small bladders.

Once onstage, the MC separated the boys from the girls. Then again, the boys from Alex. This didn't sit right with him, but the MC let the crowd know there had to be a villain for the good knights to protect the princesses from, and it was Alex.

The play began. The Valiant Knights called Alex names and chased him with swords. The crowd booed and the Princess shook with fear. The story took a wild turn when one boy came too close with the sword and caught Alex on the eye socket drawing blood. Knocking him to the ground. Alex felt rage like he did sometimes. It wasn't something that occurred naturally in him, more like an environmental reaction that comes out from large amounts of stress. Something only an abused child would understand. A desperate kind of anger that one suffers at the hands of people who are supposed to love and protect. Instead, they abuse and neglect. Alex was and is a good example of this treatment.

Feeling the blood on his forehead, Alex sprung to his feet in one fluid motion, grabbing the sword from the Valiant Knight with one hand, and socked the kid in the jaw with the other. Sending him to the ground instead.

This time the crowd booed for real. Everyone except for Tony who also sprung to his feet and cheered. "That's our Bad Little Knight!"

Alex could remember hearing his grandfather's laugh over everyone else in the crowd, even Tony's whooping and hollering.

There were maybe ten other children onstage. Valiant knights, princesses, it didn't matter. Alex put the fear of god in all of them after he was bullied to bloodshed. He looked each of those kids in the eye and decided to take back every shred of dignity stolen from him for the simple reason that there needed to be a bad guy and he happened to be the right kid at the wrong time. After the majority of the kids fell to play dead, there was only the one mean Princess who called Alex ugly. Alex, not wanting for prisoners at the moment, lunged at her too. Realizing quickly that he called her bluff, the

mean Princess fell to the ground in defeat.

In triumph, Alex raised his sword to the sky like He-Man and said, "I have the power!"

After the dust settled, and the shock had worn off, the MC had Sue retrieve her "Bad Little Knight." She politely did so.

Once back with his family, Alex's grandfather kissed him on the forehead and whispered gently, "You will always be my Bad Little Knight. Way to stand up for yourself, kid."

After getting home from the trip, Tony told everyone about Alex's new nickname.

Back at the plumbing shop over his next visit, John teased Alex. He thought the name was hysterical because Alex had pale skin. Same color as the moon. Alex cried when he felt the sting of his new nickname being twisted in that way, but with all great nicknames, the recipient's negative reaction sealed it. Alex was forever dubbed thee Knight.

When the story ends, Alex stands there for a moment holding the talk stick. The guys leap up in unison to give a round of applause.

Adam walks over to his friend. "An exquisite addition to our Dysfunctional Family Roundtable for the evening. Now Alex Walker, please hand me the talk stick."

Alex does as his friend requests. "Now, bend thy knee," instructs Adam.

Alex procrastinates. "Ok, but I feel like you're being a little aggressive right now."

Adam arches his back regally and positions the stick on his shoulder to wait. "Play along now, play along."

Alex humbly kneels. "Ok, here we go."

"Brave Alex Walker. For your efforts in life, throughout your adventures in Ambler, Philadelphia, Williamsport…then back to Ambler again…"

Adam lowers the lacrosse stick to Alex's shoulder then over his head to the other one. "I dub thee Sir Knight Alex Walker of house Polyester in the year of Anarchy. Now rise and take your fair maiden to your bedchambers. A long evening awaits you."

Julie smiles before getting up from the table. She curtsies like a princess before Alex whisks Julie off her feet and into his arms. They walk nearly to the back door as Julie wiggles from his grip.

"Goodnight, boys." She waves as they disappear into the house. The guys whoop and howl from the yard.

***

Time passes. Julie and Alex get to the second round. Hearing doors closing and lights shutting off, makes it easier to screw this time. They roll around. Taking turns. This time Julie's on top. Her magnificent tits in Alex's face. He takes the opportunity to motorboat. She giggles, but Alex knows she doesn't like it. She shoves him back to soften the mood. Her back arches. He grabs her hips. The moonlight beaming in from the windows. A man in a trench coat and hockey mask staring at them from the roof. Stroking himself in the moonlight.

Alex moves quickly. Julie screams.

Alex runs toward the window. It's painted shut. For once, he curses air conditioning. The guy escapes down the tree.

Alex dives out the bedroom door, down the steps, through the kitchen and storms into the backyard, chasing the guy into the alley.

Jesse and Chad catch up to him. "What happened?" asks Chad.

"Dude, there was a guy on the roof watching us," says Alex out of breath. Jesse looks puzzled. "What did he see?"

Alex flinches. "What? Never mind that! Hey wait, how'd you guys get here so quick?"

Jesse thinks fast. "We were smoking a bedtime blunt."

Chad points at Alex's package. "Dude." Alex is fully nude still.

Movement from the darkness distracts them. A shadowy figure in a hockey mask and trench coat leaps from the bushes. He takes a swing at Alex, trying to knock his head off. Alex ducks.

Chad and Jesse scream and fall to the ground.

Alex reaches to grab the trench coat, but he's too fast. The guy runs off. Alex looks down at his buddies. "Yo, Shaggy and Scooby, he's gettin'

away!"

Alex runs toward the end of the alley. They guy vanishes into thin air. Jesse and Chad catch up out of breath.

"Why are you two out of breath?" asks Alex. "What do we do now?" asks Chad.

"Call the cops," says Jesse

"I'm not calling the cops with all the dope and booze everywhere in the house. Are you nuts?"

"So what's next?" asks Jesse trying to catch his breath.

"I don't know. I'll ask around tomorrow to see if anyone else knows about this guy."

Julie peeks her head out of the bedroom window. "Did you get him?" Alex looks up. "How'd you get the window open?"

"I unlocked it," she whispers loudly through the night air.

"And you guys call me stupid?" Jesse puts his arm around Chad as they walked back to the house.

"Pssst, Alex," Julie whispers again into the night air, "your balls are showing."

Chapter 15
Gina

The coke in Philly's good. That much she knew. As for what happened after they got in the car with Tony, Gina had no idea. Apparently, they went on a sightseeing tour of 'wonderland' as they were driving to the city. A place called Kensington. A real rough party of Philly. The one that Alex said he found Creepy Tony beating his mother when he was a child. Gina thought it couldn't have been right. It was little Puerto Rico back there. How the hell did Alex survive that? It's a place where people make pilgrimages from all over the country in search of the purest heroine money can buy. There's no room for little hobbit-like white boys around that place.

The coke periodically worked Gina up from her walking slumber as the night rolled on. Last thing she remembered was waiting in line for the afterhours club. She could still hear Tony laughing as Richard slipped his hand down her pants. His raspy high-pitched laugh. He reminded Gina of an Italian version of Judge Doom from "Who Framed Roger Rabbit" only with nicer hair. His gaunt face skewed his handsome looks. Her high took over again. The rest of the night was like a dream. Every time Tony took another drag off his cigarette his voice became more cackley. Like a male witch. She imagined his dick as the broomstick. Him holding it out for her to take a ride. Smearing it with ice cream. Zilla doing the same. She held Zilla's as she licked the ice cream from Tony's broomstick. Zilla then tried to ram his in her ear.

She could hear them slapping hands in the clouds above where she was flying high in the sky.

"All in the family, right, Bluto?" She heard Tony rasp from his position among the Cumulous sky cover.

Zilla howled in ecstasy from his place in the rain clouds. "What happens in Philly stays in Philly, Mr. Grinch."

Richard apologized for spilling his ice cream on her hair. She didn't remember stopping at Dairy Queen. She felt left out. Richard promised he wouldn't do it again.

Gina finds herself lying on a red couch she'd been dreaming about for a while now. Seemed like ages. The one shaped like a tongue. She touches her chest and finds some more coke. Her nipples are numb. It's exhilarating. She rubs a bit on her gums, but the taste is different. She was expecting a bitter flavor, but instead the coke is slimy and salty. What a strange night. She struggles to get up. Hands are holding her down. More hands. She dreams about pirates on a big ship. She sleeps in a hammock below deck. She rocks back and forth.

The lights dim. Hues of purple and red light up the night. Followed by glowing white lights dancing off the sides of a spinning mirror ball. She wants to dance with the lights. Dance like it was her last night on earth. The music vibrates through her body. Money rains from the clouds above. No words only the howls of wolves fill the thick air. The music pumps louder as her body does the talking. She leaves the pirate ship and drowns herself in the song "Try Again" from Aaliyah.

She lays down to dance some more. Gina's clothes fall beneath her feet making it hard to balance herself. She feels so sexy. Every man wants a woman like her. She could feel it. She would give herself to each of them, but only in their dreams.

Don't stop moving is right, Aaliyah. Too much money. Never before did she have so much cash in her purse. She opens her wallet. The picture of her and Alex looks back. The frayed edges. No money in the wallet. Only wads of bills in rubber bands. Never before did she have so much money.

***

She wakes up with a familiar taste of regret and vomit in her mouth. Her clothes intact, yet covered with glitter. Funny. Gina doesn't remember putting on glitter yesterday.

Gina looks around. She slept on the floor. Richard on the couch. His hand bandaged. She notices blood soaked the gauze in his palm.

She gets up. Her head throbbing, the dizziness kicking in. *Need water. Need to remember. Where did they go? What did they do? The excitement. The luxury. So dirty yet so hot! Hot is right. Christ, who the hell doesn't use* air *conditioning these days.* Beads of sweat drip down her face. The front door first before water. Fresh air. She looks around. *Familiar. From yesterday. Ambler?* She closes the door.

She kicks Richard. Nothing. She stumbles to the kitchen and drinks thirstily from the faucet. The water tastes like old copper. She smacks her lips for a second before going back for another long pull. There's commotion downstairs. *Isn't she downstairs already?* Gina takes another swig from the faucet.

She finds a bottle of Percocet on the counter. Pops two and has another drink from the faucet before sitting down for a breather at the ratty kitchen table.

Edward Creepy Hands emerges from the basement. They ended up at Joseph's house. Of all places. Gina looks at him through her hair.

Tony smiles. "You're alive?"

"Unfortunately." She notices blood on his right palm. Same as Richard's. "Where'd you take us last night?"

Tony lights a smoke then sits down. "On an adventure through wonderland, baby. Don't chu remember?"

"I don't remember jack shit."

A loud bang from the living room. Richard rolls off the couch and moans like a wounded werewolf. "Holy fuck…"

Tony looks over his shoulder. "Time to get up, Zillaman." Richard writhes in pain for a second before rallying to his feet. He turns back to Gina and shoots a side thumb toward Richard. "That's my new roll dog. A *Good Fella* you got there, sweety."

"Yeah, I'm sure." She calls to Richard. "We need to go. We were supposed to meet your dad at the shore after the party last night."

"Oh, plans have changed. Zillaman and me have some friends to meet this morning. You'll need to wait until we're finished."

"That's fine, but I'm either going to the shore or I'm going back to Williamsport. I'm not staying here."

Richard stumbles into the kitchen and opens the fridge. He finds orange juice. Not giving a crap, opens the jug and drinks heavily.

When he's done, the jug drops on the table. Gina jumps from the ruckus. "Take an Uber if you can't wait."

"How am I supposed to do that?"

117

"Check your purse." Richard turns to Tony. "I'll be ready in a few, but I need some cologne and toothpaste."

A knock at the door. Richard answers. It's Alex's Dad. He looks pissed. "What are you doing here?"

"I could ask you the same," says Richard with defiance.

John barges his way in past Richard who looks puzzled by the blatant lack of fear. "You stepping to me, old man?"

"Nah, kid. My son already did that."

"Yeah, and he got served with a keg to the face."

John turns to Gina. "Looks like someone got served on the face alright."

Richard shudders. "Ooh, burn. Now I know where Alex got his attitude from. Fun times with Bilbo Baggins, huh?"

Tony steps in. "What're you doing here, John?"

John picks up the bottle of perks. Name unknown. "Looking for Robert. He's late for work."

Tony gets close. Grinding his teeth. "Robert's sleeping safely in his bed. Comfortably upstairs."

John cold cocks Tony in the face. Richard tries to rush him. John pulls out a pistol. Richard puts his hands up. "Alright, pops. Alright. Sure you want to go this route with us?"

"With us?" John either pointed the gun at Tony or the floor, Gina couldn't really tell. "You think because Tony's asshole blood brothers in Kensington made you a member of their circle jerk, you can walk into my town and throw your weight around?" John points the gun back at Richard. "Huh?"

Richard points his finger at John. "When my father hears about this..."
"He'll what? If he had any clout, you would've cut your soft hand long

ago, and I got news for ya, kid. Daddy ain't nothin' but a bank account with a pulse."

"Better than a loser who plays with people's shit for a living," says Richard through grinding teeth.

Gina watches Tony get up carefully. Tony sits. No blow back. Strange.

She sees John look down for a second to reflect on his life.

John picks up the bottle of pills and looks at it again. Spinning the orange plastic cylinder in his fingers. "Yeah, maybe." He pockets the bottle of perks and puts away the gun. Then sees the cash pouring out of Gina's purse.

He shakes his head. "Good luck in the ho business, baby."

He walks right toward Richard who stands directly in John's way. John stops and looks up at the giant man-child. "Get the fuck outta my way, Zilla." Richard thinks twice then steps aside.

John walks up the stairs and calls for Robert.

Richard looks at Tony with disappointment. "You gonna let Poppa Smurf punk you like dat?"

Tony wipes blood off his lip. Gina couldn't tell if the dried blood on his palm was his or Richard's at this point.

"He and I go back farther that I care to remember. He also takes care of my boy."

"Why don't chu take care of your boy? You let your ex's ex do it? What kinda fucked-up orgy is dis anyway?"

Tony looks at Richard with raw emotion. "The kind you just bonded into young Jedi."

Gina hears angry footsteps upstairs. John yells at Joseph. "No more drugs!"

John ushers Robert down the stairs and out the door. Slamming it behind them. Gina wants some orange juice.

***

It's night time. Joseph orders them a pizza. Gina walks to the corner store to pick it up. Julie's there. A cold chill goes down her spine. Gina could feel Julie's look as she opens her purse. *Damn.* Still filled with strange money. Julie could see it. *Is she looking at the picture of her and Alex or the wads of cash?* Gina closes it quickly and grabs the pizza from the bearded lady behind the counter.

Gina almost makes a clean break before Julie speaks. "Make all that money with your tits or your ass?"

Gina's attitude spikes. "Same tits and ass that fucked your boyfriend while you were at work a couple weeks back."

"He's better than you, ya know. Alex. He's better than both of us. Too bad you'll have to watch someone else marry him."

"Someone like you? Because you're sooo special, aren't you? Have you told Alex why you're in Williamsport?"

"Maybe I have."

"Or maybe someone else will do it for you." Gina gets in the last word.

119

***

Richard shows up at 10:00 with a new duffel bag. He and Gina are going to Avalon after all.

Looks like her luck's changing.

Chapter 16
Julie

Julie walks into Alex's house with a bag of sandwiches. Alex grabs it from her. "Thanks for getting the hoagies."

Jesse leans in. "What the hell are hoagies?" Julie shrugs.

***

After dinner, they sit around the table out back. Alex swigs a beer. The band smokes a joint. Julie walks up with the talking stick.

"Guys, I need to share."

Adam welcomes her into the fold with open arms. "Of course.

Dysfunctional Family Roundtable continues. Please sit." Julie sits across from Alex. She begins.

***

Back in Poughkeepsie, NY. Julie just started the 9th grade. She had friends, but Arlington High School was so big. So new. The football team. The hot guys. The parties. Julie had flowered early and began turning into a lady a year or two before. Her chest showed up shortly after her monthly friend. The boys noticed. So did the girls. It's a strange phenomenon when all girls aspire to look like a bombshell then when someone actually turns into one, their outlook on life conveniently changes. Julie took her digs with stride. Like a lady should, her mother used to say. Before she died in a car accident that is.

Julie had gotten used to being raised as a single child by an eclectic father. The house had magazines stacked up above her 5'5"

head. As her chest grew, the year before, her vertical stopped simultaneously. Tools piled up in odd corners of the house. Being self-employed running a fiber optics cable business had its ups and downs. Dad got into wiring data centers back in the '90s. Then when Mom died in '09, they were pretty much on their own. Sure extended family was there to help babysit when he worked late or traveled, but it's just not the same. Different kind of love. Different kind of attention.

Julie found drugs, alcohol, and sex at 13. Not with a whole lot of partners. Not in strange ways or with much older men. Just guys she knew since childhood. People she trusted.

Then there was high school. Homecoming. The bonfire, the night before the big dance. She met the star quarterback. Thee guy! Tommy Bradford. Up for Homecoming King no less. He invited her back to his place for a party. She thought he was sooo cool and sooo hot! Of course Julie accepted.

The party raged. Drugs, booze, strip poker, music. Wyclef Jean. "Staying Alive." A remake of a classic.

The music flowed through Julie. Her top on the floor. Pants next to them. Wearing only a bra and underwear, Julie felt comfortable and free with her new friends. She got up and danced. She made her tits bounce with the bass. Tommy noticed. He went to the radio to pump up the volume. Julie twerked a bit with her tight ass. Not good because for one she was a kid and for two white girls shouldn't twerk. However, her milkshake brought the boys to the yard. Tommy followed suit.

As the bass kicked through Tommy's parents' overpriced sound system, he ground his crotch into Julie's underwear. So much that everyone cleared the room. By the end of the song, they were alone. On the couch. No more bra and underwear. No more party. Just quick sex and a kiss good-bye. Tommy had a friend drive her home.

The next day Julie got a phone call from Meg Hope. Turns out Tommy *was* dating the Homecoming Queen after all. He lied. They were never on a break. She was out to dinner with her parents last night. She threatened Julie. Called her a slut, a whore, an ugly bitch…so many words. So vile. Julie stayed home and cried. She was going stag with some girlfriends anyway, but still. She missed her first big dance.

At school, the following Monday, she was met with looks. 'Slut' was written on her locker with a Sharpie. At lunch, some of the older girls threw food at her. Meg's younger sister, April, picked a fight with her. She pulled Julie's hair so hard, a clump fell to the floor.

Nine months later, the baby came. The adoption agency said she could keep a record of her son's new home. She tucked away the address in a drawer under her sweatshirts.

The next year, Julie started in a Catholic School across town. Sure some people knew, but it was a fresh start.

After graduation in 12th grade, she decided to enroll at Franklin Tech for Nursing. She got a job waitressing at the Rainbow Room. A block from her son's bus stop. He was in kindergarten last year. Finished up school right when she and Alex met. Julie never interferes with Jackson's life, but she watches him from afar. Lovingly. Wishing he'd been born out of love.

***

Tears stream down Julie's cheeks. They glisten in the moonlight of Alex's backyard. She could feel Alex nuzzle in next to her. Holding her tightly. She puts her head on his shoulder. Chad nuzzles in on her other side. Adam hugs them from behind. Jesse and Rick join in for a group hug. Julie giggles. Alex fights off tears to giggle with her.

"Now we're all one big family," says Adam among the human sandwich. Julie nervously laughs while wiping away some tears. "Yeah. One big,

fucked-up family. Where did we go wrong?"

Alex looks Julie in her eyes. "We didn't go wrong. Everything we've done led us here together. We did everything the best we could."

Chad closes his eyes and rests himself on Julie's side. "I love you guys." "We love you too," say Rick and Jesse in unison.

"You guys want to do a shot?" asks Julie hoping they all forgot the story already.

Her question is answered by a unanimous "Yes!"

As the guys walk toward the kitchen, Julie feels Alex stopping her from following.

"Thank you for sharing tonight. You did the only thing you could." "You don't think I'm a slut?"

"No. I love you."

Julie's heart skips a beat. It's the first time Alex said it. It! "You do?" She wipes a few more tears away.

"I do. I love you and I'm so happy you're here with me. With my crazy

123

family."

She wraps her arms around him. "Goofball. You made your words rhyme."

Alex put his hands on her waist. "Because you make me feel poetic. I can't help it. Would you run away if I wrote you poetry?"

She kisses him gently with a smile. "Maybe, maybe not." He kisses her back. "Good. Maybe I will one day."

"Maybe I'll like it." She kisses him deeply. The world fades away.

***

The moonlight's beautiful from Alex's room. Alex lay asleep next to her in the single bed. Comfy enough for now, but maybe a bigger mattress would be necessary if she's going to spend the summer here. Already planning her next steps. Loving Alex. Being with him. Starting over again in a new place with a new family. It's all she ever wanted. Away from New York. Leaving Jackson alone in Williamsport. *Ambler's not so bad*, she thinks. A little gritty. Lots of stone. People who refuse to shorten the names of others. Joseph and Robert are good examples. So proper yet so down to earth. Good people. Different, but not bad. Everyone has their issues. Julie can deal with Ambler type problems.

She gazes at the moon. The gray spots. The face. How the beams of reflected sunlight come through the tree. Something moves outside. The hockey mask and trench coat guy! She freezes. Terrified. Paralysis kicks in. Her jaw not working. Her phone on the nightstand. Plugged in. Just out of reach. She didn't know if he could see her eyes open. He grips his uncircumcised shaft tightly. Shaved pubes. Quickly pleasuring himself to her bare chest. Julie makes a pact with herself to stop sleeping naked in this room. Tee shirts would be a must from now on. She let him finish. He splattered some on the screen before scurrying off like a perverted "Darkman."

She cries in her hands when he leaves. Alex wakes. "Julie, what's wrong?"

"He was outside again."

"Who?" Alex looks around suspiciously. "Darkman…the guy in the trench coat."

"Just now? The hockey mask guy? Why didn't you tell me?" "I don't know. I'm so scared."

Alex picks up his phone from the stand. It's plugged in next to hers. They both do that so they could look at their apps in the morning. He dials 911.

"Hello, I'd like to report an intruder at 443 Church Street."

***

Alex calls his dad too. He and Robert show up right when the cops do. It's Officer Logan. The guy who wears the Superman shirt under his uniform. According to Alex, he and Uncle Scott had a run-in one night. Julie could see how he took Scott down. The guy's jacked.

She gives her story. Alex gives his story from the previous night.

The cop looks suspicious. "It happened the first night and you didn't call it in?"

Alex thinks fast. "We didn't know what to do. Not a whole lot of experience in this area."

John comments to break the awkwardness of the situation, "It was after the block party. There may have been some post festivities that clouded their judgment."

Officer Logan backs off. He and John know each other well. "Keep the underage drinking to a minimum, Alex. Please don't make us go through this again."

Julie thinks about Alex's next addition to the Roundtable. There is definitely a good story here.

The cop has all he needed. "John, we'll get him. Everyone go home and sleep well. I'll have a car patrol the alleys for now on." He gets in the squad car and drives off.

Julie could feel Robert's look. From the corner of her eye, he adjusts his package. Julie assumes he has a case of morning wood. It's 2:00 am after all. Maybe the guy has to pee really bad.

Alex's dad turns to speak, "I've got an idea. I'll make sure you're safe, OK, Jul'?"

"Yes, sir. Thank you for the help." He gives her a hug. It's surprisingly warm and affectionate.

"No problem, honey. Stay safe tonight. Robert and I got this."

Chapter 17
Gina

Gina and Richard get to the house around 2:00 am. The drive lasted forever. Richard took back roads to avoid cops for whatever reason. She got to play her music though. It was Brittany and Christina all the way down. Disney Channel champs! Gina was in heaven.

When they arrived, Richard unloaded everything but the duffel bag. Once inside, he shows her the bedroom, but does some coke instead of sleeping.

"We gotta date with some people at the beach in an hour. You're comin' too. Want a bump?"

"I want the bed, Richard. Why do I have to go too?" "They're expecting you after last night."

"Who is? I don't remember anyone new." "Yeah, baby. That's why I love you."

Gina rips through her bag to find a long-sleeved shirt. It's unseasonably cool outside. "Yeah well, the feeling isn't mutual, pal."

"It betta be. I'm all you got." "Oh, no you're not."

"What chu gonna do? Run back to Dudeman with that ratty pic in your wallet? He ain't never gonna trust you again. It's you and me now, babe. Like Bonnie and Clyde."

"More like I'd rather run and hide." She puts on the sweatshirt over her blouse. Richard promised they'd go to a bar called the Princeton on the way down. They missed last call by an hour.

Richard smiles. "Nice bust." He reaches out his hand for her to take a bump. She does. Without it, sleep would be inevitable.

"You talking about my tits or my words?" "It don't matter. Almost time to go."

***

Richard drives his rice burner slow and steady. No one is to travel over 25 miles per hour anywhere at the Jersey shore. He rolls into the really wealthy part of town. Ocean front houses with private beaches. He makes a left on 61st Street and pauses in front of the narrow entrance to the beach. A sign reads 'No Vehicles Allowed.'

"Richard. Are we allowed to drive up there?" "Just wait for it."

He proceeds slowly. The sand and gravel crackle under his racing tires.

* * *

The moonlight on the beach takes Gina's breath yet her heart races. Could be the coke. Could be the anxiety. Richard specified, "No music. We wait. Windows down. Watch the rearview for the signal."

Gina shivers in the cool breeze. She admires the house in her rearview. Its white whimsical exterior. Spiral staircase leading up to the porch off the back of the house. The flags flapping in the wind. Princeton Orange. Ireland. Italy. America. The porch light flickers three times. *Weird,* she thought.

Richard pumped the break three times. The red brake lights surrounds them in the darkness.

Gina panics. "What are you doing? The cops will come." "Yeah, I know."

The light flickers again. Richard responds with his brake lights again. "Stop it. They'll see us."

He grinds his teeth. "I know! Shut up and be cool."

A car rolls up the path behind them. No headlights on. Moonlight reflecting off its roof. The cops! "Oh my god, oh my god, oh my god!" Gina goes for the door handle. Richard grabs her arm with his death grip. Her wrist bones pop a little.

"I told you be cool. Stay still and stay put. They're expecting two of us, but you don't have to get out if you don't want."

The cruiser stops a few feet behind them. Gina could hear the car gears hit before the engine shuts off. The cop gets out and looks around. He flickers his flashlight three times before approaching Richard's window. He waits a few beats before leaning over.

Gina could smell his coffee breath. "You got something for me?" A crooked smile comes across his face. Gina thinks he looks very Irish American. When he smiles, the side of his lip drops like Popeye. Gina remembers Alex's

127

Uncle Scott from the Christmas party last year. He had the same droopy smile.

Richard motions behind them with a side thumb. "It's in the trunk." "Get out and open it." Richard follows orders.

The cop looks at Gina. "Her too."

Gina freezes. Richard gives her the look with teeth grinding again. "Get up and get out…now."

She follows orders.

Richard pops the trunk with a push of a button. The duffel bag sits still in the trunk light. Waiting for orders as well. Richard reaches in to grab it. The cop stops him.

"Not so fast, newbie. What's in it?"

A bead of sweat runs down Richard's temple. He hems and haws for a moment. Not sure of what to say. Then his personality kicks in. "My motha's dirty laundry."

The cop chuckles a little. "Good boy. Now hand it over." The droopy smile now more pronounced. Gina wonders if there's something in the water that causes mild paralysis in his face. She could smell the sulfur in the air. Maybe that's it.

The cop takes the bag. His hand on his gun. Carefully. Methodically.

Then backs up. "Close up and get the fuck out of here. We'll be in touch."

Richard, not very bright, responds accordingly, "You gonna give us a tow. My car tires look stuck."

The cop let out a sarcastic breath. "Yeah OK, buddy." He gets in his car and slowly backs up and creeps off.

***

4:50 AM. The sun would be rising in less than a couple hours. The car needs a push and she can't drive stick so Richard asks her to get out.

She does some more coke for strength. The car moves ever so slightly without making too much noise. The tires do small burnouts in the gray sand.

Richard revs the engine as quietly as possible. He yells at her with an impossible whisper. "Push fuckin' harder. Put your coke muscles into it."

Humiliation and the burning pain in her muscles allow Gina to find the primal strength necessary to beat the odds. The potential sunlight stranding them out in the open. The embarrassment and humiliation of being caught. The car shifts again. Abruptly moving now. She slips. The tires burnout louder now with a slight screech. Wet sand blows in her face and hair. Getting in her eyes. *The pain!*

"Yeah!" Richard lets out a celebratory howl. He keeps going. Leaving her to wallow in agony. Through slanted eyes she sees him make it to the broken blacktop path. He stops to wait. Tears in her eyes, she makes way for the Toyota Supra. Hoping this trip would be over soon.

Chapter 18
Julie

7:00 am. A knock at the door. Julie doesn't hear anyone answer. Louder this time. Julie gets up and adjusts her tee shirt. No more sleeping in the nude.

She looks at Jesse and Rick passed out on the couches in the front room.

Not even a twitch from either of them. Typical rock stars. Out cold.

No Adam. He must've taken the van and slept at his parents' house. He refuses to sleep on the third floor. It seems haunted. Three empty bedrooms. Everyone refuses to spend nights up there. Julie thought she could hear footsteps in the middle of the night.

She opens the heavy door. It drags on the carpet stopping before opening all the way. John and Robert walk right in.

Julie leans back. "Well, hello."

"Hey Jul. Good morning. We brought coffee and donuts." John motions for Robert to hand 'em over.

He does so with an awkward smile. "He...here J...Julie."

She takes them graciously. Not remembering Robert having a stutter before. "Thank you, Robert. I'll wake Alex."

"You'd better. We need to set up some cameras to catch Darkman outside Alex's room, and above the back porch."

"Cameras, wow. Beefing up security, huh?" she asks. Thankful that John's taking her safety to heart. The man is surprisingly secure and trustworthy. After all the stories Alex told, he sounded like a gruff a-hole, but really, he's just a goofy dad.

"Yeah, I'll have Robert link 'em to your phone when we're done. I gotta drill some holes for power then we can wrap it up." John drops a tool belt from his shoulder to the floor. He unlatches it to wrap around his waist. Then heaves it to the front, adjusting it correctly so the buckle is aligned with his zipper. In certain lights, John looks just like Alex. Other times not so much. Right now as he works, she can see the resemblance. The facial features. The cold determination on his forehead. The same look that Alex gets when he does the roadie work for the band. The showered smell, slightly sloppy hair doo. Old-school guys. Hard-working, playing hard. She appreciates that in men. Her man. That rugged sexiness goes unnoticed in today's hipster crowd. Getting lost in a sea of electronic stores and yoga studios. A song pops in her head. Once they begin working, she'll play some music.

"I'll wake Alex up."

John points to the couches. "What's up with these slobs?"

"Good luck with that." She scampers upstairs to their room. Downstairs she could hear John turning on his drill. She imagines him doing it right next to Rick's face with positively no reaction.

***

After about an hour, Alex gets up and has coffee and donuts. Listening to his dad drone on about sleeping in on a work day. Just because the house is paid off doesn't mean he can sleep his life away. Julie could see Alex had stopped listening about 10 seconds in. Once he'd gotten some food in his belly and his teeth brushed, Alex was ready to pitch in. Almost in time for the guys to be done. Alex is no dummy. He timed it perfectly. Alex played it off like he was listening to the lecture the whole time. Methodically eating his breakfast. Taking his time. Then sliding into the role of helper to run back and forth to the truck for stuff. Smooth as silk.

Julie sits on Alex's bed watching them work on the porch roof just outside. She plays some tunes from her phone. The Paula Cole song, "Where have All the Cowboys Gone?" that ran through her mind earlier. An ear worm that wouldn't go away without delivering the actual song from her brainwaves.

The windows open to their work area. Julie could hear John singing along outside. It's a song from when he was growing up. He must've been in his teens or twenties when it came out.

Robert kneels outside Alex's window, the same one Darkman shot webs at the night before.

He crouches down to tuck the wire close to the wall. Then she sees it. The intensity of his look. Averting his eyes whenever she would try and strike up conversation. She tries not to look, but he keeps adjusting his package. She has to look now. It's hard? Really? Then he reaches between his legs for a screwdriver and it all falls into place. *Robert is Darkman!*

Julie isn't 100% sure. It feels like a heavy accusation, but also feels correct. Or wrong. Whichever. *It's him!* Not bothering to turn off her phone, she runs toward Alex who's out front getting something.

Chapter 19
Gina

The morning is brutal. Getting only a few hours' sleep before Richard woke her up for the beach. She had to yak in the bathroom first before doing anything else. Richard didn't bother to hold her hair. He only pointed to the toothpaste when she was finished.

She goes to the kitchen to hydrate. She says hello to Sue and Peter as she pulls out a jug of Pedialyte. No class necessary. She sucks it back like it's her job.

Peter opens the conversation with a particularly condescending tone, "So, what are your dreams in life?"

"To sell Pedialyte to desperate college kids with terrible hangovers." Peter squints his eyes. "You're studying Nursing, right?"

"Yup. My final year awaits me back in Williamsport."

"Interesting." He turns to Sue. "Doesn't she have the most adorable accent?"

"Oh, yes. I need to confess something. I try to imitate it all the time. It's so cute."

Peter agrees, "The cutest. Hey, you're from Kentucky originally.

Family's in Pittsburgh now or somethin'. What does your father do again?"
"Dad restores old furniture. Does some ornamental carpentry on the
side."

Sue chimes in, "Oh, that's a great job for someone like him."

Whatever that's supposed to mean, Gina thinks to herself. Last time she checked, Sue lived in the slums of Philly for more than a few years. Not like Ambler's Bellaire either. If she really wanted to be nasty, Mr. Zilla doesn't exactly own the biggest house in town. Fuckers need to step off.

Gina grits her teeth and abruptly excuses herself before having the chance to intentionally offend someone.

***

On the way to the beach, Richard takes Gina to a little breakfast spot near the five & dime store in the center of town. Slack's Pancake Shack. There is a chain of them dotted throughout the shore towns south of Atlantic City.

Outside, on their way in, Richard says hello to the owner and his much prettier wife. He introduces himself as Jordan. Gina thinks the guy looks more like Rocky Dennis from "Mask." *Apparently, money can buy happiness,* she mused.

While Richard and the Dennis' finish their small talk, she feels a stare on her left. From a side-glance, Gina notices a familiar face of the Walker type. Alex's grandfather is having a solo breakfast at a little café table 10 feet from her. She hides under her hair to avoid his glance. There was no eye contact. She nudges Richard. He gets the memo. They say their good-byes and usher themselves a few steps closer to a plate of hot cakes.

Slack's resembled something that at first appeared to be aged, but as Gina takes in more and more of the scenery, it feels like she had stepped into a time warp. Not of the "11/22/63" kind. Gina doubted there would be a portal to be discovered in the cold box, yet there's a chance Stephen King himself may have visited this place over the course of his travels. More like a place where beach décor goes to die. Beautifully tacky.

The tables have placemats with local advertising. She notices one for a church. Gina loves church music. Reminds her of childhood in the South before all the madness and hysteria of her life kicked in overdrive.

A teenage waitress approaches with coffee. Richard looks thankful.

"Hey there, sweety. I'll take pancakes with a side of bacon, four eggs over hard, a thing of scrapple, and a large chocolate milk. My lady will have a short stack, a small OJ, and a side of Taylor Ham."

Gina feels the need to correct him, she can speak freely on this matter.

After spending a year with Alex, "It's called Pork Roll."

Richard looks up from the menu long enough to roll his eyes. "Not where I'm from it ain't."

The waitress joins in the fun. "Well, actually, here in Avalon, we all say Pork Roll too."

Richard laughs. "Sure they do. As long as they like 5% tips, that is." The waitress submits, "Ok, it's Taylor Ham."

Richard looks at Gina. "See! Victorious again."

Gina wants the waitress to go away. Richard is an unbelievable asshole when he's feeling competitive. She shrugs her shoulders and scrunches her nose with a smile. "Ok. Sounds good."

The waitress scampers off.

From the kitchen, a strangely handsome, middle-aged man wearing an apron comes toward them. Richard sees him coming. He rises up from the table for the necessary greeting.

The handsome man speaks first, "Bluto! How's it going?"

Bluto. Yuk. Gina's detective skills noted they all must be part of the same social circle. The horrible nickname Tony called Richard yesterday tipped her off. She hates it.

"JC. My man!" They slap hands before hugging and kissing on the cheek. "Got some business in town or what?"

"You know it, buddy, and looking for a good time when I'm off later."

Rocky Dennis walks back in. He does a head jerk in their direction. JC backs toward the kitchen in response. "You know where to find me, brother. Good to have you in town."

Richard sits down.

Gina looks at him suspiciously. "You two seem to go way back." "Yeah, all the way back to Kensington the other night."

Gina ducks her head. "Oh my god. Does he know me?"

"Relax, baby. Real men don't acknowledge things like that after having a good time together. It's all peace and love in a junior varsity surfer town like this."

Gina can't understand how all these people are connected. *Damn those drugs.* She misses out on all the little interesting facts when blacking out. Gina makes a mental note to bring more coke to keep her on Planet Earth next time they fill the eyedropper.

***

The beach is glorious. Richard carried nice chairs and clean towels for them, and made Bloody Marys in good insulated cups with lids. A separate cup of olives and pickles. Snack bags full of pretzels and chips.

In the ocean, she admires Richard's physique. She understands why he got into Professional Wrestling and Jiu Jitsu. What a body, and a face to match. He looks like a movie star.

She decided to move her bathing suit top every once in a while to see if he was looking. She catches him from time to time, but his attention is mostly on his phone. Texting. Constantly texting now. Must be his new BFF, Tony.

"Hey Richard, wanna go for a walk with me?" "Nah, bae. I'm workin' somptin' out."

"Oh, yeah. Like what?"

"I gotta stay in Philly for the summer. I may have gotten you a job here too."

"And what makes you think I'm up for having a job here?" Realizing she's about 90 miles from Philly at this point, but everyone around here seems to be from there too. The Jersey Shore below Atlantic City is really just an extension of Philly.

"Because you liked that purse full of money so much when you woke up yesterday." He's right. The money is more than she'd ever made at once. Maybe more than she'd ever made in a year. Up until now, all her money came from her dad or student loans. The brief gig at the BonTon back home doesn't count. She only made 15 bucks an hour and lasted just one season. Gina worked over the summer after senior year to pay for new clothes for college. Dad would never foot the bill for the ones she wanted. BonTon and Boscov's didn't have designer bags and tops. She ended up getting knockoffs from the farmers' market, but close enough.

"Richard, I really don't remember a whole lot from that night. Was I dancing nude again? I can only remember the song and all the hands on me."

Not looking up from his phone at all, he balances his time between her and texting. "Right, Aaliyah. Great choice, by tha way."

"What's the job, Richard?"

"You'd be dancing at a club by our new place." She sits up like a meerkat. "We're getting a place?"

"Yeah. In a neighborhood called Fishtown. Right by where we were da otha night. It's a studio above some non-profit that's affiliated with my work."

Gina has no desire to ask what that means. Her heart flutters. A new adventure. Richard is so exciting. She leans back down on her towel taking in some rays. If she's going to be dancing, a nice tan would be essential.

Chapter 20
Alex

Julie becomes a bit hysterical out front. She insists Robert is masquerading around the rooftops of Ambler as Darkman. Alex feels sympathetic toward her. He's angry, but also sad. *What if she's right?* Robert never had a girlfriend. Alex knows he isn't gay, but always thought his pseudo adopted brother was asexual. Maybe not. If he's out roof wackin' to Julie, then maybe he's just an unsexed maniac underneath it all. The kid had a terrible beginning.

***

Being kidnapped by his mother at the age of 4, Robert's first memories were of loneliness. Not really knowing his father. His mother getting hooked on dope then disappearing into the night. The cops finding him wandering the streets. Tony rescuing him, which was a bright spot, sort of.

Sue and Tony moved back to Ambler finally a couple years prior when Alex was 12 and Robert was 10. On the Dresher side of Ambler. Robert and Alex were together mostly in those days. Alex went on to live with John soon after. When kids turn 12, the child support system gives the opportunity for the kid to pick the parent. Alex was convinced that moving with his dad was the right move.

John had met a woman back then. They flew out to Vegas and got married. At first, it was OK. Alex lived with her for two years. She grew fresh vegetables in the backyard along the garage wall. Alex had homegrown lettuce on his sandwiches every day for school lunch. She would wash the lettuce then put the dripping leaves directly in the sandwich. Not much experience with kids. Alex once overheard her saying how much she hated kids. He prayed that she would love him. Maybe she could change.

After two months of the same soggy bread and turkey over and over again,

Alex had the audacity to ask for something different. She didn't like that one bit. When John had to work 60 plus hours a week, the new wife called Alex an ungrateful loser and gave him the silent treatment for weeks on end. He mostly hid in his room playing video games. Homework wasn't getting done at all. Alex was afraid of her. She was a monster. Screaming at him for leaving dishes on the counter or treating him like a ghost. Walking past him like he didn't exist.

Robert was only a few blocks away still at Sue and Tony's apartment. Alex escaped to their apartment whenever he could. At this point, he and Robert were mobile so being trapped inside with Sue and Tony wasn't as bad as it used to be. Plus, they were allowed to do what they wanted when they wanted. Alex would crash there on weekends, sometimes sleepovers during the week if possible. He could still manage to make it to the bus stop on time from there if he got up early enough.

The new wife turned out to be schizophrenic. Alex remembered going into the master bathroom and finding the medicine cabinet filled with pill bottles. From top to bottom. The brief marriage ended when she tried to murder John in his sleep one night with his own gun. Alex was 14 at this point. After John wrestled it away, she threatened Alex's life too. Alex could remember her rushing into his bedroom. Pulling his clothes out of the dresser and throwing them on top of his bed, while Alex lied still, awake and terrified from the madness. Alex and his dad made a break for William's house that night. After the dust had settled, John swallowed his pride and asked Sue to take Alex for the summer. School had ended a few weeks prior so not a huge deal in that sense. Gave John some time to sort out his differences with his new (soon to be Ex #2) wife.

Alex and Robert were inseparable that summer. They fell in with Jasper and Heather. Sleeping out all the time. They built a fort in the woods back by the sewage plant out of all the junk people dumped on the tracks.

No one would ever look for them back there. The Wissahickon Creek flowed nearby. A terrific place to hide, smoke cigarettes, and have circle jerks. Heather did not attend those, nor did Alex even think she knew about them. Alex remembered it was Jasper who convinced them to do the jerks in the first place. Apparently, his older brother and friends would watch porn in the living room when their parents were in bed. Jasper learned firsthand the tricks of the perversion trade.

Then as Alex and Robert pulled out their adolescent appendages to have a pubescent semi-public masturbatory session, Jasper would only do it under his pants or with his shirt covering. Alex thought it was disgusting watching Robert. Growing up together they'd often change in the same room, have baths together or run naked through the sprinkler out back. His uncircumcised pecker kind of looked like the trunk of an elephant. Alex and Jasper began referring to Robert's ding ding as a mutant won-ton, or Alex's favorite, Mr. Snuffleupagus.

When Heather was present, they'd watch movies or go get pizza together. She would hang at the fort only sometimes. Mostly, they'd all sneak out in the middle of the night and rendezvous in the alley behind Alex's dad's house. One of the garages had doors that didn't completely close. Old wooden ones. Not like the roll up kind from today, but double doors that slid back sideways on wheels. They would meet in there and sneak over to Pork Chop Hill.

A house owned by an old man who had a famous beer fridge in his garage. Old Man Pork Chop would leave his garage door open and light on all the time. He'd sit in his rocking chair on the front porch with a Salt Rifle during waking hours. Alex swore the rocking chair would move by itself at night. Rumor had it, Pork Chop would sleep inside with one eye open, waiting for some unlucky kids to raid his beer fridge so he could pop them in the ass with huge crystals of salt.

Alex and Robert contemplated how they could pull off the heist of all time. Jasper and Heather followed along for the excitement, but weren't filled in completely. It was on Mischief Night they put the plan in motion.

They were all the best of friends, but there was more. Alex's belly fluttered when Heather looked at him. It happened a lot. He didn't really understand it. Being 14 and not having much experience with girls. Heather was someone new to him entirely.

Then one day she mysteriously and secretively passed him a note. It said 'I love you' with a big red heart that was colored in with a special pencil she had in her art kit. Alex knew the pencils well. They spent hours watching movies together and drawing their favorite superheroes. She and Alex bonded over their shared love of comics.

They became boyfriend and girlfriend. Jasper began getting bratty. Heather wanted to kiss Alex, but wouldn't do it unless they were married. She insisted on having a wedding in the field at Madison Elementary before they sealed the deal. Alex remembered it well. Like a warm soft place in his data banks. Among all the trash piles and leaky pipes of his memories finally existed something beautiful. Something pure.

It was in late August right before high school began. They bought rings from bubblegum machines. Robert was Alex's best man. Jenny Harrington, from Park Avenue, was Heather's maid of honor. Jasper the priest. They exchanged corny vows then kissed for the first time. Then again. Then again. It was magical.

School started. They were a couple at first. Passing notes and hugging a lot. Oh, how he loved that time in his life. Even if it didn't last long, Alex caught a glimpse into a normal childhood. It was an important time to him.

By Thanksgiving, John's new wife was gone with about 10 grand of his life savings, his sports car, and his pride. She managed not to kill anyone and was never heard from again. Naming her would be a waste of time.

Alex moved back with his dad the same weekend Tony went to prison for getting caught with heroin. Sue didn't want Robert nor could she afford him on a secretary's salary. Robert's birth mother had never come back.

One fateful fall morning, John found Robert sleeping on a bench at Knights Park. John was hired by the mayor to service all the drinking fountains and public bathrooms in town. He'd gone to Knights Park to shut off the water for the winter and found Robert alone and shivering. John knew the kid well. It broke his heart to see such a thing. He took Robert in and made him a ward of sorts. Like a Robin to his Batman, only without all the money and cool gadgetry.

This is also the era when Alex and Robert began experimenting with drugs. Joe used to escape from rehab randomly to go on a quick bender. He'd disappear to Kensington for a long weekend then pop up in Ambler when he was ready to go back. One time around Christmas, he left a few dime bags of weed behind, which Alex found easily in his room on the third floor. Alex knew the hiding spot well. Over by the radiator. Pull up the carpet flap and reach down into the floor cavity. There were porn mags, knives, rolling papers, and bags of weed.

He and Robert began by smoking loosely-rolled joints and coughing till the point of vomiting. This lasted over the winter. He tried hiding it from Heather, but Jasper ratted him out more than once. She grew distant.

Things changed for Alex and Robert one night when they ate a bag of magic mushrooms. It was Memorial Day of 9th grade. Tony was getting out soon and Robert wanted to celebrate. He coaxed Alex into searching for the legendary bag of shrooms hidden deep in Sue's couch.

The legend of the couch shrooms began when Gabe and Diane threw a New Year's Eve party. Sue was off visiting her dad upstate. Alex and Robert were forbidden to go, which was fine. They hung with Heather and Jasper someplace else.

All the older kids in the neighborhood stopped over. The cops came. Once Diane heard them knocking with a flashlight, Gabe shoved his bag 'o shrooms in the side of the pullout couch. Apparently, these particular sticks of fungus were dipped in something. A chemical maybe, PCP, no one ever confirmed, which would have gotten Gabe locked up.

The shrooms were in there for months. None of the older kids could get their hands far enough down without getting skinned knuckles on the metal slats inside.

Alex one day, on a dare from Robert, reached in with his 15-years-old sized digits, and hit the jackpot! Gabe had told them so many stories about seeing bright colors in the sky, watching cartoons so vivid they'd jump off the TV screen, or even seeing the walls melt. Sounded like too much of an adventure for the two boys to pass up.

He and Robert ate them in the fort. They were nasty. Tasted like crap coated with bug spray. Luckily, Alex palmed some beef jerky and a small bottle of ice tea from the corner store. A terrific chaser for cow shit fungi.

That night was a trip, in a literal sense. It took a while to kick in. They began feeling the effects when their bodies vibrated. Like every molecule in their physiology danced at once to a funky tune. Once it got dark, they escaped the haunted woods and found themselves kneeling together behind John's garages. Not inside, just kneeling in the alley. Talking about the sidewalk. Avoiding concrete. Scared of falling in the cracks. After the rocks beneath their feet turned to lava, they made their way to the corner store for some candy.

They couldn't work up the nerve to go in the store. The neon lights in the window kicked off a vibe that freaked 'em out. There was no breaking that force field, so they made their way for Knights Park instead.

They bumped into Heather and Jasper nearby. Alex couldn't form words and looked around wide-eyed and crazily. Robert tried filling the awkwardness with terrible impressions of people from back in the day. Like Pee-wee

Herman for example. The impressions killed with Alex back in the alley. The childish laugh combined with the mania from the shrooms came out crazy wack funky. Jasper pulled at Heather to go. Calling them losers without actually speaking in their direction. Heather agreed with Jasper. She yelled at Alex for becoming such a 'loser druggie.'

Their trip went downhill from there. After parting ways with Heather and Jasper, they made for the open field by the fort. Their trip peaked when a space ship came down over their heads. The bright lights spun and made whirling and whooshing sounds. The colors. The terror. He and Robert both saw it. They ran like in a dream. Trying to move faster, but feeling like slow motion. The harder and faster they ran, the slower their bodies moved. After a while, they were forced to crawl toward the woods. They regrouped in the fort for safety. They stayed there until dawn. When they finally got back to Alex's dad's place to go to bed, it was breakfast time. Alex felt like a few years were shaved off his life.

Heather dumped him for Jasper the following week. She passed him a note that said, "Fuck you! Druggie asshole!"

***

Alex and Robert both went off the deep end that summer.

It went sideways for Robert first. His problems amplified when Tony got out of prison in June.

Robert begged John to let him go back to the apartment with his dad for the new school year. Tony and Sue seemed to have things together. Tony got a job at the local recycling plant, a normal nine-to-five, the same place Sue was working as a secretary for *the boss*. It lasted for 30 days.

Tony tried to keep it a secret from his old crew when he'd first gotten out. It was impossible. After two weeks, they were at his front door. A party had been set up at Daydreams, the dirtiest strip club in Kensington. The following day, Robert found Tony drooling on himself during lunch. A puddle of mouth juice all over his grilled cheese. Robert was real sad. So sad in fact, that when he found a bag of magic dust in Tony's left pocket, he made himself a man-sized line on the kitchen table and snorted it.

Alex found Robert foaming at the mouth a few minutes later. Alex was due for lunch with he and Tony, but had gotten side-tracked when he couldn't get the day's tin foil bowl to work correctly.

That day at the hospital, the doctors said Robert was lucky to be alive. If there was any fentanyl whatsoever, he wouldn't have made it. John swore if Robert survived the overdose, Tony was out for good. His lawyers would make sure of it this time. This is also the day Joe found Jesus and became Joseph. He loved Robert too. Joseph went with Tony the day Robert was found wandering the streets of New York alone and scared. He was like a second little brother to Joseph.

Alex didn't find god or swear any allegiance to anyone or anything. He slowly started to unwind. All the years of abuse, stress, heartbreak and now the booze and dope, had given his young mind the last strike it needed to break.

Alex started talking to people who weren't there. Punching the air on his way to the corner store while on a mission to find and kill every Smurf in the village. Like he was Gargamel. Heather ran when she saw him. Jasper challenged Alex to a fistfight at Knights Park.

Jasper's older brother, Jason, made sure it was going to happen. The older group of guys waited for Alex out front of the house on Church Street. They'd all gotten to know each other over the past couple years. Alex played lacrosse with some of the guys, and felt he knew them pretty well. They walked him down to the park like they were still friends.

Alex's heart pumped on the way there. He wanted desperately to run away, but the Moon Knight side of his personality told him to stay. Alex told them to call him Marc Spector for now on. They laughed and slapped hands. A teenager pretending to be a superhero with multiple personality disorder should never be a joke.

The older kids surrounded Alex and Jasper. Heather was there with Jenny and some older girls. Everyone wanted Alex's blood. A teenager suffering from a public mental breakdown was to be meat for the social beast. There was no room for hugs, forgiveness, empathy or understanding. Only fear and rejection. Fear of becoming someone so heinous. Insanity and weakness had Alex. He needed to be stamped out. Ultimate rejection. Deserving to be shunned forever. Win or lose, Alex would be ruined. They knew it. He didn't. Alex walked out there with his Moon Knight tee shirt on he got from the comic shop. The shirt was loud and proud. Not in a good way. Jason warmed Jasper up just outside the circle. When he was good and warmed up, Jasper ran in full speed ahead. He wound up and tried to take Alex's head off with the first punch. Alex instinctively ducked and tripped Jasper all at once. A move he learned from a kid who used to beat him up back in Kensington. When he jumped on Jasper, Jason's buddies got a couple shots in on the back of Alex's head before pulling him off. Alex tried not to cry when he felt them hitting him. Jason pretended to stop the cheap shots before the fight resumed.

Jason told them to stand toe to toe like boxers. They did. Alex got punched in the nose. Jasper got a bloody lip. It got worse. They grabbed each other by the shirts and fought like hockey players. Alex pulled more as he punched harder. Jasper repeatedly tried to knock Alex out by punching him in the chin, temple or side of the neck. Alex went after Jasper's eye to give him the shiner of his life.

They fought so hard Alex ripped Jasper's shirt off. Someone from behind Alex, pulled the Moon Knight tee shirt over his head. Jasper took as many brutal shots as he wanted. Alex struggled to get the shirt off, but couldn't. Someone else was punching him from behind. Hitting him in the back of the head. Then someone from the side. Then the front. Then the other side. First Alex's arms went numb trying to swing back. Wildly. Blindly. Then Alex felt something like a rock hit him in the forehead, his legs gave out.

Alex heard his dad's voice. He remembered the feeling of people being pulled off his limp body. The shouting. Threatening words. Alex remembered thinking his dad was weak for crying. John took Alex directly to the doctor for a checkup.

Alex felt like a warrior. It was all in his mind. He needed 16 stitches along his hairline from being hit with a brick and two weeks' rest from the concussion.

Sue refused to stay home from work to pitch in. William was in Avalon with Karen at the time. Diane stayed with him sometimes, but Alex was broken both mentally and physically. Alex would periodically sneak his weight set out to the front porch and do curls like he was a gangster in a Dr. Dre video.

The cops came when the neighbors were frightened by Alex's grunting and groaning.

That was the day Alex was taken to a psychiatric facility for youths.

He was in there for six weeks. By that time, Robert had woken up and was in a facility of his own, somewhere else. They both were put on medicine. John signed forms to let the doctors treat the boys however they could to "fix them," which is the phrase John used. Hopefully, not what the doctors would say. Alex drooled on himself for the first two weeks of his inpatient treatment. He fell asleep at the table when his dad came to visit for the first time. John yelled at him for not going to bed early enough. He didn't understand what Lithium did to a person. Not even if it was his own son.

It took until the winter to get them out of the mental health programs and back into the Ambler public school system. Neither of their lives were the same again. Robert and Alex swore off everything but alcohol from then on.

Robert promised John that he'd never do anything like that again. He didn't have many friends after that. Robert only hung with John and Joseph or maybe some older kids Alex's age. Robert started the 9th grade the following year and aspired to be a plumber like his family.

Alex worked daily to piece back together his life over the remaining two years of high school. It was the decision of his principal to put him in the emotional support class, which meant he was in the same classroom all day long.

His teacher found a ray of light in Alex that had never been discovered before. His love of Art. It was in her experience to let children pursue what they excelled at in life. Got him to read books, cover to cover for the first time in his life. Asked him to draw whatever popped in his mind. So he drew a woman with large breasts. She didn't laugh or get angry. Just gently asked him to keep it PG rated during school hours. Then he started drawing album covers of his favorite rappers. Kanye West, Eminem, 50 Cent. He could sketch people almost perfectly.

The following spring, she convinced him to go out for the lacrosse team again. Get back in goal. It worked for a little while. Until he played Dresher and recognized a few of the guys who'd jumped him with Jason and Jasper. Alex broke his goalie stick over the one kid's helmet. He was ejected from the game and asked not to come back.

Senior year brought new adventures for Alex. His teacher asked him to go out for the wrestling team this time. Alex was surprised when Heather joined and became one of the head cheerleaders for the team. It was late in the season when Alex won a few matches. He wasn't very knowledgeable in the moves department, which put him at a major disadvantage compared to the Hitler youth that had been plugging away since they were sperms. He did have natural strength, speed and stamina. This allowed him to catch more than a few sloppy kids and pin them in the first period. Alex felt like a young white, Mike Tyson.

Knock 'em out early or lose the long game. It was after his big win against Dresher that Heather invited him over late one night.

She and Jasper must've been on a break. Or maybe she was just drunk and horny. Either way, he randomly got a booty call from his old flame and was much obliged to sneak out for old times' sake.

He could see his breath in the cold winter air on the way over to the alley behind Southern Avenue. She left the basement door open for him. She took his hand and placed a shushing finger over his lips.

"My parents are sleeping. Be quiet and walk softly." She led him upstairs.

The inside of her room was warm and inviting. It smelled like Brittney Spears' perfume. Alex knew the smell because it's what Heather wore the day they were married a few years back. She let go, and knelt by her phone. She hit the screen and put it down. A green light from her alarm clock illuminated the room ever so slightly. She looked radiant. Like a female Green Lantern.

She changed quickly as Trey Songz filled the night air with "The Sheets…Still."

Heather walked up to Alex slowly wearing a white button-down with nothing but panties on underneath. Alex could feel her perky nipples rub up against his chest when she closed in. She put her hands on him. Tickling his shoulder then running her Lee Press-On nails through his hair. "Hey buddy, it's been too long. Couldn't help but call. You looked so good in your singlet today. I had to see what's underneath."

She grabbed him in a way she'd never done before. He liked it. A lot.

Heather raised an eyebrow and stepped back. She unbuttoned her shirt and let it hit the floor. She and Alex had fooled around some back in 8th and 9th grade, but he'd never seen her like this before. Her black panties looked awesome with her long blonde hair. Her nipples seemed to glow in the green light. Alex wanted to be her hero in the worst way. She put her arms around him. They kissed.

Heather pulled Alex to her bed. The song played on. That night Heather took Alex's virginity. It was beautiful. A dream come true for Alex. He had his girl back. His best friend. His wife!

The following Monday at school, Heather acted like she didn't know him. Alex was crushed. He began writing her letters. Jasper found one a few weeks later. He read it aloud in study hall.

Jasper stood up in front of what felt like half the senior class. "Oh, Heather.

My Heather. Oh, how you glow in the green light. You say it, you feel it. With me, all through the night," he continued. Everyone laughed.

Heather grabbed her backpack quickly to storm out, but before she did, leaned in to speak softly to Alex, "Way to kiss and tell, lover boy."

Alex remembered working hard from there on to get out of Ambler. His teacher had him fill out applications for college when the school year began. The only acceptance letter came right before Easter.

Alex felt disappointed when Franklin Tech was the only 'yes' he got. His teacher explained to him that art school wasn't a good path for a person to take in life. That most artists end up working in office buildings with mountains of debt. Learning a trade was the way to go. He could pave his own way in life by becoming a small business owner like his dad. Alex listened and enrolled that same day.

John was so upset with his son for being shunned by the kids at school. He felt like the kid had betrayed him by becoming such a loser. Robert bounced back without a hitch. Joseph cleaned himself up nicely. Then there was Alex. The drooling idiot.

***

Alex fights back the urge to call his dad after talking with Julie. He decides to walk over to Joseph's house and check Robert's room. He finds nothing. Then he remembers, his dad moved Robert after the block party. He makes way to his dad's place over on Euclid.

Alex walks in the front door and looks around. The morning sun radiates in the foyer through the stained-glass windows. Creating a kaleidoscope of colors on the polished hardwood floor. The house smells of dried flowers and aftershave. An interesting combination from years of Karen clipping roses to John's after-shower smell.

Alex puts his hand on the large carved spindle at the bottom of the curved stairway. He looks up to the crystal chandelier. More colors cascading down the walls toward his current position. He ascends.

Robert's room smells like old pillows, sweat, and regret. He checks the closet first. Nothing. Under the bed. Nothing. Alex sits down thinking how wrong Julie was for blaming Robert. Then he remembers something. The chest in the attic. Where William let Alex and Robert stash their comics. It became a catch-all for their private stuff. He goes to the third floor to find it.

The third floor is a wide-open area. It was John's room in high school, but had been used for storage ever since. The chest is off in the corner under some cardboard boxes. When Alex gets closer, he notices handprints in the dust. When he removes the boxes, he sees a smear of dust clearly caused by dragging something off the chest. Alex pauses before opening it.

***

Back at his house, Alex finds the guys holding court at the kitchen table. They're trying to figure out where they could practice for the upcoming show. Alex suggests one of his dad's garages. The one in the back. Where he, Robert, Heather, and Jasper used to meet up. The nostalgia makes Alex feel warm and fuzzy. They agree.

Alex calls John to ask. Luckily, it was the only garage that's still empty. The others are used for his plumbing supplies. John has some stipulations. Since the house wouldn't be Alex's officially until he graduated the following year, they would have to pay rent and soundproof the garage themselves. The guys unanimously agree. Julie even offers to get a part-time job bartending at an Italian restaurant on the main drag to pitch in.

Alex feels happy for the first time for as long as he could remember. His summer just fell in place.

***

Darkman made another appearance outside Jasper's house. Alex knows this because it made the paper. The writer interviewed Jasper and Heather. The headline read: "Peeping Tom in Hockey Mask Harasses Sleeping College Kids." He couldn't believe it. Robert should've known better when he found the empty trunk. He must have a backup costume somewhere.

Alex decides it's time. He walks to John's house to talk. It's around 5:00 so both of them would be home to shower.

When he gets there, Robert and John are eating cheesesteaks from the corner store in the kitchen.

"Hey, guys. Sandwiches smell good."

John pulls out a chair. "Sit. We got plenty. Joseph didn't feel like wheeling himself over so there's extra."

"Sure, Dad. Love to."

The cheesesteaks taste delicious. Cooper Sharp with sweet peppers. Then another with fried onions and mushrooms. A third with cheese wiz and hot cherry peppers. Alex had a quarter of each.

After dinner, Alex decides it's time.

"Dad, Robert has something he wants to tell you." Robert straightens up. "I do?"

"Yes, you do. About the costume you have in the chest up on the third floor."

"There's no costume up there," says Robert confidently.

"I know. Wanna know how I know that?" A rhetorical question. "Because I found the hockey mask and trench coat, and threw them out."

John turns to Robert. "What?"

Robert panics. "No, I swear. It's not me. If Alex tossed away the stuff, then how was there another sighting?"

"It's him, Dad. He must have a second costume hidden somewhere."

John lunges at Robert. It takes a second or two for John to pin Robert on the floor. Slightly strangling him. "You little fucker! You lie to me?"

Alex pulls his dad off. Robert begins sobbing. "I'm sorry, I just want a woman so bad. No one ever pays attention to me. I don't go to school anymore. No girls in town talk to me because I'm the overdose kid. Then all I do is work. I got no one to talk to besides plumbers. It sucks!"

"You need help, Robert."

John agrees, "I second that." He holds out his hand to help Robert to his feet. Robert accepts.

***

The following week, Alex and company are invited over to John's place for family dinner. It's a Sunday so John makes London Broil with Catalina.

It took some convincing, but Julie came too. Alex had a long talk with her about Robert. Where he came from. What happened. Julie got it, but he could tell she still feels squeamish.

When they get there, a beautiful Asian girl helps Robert set the table.

They seem close.

149

John introduces her to the crowd, "Guys, I'd like you to meet Robert's new girlfriend, Pearl. They've been pen pals for so long now, she decided to come over to America and stay with us for a while."

Alex knows his dad too well. He's lying through his teeth. If it were true, Robert would introduce her himself.

Pearl bows slightly. "Hello everyone. It's nice to meet you all. Can't wait to watch the band's next gig. Robert and I will be there for sure."

Julie lightens up after meeting Pearl. Alex leans in. "Dad's got this." "Your dad bought Robert a mail-order bride?"

"A Walker will do anything to save a life, Julie. Anything."

"Good, because I would've killed your brother myself if I had to see his pecker one more time."

Chapter 21
Gina

Daydreams could've been farther from what Gina imagined. The place smelled like old beer and *broken* dreams. The kinda place where frat boys would wheel in a keg on a red Radio Flyer wagon. Where the guys got touchy feely but not in the back, up front where everyone could see. Oh yeah, and the girls dance fully nude.

There's a more intimate bar in the back where the high rollers could hang. They used to call it the Champaign room, but that would imply a private party was necessary. Not at Daydreams. This place is called the Golden Shower. Classy. Just about anyone could slip the bouncer an extra 50 bucks and bada bing! You're in. Nothin' to it.

Only in this case the bouncer is Richard, and Gina got to dance in the Golden Shower from her first night. Made the other girls jealous. The only friends she made so far were on stage during the girl-on-girl live sex show. Richard would sit at the end of the bar counting the money while Gina was up on stage strutting her stuff. The night juice in the eyeballs was essential for her first week then the place kinda grew on her. Not like a fungus per se, more like what she imagined Stockholm syndrome to be like. Richard isn't exactly her captor, but he definitely says they'll be staying here as long the money rolls in. And boy, did it ever.

They couldn't spend the cash on anything glitzy. No new cars or jewelry, but man they have dinner at the nicest restaurants in the city, order whatever they want from the menus, and party harder than ever before. They go from one bender to another and Richard is bigger than ever. Impotency from the steroids, yeah right. Viagra took care of that. No sleeping from the coke. Ambien took care of that. Panic attacks from the hangovers. Zoloft for that. One morning, Gina came out of a particularly bad hangover from Bike Week.

Her and Richard went long and hard on a three-day bender from a bump of meth. Doesn't take much of that stuff to get the motor humming.

Gina learned to separate herself from the memories and live in the moment. She thinks back to her Ethics teacher at Franklin College. A tall, average-looking man from Brooklyn. He decided to become an Ethics teacher when he was in college and went home for a weekend to hang with his buddies. One particular friend decided to go up on a roof and toss bricks over the edge.

When her teacher asked why he would do such a thing, the friend replied, "Because it's what I want from life right now. Aren't we supposed to live to be happy? Right now, this is what makes me happy." Stuck in a moral conundrum, he began studying ethics day and night to prove his friend wrong. After years of study, he only sided with him more. Her teacher was such a nice and funny man, no one really took the story seriously, but the argument made a lasting impression upon Gina's mind. At this point in her life, if screwing bikers for meth made her happy then so be it.

She looks at herself in the mirror. Smiling. No lipstick on the teeth. She checks her top. Slightly too small, yet leaving enough for the imagination. Her hair bouncy and beautiful as ever. The picture of her and Alex on the mirror. Harking back to a different time. Saturday movie night and microwave popcorn. Snuggling up and kissing for hours. Now she has Richard. Now she has more cash than she could spend.

The bouncer knocks on the wall. "Belle! You're up!"

Gina kisses her hand and lightly taps Alex's fading face. Always once for good luck. She snaps on her high heels and makes way for the stage.

***

After her shift, Gina sits at the bar having a drink. She could give more lap dances if she wants, but Richard waves at her as if to say, "You made enough tonight."

Gina feels *just OK* about things. The money's good and so's the partying, but there has to be more she could be doing. She looks at Richard standing at the end of the bar counting wads of cash.

She feels a familiar touch. A man's touch. Massaging her shoulders.

Tony kisses her on the top of the head. "Sup, my Southern Belle?"

"Hey, Big Tone. Got in late tonight."

"Yeah, had some things in town to do. Gotta speak with Zilla. Talk to you soon, baby."

She watches him slink over to Richard. They slap hands and greet like old friends. Tony quick counts the money. She could read their lips.

"You're short, Bluto. Where's the rest?"

"Business is good, Mr. Grinch. I'll make it up tomorrow night. We got three girls scheduled for a live sex show up on stage."

"That's tomorrow. What about tonight?" "I got what I got."

"You gotta run more shipments to make up for this."

Richard cops an attitude. "I already told you, I'll make up for it tomorrow."

Tony points in his face. "Tomorrow ain't good enough. I got people lookin' for the money tonight."

"What the fuck, bro? You ask me to turn my girl out then point at me for being a few grand short?"

"Don't blame that shit on me. That girl was turned out long before I showed up."

"You got some balls speaking to me like that, Tony."

"I got what?" He gets in Richard's face. "You fuckin' mook. You walk in here looking like the offspring of the barbarian raids of Rome and talk to me like that!" Tony flexes his back muscles. "Motherfucker, I own you."

Richard laughs. "Yeah, OK. Sure you do. I'll get my dad up here and we'll square things off sooner or later."

"We'll square things off when you get my money." Tony storms off.

Richard looks pissed. He orders a shot of Fireball then throws the empty glass against the wall. It shatters in a million pieces. Tiny shards of glass rain on the concrete floor.

153

Chapter 22
Alex

The gig ends at 11:00. Alex finishes packing the van in less than an hour. The guys call it quits for the night. Alex and Julie want an adventure. It's been all work and no play for a couple weeks. Julie is working a lot tending bar, and the guys are constantly trying to write original music. It isn't happening for them, but they are getting gigs all across the city. June went by fast and July is winding down.

After the block party, Adam's mom pulled some strings with her old colleagues to get them a shot at playing Festival Pier in South Philly. It worked great. They rapped, they rocked, and they sang the shit outta some old-school ballads. No one has ever seen anyone quite like Polyester Anarchy before. People don't know what the hell to make of them except for the fact that they bring the house down.

Tonight's gig was at a bar near a small airport on the northeastern side of the city. Rumor has it the Drill Sargent from Full Metal Jacket was the original owner. Alex could see that being true. There was enough war memorabilia around to make a good case for it without actually asking someone.

He and Julie need some alone time. Alex knows just the place. A strip club nearby. A place that wouldn't card him. Julie, being slightly older than Alex and having an unbelievably bubbly personality, easily gets a couple six packs from the bar before they leave. Alex had been driving Julie to gigs lately. He saved enough over the summer to not only keep up with the rent but to buy himself a decent car. A Jeep Wrangler. He and Julie make their way to the strip club in style. Top down, and hormones raging.

***

They wait in line. Julie has the bouncer pegged for an idiot. She works him like magic. Unbuttoning her top a bit. Smiling and squeezing Alex's ass as she tells the bouncer it's their anniversary and they're looking for a good time. She does her patented wink and the guy lifts the yellow velvet rope.

Inside, Alex feels his feet sticking to the floor. Joseph had told Alex stories about this place. That him and his buddies felt like they were remaking "Porky's" on their first trip. Only it wasn't a Riverboat, and Porky Wallace was nowhere to be found. Plenty of strippers though.

Once inside. Alex and Julie feel cramped. Someone purposely spills beer on Julie to make conversation. After she politely declines his proposition to screw outside, she pulls out a 100-dollar bill.

She points back toward a yellow lighted doorway that reads, 'Golden Showers. $50 Each.'

"Doesn't that mean you get pissed on?" asks Alex condescendingly.

"It's a gimmick. Come on, Mr. Knight. Let's go have ourselves an adventure."

***

Alex and Julie grab the last two seats at the stage.

The Golden Shower room is eerily erotic. While the name itself implies being pissed on by your favorite stripper(s), there is a familiar purple hue to the lighting. The song. The way the base rolls. The brass complimenting the keyboard strokes.

Alex thinks the song is slightly too obscure for the Coors Light crowd with their hats turned backward and cut-off tees.

He turns to the bouncer who has the mic up on the long stage, which wraps around to the dressing room like a tongue-shaped runway.

"Now, without further ado, I give you: Your Southern Belle!"

Then out she walks. In all of her glory. Black high heels, and a bikini a size too small. Gina steps foot over foot and messes up her hair on cue. She doesn't see Alex and Julie sitting there nor does anyone think it odd that both their jaws are resting on the sticky floor.

A laugh. Alex could see someone pointing at him from the corner of his eye. That familiar cackle. He turns and there is Zilla. Counting his money, laughing, and pointing at Alex all at the same time.

Gina slams herself on the stage and starts grinding her ass to "Digital

Witness" by Saint Vincent. A song only Gina would listen to.

Zilla lets it go for a minute before getting her attention. "Yo, Belle!" She looks over pretending to lick her fingers.

"You got some visitas."

Alex and Gina lock eyes for what seems like an eternity. He thinks there's a twinge of anger on her face. Could be the glitter. It accents her laugh lines in a way that makes her seem smug.

Zilla breaks their high noon stare down. "Dudeman's first in line for golden showa tonight. Time ta get it in, bra!"

A lonely tear drips down Gina's cheek.

Alex feels Julie tug on his arm. "Time to go, baby." He submits. "Yeah, I guess it is."

On their way out, Alex turns for one last look. He needs to make sure it wasn't a dream. When he does, Gina runs off the stage with her face in hands. Zilla holds up two handfuls of money acting like it isn't enough. "Belle! You can't leave yet. You're up for the sex show next!"

Alex is dumbstruck. Of all the gin joints in all the world…he feels Julie pulling him further away from the madness. "Alex, fun's over. We gotta to go."

Chapter 23
John

John needs to give the elevator guy the final installment of the money. 48k flat. The damn kids did it. It'd been over a month since the block party. The total raised came to 35k. John pitched in the last bit to make it even. He was happy to do it. John does well for himself, but it's tough keeping that much around in cash. Even if he could float the full amount, someone would know he has it. Between the boys and Tony being back in town, there would be a snitch somewhere in the ranks.

John stops his truck in the alley between Southern and Park Avenues. The elevator fits perfectly along the backside of Joseph's row home. Even has some room for the new van in the driveway. That part was easy. The van's a lease from the Ford dealership in town. John helped those guys install their sprinkler system last year. They were four months behind with payments, so John squeezed 'em for a used van and got 'em to throw in the hand pedals at no extra cost.

Ed Murray was dragging his feet in court. The settlement wouldn't likely happen until Christmas. What a present. Would a guy rather have a million-dollar settlement and lose his legs? John feels happy with all the choices he made up until this point. If Alex wouldn't have gotten into that fight, Joseph may still be whole. Ah, there's no telling if time travel could heal those wounds. Even still, a goddamn DeLorean would be fantastic right about now.

A lady walking her dog is starring laser beams at John, who realizes he's been brooding in his idling truck for a few minutes now.

He puts on his social mask. "Hello, Mrs. Whittaker. Very nice to see you again."

"Don't you know about global warming, Walker? Shouldn't leave your truck running like that."

John turns off his truck. "Thank you, Mrs. Whittaker. Have a nice walk."

"My sink's still dripping. Maybe I shoulda called a real plumber."

"I'll be over on Tuesday, OK? No charge."

"Hmm. Shoulda fixed it right the first time then we wouldn't need to be speakin' right now."

"I understand. No problem. Thanks again."

John swears he heard Mrs. Whittaker fart on the way by the truck. The old bat. Probably can't control her bowels at this point. John knows her heart isn't good these days. Last time he was over, the toilet was so clogged by her concrete shit from the meds, he could barely get a drain snake through it. Old people have the toughest shits on the planet. Hands down.

***

Joseph's house doesn't look so hot on the inside. It's been about a week since he'd been over last. John walks in through the newly installed alley door that replaced the garage. The elevator had to be installed smack in the middle of the overhead door. John had his contractor weatherize the area like an outside wall to finish the space as a bedroom for Tony. John wasn't comfortable telling anyone about covering that fee out of his own pocket, considering the history between him and Tony. It's something that simply makes sense from a square footage perspective. Or at least that's the story he's sticking with from here on out.

Tony set up shop in the other basement room. Sleeping in an easy chair. John thinks of how strange the sleeping habits of some people could be. Then there's the smoking in the house. All the butts in the ashtray. Not even on a table. Right there on the fabric arm of the smelly old chair. His aging Armani shirts and designer jeans piled up in the corner. The clothes basket laying empty next to the pile. How did Sue ever fall for a guy like this? Luke's words ring out in John's memories. "Tutto spettacolo, non andare" he used to say about his son. It's Italian for, "all show, no go". Handsome, athletic, but beyond that, not much going on upstairs. Luke's cold assessment of his own boy is spot on even after all these years. John moves on to go upstairs.

Empty pizza boxes and plastic bottles cover the kitchen table and counter tops. The powder room's a mess. Shitty paper left on the ground next to the toilet. Even in moments like this, John has to resist from calling the toilet a 'John.' He stops internalizing his endless struggle with humanity long enough to continue his review of the home.

John regrets giving Joseph a weekly allowance for a cleaning person. For a while, things were presentable, but now it's clear the money's being used for other purposes. A nurse is what Joseph really needs. Or maybe another mail-order bride who won't mind taking care of a paraplegic while also committing to a person who may or may not consummate the marriage. This idea needs to be revisited later.

John walks through the living room, which only has a TV and a couch. This must be where Joseph does all his thinking. Not much trash in here. Must be keeping up appearances for the off chance he'd have someone knock at the front door. Interesting how someone would vacuum a single room in an effort to distract others from a very obvious mess. One that's clearly visible from the same room. *Idiots,* John thinks to himself.

John b-lines to Joseph's bedroom to find his son taking a dope nap in bed. 1:30 in the afternoon. He attempts to wake Joseph.

His eyes open seemingly awake. "Jesus, Dad. Stop, would ya? Why do you always have to…" Joseph falls back asleep before finishing his sentence. Drool pouring out. John opens up his night table drawer. The empty pill bottles. Some legit for his arm. The back pain non-existent, unless Joseph managed to fuse his lower nervous system back together like a werewolf.

Unlikely. The other pill bottles are the problem. Names John didn't recognize. John knows the problem. He already had a 'talk' with Tony about the mess. There was no keeping Tony away from Joseph. Things are bad enough for the kid, having another ear to bend could help, but this is something else. The drugs complicate things to the point of no return. It's hard enough to put into perspective the desperation Joseph must feel in his situation. Then telling the kid he has to fall in line and behave like nothing happened. Like the show must go on is not going to be a conversation that is easily accepted. If John's even able to scratch the surface with such a talk. John drops the pill bottle back in the drawer and closes it.

He lays down next to his son. Looks at him. Remembering when Joseph was a baby. Such a beautiful time in life. So many hopes and possibilities. John thought his boy could have any future he could imagine. Astronaut, politician, doctor, a lawyer. Maybe he'd become an Executive like his Grandfather William. He could also become a plumber, if he'd so choose. To take after his dad in the family business. A future that nearly came true. Then life took over.

With all its ups and downs. So close to achievement, being self-employed. Having only your customers to answer to. Naysayers like to pick on those who are too independent to manage. John was too independent to manage. Yet made a terrific entrepreneur. In his own mind anyway, which in a sense is the most important perspective.

He strokes his son's head. His hair cut short. Greasy from not having an easy time showering. John finds a small towel in the clothes basket not far from where he was laying. He gently places it under his son's cheek to catch the slobber. John fights off tears as he watches Joseph sleep. So vulnerable. Not so much different than a baby. If babies slobbered on themselves from opioid abuse that is. John stops teasing himself long enough to try and formulate a plan. How can this possibly get better? He closes his eyes for a quick second to process. Just for a second.

***

John feels something scratching his ankle. Something strange. It hurts his skin. John realizes he'd fallen asleep in bed with his son. The current situation must've taken a lot out of him. He looks around trying to clear his mind. The sun had fallen lower in the sky. He looks at the alarm clock. 5:30. Past quitting time. He wonders if Robert has locked up for the night.

He feels the scratching again. Joseph's toe? Scratching John's ankle? Not only scratching his ankle, but the vampire nails that had grown where the end of Joseph's toes used to be had actually drawn blood.

John speaks aloud, "The fuckin' toe's movin'."

He jumps up. Joseph rustles from his stupor. He shakes his son. "Joseph.

Aw fuck it. Joe! Your god damn toe! Look at your god damn toe, boy!" Joseph's eyes focus a little. Not completely comprehending.

John decides to drive it home. He takes Joseph's head and angles it to his own toe. "Look at your fuckin' toe! It's moving! It's moving! It's like a Christmas miracle!" John doesn't care if Christmas is two seasons away. His boy may have just received the gift of a lifetime!

Chapter 24
Sue

The summer is Sue's favorite time of year. Staying at Peter's shore house in Avalon has been a magical experience that Sue wishes could last forever. Finally, her prince has come to rescue her from the dragons that plagued her life for decades. Financial, social, sexual. All her needs are being satisfied. Almost like she's being paid back tenfold. In a good way. For all the hardships she'd suffered.

Sue's upbringing was tough. Her parents rejected her growing up. They always wanted a boy. After Sue was born, the doctors said her mother would never deliver another child. It explained her tomboy like behavior early on in life. Her father always treated her fairly, her mother was not so nice. Sue felt like Cinderella growing up. Forced to cook, wash the dishes, wash the clothes. She had to cater to her father's expectations in order to get out of the house. That's how the sports came in the picture. Eventually, she ended up a cheerleader. That suited her looks far more than tossing around the football with the Ambler ruffians after school.

It was her vacations in coal town with the distant family that changed her. The slightly older cousin who played too rough. Who used to corner her in bedrooms. Alone in the dark. She was only eight at first. He was 13. There was nothing she could do. She was alone and scared. He was so much bigger than her. He would plead to Sue's aunt for his favorite cousin to spend another week as soon as they could. It warmed Sue's parents' ignorant hearts that the extended family loved her so. This went on another four years. Two weeks each year, and some holidays, Sue would have to endure the suffering. The hurt.

The adult feelings that she had no idea how to handle. It twisted her in ways she refused to imagine, but had no choice because things like that change children forever. It makes matters worse when a child finally finds the courage to tell and becomes the monster of the family. This happens quite often with shy young children who are abused. The abusers are usually very funny, charming and bright. They know exactly how to get what they want and aren't typically afraid to say or do whatever it takes to get it. This is exactly what happened when Sue tried to tell her mother and father before going to coal town to celebrate her birthday with the extended family.

Her cousin being 17 at this point really got aggressive the year before and Sue found blood in her underwear for days after. When her mother said she'll go to hell for playing with herself like that, Sue stewed over that particular painful experience until she had no choice but to tell. Her mother called her a liar. Her father, a whore. This is what echoes in Sue's mind when she was told John Walker was the one for her by those same people. Sue really did love John. Still does. He was awesome. The way he'd drag race his Nissan 300ZX against the rich kids from Dresher. He won most of the time.

No matter what car they brought, John would figure out a way to win somehow. Sue thought it was his patented Stink eye. He had a way of shooting people a look that scared the piss out of his enemies. He's not a big guy by any means, just batshit crazy. It was his Eddie Haskell routine that charmed Sue's parents mostly…and his father's money. Only John wasn't meant to be an Executive like his dad. He was made to wallow in shit like his hero, Luke. It was the forceful, "You need to shut up and settle down with John Walker. He's the best you're ever gonna do." She could remember the words of her mother clearly. Like they were spoken just yesterday.

Her mother died of cancer right after the divorce. It was a tragic end. Too bad Sue couldn't bury the pain and rejection with her.

She is more at peace with Peter around. He's not tough like John, or as man pretty as Tony, but he's smart and dapper. He is a handsome man, just different in his own way. The money helps, but Sue really enjoys the time she spends with Peter. Now, if she could only erase Alex. Not really erase him, but maybe erase the bad juju between him and Richard. This would help move things along nicely. Maybe since it's nearly the end of the summer, Sue could start mentioning Thanksgiving. Sue would rather spend Halloween with Diane and the baby, but a bigger holiday would work. Christmas is too big. Thanksgiving is just right.

Chapter 25
Gina

Gina's summer had turned into a blur. The drugs have gotten worse. The partying is 24 hours a day. Richard parties with the bikers now so he's constantly on something major for what seems like days at a time with no rest then he'd crash for god knows how long until he could stand on his feet again. The strip club was sexy for a minute, but now after being a glorified call girl for Richard's biker and mafia friends, Gina needs an escape.

After hearing the organ music playing beneath their apartment since early morning, Gina feels the urge to investigate. With Richard being out cold, it's her shot to get away, and meet some straight edge people for a change.

She dresses in sweats and a clean tee shirt with a bra that fits properly. The undersized pop top bras she'd been wearing at Daydreams were giving her terrible back pains. She actually craves normal bras whenever possible. The thought of a breast reduction has crossed her mind lately. Had she been a lot older, it would probably be a reality.

She creeps out of the lonely cold apartment. As she gets closer to the music, Gina feels lighter on her feet. Like something is calling to her. Her pace quickens. Her back arches, but not in a sexual way, more of a needy confidence. Gina desires to be around people that treat her like a person and not a play thing. The hallway from the condos to the common area is made of industrial concrete. Colored with a slight hue of beige. The ductwork above her head, as in the condo, exposed and spiral looking. Very much the style of new buildings in Philly. Modern and clean with very little character.

The charm of old wood has a much warmer, richer feel. This is the difference between the city and the country. In the city, they condemn most of the old-style buildings, tear them down and replace with things like this. In the country, buildings like this wouldn't be thought of. Those old-style structures aren't neglected that way. Such a different mindset. Such a tragedy.

She finds the concrete steps going down to the next level. She remembers that day on the beach after her first excursion with Richard and Tony. Richard saying they were going to stay above 'some non-profit.' As Gina moves closer to the double doors leading inside, a bright and happy face greets her. A very nicely dressed man opens a door to let Gina in.

"Well, hello young lady. Are you here to join us for Sunday service?" asks the nice man.

Holy shit, it's Sunday! Gina had no idea the day until now. "Um, I heard some pretty music and thought maybe you wouldn't mind if I said hello." She winces a little after speaking.

"Of course, you can enjoy our lovely music. Please come right in and make yourself at home. I'm Bob."

He extends a gentle, soft hand. His breath is warm like a baby's diaper, but he seems so sweet. She smiles genuinely and returns the gesture.

"Hi, I'm Gina."

"Well, aren't you a ray of sunshine." He shakes her hand kind of aggressively, but not in a creepy way. Her elbow jiggles a bit. Like a goofy uncle that might ask you to pull his finger. "Please, let me introduce you to the girls."

Finally, some people other than bikers and dope dealers, she thinks to herself.

Bob leads her through another set of doors into the Chapel. This place isn't a non-profit. Richard's an idiot. This place is nearly a freggin' mega church.

Gina walks slowly so she wouldn't trip. Attempting to take in the room all at once could be detrimental to her health. She notices Bob, letting her go. *Such a nice man,* she thinks.

The wood, the stained glass. It's almost like the condos and industrial façade were built around this place. She knows it isn't possible, but the detail and the woodwork. It's new, but looks so nice!

"So what do you think?" asks Bob.

Gina stops looking up to scan the perimeter of the room. She notices all the adjacent rooms filled with non-perishable goods. Not donated though. Boxes of brand-new stuff.

"What is this place?"

"We're a major food distributor for Philadelphia. The government sends us containers full of goods for the Emergency Food Network here in the city.

With a portion of the income we earn from distributing the goods to food banks, we're able to finance the church."

"Isn't it usually the other way around? Church then food stuffs?"

"We're an unusual non-profit in that way. Some people joke that we're actually in the CIA moving guns and drugs through the country. Way more fun doing that, right?" Bob flashes the crazy eyes as he finishes the sentence.

Gina tries to ignore the man's odd sense of humor. "Wow. Sounds like a great plot for a movie."

"Sure does. You write it, I'll direct it. Gotta be more money in the entertainment biz than running a charity, you know?"

"Sure, but don't you think what you do is more rewarding. Like in your heart?"

"Ah, maybe. Some days I pray to god and feel grateful for the opportunities I've been given. Then other days I wish I was on a beach in Malibu."

"What about today?"

"Today, I'm just happy to be on this side of the dirt."

Gina could feel herself twitch a little from the hangover. Bob's hot breath combined with the operating room lighting above makes her dizzy.

Bob put a gentle, non-creepy hand on her shoulder. Comforting. "Hey. Let's walk a little. There's some people for you to meet."

Bob leads her to a group of cackling Betty's in what seemed to be a sewing circle without the needles or yarn. "Hey Margi." A betty with died black hair turns around. "We have a guest today for service. Gina, I'd like you to meet Mar-gee." He over accentuates her name to be sure Gina wouldn't mispronounce her brand.

"Hello, Gina. Aren't you a pretty one. I'd bet all the boys give you their phone numbers?" Margi giggles like a school girl. Gina wonders how well that joke killed back in the '60s. She decides to be polite to the nice lady.

"They sure do." They giggle together immaturely. "Thank you for opening your doors to me. I'm just a southern girl at heart and well, when I hear those church bells, I coma runnin'."

"You know, I can hear the twang in your voice now, and you are just prettier than ever. Please come sit with us girls we have been dying to see some younger blood in here. It gets so stuffy with these old ladies sometimes. A nice little thing like you will help brighten up these stiffs real quick."

Margi and Gina sit and talk with the old Betty's for a while before church begins.

It's all so tender. The music. The sermon. Bob turns out to be the preacher. He seems like such a normal guy, but in a good way. In a wholesome way. She takes his business card on the way out. *What a pleasant surprise.* she thinks.

After church, Gina finds Richard waiting for her on the couch. "Where you been?" He doesn't even bother to look up from the TV.

"I went to church."

"You mean that non-profit downstairs?"

"No, Richard, it's a church. You should come see for yourself." "I don't need to see it. It's a non-profit."

"What are you talking about?"

"We own this building and everything in it."

Gina couldn't help but notice Richard's accent disappears when he comes off a bender. "Who's we?"

He shuts off the TV and stands up with a grunt. "The people who own this place. Don't ask questions that you don't want answers to. I'm going for a shower." He tosses some cash on the table. "Go get us some food. We gotta make anotha run tonight."

There's the accent again. she admits to herself.

***

The ride down is chilly. Summer winds down. School's going to start back up in a few weeks. Gina hopes there wouldn't be too many more of these trips. She's grown tired of Philly, and the shore for that matter, during their current adventure.

When they arrive at the desolate entrance to the beach, Richard slows down and turns off his lights like he'd done before. He slowly drives onto the beach. More methodically than she remembered. Almost like he'd done it a hundred times since. They pull to a stop. Windows down. This Gina remembers well. It's always chilly on the beach at night in Jersey.

They wait. Longer than before. It feels like forever. An uncomfortably long time. In absolute silence.

Somehow Richard managed to turn the lights off to the clock so nothing glowed when the car is off. It could've been like that before. Gina doesn't remember, but gets antsy from the wait. Then she hears running.

166

Someone grabs her by the hair. She tries not to scream, but the fear is impossible to overcome. All she sees is Richard grabbing the gun from the guy's hand to beat him across the face with it. Richard launches over her, opening the door, clutching the guy by the back of the neck in one flawless motion. Richard flies into a rage, slamming the door into the guy's head, over and over again until the body falls lifeless to the sand. Gina starts to panic as she watches the man's body slump to the ground. The gun beneath Richard's feet.

Richard knelt by her side. "I got this. Quiet down. We're leaving tonight."

She could see blood streaming down his hand. Gina dips her head as Richard kisses her gently. His blood dripping steadily on the sand. Richard pops the trunk. He picks up the guy like a side of beef and tosses him in.

Richard pulls the phone from his pocket to make a call. "Hey, dad. I know it's late, but I'm in need of *groceries* right now."

***

Gina sits down on Mr. Zilla's comfy leather couch. Sue comforts her while he and Richard speak in the kitchen. She could hear everything.

"It was that Tony guy dad. He made me back in Philly last month."

Peter smacks Richard across the head. "Whattya mean he made you. That can't happen twice."

"Dad, I know. We had a lot going on. I stayed at a condo from our people for a while. They knew I was family the whole time."

"Those gavones are not our family." Peter takes him by the shoulders. "They are the people we own."

"Dad, their just trash from Philadelphia. Ambler. Gina and me were just havin' a good time. Country bumpkins compared to us. It was nothing. They don't even know us."

"They do now. One of them tried to kill you. Are you kidding me? Getting wrapped up with these people. Sue is one thing, but hanging with her Ex of all people? And now you may have killed someone because of this situation? There will need to be consequences here, son. Do you understand me?" He grabs Richard by the hair. "Huh, do you?"

"Yes, Dad."

He looks at Gina without letting go of the hair. "And whatta 'bout her?"

Peter lets go.

"She's OK, Dad. We never showed her anything. She just danced and got stoned."

"You brought a junkie to help you sell dope?"

"She's not just a junkie, dad, she's my girlfriend. I love her."

"Love. Whattya know about love? Fuckin' kids. Mother Mary of God!" "What's next, dad."

"What's next? I'll tell you what's next. Take your car to this address." He whispers something to Richard. "Then you come back here, pick up the Caddy and head back to Williamsport."

"Sorry, Dad."

"You're sorry? Now, I gotta clean up this fuckin' mess you created." Peter pauses to pace around the kitchen. "You know, it was one thing when that plumber pulled a pistol on you and that Grinch lookin' muthafucka for getting his invalid son hooked on perks. Now, it's something else." Peter kisses his son the head. "Don't you ever fuck up like this again." Peter wags his finger in Richard's face. "This kind of stupidity topples empires. You're gonna keep your nose clean for good this time. No more dope. No more hookers and no more fightin'. You hear me?"

Gina hears him loud and clear. She never knew the Zilla's cared so much about each other. It's also a revelation that Richard loves her.

Chapter 26
Adam

The summer is coming to a close. One more big show. At a B-list venue. The Electric Factory. Adam could remember his first concert at the venue. It's a place where bands at the end of their careers typically go to play for older audiences or large groups of 14-year-olds. He thinks back to his first concert. GWAR. So funny. The puppets, the fake blood. "The Road Behind" was his favorite song off their album America Must Be Destroyed. An oldie, but a goodie. It was really what turned him on to 90s music to begin with. His mother's friend from college was an original band member. Adam got backstage passes. Witnessing the behind the scene's action would lead to his love for the stage.

The second act he saw at the Factory was Rusted Root. "Send Me on My Way" is the other throwback song, he put on the list for tonight. After that show, his musical taste was sealed forever.

The '90s must've been beautiful, man. Adam loved everything about the decade. From the evolution of Rap to Hip Hop, Heavy Metal to Grunge to Alt Rock to Rap Rock. The reemergence of bell bottoms and 70s style. The polyester. The anarchy of the riots, the trials, the impeachment. Polyester Anarchy forever.

Staying with Alex was illuminating to say the least. He bounced back and forth from mom and dad's place to Alex's house when there was a bed open on the second floor. Chad would often go back to Williamsport with Jesse. Rick disappeared to his parents' place in South Philly sometimes. It was a comfortable environment. It was also really nice to see Alex move on from the Ex. After Dick Biter Gate, Adam was shocked to see how far a little bit of love and attention could go to heal a person like Alex. Someone with his scars. The Walkers became human after all.

The stories Alex told were true, but there's always another perspective.

Another side of the story. His crazy dad being the actual glue that holds everyone together, another shocker. His mom, and her abusive parents. The sister's bad relationship with the (former) stepfather's cousin. The brother. The step/half-brother or whatever that mess looks like. Then there are the full stories about Alex's high school experience.

After listening to Heather and Jasper retell 'the Ballad of Alex Walker' the night of the block party, Adam had a whole new way of looking at his buddy. Understanding why Alex fights as hard as he does. Why he's this kinda 'Mad Max' type character is the grand scheme of teenage angst and social imagination. He was betrayed, abused and neglected by nearly everyone he ever loved. The kind of survival skills a person would need to avoid suicide after what Alex suffered through must be immense. Adam has a deep respect for Alex. Even the level of forgiveness he exhibited by inviting people like Heather, Jasper and Tony to his house for a party.

The older brother Jason and some former lacrosse buddies even stopped by, and these are the people who nearly beat him to death.

It's a miracle Alex doesn't have severe brain damage from being cold cocked with a brick! Adam wants to make his first original song about the story of Alex, but he has to disguise it somehow. Less in his face. It's interesting that Alex used to write Heather poems after she took his virginity. Adam wonders if Alex is secretly a poet too. His love of art makes sense. Being in touch with that side of your emotions is something most guys are afraid of for risk of being called gay. People who tap into those feelings freely have a special kind of relationship with their personality, and are comfortable with certain things others are not.

If Adam could somehow convince Alex to help him write the song, he'd split any profits that would come back to them in the future. Adam always vowed to pay Alex back for helping him with Unicorn. The night that anti-Semitic member of the SBD Hitler youth fucked with him for being a Jew. What is this 1940? Adam felt steam coming from his ears thinking about the rejection. It's a religion. Only idiots hate other people for the differences that divide us. Take Rick for example. The other guys have no idea what nationality he is. Rick's parents are Muslim! It was something he and Adam established the first day of school. They met in their Culture and Society class. Their views on religion and politics were strangely similar.

Adam's religion being obvious, Rick confided in him about being Muslim.

Not that he was ashamed, but it's a tough pill for some people to swallow. A Muslim and a Jew hanging together. Then after rocking out on their guitars in the courtyard one sunny afternoon, in came Jesse and Chad. Chad tipped over a recycling bucket and Jesse provided some human beat box vibes. It was probably a combination of their lack of practicing, and their look that prevented them from getting gigs anywhere besides the Rainbow, but it worked.

Chad opened the door, then Adam and the guys built the vibe together on stage. No one, absolutely no one, in this world, is more forgiving than the LGBTQ community. Talk about a warm environment. The band could not have done it without them. Not to mention, most of their gigs this summer were in gar bars courtesy of the kindness and direction of Silvio. 15% of the door money didn't hurt either.

Now they're playing the Electric Factory to close out their summer adventure. Adam feels like he finally made it. A fist full of cash and a chest full of confidence. This has to be what success is like. Sure he could flick his wrist to sell insurance with his dad, but this is the stuff dreams are made of.

Adam notices a homeless person holding a sign for 'Spare Change' only a few yards away. He pulls out a five and gives it to the guy. The man responds with a look of genuine appreciation.

He walks around the nearly empty street. Adam requested the guys show up early. He took the train in to have breakfast with his mom at the Continental Diner in center city. After a nice long hug and lots of praise for his accomplishments this summer, Adam parted way with his maternal life guide for what was going to be the biggest night of his life.

Rick pulls up first in his rape van with Chad and Jesse riding shotgun. They must've abandoned the unsecured easy chair sliding around in the back for risk of getting a bloody nose when Rick slams on the breaks. Alex's dad gave it to Rick as a present over the summer. Weird gift if you asked Adam. That chair is a death trap.

Alex and his high potential life mate, the ever bubbly and lovely, Julie roll up in his Jeep Islander. The exact Jeep Wolverine drove in the X-men cartoon from '93. How Alex scored that gem, Adam would never know, but it represents exactly who they are. The '90s, man. Fuckin' A!

They all park and jump out in rhythmic harmony.

"Gentleman." Adam motions to the sign of Ben Franklin extending his cartoonish arm toward a yellow lightning bolt. "Behold! Our church awaits. Please gather under Ben, please."

They circle in close.

Rick speaks first. "Adam's always such a showman."

"Yeah Adam, without you, I wouldn't get excited for things like this at all." Jesse adds with sarcasm.

Chad leans in to his best buddy and ambiguously gay partner, "Hey buddy, why don't you tell them who's really getting you excited these days?" "Yeah." Jesse looked down at the ground before formulating a response.

"Sooo, probably a conversation for us to have offline."

"Offline." Chad says smugly. "I'll give you an offline." Chad grabs a chunk of Jesse ass with authority.

Jesse smacks it away. "What the fu…Knock it off." Julie gets a little embarrassed. "Oh boy, here we go."

Alex jumps in. "Would you guys reel it in for a minute. Adam asked us here for a reason."

Adam snaps out of his daze. The hijinks with this crew never cease to amaze him. "Ah, yeah. Thanks, Alex." Adam readjusts his stance. He motions to the sign. "I asked you all to come early to get a pic for my scrapbook. This is the closing show and the biggest venue we've played all summer."

Alex chimes in, "But not the biggest crowd."

Adam acknowledges the truth. "Nope that honor goes the block party." "Hear hear," Jesse adds.

"This picture," Adam continues. "Is of us. For us. In order to remember where we came from. A reminder to bring us back together during whatever rough times may lie ahead."

Chad looks around. "Guys, who's going to take the pic?" Julie steps up. "I'll do it."

Adam waves her off. "Absolutely not. You pitched in this summer just like the rest of us. You've earned the status of honorary member." Adam looks over to the homeless gentleman. "Hello again, sir. Could you help us with our picture, please?"

The man is more than accommodating and surprisingly good with a smart phone. The picture came out exactly as Adam had hoped. A moment captured in time. Polyester Anarchy has arrived.

Chapter 27
Joseph

His dad is experiencing an unusual mood. The music blares in the truck on the way home from the hospital. The night air fills with "Feel Good Inc." by the Gorillaz. The song crackles from the blown speakers. Joseph laughs at his dad singing along. Or rapping or whatever sounds he makes with his face.

Joseph thinks his dad looks extra crazy when openly happy. "Feelin' good, bud? I know your fuckin' toes are! Whoo!"

"How is it possible you're happier than me right now, dad?"

"Because I made you from the super sperm! Yeah, sing it boys!" He cranks the volume again, letting off before the speakers break up.

Joseph turns the music down. His dad looks at him like he's nuts. "Dad, you do realize the doctor said there's only a slim chance that I'll walk again. That's like a fraction better than I was yesterday."

"Nonsense. This is a sign from god, my reborn son. Take it and understand that miracles do happen and dreams can come true." His dad turns up the radio again.

Joseph starts to get annoyed at this point. Fun is over and reality kicks in. This battle is one that he'd have to fight alone. Sure his dad would be there to encourage him, if that's what you can call this present situation, but the odds of him feeling his dick again are slim to none.

The song ends. They pull up behind Joseph's house. His dad jumps out to get the chair from the back.

"Holy crap, I thought that ride would never be over," says Joseph struggling to get in position.

His dad helps him from the truck to the chair. "Ah, deal with it, kid. You're on the road to recovery. Don't be such a miserable prick and enjoy the good news. It's the first you've gotten in a while."

Dad's a bit too gruff, when it comes to tough love, but he's got a point.

The pins and needles in his feet are real.

He wheels Joseph over to the elevator. He unlocks it and opens the door for Joseph to push himself in. Joseph notices the open basement door. *That's weird*, Joseph thinks. Tony was in Avalon for the week. He must've come back early. Maybe inside sleeping one off. As usual.

"How much longer will he be staying with you?" "Hasn't said Dad, but last I checked it's my house."

"Last I checked you were getting illegal pills from him and his new butt buddy."

"I'm on a new road now, dad. This is it for me. If this is real, I'm done.

For good. It's me, my healing spine and the good lord for now on."

Joseph could feel his dad circling around to get face to face for some closing words. He looks at Joseph sternly and points in his face. "Whatever floats your boat, kid. Just know that from here on out. You write your own ticket. You got that?"

Joseph manages to raise his voice loud enough to talk over the sound of John aggressively getting in his truck. "I got it, Dad."

"Good now get some sleep. Your new sister-in-law will be here first thing in the morning to get you ready for work."

"Can't wait to see, Pearl, dad. Hope she smells like kimchi again."

His dad hollers from the truck. "It's a delicacy where she's from, my boy. And don't rain on your sorta brother's parade. The girls' been breaking him off some. You should be happy for him."

"Seriously, dad?"

"Well, yeah. Robert moans louder than she does. I try to bang on the walls for them to stop, but they've been screwin' like rabbits."

"That's it. My ears are going to bleed if I don't go inside right now." Joseph turns himself to get in the elevator.

His dad shouted some final parting words. "You're next, bud, first the feet then the d…"

Joseph slams the door to the elevator quickly before the ending of that sentence has a chance to penetrate his eardrums. There's no unhearing certain things.

***

An alarm sounds. Joseph opens his eyes. Still nighttime. He looks for the clock. Over his shoulder. 4:40. *Can't be the alarm clock*, Joseph thinks. The sound cuts through the thick air in his row home. Smoke. A lot of it. The red flashing and the smoke together make Joseph feel disoriented. He reaches for his chair and misses, hitting his face on the floor. The dull pain accompanied by the flash of light didn't help matters at all. His falling body topples the chair over, blocking the doorway. Joseph only has the use of one good arm. The reattachment worked, but nowhere near being anything more than a T-Rex arm. He could grab things with his fingers and give a passable handshake if he dared to endure the pain.

He uses the good arm to pull himself. Elbow first. Dig in. Pull! Elbow first. Dig in. Pull! Shit, the chair. He struggles to collapse it to get by.

"Tony! Help! Someone help!" Joseph could feel the intense heat under the smoke at the floor making his arm and chest hot.

"This is bad soo bad! Oh, god. Oh, god please no!"

Chapter 28
John

John races to Joseph's house like a bat outta hell. His buddy on the force gave him the call. Said there was no time to waste. John yelled for Robert before leaving. Told him and Pearl to call Alex and get his ass outta bed too.

The flames shoot from the windows. No sign anyone got out the front. Sheer terror courses through John's veins. He tries running to the front door.

A fireman stops him. "No way in. Go around back!"

John sprints up Southern and takes a flying leap over someone's flower bed as he turns the corner on Park to find the alleyway. He nearly slips on some gravel before making his way closer to Joseph's back door.

The elevator door is open. Firemen pull someone out. It's him! They take Joseph to safety.

John falls to his knees in tears. Blubbering like he'd never blubbered before. "Holy shit! Joseph! You're alive. You beautiful son of a bitch, you're alive!" He hugs his son's nearly lifeless body. Then John realizes that half his body is lifeless. The top half is fully responsive. *Yes!* He may or may not have outwardly cheered.

"Dad." He points to the back door. His lip quivering. "Tony's still in there."

John pretends to give a shit. He knew this fire was Tony's fault as soon as he got the call. Those cigarettes on the armchair. He slobbered on himself again and left one burning. John holds his son tightly while brooding without regret this time. "Motherfucker finally got what was coming to him." John realizes this was actually said aloud.

John locks eyes with Joseph who manages to look even more horrified. "Dad! What did you say? Tony's dead for god sakes."

"I said, maybe the axe chuckers ran him out of there in time?" said John as he looked around over dramatically. John needs to think fast. If Joseph didn't believe him there's a good chance he'd get blamed somehow. "Did anyone else get out?" He bellows to a firefighter nearby.

"No one else, but him. He's a lucky kid. If that elevator didn't get built with a one-hour fire rating, it may have gone very differently. John suddenly remembered paying the extra money to make it fireproof. Maybe Joseph's onto something with this reborn Christian stuff. He'd have to remember to kneel down in nature soon and reacquaint himself with the almighty to say thank you.

Alex and his gang run up behind them. "Dad! Dad!"

"Over here, Alex." John rocks Joseph in his arms. "He's alright. We're alright."

***

John gets called to the police station the next day. They would've brought Joseph in too, but he's currently laid up in a hospital bed in Chestnut Hill.

Tim Logan meets him at the front desk. John thanks Tim for calling about the fire. It was a matter of life and death. Tim came through for John so many times in the past. Like the night Scott punched out his squad car window for Joseph and Tyrone, who were legitimately locked up in the back on Mischief Night a few years ago.

Tim had moved into his starter home on Orange Ave before that night. They were tight for cash, and having serious drain issues. A giant maple tree needed to be removed and also the drain under it had to be fixed. It was a $10,000 job. It would've nearly bankrupted Tim and his wife. John gave him the labor cost for free. Tim never forgot it.

"Hey Tim." They shake hands showing genuine respect for each other. "Hey John. We got an issue with the fire."

"What kind of issue?"

"Come on in. We need to sit down with the Chief." "The Chief? Oh, Christ really."

"'Fraid so, bud. Follow me."

Tim leads John to the Chief's office down the hall of the old Mattison Elementary School, which was turned into a Municipal Building recently. John remembers these halls from childhood. Growing up with Tony and Sue. Having recess where the squad cars now park. *My how things change so much.*

He realizes while making peace with the flow of life.

Tim opens the door to Chief Cook's office. He stands to shake before asking Tim to close the door for the talk.

"John, are you familiar with Tony Mangles' involvement with organized crime?"

"Somewhat, I suppose. His old lawyer that used to pressure me for child support, was apparently connected to that group. Over the years, I've done my best not to speak to Tony. Especially, about something of this nature. He turned on me so badly when we were young, if it wasn't for Sue and the kids, we'd have never spoken again."

"Right well. Tony Mangle may have turned on the wrong person recently."

"How so?" asks John.

"Well, John, we're currently investing his murder case at your son's home," says Chief Cook.

"Murder?" John gets flustered. "Tony died in a fire…right?" "John, your sons' home is also being investigated for arson."

He has no choice but to believe it now. "You mean it wasn't a cigarette?" "No, it was not a cigarette. Our investigators found a residue surrounding

his body. On the arms of the chair, around his head, around his crotch, on the floor. After further analysis, it was found to be alcohol. The flame point started at his crotch area in the chair."

"Could it have been a suicide?"

"No, John. Tony Mangle was shot in the back of the head at point blank range while Joseph was asleep upstairs. The perpetrator then poured a bottle, of what we believe to be a very strong rum, all over his body then threw a match. John, your son is lucky to be alive."

"We understand you and he were at odds a few weeks back. A young man named Richard Zilla, who was seen with him numerous times over the summer, has told of us of a particular altercation involving the three of you and a pistol."

"Yes, that's true. Tony had been giving my son drugs. Joseph was clean while Tony was gone, after he'd returned and got Joseph hooked again, I may have hit him in the face."

"Then pulled your gun on Richard Zilla?"

"Yes. My registered pistol was pulled out in a house in my name because I felt my life was in danger with Zilla present."

"Zilla and your son, Alex, had a serious altercation at school, yes?"

"Yes, Zilla and Alex's ex-girlfriend were caught in the act. Alex felt the need to stand up for himself against Zilla, who by the way, is a much larger, nastier individual."

"I know Alex's story, John and I know you. I also know that you were home at the time of the fire. I have two eye witnesses who saw you go home, park your truck, then saw your light turn on when Tim called. The next report has you running to your truck. Your story is sound, and we'll have to revisit this another time when there's more evidence."

"Understood. Am I obligated to stay?"

"You are not, but it would be wise to stay in town for a while just in case."

***

Driving back, John feels like he's been hit by a train. Putting it all together is impossible. He doesn't get it. The story is too much to take in all at once. How could he tell the boys? Diane, Sue. Robert! This is an absolute mess.

***

John has to do interviews with the TV News, the papers, more statements for the cops. The house would take a year to fix. Luckily, arson falls under the insurance blanket. It even covers the cost for the elevator, another thing John paid for at the last minute. Thankfully.

The funeral is held a number of weeks later. People line up around the block to see Tony off. He actually had a lot of people who cared about him. Robert was the first there and the last to leave. John does his best to stay with Robert. It's what he wanted. Pearl had comforted him in a way that no one else in his life has been able to until recently. The kid decided to drop out of high school and go to work. As his guardian, and his boss, John decided to give him that much. The kid suffered enough. Right now he wants to be with John and Pearl. The kids at school never mattered much to him and he had his heart set on working and getting married in the future. Hopefully, the distant future.

The Zilla's show up with Sue. John meets with them cordially. Not spending too much time and moving on quickly to the next grieving acquaintance.

Diane shows up with Tyrone, not Gabe, which surprises John. He could remember them hanging out at the block party, but if they're dating, he'd been the last to know.

Gabe and his mother walked through with the baby. Sitting near Diane in the crowd, but just far enough away. John could feel the tension.

Joseph stays near Robert and Pearl the whole time.

Alex and company make a surprise appearance. John told him to stay in Williamsport, but Alex didn't listen. They are there and gone before John could even think about complaining of how he'd be missing classes for making the trip.

At the burial, Peter Zilla breaks from Sue's side long enough to speak with John personally. "Tough break for an old friend, huh?"

John could see Chief Cook and Tim Logan watching their interaction from a distance.

John rolls his eyes after smelling Peter's cologne. Listening to his words is actually worse. "Peter…you, me and Tony, we all share an Ex. I'm sure you probably know some good stories about both of us at this point, but tell you what, if you're going to open that big mouth of yours, I really don't really give a shit about your opinion."

"Well, she's not exactly an Ex in my case." John licks his teeth. "Not yet, she isn't." "You know what plumber…"

"Ooh. Now, it's getting interesting. It feels like a threat's coming my way."

"If I was gonna threaten you, I woulda did it after you pulled a gun on my kid."

"The same kid that tried to bully mine to death? The same one that helped get my other son back on drugs? That kid?"

"I don't know much about that, but my advice for you, Walker, is to watch yourself in the future."

"Is that right?"

"Yes, it is. And furthermore, maybe I am just a bank account with a pulse. However, I am also someone that always balances my checkbook if you get my drift."

"Oh, there's the threat I was waiting for. It sounds as if you're passive aggressively taking responsibility for Tony's death. Am I interpreting this correctly?"

"Not at all." Peter slaps John's shoulder to show sympathy. "Again, my condolences." Peter Zilla slithers back to parts unknown.

John feels sick. Peter's voice was unsettling. John cringes. Something's seriously wrong here.

Chapter 29
Alex

The first half of the semester had come and gone. Alex worked to expand the band's venues in Williamsport. After their resume building from over the summer, they were in a much better spot to get into the bigger venues at school. The Cell Block is on the top of Alex's list. It's one of the state's oldest prisons. Abandoned for decades until some very smart Franklin Tech graduates presented a business plan to the Williamsport Bank to build a bar and music venue on the prison grounds. A major design piece was removing the bars in between the cells and installing tables where the beds used to be. Long story short, it worked, and it worked well. The Cell Block had been the town's biggest draw for years. The guys who owned it, legends. They became the golden standard for blue collar kids becoming serious entrepreneurs.

There were no try outs this time. No snide comments about their look or the songs. Alex created their fan page gradually over the summer. Highlighted with lots of memorable moments including Adam's closer for the summer at the Electric Factory. Sinéad O'Connor's "Nothing Compares 2 U." Adam's voice sounded great even through the phone speaker. The guys at the Cell Block booked Polyester Anarchy for five prime time spots throughout the school year. Four Saturday nights, and most importantly, the night before Thanksgiving, the biggest party night of the year. Adam and Rick have something special planned for that night.

Sue had talked him into coming to Thanksgiving dinner at Peter's shore house. He'd sold his place in North Jersey and set up shop in Avalon full time. Alex committed to dinner, but he didn't want to ride with Richard or stay there. His grandfather said he could crash at his place by the bay instead. Richard had said to Alex that sleeping at a house near the bay should be beneath him if a house on the beach is available instead. The half assed invite creeped Alex out and offended him all at the same time.

Zilla and Gina are also more of an item this year. Zilla gave up his position as Frat President and moved in with Gina instead. They stopped partying and attended a mega church outside town regularly. One where the people would pretend to writhe in pain, and roll around on the ground to expel the demons. Alex's grandparents on his mother's side were into that sort of thing also. When they moved to coal town when he was a kid, Alex remembers his grandfather inviting their preacher over for dinner when he was up for vacation one time.

The preacher held a bible in one hand, high in the air, and placed his hand on Alex's head with the other. He claimed Alex wetting the bed at the age of eight was from the demons that occupied his body. Jumped into him from the slums of "Filthydelphia." The memory of the preacher was scarier than demons. The guy moved like he was being electrocuted. Alex's grandparents shook him back and forth to mimic the motions. The exorcism didn't work. Alex stopped peeing the bed after Tony stopped beating his mother. In front of Alex, that is.

Alex and Chad moved out of their place and got an old Victorian home with the other band members. It was a gigantic place with plenty of bedrooms. The basement had a kegerator and bar for parties, and was nearly soundproof for band practice. There's even a study! A real study with old dusty books and a big wooden table in the middle of the room with two ornately decorated pocket doors that opened and closed sideways, reminding him of a smaller version of dad's garage back home. The one where he and his first gang used to meet up for their late-night excursions. It was in this study he and Adam wrote Polyester Anarchy's first original song.

Adam seemed to have given up on the central members for inspiration. He snooped in Alex's room one day when they were playing video games. Alex was distracted while playing an NES classic, "The Legend of Zelda." Adam opened up his black and white composition book and found his poetry about Gina and Heather. Adam asked if he could piece some of them together in a song. They ended up sitting together for hours in the study. When they were done, Adam had a full song and the bones for some others. Alex didn't think they were that good, but Adam kept a tight lip about it.

Julie and Alex's relationship had gotten serious. They continued to spend all their free time together. Her clothes were in his room now. She showered there and bought groceries for him and the guys. It would've felt wrong if she didn't. They had so many adventures over the past few months. To the others she's just one of the guys. To Alex, she's amazing.

Alex's school work is going according to plan. He was all caught up from his mistakes first semester and on schedule to graduate with his class. His grades are above average, or close enough anyway. His GPA has to be at 2.0 in order to graduate in June. He bumped his grades up to a 2.8 by choosing writing enriched electives. All relevant to the trades, as is customary at Franklin Tech. A sociology class on Work and Culture, one Adam and Rick had taken together. Another on Technology and Society, that studied Henry Ford and his application of the Scientific Method to create his Assembly Line for the Model T. The other being the Ethics class that Gina used to talk about a lot. The teacher's as great as she said. The brick story from a rooftop of New York kind of made him a rock star to his students.

As Alex walked to his Heat Pump class, he thinks about his life. How happy he is. Maybe for the first time ever. He remembered being happy-ish with Gina, but the partying always kind of scared him. He wasn't into the hardcore drugs and all the blackouts made him feel like he was going to wake up with genital warts one day. He never did, fortunately, but it still ended badly enough.

His walk continues. Things are looking up these days. That's for sure.

***

Alex pulls up his Jeep behind the Cell Block.

Rick waits by the rape van. They slap hands and lean in for a bro hug. "Sup, bro," says Rick excitedly.

"Sup, playa," Alex responds. The quiet moments between Rick and Alex let them flex their wannabe street sides. Neither one are gangsters by any means, but it's still fun imitating their musical gurus. "Gotta git it tonight, huh?"

"Tonight's the night, baby. We gonna bring tha house down or what?"

"Whattya mean we? I'll be standin' in the crowd with my lady. You motherfuckas, the ones that need represent." Alex shakes his head as Rick hops in the van to start unloading. "We. That shit's funny, bro."

Rick leans back to get in close to Alex's face before grabbing any gear. "And bring it we shall. Biiaatch!"

184

Rick tosses a drum case to Alex. They stay in character to build momentum.

***

The stage is set on time. Exactly 30 minutes before their first set. Polyester Anarchy will do one full set at 10:00, have a break, then the closer at 11:30. The guys are pumped and ready to rock.

Alex sees Julie with drinks. She hip checks a girlfriend playfully on her way over. Sodas only. No busts from the Liquor Control Board on a night like this or ever for that matter. She makes her way to Alex. He takes the coke. "Thanks, baby."

She gives him a kiss. "Hope you like it." She drinks from the little black straw from the plastic cup. Squints her eyes a little before swallowing.

He takes a swig. "Captain and coke?" He asks. "Shut up. Be cool and be thankful."

Alex shrugs with a smile and takes another sip.

Moat's greasy fat ass gets up on stage to MC. He'd been a bouncer here for a while. Side hustles include taking Sunday sports bets and selling weed out the back door. Must've gotten promoted to mascot recently too.

"Ladies and gentleman. I'd like you to give a big round of applause, for the most cultured band in American history! Tonight, I give you! Polyester Anarchy!" Moat spreads his arm out in a chivalrous gesture and bows slightly as he backs off the stage.

The lights shut off. The crowd looks slightly confused. The sound of a cell door locking. Rick's voice rings out through the mic. "Welcome to Death Row mothafuckas." The spotlight turns on. Focusing on Jesse at the turntables. He begins scratching. The light reflects off his Yamaka. His fake sideburn braids dangling over the records. The blue and white shawl draped over his black button down. Doing his best Dr. Dre impression. Mixing old school gangster rap. People cheer Jesse on. Turntables are rare for bands like this. Spectators in the crowd seem genuinely impressed.

Another spotlight. This time on Rick. "What's up Dre." Jesse responds. "What up."

"I got something to say."

Jesse lets the album spin for a second before the bass drops. The stage lights come on. Adam, Chad and Rick step up to the front of the stage, and punch the air as Rick spits the first verse to "Fuck the Police" by NWA.

Damn! Alex says to himself. This is powerful. This music. In this ancient prison. The crowd is hype!

Julie leans in to press his ear down. "Fuckin' amazing!" He talks in front of her face. "I know, right!"

Rick finishes his verse and tosses the mic over his head. Stepping out of the way for Chad to catch it and take over. His fake red braids sloshing back and forth as he did.

"That wig glue's impressive!" Julie shouts.

Alex smiles. The guys themselves are impressive.

When Jesse stops mixing long enough to say his part, Rick tosses Adam the mic.

Alex looks around. Most of this crowd never even heard of NWA. They were born years after the group had broken up. Completely missing the impact of Gangster Rap on the country. Alex could include himself in that age group, but was also surrounded by people who regularly listened to the music. Tony, his dad, Uncle Scott, even Joseph and Tyrone used to play it. Alex knows it well. He's glad Rick liked the idea of doing West Coast Rap back when he first mentioned it.

The guys moved in unison as they wrapped up the song. Adam still has the mic.

They all got together and punched the air again. "Fuck tha police!" Cheers from every angle of the Cell Block fill the air. The vibe's terrific. Jesse spins a new song. "I Wanna Do Something Freaky to You" by Leon Haywood catches Alex by surprise. He's surprised Jesse slowed it down so quickly, but given it's the original music for "Nothin' but a G Thang" the switch totally made sense.

***

The set was unbelievable. They closed with "Gangster Party" from Tupac and Snoop. People ate it up.

Alex and Julie move outside. She wanted to talk.

"Hey, bud." She often calls him that. It's what everyone call each other in the group. "Wanna ditch Zilla and come to Thanksgiving with me and my dad?

186

It's just the two of us, and I'd love to have you." She scrunches her nose. "Plus, I'd really like you to meet my dad." She winces a little.

"I know. We really need to do that soon." Alex wants to blow of Zillagiving for Julie, but also wants to make his mom happy. She was calling him again. Alex welcomes the chance to have her back. This would ruin everything.

Julie expresses her concern again for the 'no girlfriends allowed' message Alex previously gave her about the dinner in Avalon. "Alex, I'm just going to come out and say it. I don't' want you to go."

"No kidding."

"I get it. You want to reconnect with your mother. Who wouldn't, but at what cost?"

"What do you mean?"

"I mean, you and Zilla are mortal enemies. This is clear to all of us. Now, by some wild stroke of fate, you also share a familial bond, which is kind of frightening."

Alex feels a twinge of fear from talking about Zilla so much. It was there the day they met and still digging away at him after all this time. He's afraid to agree with Julie to run a risk of her finding him weak, and therefore, less desirable.

She looks him in the eyes. "Tell me you want to go to their house. Tell me you aren't crapping your pants every time you think about it. I would be."

Alex refused to admit defeat. "I'm not crapping my pants, and I'm not going to turn and run from this."

"Ditching them for me isn't running. It's being sensible. It's keeping yourself safe."

"Stop it."

"No, I will not stop it, and I won't stand by and watch you two kill each other."

Alex's fear changes to frustration. "Nothing will happen. Our parents will be there."

"Fine. Do what you want. I'm going home to pack. Are you coming?" "I'll be there in a little bit."

She kisses Alex on the cheek and leaves abruptly. Alex goes back inside to watch the last set.

The guys began their second set while Julie and Alex argued. All East Coast Rap for balance. By the time he'd come back in the band was halfway through Diddy and Mace's "Can't Nobody Hold Me Down."

Rick has the mic.

They all have mics out at this point. The tossing back and forth is a great move to warm up the crowd, but after a while it gets old like anything else. Adam's up. Rick chimes in for Diddy's lines.

Alex zones out. Maybe he's the one who ain't ready to rock the derby. I mean how could he spend time with people who had treated him so badly? Why is he so desperate to reconnect with his mother after all she'd put him through? The way she was talking about Alex with Diane and Joseph after his fight with Zilla. It was like she was Zilla's mother and not his. She called Alex *a monster* for Christ sakes. All he wants, in his heart, are for things to be normal. Just like "Leave it to Beaver" with Ward and June Cleaver. They had all the answers. Wally and the Beav had such a great childhood. Even the reunion show they came out with in the 80s had them still living good lives. Alex wanted him and Joseph to be Wally and the Beav in the worst way. Anything other than who they are. What they are. A horribly dysfunctional mess.

***

Alex finishes packing the van and says good-bye to the guys for the holiday. He waves to them as they drive off. Hops in his Jeep and nothing. The car's dead. The battery had been draining for a while. Jesse told him to watch the alternator last time it happened. Alex forgot.

He calls AAA for a tow. Julie is gone when he gets home.

In the morning, Alex calls his mom to let her know his status. She texts him Zilla's number for a ride. With his balls in his throat, he makes the call.

***

3.5 hours in the car with Zilla down. Two to go. Once they reached Philly, it was all downhill from there.

Zilla's rice burner looks immaculate. Detailed to the point of OCD. Besides the mumble rap, the conversation is basically non-existent, which is fine. Zilla changes the music. Cypress Hill, "Hand on the Pump" comes on. Zilla turns it up. The system in his car impresses Alex. Clear treble, good base. Alex enjoys this part of the ride.

"Reminds me of your homies? Know what I mean, Alex?" Zilla smiles then looks back at the road.

Alex feels like talking now. "Sure. Right up their alley." "They played the Cell Block last night, no?"

"Yeah. Good show. They did all gangster rap. It was very appropriate." Zilla perks up. "Like Death Row Records stuff?"

"Not only that, the second set was all music from Bad Boy."

Zilla swipes his finger across his phone. A green bar of light flashes on the screen, over and over again. Alex doesn't think much of it. Maybe it's a timer or something for the music. Alex wishes he could count the seconds until this day ends.

"Man, those Jew boys sure know how to rap and rock, huh?" "Adam's such a good guy. He's really the only one who's a Jew."

"No kidding. You mean the faggots and the dark-skinned dude aren't Jews too? That don't even make sense. Why would they do that?"

Alex chooses to ignore the way Zilla's described his friends. "They all admire Adam and his people. I do too. The trouble is, that none of us understand Judaism all that well. It's kind of an exclusive culture."

"Exclusive? You mean like Jews won't let you join their club?"

"Nah, man. They've been through a lot. Been on the receiving end of numerous genocide attempts through history and they just don't trust outsiders very much, and for good reason. Thankfully, they were smart enough to survive. Their numbers are only about 1% of the global population, but maybe things are getting better in the world. Maybe people are learning the differences between us are what makes people beautiful."

Zilla sneers. "They survived by hiding in attics and basements. Haven't you seen "Inglorious Bastards?""

"Dude, that's fiction."

"I know. Just kiddin' ya. Those fuckin' Jews are lucky they even made it through all that stuff, right?"

"Those fuckin' Jews…" Alex repeats Zilla's words condescendingly.

189

"...have done everything they could to rebuild their community." He feels frustrated and wants this talk to end now. "You know what? My buddies. Adam and those guys. They may only pretend to represent Judaism, but they bring that shit every time they're on stage."

"Yeah, those guys are pretty crazy. You see them makin' it?"

"They've come a long way from the losers they were made out to be last year. The guys at the Cell Block wouldn't even take their calls."

"What changed that?" "I did."

Zilla smirks at Alex as he swipes his finger across the phone again. The conversation ends. He points to the radio. "Good tune, right?" He turns the music up.

Oh, Alex began imagining a funeral. He just hoped it wouldn't be his own.

***

They get there by early afternoon. The ride ends with Zilla pulling Alex's bag from the car and drops it on the ground before Alex could grab it from his hand. Zilla walks toward the mansion like nothing's wrong. Alex swallows his pride, and picks up the bag. *This is going to be interesting.* Alex says to himself.

Mom turns out to be extra cold when he walks in. "Well, hello Alex." She looks at his Eagles sweatshirt and Jeans. Glad you decided to dress for the occasion." She laughs heartily. So do Peter and his clone.

Alex is seriously humiliated. "Mom, did you bring me here to insult me in front of your new friends?"

"Oh no, sweety. These are not just my new friends. This is your new stepfather and stepbrother."

"What!"

Peter moves in to confirm. "Sure, buddy. We got married at the Courthouse last weekend. Nobody told you?"

Sue flashes a huge diamond on her finger smugly.

Alex looks shocked, sad, angry and heartbroken all at the same time. "You did that and didn't tell me?"

"Diane and Joseph could've. I'm actually surprised they didn't." She says without regret.

"You mean my brother and sister were there and I wasn't even invited?"

Sue shrugs. "Peter's assistant sent an invitation to your house."

Peter chuckles. "You know what? It may have been the Ambler address. My mistake."

Alex couldn't believe his ears. His mother whisks herself away to the kitchen.

Peter puts his arm around Alex. "Hey pal. Don't take it personally. We'll have plenty of time to catch up."

Zilla Jr. chimes in, "Yeah. Just the four of us."

Alex wants to crawl out of his skin. He fights back tears thinking of spending the next half day like this.

His mother comes back with a tray of hot food. "Stuffed mushrooms anyone?"

That's the last straw. "No, I don't want any of your stuffed mushrooms." Peter holds out his arms. "Come on, pal."

"I'm not your pal, and I know you threatened my family at Tony's funeral," says Alex with clenched teeth.

Sue gets angry. "That's a lie!"

"No, it's not! I saw dad's expression when you cornered him. I know you said you always balance your checkbook. What did you mean by that, Peter?"

Peter puts an arm around Alex to close talk. Alex flinches aggressively. "Get off me!"

Zilla Jr. steps up. Peter extends an arm up to stop him.

Peter turns toward Alex with his hands up like he doesn't want to fight. "Listen, son."

Alex cuts him off. "I'm not your goddamn son."

Peter laughs. "Yeah, that's for sure, but listen kid. This…what you're doing right now… is probably why you shouldn't have come to the wedding. Maybe that's why you may or may not have been excluded."

"May or may not have been?" Alex parrots back. "You're not even man enough to fully reject me. Dad's right about you."

"Your dad's nothing but a loser," remarks Sue.

Alex looks at his mother coldly. "Just like me, huh, Mom?" Zilla Jr. laughs. "Got that shit right." Sue laughs along with him.

Alex feels cornered. Abandoned. A familiar feeling. Comforting in a way that a kidnapped person might find a dry corner in a cell full of piss and shit.

Alex grinds his teeth. "Fuck you people."

Zilla Jr. leans in to grip Alex up but his sweatshirt. Growling through his teeth. Sue jumps in to separate them with a spaz attack. She swats at Alex, hitting him in the face. Her ring cutting Alex's cheek. Peter grabs her. She gives a scream that comes from her toes. "Get out!"

Alex turns and walks out. Tears pooling in his eyes. He hears the door open. Someone walking fast behind him. He turns around. Ready for anything. It's Zilla Jr. Alex's balls rise into his throat again, but he's greeted with a smile from ear to ear across Zilla's smug face. Looking as if he's about to apologize. Maybe it was all just a big joke. They could go on with their lives and be one big happy family. Like everything could be erased and a whole new present could be written based on how Alex would've wanted for himself.

Zilla holds up his suitcase and drops it again. "You forgot this. Later, Dudeman."

Alex watches the suitcase drop in slow motion. It hits the ground. He pulls out his phone to call an Uber.

***

$450 later, he arrives in Poughkeepsie, NY. Julie lives in a well-manicured split-level home on a quiet cul-de-sac. She meets him at the curb with open arms. He's so happy to be out of Avalon. To be here. Anywhere but Avalon. He'd never feel the same way about that place again.

Julie's dad greets them at the door. Earl sticks out his hand to make Alex's acquaintance.

"Hey, Alex. Come on in. We kept it warm for ya."

They go inside for dinner. Earl slept at his girlfriend's house that night. Julie was right about him being a packrat. Magazines and boxes are stacked in every corner of the house. Half-finished home improvement projects here and there. Tools and saws litter the living room floor. Julie jokes that there is a fireplace downstairs somewhere. Alex doesn't see how that's possible. Then she moved some things aside and, voila! There it is.

She and Alex make a fire and watch half an old movie. They kiss and hold each other for a while. Alex could feel her holding back an 'I told you so' all night.

Julie turns off the TV and takes him upstairs to her bedroom. They have privacy to do what they want. They take full advantage.

The next day, she and Alex make the trek back to Williamsport.

Chapter 30
Gina

The holidays come and go. Christmas in Avalon with Richard's family was beautiful. The drugs are gone. The violence gone. All that remains is hope, faith and purity. She avoids her old friends and haunts like the plague. Last semester, Richard stopped going to frat events and settled in with her and the Church.

Spring break is coming up. Gina heard that Alex and his crew are using the proceeds from their gigs at the Cell Block to fund a trip to the Bahamas. She'd feel jealous if the trip it wasn't laced with a non-stop party.

School is almost over for them. She and Richard both decided to wrap up their studies. Gina's nursing program is ending in June and she decided not to continue. Richard chose to end with his Associates degree instead of the Bachelor's he originally wanted. Both want to pursue careers in the seminary.

Richard is electric in front of the crowd. He'd drop his accent and imitate his father's professional rhetoric very well. He has a terrific memory and could quote numerous books from the bible on cue.

Gina bought a new computer with editing software. The preacher at their church asked her to start editing together various videos and hymnal recordings to sell online for members of their flock. She thought of a few that she planned on finishing today, but the computer is nowhere in the living room. She looks all over the apartment before finding Richard using it in her bedroom.

"Richard!" She calls to him. His response delayed due to the headphones. "What are you doing?"

"I'm working on a sound bite. Give me a few and I'll be finished. OK?" She loves his new speaking voice. So smooth. "No problem, sweety.

Carry on."

He smiles and puts back on the headphones. Gina goes back to the living room for prayer.

Chapter 31
Julie

The plane ride to Bahamas was quicker than she remembers. Last time Julie was 12 with her parents. A trip filled with cornrows, virgin daiquiris, and her first kiss on a beach with a boy from Delaware. Lovely memories.

Alex looks unusually relaxed by the pool. After breakfast at the hotel buffet, they'd settled down for poolside Bloody Mary's. The guys are off for an excursion on a Pirate Ship. Julie pauses to think about the conversations that would occur with Rick and Jesse on that boat. Probably something about how Jesse and Chad are butt pirates. Then Chad would reply with a gross quip about how Jesse's butt is the thing of dreams for men on a pirate ship for months at a time.

Then Rick would say how he knows of a couple people who would love to be stranded on a ship with sweaty men for months at a time. Then Adam would tell them to all shut up and listen to the guide. Meanwhile, helpless parents with small children look at them with jaws on the floor. She giggles at the thought. Can't be far from the truth.

She sees Alex perk up. "What are you laughing at over there?"

"Just thinking about the members of Polyester Anarchy on a pirate ship with a bunch of helpless tourists."

"Helpless like they won't be able to wash their ears after hearing Rick terrorize Jesse and Chad for two hours?"

"Yes! That's exactly what I think. Are you happy to be rid of them for a little while or what?" she jokes.

"Little breaks from each other's probably a healthy thing for all of us." "I concur, doctor."

She looks past the palm trees from the pool to the ocean. It looks bright blue and clean. The entrance to the beach not far from their seats. A wooden pole with a picture of a jellyfish catches her attention for a second, then the ocean again. So beautiful.

She nudges Alex. "Wanna hit the beach?"

"I'd rather go to the bedroom." He winks at her from behind his Bloody Mary glass.

"We can do that after. Come on." She jumps up and extends her hand. He takes it. "Sounds good, baby."

***

The ocean's as blue and clean as she wanted it to be. The beach is a different story. She couldn't understand why there is no one else. Just them and the ocean. The waves crashing into her. Alex riding them in like he was back in Jersey. He rides a wave to her. She puts her arms around him. A patch of seaweed closes in on them. They embrace for a loving kiss.

She pulls away slowly. "Aren't you glad we did this? Aren't you so happy about where we are? About to graduate. Living the life here in Bahamas on Spring Break. Isn't life beautiful?"

The seaweed gets closer.

She puts her hand in his bathing suit. "Hey, wanna get kinky in the ocean?"

Alex looks around. "Hell yeah. No one's watchin'."

They lower themselves so only their heads are out of the water dropping their bathing suits. Moving with the motion of the waves. Hands, legs, Alex moving the way she loves. Their motion brings the seaweed in. Then she feels the burn. It starts as only a little shock on her leg. Then up to her ass and on to her back.

Lifeguards run to them from the pool area waving frantically trying to get their attention. Alex grunts. "Ow! What the fu…" He tries to toss the seaweed, but instead puts his arm directly in the tentacles of a Vietnamese Man of War. He shouts with pain.

Julie turns around. There's one on her back. Another on Alex's back and all over his arm.

The lifeguards wave them in.

She feels Alex lift her up and pull her out of the water. She can't tell if her legs are working or not. Couldn't remember if she'd passed out for shock or if she had drowned and was being carried to the boatman on the River Styx.

She could feel hands holding her down. Her bottoms are gone. She looks for Alex. They're holding him down too. Julie sees one of the lifeguards unzipping his pants. Then another unzipping his pants next to Alex.

Julie has a sense of dread. "No! Help! They're gonna rape us! Help!" Then she feels a warm stream of something salty on her face. Her arms,

her back, her legs. She and Alex are being pissed on by the Lifeguards. The Golden Shower ends. She wipes the piss away from her eyes along with her hopes and dreams.

One of the lifeguards tosses a towel on her. "Cover yourself up! You should be thankful!" They shake their heads at the stupid Americans and walk off. She notices Alex looking at something. Then realizes they have an audience. People from the pool are staring at them.

"Look Jul. We got some fans."

"Shut up, Alex!" She gets to her feet and wraps the towel around herself.

Julie storms off to go shower for real.

She could hear Alex high fiving some guys as he trails behind. *Men are such pigs.* She thinks to herself.

***

Back in the room she cries alone in the shower.

***

The night's warm and inviting. Not unlike the steam of piss that relieved her pain from sea creatures earlier. The few drinks Julie had, had helped her loosen up. Alex finishes setting up the band's instruments and joins her side. She shakes an empty cup.

Alex gets the hint. "Ok. Let's get some drinks."

She takes his arm. They walked together to the bar where they find Rick and Adam talking with some guys from the pool.

The one with the mustache recognizes her. He taps his buddy's arm. "Dude, look. It's the couple that got pissed on today."

Rick's eyes light up. "What did you just say?"

Stash face speaks again. "Yeah, they both went swimming on jelly fish beach. Then the lifeguards pulled them out and had to piss on them before they went into shock."

Rick couldn't contain his laughter. Adam raises an eyebrow. "You mean, you actually got…ehem…a Golden Shower?"

Julie could see Alex getting a little pissed. "Yo, man. Easy with the Daydreams jokes, alright. Julie's right here."

Julie feels angry too. "They didn't piss on each other at Daydreams…" she trails off. "It kinda smelled that way though."

Adam could barely contain himself. "Julie, you've been hanging with Alex too much."

Alex leans in. "The adventure's just beginning, motherfucker." Adam laughs again. "Yes, that's clear to us."

The MC catches their attention. "Ladies and gentleman. Please give a warm round of applause for tonight's entertainment. The one. The only. Polyester Anarchy!"

The conversation ends. The band runs on stage.

Julie uses the audience distraction to order a couple drinks.

Adam takes the mic to warm up the crowd. "Hello everyone and hello Bahamas!" People cheer. "I'd like to dedicate our first song tonight to our good friends Alex and Julie. Two people who are very much in love and at the beginning of their adventures together."

Rick picks up the base. Adam puts on his guitar.

Alex knows the song as soon as he hears the first cord. "Ironic" by Alanis Morrisette. So poetic.

Julie had to laugh. It was too strange of an experience not to. Adam has a great sense of humor. She sees Alex relax a little when he realizes she isn't pissed anymore.

Julie raises her cup to cheers Alex. "Here's to golden showers, bud." Alex stares at the stage with a blank expression. He clinks instinctively.

"Yeah. To golden showers."

Chapter 32
John

John loads up his truck. The settlement from Ed Murray came in over the holidays. $800,000 after lawyer fees. Enough money for Joseph to rebuild his life. John started with investing more than half in retirement savings for him. Take that plus the insurance money to rebuild the house, Joseph has a new path. One he could pursue while the real healing begins. His physical therapy has made leaps and bounds since last summer. First it was his toes, then his feet got pins and needles. Now he can feel his knees again. Not walking yet, but feeling is enough to provide hope.

John can be out more working now that Pearl has the office in order. She does all of his billing, keeps the place in order and even cleans regularly. She and Robert are now engaged. John hadn't told him yet, but Joseph purchased one of Tyrone's fixer uppers on Church Street near Alex. He'd wait for the right moment to reveal that one.

Joseph's house is about finished. The elevator is in good shape. Mostly cosmetic stuff and removal of the smell. The house was gutted and completely redone. John made sure that with the garage area being part of the living space, Joseph had a full bathroom added down there and a nicer one rebuilt upstairs. Another week or so until the floors are done then paint.

John's thinks about being an empty nester. *Oh, how glorious it would be.* His phone pulls him from the daydream.

He recognizes the number. "Walker Plumbing."

"John, it's Tim. We need to talk. Can you come to the station today?"

"Sure, Tim. Should I bring a lawyer?" Tim grunts. *"No. Just yourself."* Click

***

The station is quiet when John gets to the front desk. A young female officer escorts him to Tim's office.

They shake and sit. Tim speaks first. "Have you spoken to your Ex-wife lately?" "Which one?"

"Sue Davies. Now Sue Zilla." "Nope. Not a word since last fall." "Around when they were married?" "Yes."

"Do you know anything about her husband Peter?" "Nothing really?"

"You and he spoke at Tony Mangle's funeral, correct?" "We did."

"Can you tell me what he said?"

"I can, but it wasn't anything you can hold him to." "What do you mean by that?"

"I felt like he implied something, but I can never prove a feeling." "Does Sue have anyone besides her children?"

"Only some extended family upstate." "Any friends?"

"She never kept many friends. What's this all about?"

"After the Tony Mangle's murder, we began investigating all potential suspects. This led our search to Avalon, New Jersey and the Zilla family. After working with their department for a while, we decided to kick the case up the ladder. The investigation has now reached the federal level."

"The Feds? Really? This sounds bad."

"Yes, John. I'm telling you this because you're my friend. My suggestion is to try and keep your children from the Zilla's or Avalon for a while. If they come to visit, please let us know."

"No problem. Anything else?"

"Yes. You'll be in Williamsport for graduation in a week, right?" "Yes, Alex and his girlfriend are finishing up school now."

"Keep Alex away from Richard Zilla. Any outside interference would be very bad for all parties."

***

John zones out on the way back to the house. *Shit. Maybe Peter Zilla wasn't bluffing. At the moment, he sounds much more than a bank account with pulse.* John says to himself.

He feels for Sue, but only so much. She's rotten to the core. She deserves what's coming her way. However, that's something he could never let out. His children would only suffer more.

Chapter 33
Adam

Graduation Day. The robotics program was illuminating. Adam loved his education. Over breakfast this morning, his dad joked about how Adam should build robots to sell insurance for them. Adam felt like that would be a great theme for Polyester Anarchy's first music video.

Adam made sure his direct number was on the bottom of concert posters for something like this. Alex insisted. It was one of his better ideas.

Jerry Medina worked with bands like Blink 182 and Linkin Park back in the day. His label's looking for a new act, but he wants a hit single first. Luckily, Adam has one locked and loaded. The song he and Alex wrote. After finals, Adam cruised up to the Big Apple to meet at his building and talk business.

***

Jerry cued up the song on his phone and played it through the speakers in his office.

"What's it called again?" he asked.

Adam felt the sweat drip down his ribs. "Too Far from You."

The music began. Adam got chills as he heard Rick's bass grove kick in. His guitar and Chad's drums kicked in before slowing down for Adam's lyrics.

...This world is what you make it to be, The ones who you love, are the ones who you fight, The laughter don't make it right, why so cold, The reasons for living become old and blurred, The way to make it is to break the walls down, Leave it all behind, seething faithless letting go, Feeling neglect in your soul, let the tears roll...

Jesse kicks in with the scratching. A mixture of old and new. Rick hits the base groove a few beats in before rapping the chorus.

...My angel's here to take me away, I loved you before we met, Loved you so much my face gets wet, Love is why we waited, I know the feeling true, Why can't everything be me and you...

Adam's voice coos the next verse over Chad's drum beat.

...I picked you up too late one night, It's not cool how your friends always want to fight, Was I only allowed to love you a certain amount that night, No need for fright, My rep can't hurt you, Just remember who I was to you, No matter what my jaw felt, The love never gets old, just too far to hold...

Rick comes back to battle Jesse's scratching over the next chorus.

...My angel's here to take me away, I loved you before we met, Loved you so much my face gets wet, Love is why we waited, I know the feeling true, Why can't everything be me and you...

Adam came back for the bridge.

...We're drifting too far into the mist, Knowing just how special we were. Missing you more now. Needing your love. You're face only a blur...

Rick and Jesse rap together for one more chorus and the ending.

...My angel's here to take me away, I loved before we met, Loved you so much my face gets wet, Love is why we waited, I know the feeling true, Why can't everything be me and you...

...My angel's here to rip me away, I loved you since we met, Love you so much my face got wet, Our love never lasted, I knew the feeling true, Why can't everything get back to me and you...

The music fades.

Jerry sits in silence for a minute. Adam sees him glaring at the Yamaka. "Drop the shtick. It's time to go pro."

***

Adam feels terrific. He waits by the bathrooms for Alex. He sees Zilla from a distance.

Adam feels his phone vibrate. A message from Zilla. *"Never trust a Walker. Listen to this and make your move."* Adam opens it and listens.

"Man, those Jew boys sure know how to rap and rock, huh?"

"Adam's such…a Jew…Thankfully…Those fuckin' Jews…Their numbers are only about 1% of the world's population…The trouble is Judaism…'s…an exclusive culture."

"No kidding."

"They've come a long way from the losers they were last year. The guys at the Cell Block wouldn't even take their calls."

"What changed that?" "I did."

"Yeah…You see them makin' it?" "Nah, man."

He looks back up for Zilla, but he's gone. Steam comes out of Adam's ears. He trusted Alex. How could he do this? It was since Bahamas that he and Julie became distant. Alex began spending more time at her place. Missing the last gig, making the band work double time to set up and break down. Now this. *Fuckin' Jews, huh? Dammit!* Adam seethes.

Alex saunters up with Julie. "Hey Adam. Congrats," she says. "Yeah sure. Can't wait to leave this hellhole." Snaps Adam.

"Ok. Sure." Julie looks confused, but continues onto the bathroom. Adam fumes, as he looks Alex in the eyes. "Alex is this you?"

He holds his phone up and presses play.

Alex's face twists and contorts as he listens to the recording. Adam drops his phone when it ends. "I'll repeat, is this you?"

Alex looks dumbfounded. "Well, yeah but…"

"No, buts. That's you! You called us 'fuckin' Jews' and you know it!" "No, I didn't. I remember this conversation. It happened over Thanksgiving break. With Zilla, no less. Dude, this is wrong."

"How is it wrong? It's as clear as crystal. This is you and you betrayed me. You are out of the band, Dudeman. We are finished!"

Adam storms off. He couldn't believe the audacity. The disrespect. The lack of love. How could Alex do such a thing? Adam would show him. That song they wrote. It's going to be huge. Alex would have to hear it on the radio by himself. He's out and would be lucky if he receives a dime of the money after this nonsense.

Chapter 34
Julie

Julie could hear Adam harping on Alex from the bathroom. She finishes washing her hands then goes to his side.

"Everything OK?" she asks. "Not really."

"Let's go outside and talk. Come on." She tugs at his arm.

Their parents have already gone. Alex and Julie are supposed to stay at the house with the guys tonight to celebrate. Everyone graduated today. Alex, Julie, Adam, Rick, Jesse. Even Zilla and Gina. Done. 2-year Associates degrees and out. Good part is half the debt and jobs that pay as well, if not better, than those from a more expensive 4-year college or University. Plumbers, HVAC guys, Welders, Nurses, Chefs. All is well on the possibilities front.

They sit down on the curb alongside of the building. Alex speaks first.

"I can't believe one person can cause so much damage in a somebody's life. I'm at the point now where I'm trying to understand why Batman never killed the Joker."

"That Joker. He sure is trouble."

"I'm serious though. How the fuck was I supposed to know I'd be recorded during a drive to Thanksgiving dinner? I wasn't even talking bad about him or anyone else. I was trying to help that idiot understand why tolerance is important."

"More irony, huh?"

"Yes. A giant unhealthy dose of irony or bad luck or ill intentions or whatever you want to call it."

"People suck, bud. Sorry this happened to you."

Alex wells up with tears. "After all these years. I finally found another group of friends that I click with. Then this nightmare of a human being comes out of nowhere and rips everything away from me."

206

"Not everything, Alex."

He looks at her without expression, then softens once their eyes lock. He puts his arm around her. "Sorry. You know how important you are to me."

She puts her head on his shoulder. "I'm pregnant." "Just in time for graduation, huh?"

"Yup. What're we gonna do?"

"I got a place. Wanna come over?"

She could feel warmth and humor rush back. It tickles her on the inside. "I don't know. Those Ambler people are pretty tough. Think there's going to be anyone to protect me if Darkman returns?"

"That sounds like a job for Dudeman." "I love me some Dudeman."

Alex hugs her tighter. "He loves you too." That settles it. Ambler or bust.

Chapter 35
Gina

Graduation came and went. Gina and Richard moved to a place in Avalon near his dad. She found them a nice church in town. Beautiful, wealthy, very white people everywhere. Not like she isn't used to being around lots of people of her own tribe, it's just that, Gina doesn't really understand them. Being a person of God, you shouldn't separate yourself from others based on wealth or material objects.

She understands the importance of tithing and how that sort of thing can elevate someone in their community. Richard spared no expense in getting himself recognized once they committed to their church. It took him about a month to get himself a job as Assistant Preacher. A feather in his cap was not having to live in the church's residence set aside for such a position. He decided the church could rent that out for additional income instead, and so they did.

Gina looks at her phone. 4:00. Sue would be coming for dinner in a bit.

Richard and his dad are out with friends. Gina enjoys the girl time.

She doesn't have to get a job just yet. Richard's father is pretty much footing the bill for everything so far. The income Richard receives from the church amounts to spending money for the two of them. She got a car. Not an expensive one. A cute one. A supercharged Mini Cooper. Faster than a demon and comfy like a couch on wheels. She loves it because Richard hates it. His big body all scrunched up in there like a jack in the box. Makes her laugh when he bitches like one of the girls.

Richard's amazing on stage. His current position requires him to manage the youth groups, Sunday school and community outreach. The Preacher, James Haws, is a nice guy. Gina could tell, but there's something off about him. Gina got an aggressive vibe here and there. He's a guy who found his calling while on an acid trip back in the early 90s. He was walking around a shopping mall and wandered up to one of those kiosks with Magic Eye posters. When at first glance, you only saw random colors, but if you stared long enough an image would appear.

Apparently, James was the only one he knew who could never see the images. James mentioned, while telling Gina and Richard the story, how he even sat with his younger sister and went through books of these images. She'd point to a train or a plane, and James would see nothing. Then in the mall, Jesus appeared to him on the cross. There were about 30 other images for sale at the kiosk. James at first thought it was a fluke. He looked at each one intently. Then after going round and round, for what he said seemed like an eternity, there He was again. The image of Jesus. The only one James could see. Afterwards, he quit partying and joined the seminary. Just like that.

Sue is really the only friend Gina has outside the church. The two of them share common ground. Gina really has no recollection of the exact experiences other than something that resembled dreaming, but she and Sue may or may not have shared a man. During her partying days with Richard, all sorts of mayhem ensued. The drugs eased the pain of the memories. Blackouts worked in her favor that way. All that remains are the flashbacks. Those usually occur when driving by herself listening to music. Songs have a way of taking Gina into a state of meditation. More so than prayer could. She decides to keep those experiences to herself.

Sue walks in their two-story bungalow in the center of town. Richard would commonly say how Alex's white trash family could only afford a house on the bay. Gina would kill for a house on the bay. To be right on the water. She missed out on that part of the relationship with Alex. So much they missed out on together. Now she only has Sue to keep her connected with him. From afar. She could sneak a look at pictures sometimes, if Sue has them out. Pictures of the family would be pushed to the front of the photo albums, rotated to the back or disappear altogether. Those decisions were based on the level of depression Sue feels from day to day. All Gina could lend is an ear. Dinner tonight with the two of them would include lots of gossip and end with strong coffee.

Gina gets up to put a meatloaf in the oven. 375 for an hour. She hits cook. No wine for her, but Sue would be in the mood for some. Gina pulls a bottle of blush from the wine rack. Sets it on the counter. Looks around the open area of their Cape Cod style home, which could be considered their starter home.

209

Are she and Richard really doing this? Is this what her future looks like? Pastel colored furniture?

Anchor and drift wood décor. It's cute, but not what she's used to at all. Gina misses Pittsburgh. She'd call her dad, but he may not pick up. He hates talking on the phone and hates leaving the county even worse. He'd make a pilgrimage back to Kentucky once a year to pick up some good bourbon and that would conclude his travels until the world turns again. Gina does enjoy the company of Richard, the money, and the lifestyle. It's her inability to take it all seriously that holds her back from loving him the way he claims to love her. He may or he may not. Their relationship *is* built on lies after all.

A knock at the door. Strange. Sue doesn't knock.

Gina walks to the front window to peak through the curtains. An older man waits patiently for someone to answer. Feeling no threat, Gina decides to open it.

When she does, Bob smiles at her from the stoop. "Well, hello stranger." he says with a familiar happy tone.

She cheers up unknowingly. "Hey. What brings you to town?"

"Well, it's a bit of a coincidence, but my lady and I have a little place on the edge of town, OK." Bob tends to add 'ok' to the end of his sentences like Mr. Mackey from South Park. "I've been on assignment from the non-profit to expand business to our sister state. You know, expanding from PA to Jersey. Then I got wind of you and Richard joining the church here in town. His sermons are something else. People are really talking."

The randomness of Bob's visit feels a little off. "That's great Bob. So *what can I* do for you?"

"You know it's funny you ask. Remember my friend Tony, that connected you with the condo back in Philly?"

Gina didn't know they were friends. The feeling is getting stronger now. "Tony, right. Sorry to hear about his passing over the summer."

"Yes, well Tony wasn't the only friend I lost. My friend, JC from Slack's Pancake Shack, OK. He also suffered an unfortunate event over the summer. They discovered his car around 61st Street early one morning, and he was never seen again. My police buddies say there was some evidence that went missing after the investigation."

"I'm really sorry to hear that. Hey listen, if you'd like to speak with Richard about the church, I can connect you two."

"No, actually I'm here to speak with you. There's a house on the 61st Street beach. One with a few flags on the porch. Italy, Ireland, the US and another one." He snaps his fingers joyfully to jog his memory. "Oh yes, and Princeton orange."

The feeling Gina has turned out to be nausea.

He continues. "So that house. As it turns out, has a very nice security system, and a camera pointed right at the beach of all places. I could show you some of the video on my phone, but I just can't ever seem to get the darn thing to work right." He smiles.

She opens her mouth to speak, but nothing comes out.

He turns to walk away. "Oh, one more thing. There was a gun found in a dumpster behind a newsstand not too far from here. It had two sets of prints on it. JC's and someone else's. They didn't say whose exactly, but I bet if we checked that security footage from that house on 61st Street, the police may just get lucky and find their suspect."

Bob hands Gina his business card. "Take this and call me if you can think of anything that could help the police." She looks at the card like it's covered with a virus. She feels his hot breath on her face. "Gina, I want you to know something." She looks up at him. "None of this is your fault. You don't have to suffer because of someone else's mistakes." She nods, her mouth still open. "Call me, and I can help you figure this all out. See you in church," he says before waving and finally walking away.

Gina closes the door and slinks down on the tile beneath her feet. It feels cold on her legs. She zones out. Her life flashes before her eyes.

Chapter 36
Alex

Moving home was the right move. Trying to speak with Adam after that was pointless. All of the guys are avoiding Alex's calls. Except Chad, but even those brief conversations are awkward. Alex decides to let it go, but that proved to be easier said than done.

To let go of such a big part of his life proved difficult. He constantly thinks of them. Who's setting up and breaking down their gear? Who's doing their new posters and scheduling the gigs? And what about the song? Those lyrics came from Alex's love and pain. Those emotions took years to form words. He has to let go. Nothing good can come out of obsessing.

He thinks of Julie. Working at Chestnut Hill Hospital. In the ER. Her hours aren't much different than when she was a bartender. The baby. Julie's three months pregnant at this point. She mentioned how it probably happened over the winter. That means she was pregnant during spring break. She had no idea so drinking that way doesn't make them bad parents. Once it's clear *then* you need to justify falling off the wagon. 'Bad day at work sweety? Sure you can have a glass of wine.' 'Can't pay the bills today? Here's another.' Alex is drinking less these days himself. He wouldn't be 21 until the following year, but if people think that kids wait until legal age to become alcoholics, they're sadly mistaken.

After getting home, Alex buckled into the Walker Express. Walker Plumbing rather, and hit the ground running. Alex is the guy in the ditch now. His dad hired a brand-new excavator on the job. No more Ed Murray. He went belly up. The insurance claim raised his rates something fierce plus word got out that he's dangerous. Apparently, Ed started landscaping instead. Seems like a good move, now he can only sever fingers not spines.

Alex and Julie got closer with Diane. She and Julie would talk baby stuff. Alex enjoys watching Maria grow up. She's going into preschool next year.

Little Maria's a sassy kid. Gabe's long out of the picture. Engaging on a little more than baby momma drama. Since Diane started dating Tyrone last summer, Gabe had been locked up for evading child support. He was able to push off the hearings for a while because of his status as an economic ghost. All the cash he makes equates to squat for taxable income. It was only a matter of time before it caught up to him. A person can't drive around in a BMW and claim they make zero dollars. It just doesn't happen.

Tyrone made an interesting proposition to Alex recently. Ty has the opportunity to buy up a half a block of row homes in North Philadelphia to rehab them. His status as a minority business owner gives Ty an opportunity that doesn't come around every day, but he doesn't have the capital to do it.

That's where Alex comes in. Since the house on Church Street is paid off, Alex could take out a Home Equity Line of Credit to front him the money. Ty would give him 10% on the original investment plus pay him time and labor for whatever Alex could pitch in during construction. His dad's against the idea. John feels the venture is too risky for someone Alex's age to be involved in plus it's a dangerous part of the city. Ultimately, it's still Alex's decision. After his grandmother died, Alex had to sign some papers. Then he had to sign more after graduation. Now, the house is officially his.

Julie and he moved into the master bedroom right away. They opted to use her furniture. She has an actual set her dad bought when Julie moved to Williamsport. Alex had a bunch of shit thrown together from whatever his dad collected from estate sales. Those things were dropped off at the second-hand store for a fist full of cash right before moving day.

Alex has been seeing his mom here and there at Diane's too. She visits alone. No Peter or Richard in tow. Trouble in paradise maybe. Alex knew that relationship would be doomed from the start. They met under the worst circumstances. I mean who moves in with the father of a boy who tried to beat your son to death? Alex could acknowledge the lack of good mental healthcare among his family members. Yet, healthcare is useless for people who think they're perfect. His parents are amazing that way. No matter how big of jerks they would be to each other, their children, society in general, they each go home at night, and sleep peacefully like nothing's wrong. Like they're the greatest gift to suburbia the lord could give.

Alex himself is a big fan of mental healthcare. It's what saved his life. His emotional support teacher in high school and the various psychologists he met along the way.

Talk therapy is highly under rated, and if you're bright enough to accept its benefits, you can accomplish almost anything. Psychiatrists on the other hand. Those are the same people that put sad young Alex on Lithium when he got sent away for having a nervous breakdown when he was younger.

So quick to get people strung out on drugs. So quick to tell a scared young kid that he can expect to be a part of 'the system' for the rest of his life. That once you get diagnosed with bi-polar disease you can look forward to struggling with it for the rest of your life. Maybe what those people should focus on is prescribing hugs to their patients first before getting them all doped up on anti-psychotics. Giving a teenager Lithium. What the hell is wrong with people?

Alex could feel himself brooding. These are the moments when Julie mentions how much he looks like his dad. Alex doesn't feel much like his dad. Always so quick with a smart comment. Alex is more of a serious guy. More likely to tell you to piss off than to make a joke. Alex has kind of a zero bullshit policy. Julie says he'd make a terrible politician. Those guys need to sugar coat everything. Alex has a bad habit of telling it like it is. A career in Corporate America's probably out of the question also.

Alex walks to the kitchen, and opens the refrigerator. He takes out a can of coke. Still warm. He went to the corner store this afternoon on his way home from work. He puts it on the counter then reaches up to get a glass from the cabinet, but something catches his eye. An old nick in the cabinet door. A makeshift patch job he did to hide the spot from his dad. Alex remembers specifically when it happened.

It was a week before Heather dumped Alex for good. A chain of events led to it. One being the shroom night. Another was the spoon incident.

***

In all fairness to Heather, the spoon incident happened while she was attempting to conduct something of an intervention. She, Jasper, and for whatever reason, his brother Jason, decided to come over. Robert was excluded because Heather felt he was part of the problem. That was debatable. Alex and Robert emerged from the same powder keg. The problem wasn't with either of them. That's what teenagers fail to understand when trying to dissect each

214

other's lives. These problems don't just come from a vacuum. What they fail to notice before passing judgment is the shitty parenting causing all the turmoil to begin with.

They came to the kitchen where Alex was making a tinfoil bowl. They watched him roll the foil over a pen, bend the loose end with his finger, then roll and flatten it out with his fingertips like a pipe.

Heather sat with her arms crossed on the stool by the breakfast island. Her sneer extending so high in her left nostril, Alex thought she looked like Elvis' retarded daughter.

"Alex, we really need to talk."

"We think you're going overboard with the drugs these days," added Jasper.

Alex walked over to the sink. He unscrewed the aerator on the faucet and removed one of the screens.

Jason put his hand up to say, "Hay man, maybe you shouldn't do that."

Alex smiled and flipped off Jason before pushing the screen into the tinfoil bowel.

Jasper injected some venom to the conversation. "You know. You could sit down and listen instead of assembling your crack pipe."

Alex pulled an empty cigarette wrapper filled with weed from his pocket.

He took out a bud and packed the bowl. "It ain't crack, dude." Jason rolled his eyes. "Yeah, genius we know that."

Alex licked his teeth. "Wasn't sure if you did." Alex pulled out a lighter. Heather uncrossed her arms. "You're really going to smoke that in here?" Alex pointed upward like he remembered something important. "Oh yes,

I have a solution for such an occasion." They all looked at each other confused.

Alex reached into a cabinet and pulled out an empty paper towel roll, but not a normal one. Alex rolled some dryer sheets on the end and secured with a rubber band. He lit the bowl, took an unhealthily large hit and blew the smoke threw the paper towel roll. The room smelled like springtime linen and skunk ass.

"Ok, so that smells terrible, and I'm leaving. This has been a total waste of our time," said Jason before storming out.

"Alex, please listen, we're concerned for you. We want you to stop smoking weed." Pleaded Heather.

Alex went for the refrigerator to get a snack. He took out a pudding and opened it. Jasper blocked Alex from getting a spoon. "Did you hear her, Alex?"

Alex shoved him out of the way and got the spoon. He walked away to toss the plastic lid in the can. Heather and Jasper huddled together by the cabinets near the fridge. Both looking frustrated.

"Fine eat your pudding. We'll stand here and wait for you to get a hold of yourself." Heather crossed her arms.

Alex ate his pudding without a word. He wanted the situation to end, but he also wanted to be with Heather by himself. Those days might be over. His stomach churned at the thought. He just couldn't conjure the strength to speak. The thought of not going back to the way things were made Alex feel depressed. His new self being so strong and interesting. Heather and Jasper couldn't be more wrong. The weed opened up his mind.

Made him a whole new person. Someone heroic. Someone more like the superheroes in his comics. Like Moon Knight. A wealthy adventurer who became possessed by an ancient spirit giving him unimaginable power. Gliding across rooftops fighting crime. His crescent shaped throwing stars. Alex felt the weed gave him similar powers.

The seconds were going by like minutes. Alex could feel their glare. "I'm just over here hanging out, guys. Flexing my new abilities?"

Heather's forehead crunched together. "What new abilities?" Jasper turns to Heather. "Should we do this or what?" Heather turns to him. "Yeah, it's time."

Jasper makes his move. "Alex, we're taking a break with you for a while. It's over between all of us."

Alex licked some chocolate pudding from the spoon. "That's nice." He looked at Heather. "You want to ditch him so we can talk alone?"

A look of disgust washed over Heather's face. "Alone? Alex, I'm not so sure that's a good idea."

Jasper chimed in with a condescending tone. "Yeah, with your *new abilities* and all."

They didn't believe him. Alex could feel the power of the weed coursing through his veins. Alex wondered if his blood was green at the moment. His abilities were growing fast. He needed to prove it.

"You don't believe me? I'll prove it to you."

Jasper bit. "Ok, shoot?" He and Heather both leaned against the countertop with their arms crossed now.

Alex licked the spoon clean. He channeled all his energy into his right arm. The spoon between his thumb and forefingers. The anger. The rage. All going into that spoon. In one quick motion, Alex raised the spoon to his ear and threw it like a lightning bolt from Zeus himself. The spoon whizzed past Heather's face taking a chunk from the cabinet door. A piece of the wood hit Heather in the eye.

She recoiled from the pain. Heather touched her eye gently. Her face hiding behind her hair. Alex thought she was laughing at first. She wasn't.

Jasper raised his hands like a human question mark. "What did you do?" Alex responded with humor. "You told me to shoot."

Heather ran from Alex's kitchen in tears.

Jasper grabbed Alex by his shirt. "You stay away from her!" His face full of anger.

Alex didn't think much of Jasper's toughness or *his* abilities. He straightened his forefingers and poked Jasper in the throat. Jasper let go and stumbled backward. Defeated, but defiant.

"You're a freak, Walker. Everyone hates you." He followed Heather out the door.

He went to the cabinet and ran his fingers over the damaged portion. He thought about Shop class. His teacher gave him instruction on how to repair things like this. He went to the basement for some supplies.

In the basement, Alex found his dad's work bench in the back room. Alex remembered the smell of that room. The laundry always had a musty odor. Alex and his dad didn't have the touch to make the laundry smell like flowers. Their clothes often times smelled like the machine itself. A front-end loader that needed to be cleaned weekly. A top-of-the-line model, but no one around to use it correctly. Neither one of them had the time or energy to figure it out and often suffered socially as a result.

Alex ignored the smell and focused on the workbench. He sanded a piece of pine until there was a pile of sawdust the shape of an anthill. He found wood glue underneath the bench. He reached into the tool pouch on the ground next to him and found a razor knife. Alex used the knife to shave off a tiny chunk from the pine.

An old dish sitting on the far corner of the workbench held some random nuts and bolts. Something his dad kept in multiple places around the house for repairs. He emptied the dish on the bench and used it to mix the glue and saw dust together into a wood paste.

He took the dish in one hand and the chunk of pine in the other and went back to the kitchen.

Alex applied the paste to the cabinet with a butter knife. He carefully placed the tiny chunk of wood in the bed of paste then pressed it in with the tip of his pointer finger. The glue oozed out from around the patch job. He wet a paper towel then wiped away the excess paste.

Alex stood back and admired his work. "Dad, will never notice." He said aloud.

Two hours later, dad came home and found it after being in the kitchen for 30 seconds. Alex was grounded for a week.

***

Alex and Julie recently talked about redoing the kitchen. The light oak cabinetry and the pastel blue Formica counters looked a bit 80s. Alex grazes his hand over the old patch on the cabinet. Thinking about how much his life had changed over the past few years. The pain. The suffering. All channeled to this one seemingly insignificant blemish on the old cabinetry. Something that would stay with him until the day he died. With or without the cabinets.

He removes an ice tray from the freezer and cracks loose a few cubes. He drops them in the glass with a ding and a clang. He uses a fingernail to pop the can of coke open. He fills the glass until the froth nearly spills over. He trades the can in his right hand for the cold glass and takes a sip. The carbonation makes his chest burn in a yummy way.

Alex could hear someone open the front door. He doesn't think much of it. People often don't use the doorbell around here.

Tyrone strolls in the kitchen. "Sup lil' bro!" They slap hands and hug quick. "Daddy Warbucks ain't got you working today?"

"Nah, bud. Robert's on call this weekend. I got the day off. It's Saturday, man. Taking some me time."

"Oh yeah, you're on me time alright." Ty pulls a stool out from under the island to sit. "Hey, you think more about what I asked you?"

"Yeah, I have. Dad's not into it."

"Forget about dad for a minute. What about Alex? Is he into it?"

Alex smiles at the thought of talking about himself in the third person. Reminds him of Gambit from the X-men cartoon. Wolverine's best friend. "Alex, might be into it. 10% plus material and labor could be a nice investment for me."

Alex could see the gears turning in Ty's handsome face. Tony used to joke that Tyrone is what the guys in the *Joint* would call man pretty. His dad would also comment on Ty's looks and demeanor. Calling him *A* "Distinguished Gentleman*"* referencing an old Eddie Murphy movie from the 90s. Alex had seen the movie before. He understood the looks part of it, but he could never see Ty cheating anyone to get ahead. It's just not like him.

Ty breaks the silence. "Come on, man." Ty gets up. Alex takes another swig of his soda. "Where we goin'?"

"I'm taking you for a ride. I need to show you something."

***

They get out of Ty's red BMW and step onto the sidewalk of Hope Street in North Philly. Not too far from the spot in Kensington where Alex had received multiple beatings from neighborhood bullies as a kid.

Alex looks at his feet. Heroine needles and human shit litter the sidewalk.

Ty speaks from behind him. "I know it don't look like much now, but just you wait."

Alex feels nauseous from the sight. "Wait for what? The zombie apocalypse? Looks like it's already here." Alex points down the street. Addicts doing the *Neutron Dance* try preventing themselves from falling over after shooting heroin.

Ty puts his arm around Alex. "Gentrification's coming." Alex thinks Ty sounds like Ned Stark from "Game of Thrones". "Look at these shit holes and imagine the possibilities."

Alex grinds his teeth. "All I'm thinking of is cockroaches and bed bugs."

"Nah, kid. Think about Green Building. Energy efficient housing. Top of the line HVAC systems and rooftop solar panels. This is the future, bud. Me and you."

Alex thinks about the future. All he wants to do is write and draw. He never wanted this, but as life would have it, this certainly wants him.

Ty speaks again to drive the sale home. "You learned about all this in

219

school, no?"

"Yeah, took my LEED AP exam as part of my studies." Alex thinks back to his Sustainability classes with Mr. Taylor. A guy from the area of Pittsburgh were everyone speaks like Fred Rodgers. The Leadership in Energy Efficiency and Design offered an Accredited Professional certification as sort of a Minor that coincided with his Associates Degree.

Ty looks pleased. "You gonna put that education to work or what?"

Alex stares at the block of row homes and thinks about the mountain of work ahead. "Is it really half the block?"

"The entire row actually. A project the Mayor calls 'Energize Philly.' Rehabbing old homes to make them new again. We could make over a hundred grand per home and all ten homes on this side of the block. All I gotta do is come up with 10%, and that's where you come in."

"How can I pull the money out of my house to do this?"

Ty smiles. His shrewd handsomeness peeking through the conversation again. "I got that all locked and loaded, lil' bro. All we gotta do is shake on it."

Alex looks his friend in the eyes. Ty's not bullshitting him at all. This is serious talk. Alex feels butterflies in his belly, but shakes Ty's hand anyway.

Tyrone looks pleased. "Time to put some hustle behind that muscle."

Chapter 37
Sue

Things with Peter have gotten spooky. He is so distant. Not wanting to leave the house. Visitors at all hours. Meetings in the office behind closed doors. Peter used to include Sue in all his business dealings. She'd sit on the small bench by the door of his office overlooking the Atlantic.

Their beach. Not exactly private being in the center of town, but close enough. The only thing separating them from the sand is the boardwalk. The lovely boardwalk. Sue couldn't help but gaze at the beauty of Avalon every chance she could.

The words of Peter and his associates would fade away into the background as she took it all in. Peter would talk about container sizes and dealing with the United Nations for his shipping business. Getting goods delivered overseas and back again with a trained efficiency that only a true professional could offer his clients. Logistics is the proper name for his business. Sue didn't really understand any of it and didn't care to. All she cared about in the beginning was living in the moment. Nowadays, Sue thinks more about the future. Where the relationship's going. Why the house became so cold.

The marriage is good, but she feels alone.

Then there's Gina and Richard with their church. Gina had been Sue's rock since they moved to town. Her only friend in the world. Their dinners are getting less frequent as the weeks go by. A man named Bob, had stopped by to offer them tickets to a fund raiser. A Harvest fest of sorts. The main act is Polyester Anarchy, Alex's friends. Apparently, they have a new song that made its way to the radio. Somehow, this Bob character was able to book them before they found fame. Sue thinks about the chance of running into Alex. It makes her nervous. She doesn't want to go.

Sue has no interest in church. It never made any difference in her life. Plus, it reminds her of growing up with her parents. The way that preacher tried to cure Alex of his allergies when he was a kid. Thinking of the snakes and how that man's eyes rolled when channeling *the power of Christ* makes her skin crawl. Jesus wouldn't have frightened a little boy like that. All that preacher wanted was for Tony to peel a few hundred dollar bills off the wad of cash in his pocket. He wasn't going to even walk in the trailer without seeing the money.

Church people are full of shit. She thinks to herself as she sits on the couch by the picture window. The waves crashing on the beach in the cool fall breeze. The warm sun on her face. The cool draft coming from the window panes. Sue reaches for a blanket to snuggle up with her thoughts.

Peter and his associate end their meeting in the office. She could hear him say good-bye and close the garage door. Peter comes into the family room looking disheveled.

"You OK, honey?" she asks.

Peter rolls his eyes. "Yes. Everything's good. What's for dinner?" "Dinner isn't for a few hours, Peter. I don't have anything planned just

yet. What would you like?"

"I would like for you to act like a wife. That's what I would like." Sue straightens up. "I'm sorry. Am I not making you happy, dear?"

"Don't give me that *dear* crap. Get off your fat ass, and make me something to eat."

"Excuse me?"

"You heard me. Get off my couch, and get your chunky ass in the kitchen!" Peter looks angry now.

Sue feels self-conscious and anxious. "Your couch?" she readjusts to calm down. "I'm sorry, you told me to stop going to the gym. You told me to stop running on the boardwalk. All you want me to do is cook and clean and never leave the house. What am I supposed to do?"

Peter's eyes changed when he grabs a fist full of her hair. "Get the fuck up, and do what I tell you, woman!" Some spit flies off his tongue and hits Sue on the cheek. The pain is familiar. The anger and fear warm her in a way she hadn't felt for years. The warmth is temporary immediately followed by salty tears and self-loathing.

What did she do to deserve this? How can she fix it? Before she has a chance to speak, her body jerks to the floor. She reaches up to scratch Peter's hands in an effort to make him let go. It's no use. Her yoga pants yank to her knees as she's drug across the carpet. Her hip getting rug burned. The words out of Peter's mouth becoming more violent. The dragging stops when he throws her into the kitchen island. She hits the cabinetry head first. After the burst of light diminishes from her eyes, Peter hoists her to her feet.

"Look at you. You're pathetic. You're only good for one thing." He rips off her underwear. Sue shrieks from the pain. She feels his penis behind her. It's hard. Sue couldn't understand what would be turning him on at this point. She resists. Begging him to stop. "Please stop! Peter, no!" He doesn't care. She hears him spit on his hand before he enters her from behind. Sue feels a tear. She screams from the pain, but Peter smashes her face into the slate countertop. The flash of light returns. Sue rests her face on the counter until he finishes. A pool of bloody saliva runs from her open mouth. She could see light reflecting from the wetness on the grey material.

When Peter finishes, he wipes himself off on the back of her shirt then leaves the room quietly. Sue falls to the ground, shaking and crying. She reaches for her backside. More blood covers her fingers. She cries herself to sleep on the kitchen floor.

Chapter 38
Gina

Gina peeks out the front window through the curtains. The Chevy across the street is still there. Been there for weeks. A guy sits in the driver's seat staring in her direction. Richard told her to stay in the house while he went to the store. Gina couldn't imagine what store. He doesn't need clothes. The fridge and pantry stocked with enough food to last for weeks. The storage closet packed with toilet paper, paper towels and dry goods. Richard turned into something of a survivalist recently. It's a bit unsettling what Avalon was doing to the both of them.

Her phones rings. It's Sue.

Gina picks up. "Hey Sue. Long time no speak." It'd been a few weeks since their last dinner together.

Sue doesn't answer right away. The sound of her sobbing into the phone makes Gina feel queasy. "Sue, is everything alright?"

"*Gina, please come get me. I need to go to the hospital.*" "Where are you? What happened?"

"*I'm at the house. Peter got rough with me. I'm having trouble getting up.*" Gina rushes over to help her friend.

***

She gets to the beach house without a moment to spare and parks on the street behind another Chevy like the one she saw watching her house earlier. *An odd coincidence.* Gina says to herself. No one's inside this car though.

Sue limps from the front door to meet Gina. Her face beaten to a pulp.

Gina leaves the car on and runs to help.

Gina puts her arm around Sue. "Oh my god! What happened?" "Hurry up. He's coming."

"Who did this, Peter?" "Yes. Please hurry."

Just as Gina puts Sue in the car. Peter rushes from the front door. "Don't you take her anywhere!"

Gina jumps in the car and locks the doors. Peter tries to open Sue's door. She shrieks with fear. A sound Gina never heard a person make before. Her blood boils.

"Open this god damned door now!" "Peter no! What did you do?"

"She told you I did this? You lying bitch. Open this door!" The door wouldn't open for him. He punches the glass until his knuckles bleed.

"Gina, get out of here now!" Cries Sue.

Gina speeds off in her Mini. Peter chases them for a block before stopping. Gina could see him make a call on his phone in the rearview.

There's a call on her phone now. It's Richard. Sue sees her pick it up. "No, Gina, please. Don't answer it."

Gina ignores her. "Richard. What's going on? Sue's hurt."

Richard growls through the phone. His voice loud enough that Sue could hear too. *"Turn that car around now! My father will not tolerate this from either of you."*

"Tolerate what? Sue needs a doctor, Richard. It's bad."

"Nothing is bad. That piece of ungrateful trash needs to go back to my father's house at once."

"No. Please don't take me back there." Begs Sue.

"Richard, she can't stay there. She can hardly walk and her eye is swollen shut.

"She did that to herself. Do you understand me?"

"Of course she didn't do this to herself. What's wrong with you?"

"If you take her to that hospital, I will meet you there and make sure neither of you step inside. You remember that night on the beach, right? What I did to protect you? I'll do it again, you know. For my dad, I'll do anything."

Gina looks like she saw a ghost. She could hear Richard rambling on with more threats as she hit the *end call* button.

"Sue, we can't go to Avalon Hospital. Anywhere else you can think of?"

"Take me back to PA. Punch Chestnut Hill Hospital into your GPS. They won't find us there." Sue begins to cry. "I'm so scared. I don't know who to call for help."

Gina does. She opens her purse and takes out Bob's card.

***

They make it back to Philly in record time. Bob tries talking Gina into hiding out at his place on the other side of Avalon. She declines the offer. After recalling all the gory details of her day with Bob, she passes the phone to Sue to fill in the gaps.

In the hospital, Gina holds Sue's hand while the doctor examines her. He tests her with a rape kit to confirm things on his end. Gina can tell he believes every word of the story, but he still has to follow protocol for things like this. The doctor gives Sue a sedative to help her sleep. A policeman meets Gina to get the story. He swabs blood from the passenger's side window and takes something from the rape kit for his evidence.

When the policeman asks Gina where she's from, Gina realizes she has no home. Her apartment in Williamsport is long gone. She lost touch with Jamie after graduation. The house in Avalon belongs to the Zilla family and she hadn't seen her father or mother for a couple years. Sue currently being her only friend or family in the world. The cop goes easy on her, but asks Gina to call once they get settled in wherever they end up. Gina sheepishly agrees.

***

Gina wakes up in a chair next to Sue's hospital bed in the morning. Gina's surprised to see Julie at her bedside. Their conversation wakes her up.

The two of them lock eyes. Julie looks sympathetic. "Oh, hello. We were trying not to wake you."

Gina straightens up in the chair. "Fancy meeting you here all decked out in scrubs."

"Well, we did graduate from the Nursing program together. Looks like you took another path, huh?"

"Maybe I did." Gina's blood boils again. She could feel Sue's look. "Gina, Julie's going home soon to bring us back a bag of clothes from her and Diane."

"Why do we need her help? We can just go to Diane's house ourselves."

Julie cuts her off. "Considering the part you've played in this current situation, I don't think it's a good idea for you to pop up wherever you please in the Walker family or Ambler anymore."

Gina wants to strangle Julie with Sue's IV tube. "I'll pop up wherever I please, bitch."

"Ok, that's enough. I'll get you both some clothes and toiletries and that's it." Julie stands up to leave.

Sue pleads with her. "Julie, please. Call Diane again. We need to stay at her house."

"Oh no, you don't. I don't want either one of you bringing the Zilla's back into our lives again. You need to find someplace else to go."

"Then where do you suggest we go?" asks Gina before Julie could duck out.

"You both have fathers. Maybe try one of them."

Gina and Sue fall back in their respective places in unison. Both acknowledging the truth. Neither wanting to deal with it.

***

car.

Bob agrees to drive up that night to meet them before they leave town. They head to a diner outside Ambler to wait.

Julie shows up first with the bags. Sue waits inside while Gina packs the Julie looks like her usual smug, hound dog self. Pregnant and miserable.

Gina imagines her drooping even more after having the baby. She hopes Julie will age terribly. That Alex would leave her one day for a much younger prettier version of herself. That would be poetic.

They meet at Julie's car. A little hatchback SUV. Something that matches her working-class ass. Julie opens the hatch and points to the bags. "Get your shit, and get the fuck out of our lives."

Gina grabs the bags aggressively. "Hope you're happy with my sloppy seconds."

"Oh, I'm happy alright and so's Alex. You know what, I bet at this point, he's totally forgotten about you."

227

"Huh." Gina smirks. "Yeah right. I was the best he ever had and you know it."

"Yeah. Strippers are good at that."

"You wish you had a body like this. Good luck with your saggy tits and row homes."

"Oh, I don't need your hollow wishes. I'm pretty sure Alex and I could live in poverty and still be happier than you could ever imagine."

Gina rolls her eyes. "Yeah, you're right. Poverty is probably the best someone like you could ever hope for."

Julie closes the hatch and gets in her car to pull away. Gina feeling satisfied about getting the last word puts the bags in her Mini. She hears Julie's SUV humming behind her. It makes her hair stand on end.

Julie rolls down the window. "Good luck hiding from Dickzilla and his psycho daddy out in the woods. I gave you some sweaters to bundle up. It's going to be cold out there."

"Not as cold as it is in your bedroom." Gina fires back.

"Nah, my bedroom's nice and warm. I wake up every morning next to a guy that loves me with all his heart, and believe me. I give him everything his heart desires." Julie winks at Gina when she finishes her sentence. Gina feels rage. Julie closes the window and drives off.

Gina could see Sue watching her from inside. Gina grinds her teeth as she loads the bags in car.

After what seems like a dozen cups of coffee later, Bob shows up at the diner. He sits down with them as cheerful and musty as ever. Gina nuzzles in next to Sue to give him room on the other side of the booth to talk.

"Well, hello to you both." He says solemnly before taking a seat. "Are both of you well enough to have a serious talk? I can make a call for additional medical attention if necessary?" Bob's tone is completely different. He sounds like a battlefield medic. Gina could imagine him storming Hamburger Hill with other soldiers in Vietnam. He's about the right age for that.

Sue speaks up. "I just got out of the hospital." She takes a bottle of pills from her pocket and shakes them. "Got all I need right here."

Bob looks disappointed. "Those are good for right now, OK, but try to keep a level head for me. What we're going to talk about next will sting a little."

Gina takes over. "I don't know how much either of us can endure after what happened yesterday."

Bob taps on the table with his fingertips for a second before speaking. "Have either of you ever watched the show, 'The Sopranos'?"

Gina sneers. "Yes, we've both seen it. What's your point?"

Bob continues. "Imagine if you will, that instead of Tony Soprano being in the Carting business, he actually shipped stolen goods. And instead of having two children, he only had one."

Gina doesn't believe it. "You're not telling us that Peter Zilla is a real-life Tony Soprano, right?"

"Not exactly, but what I need you to understand is that Peter and Richard Zilla are currently on their way here to find you both."

Gina's heart stops. She feels like a hunted animal. "How would they know where we are?"

Bob taps on the table again. "Richard called the car company that provides the Mini's onboard GPS and located your vehicle. He currently has your exact location."

Gina looks skeptical. "How could you know something like that?" "Think back to our talk at your place, OK. Remember how I mentioned that we all had mutual friends? Well, I have other friends who have been very interested in the activities of Peter and Richard for some time now, and these are serious people. The kind you want on your side in a fight, if you know what I mean?"

Sue adds things up in her head. "Have you been watching us?"

"No, not me specifically, but friends of mine could have been." Bob looks out the window. Gina does too. She notices a car eerily similar to one of the Chevy's from back in Avalon. "And if you look outside, you may ask yourself if we're being watched right now. If you think the answer to that question's yes, then you may be on to something."

Gina's jaw drops. "We're being investigated?"

"Maybe. Maybe not, OK." Bob lightens his tone. "What you need to understand is that a chain of events occurred over the summer, which led you here today. These events began the very first night you and Richard went to Philadelphia with Tony Mangle."

The breath leaves Sue's chest. "Why would you mention his name?" She turns to Gina. "What's this man talking about?"

Bob cuts them off. "There's plenty of time for that later. The question I have for you both can be answered one of a few different ways." Bob spreads his hands across the table like he's dealing a set of cards. Gina's reminded of a poster in the SBD frat house of the Grim Reaper asking the viewer to pick his or her fate.

"One." He begins. "You go back to the Zillas and roll the dice. Two. You can make your way to central Pennsylvania, and hope they don't find you there."

Gina thinks about how Bob could've known they were making a break for the mountains. Is her phone tapped? Is someone at the hospital listening to them? So many questions. So much fear.

Bob continues. "Or three. You can leave the Mini here and come with me under the protection of the United States Government."

Gina squirms in her seat. "The government? I thought you were a preacher at a goofy non-profit in the city? You can't protect us. Can you?" She looks at Sue for guidance. Sue sits still like stone.

"Gina, after Richard's interaction with Tony Mangle you two became part of a network of people that do very interesting things for this country. The Zilla's have disrupted that flow of *interesting things* and now we're all sort of playing catch up to fix their involvement."

"What are you offering?" asks Sue.

"I'm offering a chance at a fresh start for both of you. In a place far from the Zilla's reach."

"Where would you take us?" Gina could feel Sue squeeze her hand. "That's not important right now. What is important is getting a sworn

statement from both of you on Peter and Richard Zilla. What happened that night on the 61st Street beach and anything else that you can provide to put both of them behind bars for life."

Gina squeezes Sue's hand this time.

Bob asks one final question. "Do you want my protection?"

Chapter 39
Joseph

Pearl suggested Joseph take a trip once he began feeling better. The fumes from the exterminator at the office made him sick for weeks. The guy with the Ghostbuster's backpack said there wasn't supposed to be any harmful side effects for people. Maybe the concoction of drugs from the doctors lowered his immune system enough to make him susceptible to things that people wouldn't normally be bothered by.

During their talks at the office, he and Pearl became friends. They talked a lot about her home country back in Vietnam. The ways of her people. The beauty of her country. Joseph really wanted to take her and Robert along for the trip once he could get strong enough to go. The feeling of pins and needles had spread throughout his lower body and into his junk. Joseph felt a surge of hope finally when he was able to willingly get *it* up. His dad joked about Joseph giving himself *the stranger* as many a great man before tried and failed.

All joking aside, Joseph is very happy these days. Things are looking up for him indeed. The money has smoothed things over nicely. He fixed up the house and gave it to Robert and Pearl. He thought it was in poor taste because of what happened to Tony, but Robert asked for it. Once he heard Joseph was going to sell it and start over, Robert asked to buy it. He thought if there was ever a haunted house to live in, it would be one with the spirit of his father. Joseph thought it was a little sickening, but Robert's not the usual teenager. He's an old soul trapped in a young man's body and Pearl's practically an alien. Her rational is strikingly logical at times. Very far removed from someone who makes decisions based on emotion. The two of them together actually make sense.

Pearl being 20, she's a bit older than Joseph's adopted younger brother, but she's also young at heart. She puts thoughtful little notes in Robert's lunch bag. She cuts his sandwiches into heart shapes. She waits on him hand and foot. She kinda worships the ground Robert walks on. Joseph is jealous in a way. He thinks the idea of a mail-order bride is way too much for the people in town to handle. Joseph has heard them joking about Robert while he shops at the corner store.

Joseph became almost invisible once he sat in the wheelchair. People subconsciously talk about his family right in front of him. Joseph digs it. Gives him a better sense of what people are really like behind closed doors. Joseph decided after over a year in the chair that people aren't good nor evil by nature. Some are just more screwed up than others. Being evil is an environmental response to negativity. Being good is a path you follow after seeing the beauty of life. People aren't one or the other. They just experience different levels of comprehension of their current situation. It's like saying a person from Star Wars can only join the Dark Side or practice Force magic. There has to be a Grey area somewhere between. That's where most of humanity exists. Joseph concludes.

Joseph wheels to the shop from his new place at the top of Church. He snatched up one of Ty's smaller Victorians for sale. Joseph added an elevator, and updated the place. It's more than half his money, but the house is paid for. His dad called him nuts when he gave the old place to Robert and Pearl as a wedding gift for a dollar. It makes him happy to see Robert smile.

The wedding was on November 1st a few weeks back. They went to Mexico for a 10-day Honeymoon. Something about the Day of the Dead appeals to the both of them. They toured the Mayan temples while there. She brought back painted ceramic skulls to decorate her desk at the shop. All she talked about since they got back has been Mexican history and the crazy shit they used to do to people in ancient times. Like using human heads for soccer games and stuff. If soccer was even a thing back then.

Pearl loves the macabre. American horror movies are her passion. She and Robert watch George Romero movies all the time. All the blood and guts give Joseph nightmares about digging ditches. He can't hack it over their place around Halloween. Robert kinda gave Joseph the creeps to begin with.

Add some Zombie make up and the thought of Robert and Pearl having rough sex in costume, and Joseph's tapping out.

On the way to the shop, Joseph rolls down the uneven sidewalks of Ambler. Thinking of Vietnam. How close he is to walking again. He could remember the feeling of his legs falling asleep when he was young. When he got up and tried to walk. The feeling of pins and needles followed by the heavy dull pain of the blood rushing back to his feet.

He thinks back to his last physical therapy session with Julie at the hospital. His legs barely moving as he held on tight to the bars on either side of him. A feeling like he's walking on a planet with denser gravity. Having to sling his legs forward like raw pieces of meat. That same heavy dull pain consuming the entire lower portion of his body. Even his junk. Giving himself *a stranger* is a walk in the park compared to this. Pulling on his dick feels like he's jerking off with sandpaper when the feeling of blood rushes in. Walking with that feeling feels like he's swimming in a pool of hypodermic needles. He hates it. The feeling terrifies him, but the thought of never walking or screwing again scares him even more.

He wheels through the gravel alley to the shop door. Next to the old garages. He looks at the old doors before ringing for Pearl. He thinks of Alex and his old crew. It was their club house back in the day. He remembers Mischief Night. Uncle Scott busting them outta the car. Him and Ty running from the cops. Hiding in the old garage, smoking a bone. Those were good times. Too bad everyone had to grow up.

He rings the doorbell for Pearl. She greets him with a smile. "Hello, Joseph. Time to make the donuts again, right?" Joseph smiles back. All Pearl knew of America before she came over last year was old TV shows and commercials from the 80s. Apparently the programming overseas is literally decades behind the US.

"Sure, Pearl. Let's get to makin' those donuts." She helps him into the chair lift on the steps to the office. He thinks more about Vietnam as the chair inches up the steps.

She calls down to him from the top. "I have commercials of the old fat man in a white uniform making donuts on my phone. We can watch over coffee."

Joseph smiles at the thought of watching blurry old commercials with her. Their time together in the office makes the place seem brighter somehow. Warmer.

Chapter 40
Alex

It had been almost two months since he and Ty visited the properties on Hope Street for the first time. Joseph had offered to lend Alex the money directly, but their dad stepped in. He felt Joseph was being too reckless with his money. John said if Alex and Ty wanted to go on a "Quest in Wonderland", they'd have to do it alone.

Tyrone connected Alex with someone at Ambler Savings and Loan. Someone he used to finance his own house in West Ambler. A place he bought years ago right after he entered real estate. Close to Diane and Maria. The bank gave Alex a Home Equity Line of Credit for $200k. Ty spit his coffee out when Alex told him the good news.

"A line of credit like that is something only Walker money can buy." *Whatever that's supposed to mean.* Alex remembers thinking to himself. They bought the houses for 10 grand a piece from the city. When they were offered the other group of houses across the street, Alex accepted. So they bought the whole block. The city took care of evicting the old tenants. The older people in the neighborhood spit at Ty's feet.

They called him an Uncle Tom and spray-painted *otay buh-weet* on the side of his car. Ty said it meant sell out in street language. Alex had no idea how those words could make that jump, but he took it at face value. Ty may look like a traitor to his own community in some way, but he explained to Alex that no one could stop Gentrification from happening. So they mine as well cash in like everyone else before it's too late. Alex feels happy to go along for the ride.

The flips are scheduled to be finished in less than six months. The houses were absolute shit when they started. Ty borrowed against the properties for construction money. They ended up with a budget of 80-100k per house.

Alex could end up with 10% of all the profits on top of what he was already making to begin with. It seems too good to be true, except for the actual work and dealing with the neighborhood. Life has a way of balancing itself out like that.

Ty wanted to rip the houses all down and build 20 new ones from scratch. It would be easier except the city ordinance wouldn't allow it. The Historical Society deemed the front of the row homes to be important enough that their integrity could not be altered in any way. Ty's way around it was to rip down everything but the front walls and rebuild from the ground up. He hired excavators to dig deeper basements. Alex's dad helped him design the plumbing systems and even pitched in for some of the costs to help his boy out. The prickly old man has a heart of gold sometimes.

Once the basements were finished and the foundations built from insulated concrete block, the framing began. Ty made sure the insulation was the best. The houses would need to be weatherized to the fullest extent to make them as energy efficient as possible. He had Alex work with some engineering students at Temple to design a cheap, but robust HVAC system to impress the buyers. Alex ended up with a system that worked like a heat pump and a gas furnace. Two stages. The beauty of using a heat pump for the first stage of heat is that the cost for energy could be offset by the solar panels. He also put in a permit request to add small windmills and Tesla batteries to get the houses off the grid.

This would push them over budget normally, but Ty worked out a deal with the manufacturer where the new owners could finance the package with a leasing deal over the course of eight years. This actually lowered their construction cost because the utility companies backed the lease with lower rates on natural gas and electricity for anyone who would enter into the agreement. Alex sat in those meetings, but felt like Ty's errand boy mostly. He didn't understand how Ty could sit in a room with all those stuffy old people, and talk them into that sort of thing. Alex had no idea what the hell a Microgrid is or even how to describe it. The classes he took at Franklin Tech glazed over things like that.

What he really learned about at school was the impact of refrigerants on the environment and how energy efficient units could save people money. This Microgrid stuff is on another wavelength. When they walked out of that meeting, Ty told Alex if all went well, they'd be having dinner with the Mayor by next summer. Alex doesn't understand what was going on around him, but he likes Ty and trusts his judgment.

It would be another couple months yet before the houses would be finished. Ty wants to get the places buttoned up before it gets much colder. With Thanksgiving coming up next week, and the holidays in December, they'd be losing daylight and workdays quickly.

Alex drives his work truck to one of the houses to check if his delivery arrived. One of the HVAC measures includes bringing in outside air to the house. The weatherization of these houses makes them extremely tight in a construction sense. Barely any air moving in or out, which means mold can grow from all the added humidity due to cooking and showers. Usually houses are drafty, and don't have this issue. When houses are too tightly constructed, you have to mechanically bring in fresh air from the outside. Alex found a unit that could both bring it in while exhausting some of the stale air from the house at the same time. The first of the units is supposed to be waiting for him inside. He needs to install the thing and get it up and running before he can buy the other 19. Ty wants to get one house going before they rush through the rest to finish by the spring.

Alex parks out front of 119 Hope Street. A unit at the end of the row. They work from left to right. It reminds Alex of the order you'd deal cards in Asshole. He thinks of that night after the block party with the guys. The song plays through his speakers. He sits and listens until it's over.

...My angel's here to rip me away, I loved you since we met, Love you so much my face got wet, Our love never lasted, I knew the feeling true, Why can't everything get back to me and you...

Rick's flow gives him the chills. Too bad he couldn't be a part of their newly found fame. Even if he did have a hand in getting them there. He turns off the truck and goes inside.

He closes the door tightly, but for some reason the lock doesn't work from the inside. He wedges a board under the door knob then looks for the box in the house. Alex could hear the sawdust crunching under his boots. The smell of freshly cut wood and elbow grease fills his nose. Alex enjoys the feeling of construction sites. The endless possibilities of what they could make. The thought of what the places would look like when they're finished fill him up inside. These kind of jobs make him feel like a future in the trades isn't such a scary place after all.

After finding the box in the basement, he hears the board upstairs kick out. He ignores it. No one would bother him here. He has no issues with anyone. That paint on Ty's car was only the one time. Then he hears footsteps. Alex freezes. The footsteps get louder like they're coming down the stairs. Alex's balls enter his throat. He sees an angry man with a knife coming at him. Alex braces himself, but can't stop the crazy person from coming his way. The knife enters his abdomen like a red-hot poker from a fireplace. He screams in pain as the man pulls out the knife and rifles through his pockets taking his wallet, keys and phone.

When Alex comes to his senses, he crawls up the steps and manages to get out the front door. The man stole his truck and everything else. Alex couldn't bang on a neighbors' door because there aren't any. He looks down at his hands. Covered in blood. He feels dizzy. Where could he go? Is he going to die here? Like this? A corner store. They called them bodegas around here. There's one close by on Front Street. Alex makes his way to the sidewalk without falling over. The pain is terrible.

He leans on a railing halfway down the block. Alex couldn't see how he could walk two blocks without bleeding to death. He thinks of Julie. He thinks of his baby. He tightens up enough to keep moving. To keep sloshing down the street far enough to find help. As he reaches the corner, he can see the bodega. So close yet so far. All he wants is to go to sleep. It feels so cold outside, if he could just curl up on the ground, he might be OK. Alex takes a few more steps before lying down. He looks up at the sky. The sun sets. Tires screech. Two beautiful Puerto Rican angels with long black hair and blue eye make-up whisk him off to heaven.

***

Alex wakes up in Temple Hospital downtown. He feels woozy from the drugs. When he tries to sit up, a horrible pain shoots through his stomach. He looks over and sees Adam by his bedside. Sleeping in a chair.

"Am I dreaming?" Alex asks aloud.

Adam opens his eyes. "Hey, bud. How you felling?" "I just got stabbed. How do you think I'm feeling?"

Adam half smiles. "Back to your old self already. Glad to see you snap back to reality so quickly."

"Adam, why are you here, and why are you the only person I can see? Am I dead?"

"I'm here because your lovely girlfriend sent us all messages to come visit in case you died. I'm the only one here because everyone else is at home for Thanksgiving dinner, and no, you're not dead."

Alex trembles. "Today is Thanksgiving? That means I've been out for almost…"

"You've been in a coma for a week. Julie and your dad were here the whole time. I told them to go home to get some rest."

"You're not mad at me still? But that recording that Zilla sent you…"

"It was a fake, Alex. Zilla pieced together parts of a conversation you had with him. He recorded you for a few minutes to get enough for the sound bite."

"How do you know all this?"

"After Julie sent out the text, Gina got in touch. Apparently, there's trouble in Zillaville. She and your mother moved away to parts unknown, but Gina was able to send me a cloud invite to a folder where Zilla kept the original recording. I heard the whole thing."

"So you know it was all bullshit then?"

"Alex, I consider myself an intellectual. The fact that a troglodyte like Richard Zilla was able to convince me that my best friend is an anti-Semite still baffles me as I sit here." Adam's face drops into his hands. "Even after knowing the truth. I still feel like an idiot."

"That's because you are an idiot," says Alex with a smile.

Adam's tone becomes solemn. "Can you forgive me for leaving you that day at school? I know how many people let you down throughout your life. I'm sorry it took a near death experience to bring us back together, but I'd love us to work this out."

"Is this a proposal?"

"No, but Jesse and Chad are officially a thing." "Get out! No way."

"Yes way. Rick and I caught them doing the nasty in the back of his Rape Van late one night when we were all shacked up in a cheap motel in Jersey.

The place only had one room left with two double beds. Guess they wanted more privacy. Only they didn't count on Rick sleeping with one eye open."

Alex laughs. Jesse pretended to be such a homophobe. "We should write another song about this. Those guys are too much."

Adam's tone changes again. "Speaking of songs. Have you heard it?"

"I have. My dad got satellite radio in all the trucks. The song's on Alt Nation all the time. You and Rick sound great on the truck's system."

"Glad you found time to listen. Did it make you pissed when you heard it?"

"At first maybe. Then I stopped giving a shit."

"I'd like for you to give a shit again. There might be money in it for you." "What money? You signed that contract after I got thrown out of the band."

"Actually, you were never thrown out. Not officially anyway. My mother and I had the contract drawn up with the record company before graduation. Inside is verbiage on how you and I would split the song rights for new music."

"You did what?" Alex tries to process the information before Adam has a chance to speak again. "You mean?"

Adam pulls a check from his pocket and hands it to Alex. Alex takes it to look at the ink. $275,000. "Holy shit, really!"

"Yup. They're calling us a one hit wonder. I don't care about the label or the fame. I miss our old act. They turned us into something we're not."

Alex looks up from the ink on the check. "And what's that?"

"An Emo band." Alex could see Adam tremble with terror. Adam hates Emo bands. The fact that his music played on Alt Nation with all the winy teenage rockers pissed him off royally. Alex laughs.

"Well, isn't it ironic?"

Adam reaches out to put his hand on Alex's arm. Alex could see his lip quivering through his crooked smile. "Don't cha think?"

***

Julie and his dad brought Alex enough leftovers to make a Gobbler sandwich. It consists of turkey, gravy, stuffing and cranberry sauce on a long hoagie roll. Alex looks at his sandwich for a moment before ravenously digging in.

He could see Julie's face as he eats. She looks radiant. The baby would be here in a few weeks. Alex needs to get his strength back to if he's going to be a daddy soon.

The doctor walks in to make his daily rounds. Alex's dad speaks up. "Hey

239

Doc. Can I get my son out of here today or what?"

The doctor responds thoughtfully. "Your son is doing quite well. He should be ready to leave tomorrow."

Alex perks up. "Tomorrow?" He says with a mouthful.

Julie wipes gravy from his chest. "Come on, bud. You're making a mess. I'm not interested in watching one of my colleagues give you a sponge bath again." She smiles and winks. "That's my job."

John cringes. "Ewe. Get a room."

They look at him funny. "This is my room, dad." Alex says plainly. Alex's dad looks at him with a slight touch of embarrassment. "Oh yeah. That's right."

Alex swallows the last bite of his sandwich. "Hey doctor. When can I go back to work? My partner and I have houses that need to be finished by the spring."

"I'd stay out of work for at least 6–8 weeks. You need to let those stitches heal. Any heavy lifting could pop the ones inside and make a mess of all my hard work. You're young, and strong. By the end of January, you should be as good as new."

"January? That'll blow our schedule. I can't wait until January."

"Doctor could you leave us for a minute?" asks John. The doctor makes a graceful exit to see other patients. Alex's dad gives him a serious look. "You are not to go back to Kensington. At all."

"Dad, you can't do this? It's my business."

"It's not your business, it's Ty's. You've done your part. You fronted him the cash to buy the places and helped him with the HVAC and plumbing. Now it's time to bow out."

"I can't bow out now. We have the other side of the block to start in the next couple weeks. I have to be there for Ty."

Julie cleans up the mess from Alex's sandwich, and makes her version of a graceful exit. "I'll be back. Fight nice you two."

Alex's dad continues. "No, you don't. Robert and I can finish your work. You don't have to go back there ever again, son." "But dad, I want to."

"Why would you want to? That place almost killed you. Now you want to go back?"

"Yes, please. It's important to me. I feel like I left a piece of myself there that I need to get back."

"Yeah Alex, it's called your DNA, and it spilled all over the neighborhood. You're not going back, and that's final."

"You can't stop me. It's my life."

"Oh, yes I can. You have a child on the way. Your wife needs you home with the baby."

"Yes, and I need the money to pay for the new baby."

"No, you don't. You just got 275 grand from your buddy, and you have all the money coming back from Ty when the houses are sold. You and Julie could stay home for the next two years, and you'd still be fine."

Alex thinks about taking a break. It could give him a chance to help Adam write another song or maybe he could begin creating the graphic novel he always wanted to do. *It's not such a bad idea.*

His dad takes his hand to squeeze it gently. "Please son. Stay home for a while. You need rest. We got this. Everything's gonna be fine."

Alex accepts the truth. He needs to tap out. He'll be a daddy soon.

Everything's about to change again. For the better this time.

***

The house seemed more full when they got home. Diane had Julie's baby shower planned for the Saturday after Thanksgiving. Alex asked Julie to go without him. At least, he was awake for it. She had him on a video call the entire time. Alex had to keep his new phone plugged in because it kept losing charge. The old phone was unrecoverable, but it led the cops to the attacker. Turns out he was just an addict looking for something to hock for dope. Alex's dad recovered his truck from the impound lot a few days after the guy was caught. The addict couldn't sell it so he left the truck in a No Parking zone while he was walking around the streets of Kensington trying to sell the tools to people walking by. The cops began searching the area and ultimately got tipped off by an old lady who wanted to see the neighborhood cleaned up. Word travels fast in those parts of town. Most people knew the story, but barely anyone would come forward to help besides her. The cops found Alex's wallet in his house. Miraculously, the phone was working, but had been broken beyond repair. It was the least of Alex's worries.

Julie sits Alex down to watch some TV and talk baby names. They'd gone over what seemed like thousands of names over the last few months. Julie had one last name to try.

"Alex." She says patiently. "What about naming our son after you?" "No, I don't want that."

She gives a look of frustration. "Why not? Your name's so awesome." Alex looks her dead in the face. "Yes, but I am not awesome."

"Why would you say that?"

"Julie, every night when I go to bed I'm haunted by my memories. Each morning when I wake up, those same issues are there to say good morning. Whenever I look in the mirror, all I see is ugliness. I don't want my son to feel that same pain. I want him to be normal. If I name him after me then he might not have the opportunity to start fresh. Another Alex Walker could mean there's another "drooling idiot" walking around 16 years from now."

Julie definitely looks angry now. "How dare you say that about yourself. The people who did this to you are the ones that're screwed up, not you! This is the moment in your life, Alex Walker, where you need to be strong for the people who love you, and stop feeling like a sad sack of shit. You're so much more than that, and all you do is beat yourself up all the time."

She's right. The self-loathing is just miserable. The issues keep resurfacing because Alex wants them to in a sad twisted way. It's like he keeps abusing himself long after the abusers have gone away. Like he feels he deserves it because it's all he knows. Tears well up in his eyes. "I just want the kid to be happy, and have a nice childhood. If we name him Alex, there might be a curse."

"The only way that would happen is if we let it happen. Alex, we are naming this baby after his awesome daddy and that's final."

Alex concedes.

242

Chapter 41
Gina

Bob had moved Gina back to the condo in Fishtown after Richard's meltdown. She and Sue then stayed at a safe house in Maryland for most of October and November. Things changed when the Avalon cops brought Richard in for questioning. After showing him a bag of reddish sand that matched his DNA, and a gun with his prints, they could pin the murder of JC on him without much difficulty.

Richard sang like a canary once he heard there was a chance at 30 years in prison. He told the cops about the non-profit in Kensington. He explained the connection between Bob, Tony and JC. The owners of the pancake shack, also connecting the strip club back in Philly.

He blamed it all on the double dealings between the mob and the CIA. How they were bringing guns and drugs in through the non-profit then shipping them out to all the low-income neighborhoods in town with the help of the food banks.

The following day, Richard was on a trip to make a plea deal with the DA. After they took him out of the car, an off-duty police officer shot Richard in the chest from point blank range. Gina remembers the cop's face from the first drop they made in Avalon. The guy with the droopy smile. Sounds like he was worried about one idiot taking down the whole network, and decided to take one for the team.

Peter also met his untimely demise in November. Once his son was gone, Peter knew he was next. After pinning the murder of JC on Richard, Peter's henchmen made the body disappear. Two of his top guys flipped. That's when Peter locked himself in a shipping crate headed for Moscow. There's no extradition laws there, and Peter's connections with the Russian Mob in New York could get him safe passage. Only problem was that Peter had to use an electric heater powered by a car battery over the seven-day journey. Peter fell asleep with the heater on and it toppled over setting his blanket on fire. He did pack a fire extinguisher in his moving chest, but that was shipped in another container mistakenly heading for Japan. Peter tried patting out the fire with his hands, but it spread to some cardboard boxes. Peter was lucky enough to die from smoke inhalation long before the smoldering fire cooked his body inside the container.

It happened right after Gina received Julie's text about Alex. Then Bob came to get them from the safe house. With the Zilla's dead, the threat was eliminated. Sue had asked Bob about Peter's money. Her being the only living relative, she felt entitled to it. Bob was kind enough to tell Sue that she should be thankful for having the chance to live a normal life again. All the Zilla assets were property of the US government effective immediately. Sue was free to return to Ambler. Bob would have an associate drive her home.

Gina however, was a different story. She was not free to go. She truly became a prisoner of her own devices. Bob gave her the option of prison, for being an accessory to the murder of his friend JC or to become a government asset running the operations of the church for him. She chose the latter without giving it a second thought.

The old Betties at the church welcomed her back with open arms. She worked closely with Margi to learn the ropes.

Over Christmas, she gets a pic of Alex's baby boy. Alex Junior is as cute as a button.

Gina decides Julie hasn't changed much. The message that comes in after the pic reads, "Loving my life of saggy tits and row homes. Eat a dick, Gina!"

She has to laugh. Julie's a bitch to the core, but Gina has to hand it to her. As much as she hates Julie, the girl makes Alex happy, and brings the best out of him. All the guy ever wanted was a normal life. Maybe with Julie by his side, he can finally have one.

Chapter 42
Alex

Spring has sprung. Baby Alex reaches his four-month picture day. Julie wakes Alex up to get him involved in the festivities. He's been up for nights on end trying to finish the first run of his comic book. He has ten issues all mapped out with eight of them finished. The inspiration that flows through him in moments like this prevent Alex from sleeping a normal eight hours at night. In fact, Alex barely sleeps at all while he's working on his art, but for Julie and the baby, he'd gladly roll out of bed to be a daddy.

When he gets down the hall to his old room, which is now the baby's room, Julie has the four-month baby signs set up all around their son on the floor. Alex thinks he looks like a Cabbage Patch Doll laying in a pile of giant department store receipts. "Julie, did you have to mummify our son with copy paper?"

She hip checks Alex out of the way to get the shot. "Shut up. He loves the smell of fresh ink." She takes more than a few from that angle. "Now pick up our son, and get your insomniac ass in the pic."

Alex does so without thinking. He picks up baby Alex and sits him on his lap. The baby coos and touches Alex's face with his tiny soft hands. Alex knows why they had those Cabbage Patch dolls scented with powder. Baby's really smell that way in real life. His son's fingers tickle the stubble on Alex's upper lip. Julie takes the shot.

***

When Julie heads out for work a few hours later, Alex puts the baby down for a nap. He gets a call from Adam about a minute later.

"Sup bro." Alex and Adam became close again since his near fatal stabbing.

"*Alex. I have news for you.*"

"Oh yeah. What kind of news you got for me?"

"*Remember the guy that got us on the radio? He wants to meet you in person.*"

"For what? I thought he was pissed at you for not wanting to put out a second song."

Alex is kind of pissed about that too. It's painful to pass up the chance at another $275k. Adam chose to go back to his roots. Polyester Anarchy was out of the Emo game, and back in their Hasidic garb once again. They are much happier doing their own thing. The money was good, but the guys hated themselves for becoming sell outs. The Emo stuff ate away at their souls too much to put out another song, and tour with a bunch of winy teenagers again.

"*At me, yes he's still pissed, but when I mentioned you, and reminded him of the band posters, he asked to see you.*"

"Maybe I shouldn't write him any songs. I don't want anything to do with those winy Emo teenagers either."

"*It's not the music. It's your comic. He loves the Dudeman concept, and wants to hear your pitch in person. I'll text you the address. The meeting is next week.*"

Click.

Alex sits back on his new leather couch and takes a deep breath. *What the hell could happen next?* he wonders.

***

Alex shows up to the address at approximately 9:00 am on a sunny Tuesday morning in early May.

Jerry's assistant ushers him into the posh office in uptown Manhattan. Alex sits on a chair in front of Jerry's gigantic antique desk. He's impressed by the craftsmanship of the woodworking, and the inlaying of the stains to make it look so rich in color. He plots to build a replica in his garage behind the house at once.

Jerry cues up "Too Far from You" on his phone, and makes Alex listen to it with him. Alex feels a pang of rejection when thinking about all he'd missed with the guys during that time.

When it's over, Jerry speaks. "You wrote this?" Alex shrugs. "Yeah, mostly."

"Any now you write…comic books?"

Alex subconsciously clutches his portfolio close to his body. "Yes, I do." "Why don't you cut the shit, and write me another song instead?"

"I don't like Emo music all that much."

Jerry lets out a condescending breath of air. "Huh. That's the same thing Adam said." He turns to look out the window of his office into the major city that appears on the other side of the glass. "So tell me about this Dudeman character you created. What's he like?"

"Well, Dudeman's a college dropout."

"Stop right there. I thought he's a superhero?" "He is."

"How'd he get his powers again?"

"He got anal probed during an alien abduction."

Jerry smiles. "And these powers materialize every time he takes a dump?"

"No. The anal cavity's how the aliens reach the human brain with their technology. The powers materialize when Dudeman's fighting the school bully in the front yard of a frat house. The powers are triggered by an extreme response to a stressful situation."

"Go on."

"Dudeman takes an empty keg to the face during the fight and the powers come out when he feels close to death from the blow."

"What are these powers?"

"He can fly and he's super strong." "Is that it?"

"No, he also farts when he's scared, but the farts are so bad people pass out."

Jerry looks like *he* smells a fart. "Uh huh. What about his friends?"

"His girlfriend, Wegotta Gyna, is always getting trapped by evil frat boys, and she calls Dudeman to come to her rescue."

"Who are his enemies?"

"There's the Bush Wacker, who constantly masturbates in public. Another bad guy is the Party Animal who crashes the pretty girl's parties to steal their beer and drugs. Then there's Dickzilla, the evil leader of the SBD frat boys."

"SBD means 'Silent but Deadly'? There's lots of farting going on in this comic, huh?"

"No, that part's real. It's an actual fraternity in Williamsport, PA where the comic takes place. Their Greek letters are Sigma Beta Delta."

"You want to create a superhero comic based on a college dropout in Williamsport, Pennsylvania? Are you nuts?" Jerry looks like he had enough.

"Maybe a little, but I think you should consider the town itself is a main character in the story. Williamsport's a strange and magical place. It's a microcosm dropped in the middle of Appalachia. A town that can scare the shit out of you one minute then make your wildest dreams come true the next. It's like no other place on Earth."

Jerry makes a duck face while nodding his head. Seemingly processing the plot. "You brought some of these comics with you today?"

Alex holds up his portfolio. "Got 'em right here."

Jerry snaps his fingers impatiently. "Hand some over. I gotta have a look at this Dudeman story."

Alex does as he's told. Jerry flips through the comics without showing any emotion. "You made these yourself?"

"I did. Took me almost six months to finish, and about three years before that to write."

"You better do better than that for your second run." Alex does a double take. "I'm sorry, my what?"

"Your second run, kid. I'm going to sell these to Vertigo comics. Ever heard of em?"

Alex knows exactly who Vertigo comics is. They publish his favorite comic of all time, "The Boys" by Garth Ennis. "Sure I have. I've been reading their stuff since I was a little kid."

Jerry leaned back in his expensive leather chair, and casually tosses *Dudeman #1* on top of the other issues that litter his desk. Alex watches it spin in the air before flopping on top of his other babies.

"Well, now other little kids can read your stuff." "That sounds pretty awesome."

Jerry looks at Alex dumfounded for what seems like a minute before speaking again. "I'll have my assistant send over the paperwork this week. Once you sign with me, we'll have Vertigo put out an issue a month for the first run. That'll give you 10 months to write the second run, but we'll need 15 issues this time. Can you do that, kid?"

Alex agrees before speaking. "Yeah. I mean yes, I can do that."

"Good, now go back to where ever you came from, and start dreaming up some new stories." Jerry swivels his chair toward the window. All Alex could see is the top of his head, and his arm extending toward the sky. "I see a Netflix series in our future, Alex Walker."

Alex feels his balls back in his throat again. He'd better get back to the land of Dysfunction to work on some new material fast. 10 months is suddenly right around the corner.

***

Julie's dad and girlfriend drive down from Jersey for the week to help watch the baby while Julie and Alex work. Alex tries to convince Julie to quit. They have some money saved up, but Julie wants to work hard now while they're young to save enough money so they won't have to bust their humps when they're old. Alex understands and keeps working himself.

Alex rides to Kensington with his dad to meet Ty. Today's the big day. Alex hasn't been to the site since the stabbing. He's dying to see the results.

They pull up to 119 Hope Street. Exactly the last place Alex had been. At first glance, the houses look very similar to the way they had when the project began. Once he and his dad get out, Alex notices the glare of the sun reflect off the new material around the doors and windows. The clean sleek look of the new capping over the double pane windows. The terracotta tiles covering the tops of the parapet walls. The newly built porches with decorative steel railings.

"Wait till you see the inside, pal." Alex's dad taps him on the shoulder to keep it moving. He could feel his dad pushing him first to offer protection. None would be necessary. The threat's long gone.

This inside of the house looks like something from a magazine. The clean look of the modern industrialized décor that attracts young professionals from all over the city gleams in the afternoon sunlight. Ty waits in the kitchen. Alex lets his hand brush over the handmade concrete countertops. The shards of recycled glass look like a kaleidoscope to him. The clean steel appliances, and the exposed ductwork in the kitchen complete his vision. It all becomes clear to Alex what they're doing here now. His enthusiasm for the project faded after the attack. Now it's back again.

Ty speaks, "So what do ya think?"

Alex looks around thoughtfully. "I think it's beautiful." "You know what

249

I think is beautiful?"

"What's that?"

"I got the last one sold this morning." "No, you didn't!" says Alex excitedly.

His dad pats his shoulder again. "He sure did, bud. Ty did it."

Ty leans in to put a hand on both of their shoulders to complete the circle. "No, John. We did this. Team Walker."

Alex likes the sound of that. Team Walker. Has a nice ring to it.

Chapter 43
Joseph

The flight to Ho Chi Minh, Vietnam took 32 hours. Between layovers and time in the air, Joseph's head spins when the plane lands. There's only so many hours a day a person can spend reading or playing games on their phone.

The conversations with Addie began around Christmas. Pearl had her sister on a video call, and she passed the phone to Joseph when a timer went off in the kitchen for the ham. Joseph remembers Addie smiling at him for the first time. She looked so pretty. Pearl let them talk for over an hour while she fixed dinner for the family.

Addie and Joseph both have a love of movies. Old and new. Addie saw all the Superhero movies the first night they came to the theater. Joseph told her about different sites where she could watch movies from home. Some could even be found for free if she tried hard enough, and didn't mind seeing shadows walk past the screen or people coughing and chewing throughout. She declined. Going to the movies is her favorite thing. The popcorn, getting a *soda*, and a box of thin mints. The sound effects, and the emotion that consumes you during the film. In her mind, there's no other way to watch a movie.

Over the next six months, she and Joseph talked at least twice a week. Texting pics back and forth. Talking together until one of them would fall asleep at night.

In April, Joseph agreed to take the trip. A new Batman movie's hitting the theater on the first day of summer. They both love Batman. The fact that a guy in a fancy suit could hang with others in the Justice League, who are basically gods on Earth, made him the greatest character of all time. They liked to discuss the correlations between the DC superheroes and the Greek gods of old. Superman is Zeus, Wonder Woman Athena, Aquaman Poseidon, and Batman Hades. Presiding over the slums of Gotham much like the devil in hell.

A core member of the original team, damned to a solitary life watching over the scum of the criminal underworld.

The plane lands at 2:00 PM. Joseph grabs his walking sticks inserting his hands into the loose metal bracelets at the handles. A lady next to him, helps Joseph to his feet.

Once he makes it past the terminal, he sees a lovely petite woman in a tight black body suit with a headband that looks like cat ears holding a sign that reads, "Joseph Walker, your Catwoman awaits."

Joseph takes a long look at Addie before giving her a hug. He feels butterflies in his stomach. Addie makes him feel whole again.

Chapter 44
Alex

Alex and Julie walk the baby stroller to the center of town for Ambler Music Fest. The weather on July 4th is hot and humid. When they left the house, the smell of the sewage plant at the end of Church Street was horrendous. The smell comes and goes with the direction of the wind. On clear, humid days with little wind, the smell lingers something fierce. Once they got a few blocks away, the smell dissipated.

Alex asked Polyester Anarchy to headline the festival. Adam reached out to the festival supervisor to secure the gig.

Julie and Alex reach the festival with minutes to spare. His dad waits for him by the stage. After they say hello, his dad motions to a group of people behind them.

"There's someone who wants to say hello."

Alex turns to see who it is, then spots his mother holding Maria with Diane and Ty. Sue and Alex lock eyes.

Alex's dad speaks again, "Be nice. She's been through a lot." "Yeah, so have I."

"Go easy, kid. You need to be the bigger person." "That should be easy."

"I raised you better than that. Tuck that anger away for some other time.

Walk over there and be cool. You have a reputation to uphold now."

Alex does as he's told. He thinks about the Ambler Gazette doing a front-page article about his life back in May. Talking about his upbringing, his education in the trades, and his recent success as a writer. Calling him one of the area's top young professionals. The article was flattering, but makes Alex cry when he reads it. A bittersweet tribute to a highly dysfunctional life.

Sue hands Maria back to Diane. Alex sees her readjust herself to be ready for an awkward hug. "Hello, Alex." She says abruptly.

"Hello, Mommy Dearest," says Alex sarcastically. It's a movie reference harking back to his days as a kid growing up with his mom watching old films. Alex calls her that to get a funny reaction, but it does the opposite. He sees tears in her eyes.

Sue's lip quivers before speaking. "Always quick with a joke. Just like your daddy." She wipes tears from her cheek. Alex regrets making her cry. He always wanted her love, he just never knew how to get it. Maybe things don't have to be so complicated. Maybe they could just take each other at face value.

He reaches out to give his mom a hug. "Sorry to hear about Peter, mom. I know you were happy in Avalon."

She holds him tightly for a long time before letting go. "Not really, Alex. I spent my entire adult life running from the things that scare me. Commitment. Security. Motherhood. All these things that could've helped you have the life you always wanted. I could've done those things for you, but I was too scared to sit still to be there for you."

"I do have the life I always wanted, mom. You should see that now. Being here with us today. Back in Ambler. This is your home. Be happy with the way things turned out. Now your family has you back."

Alex hears someone call his name. He turns to see Julie, talking with Heather and Jasper. They reconnected the night of the annual block party a year back. She and Jasper bought her parent's place on Southern Avenue. Just down the street from Robert and Pearl.

He sees Uncle Scott talking with his dad. Scott hadn't been back to Ambler for a couple years. Living a transient life as a professional wrestler and part time reality TV star. Alex and Julie had been watching him on the Public Access Channel, loving his new look. Scott had since dropped the "Ruthless Aggression" routine, and grew a green mullet instead. The hair reminds Alex of childhood. When Scott would dress like Captain Planet for his birthday parties. *Such a goof.* Alex hadn't seen his uncle much since the day after the Zilla fight, only having dinner once when Scott was in Williamsport for a match. Looks like Scott finally found his place in the world. Alex thinks it's good to have him back.

Julie hip checks Alex. She hands him the baby. "Someone took a dump in his pants, and it's daddy's turn to change the diapy."

Alex takes the baby instinctively. "And what's mommy going to do?" "Mommy's going to get a beer, baby! It's drinky time." She smiles and winks at Alex before disappearing into the crowd with Heather by her side.

Alex looks at the baby version of himself with a solid feeling of affection. Being a father changed Alex for good. He finally has the life he always wanted.

**

Polyester Anarchy reigns supreme over the crowd at the music fest. Adam and the guys come out in their signature garb and light up the crowd.

They open with "Too Far from You." Adam signals Alex out in the crowd to thank him for all his hard work. They couldn't have gotten this far without him.

When Adam later grabs the mic to say, "Gunter Glieben Glauten Globen," Alex feels his balls in his throat again. He goes up on stage anyway and follows through with the act for old times' sake. It goes better than last time. He feels happy to do it when all is said and done.

Adam closes the night with "So Far Away" by Stained.

Rick opens the song with a guitar solo. Adam steals the attention with the lyrics next.

Alex looks around at the faces in the crowd. These people. Their lives. How everyone intertwines. The six degrees that separate them all are also what makes their lives so full. Alex complained growing up that the suburbs lacked community. That's why he thought everyone got so messed up along the way. Now he can see the err in his ways. Now he sees his family. Alex's community doesn't exactly suffocate him these days, it feels more like a warm embrace. Alex comes to an internal conclusion. *Life is beautiful.*

**

The after party is a blast. Alex's original crew stay late night playing Asshole with Uncle Scott. Alex finds it hard to believe the game had been around since Scott was a teenager. His strategy stinks. Scott goes out last and becomes Asshole every single time. When Adam becomes President, Scott's responsible to fetch beers. When Alex is President three times in a row, he institutes the *Colonel Klink* rule, which means the Asshole has to hold a beer cap in his eye like a manacle for the whole game. Each time the cap falls, the Asshole has to drink.

After ten rounds, Scott seemed to be impervious to the effects of alcohol.

Alex calls for a Waterfall. They all chug beers. Scott chugs two.

Rick calls for flip cup. Scott plays on a team by himself and laps everyone.

They pulled out a bottle of Fireball. Scott drinks twice as much as anyone else without flinching.

After a few hours of trying to get Scott drunk, they gave up and ask him to tell stories instead. They want to hear "The Adventures of Scott." Adam hands Scott the talk stick. Julie asks Scott to tell the story about Mischief Night instead. Scott declines.

He hands the stick to Alex. "This is your story, bud. You tell it."

Chapter 45
Mischief Night

Alex and Robert cut school early on October 30th. Mischief Night in Ambler's a special occasion. He and Robert met in the bathroom on the side of the building near the woods. They count their lunch money. More than enough to buy eggs at the corner store. They waited for the Study Hall bell to ring after lunch then ran like hell once the halls cleared.

They were supposed to rendezvous with Heather and Jasper at Alex's garage after school. On the way, Robert tried to convince Alex he was going to get laid tonight by Heather at Jenny's party. Alex didn't believe it. He and Heather had only kissed. She let him put his hands up her shirt once, but not for very long. Either way, Robert told Alex they needed to stop at the old pharmacy on Butler Pike to steal some condoms just in case.

When they get to the pharmacy, the place almost looked vacant. Alex and Robert try to walk in quietly, but an ancient bell rings when the door closes behind them. The living mummy behind the counter watches them. All Alex could see was his white hair and beady red eyes over the top of the newspaper, staring lasers at them. The phone rings, he takes a prescription. They pretend to read comic books until the pharmacist disappears to the back. Robert tapped Alex. Now's their chance. They make way to the condom aisle.

Alex looks at the condom boxes cross eyed. He has no idea what to pick. "Get the blue ones," said Robert pointing at a Trojan box.

"Ok, how about this one?" Alex showed Robert his choice.

Robert took it to read the label. "Ribbed for her pleasure. Yeah, get this one."

Alex looked down the aisle for the pharmacist. Still in the back. Alex shoved the box down his pants. He and Robert turn to leave. They took a few steps toward the door. It looked like they're going to make it. Alex could see him and Heather having the night of their lives already. As they got closer to the door, the pharmacist reached his zombie like hand out and grabbed Robert.

Robert screamed. "Oh my god! Get him off me!"

Alex rushed in to hip check the pharmacist to push him away. The guy moved back to dodge Alex. He tightened his grip on Robert.

"Hand 'em over, kid."

"No problem." Alex pulled the condom box from his pants and tossed them at the guy's face. The pharmacist let go of his prisoner long enough for Alex to grab Robert by the shirt and pull him out of the store. They made a break for it.

The pharmacist put his head out the door to yell at them. "You punks better run!"

Alex and Robert waited for their friends to meet up at the garage. Like clockwork, Heather and Jasper showed up exactly 20 minutes after school ended.

"It's Mischief Night. What's the plan?" asked Jasper. "We rob Old Man Pork Chop's beer fridge," said Alex.

"Are you nuts? Old Man Pork Chop's gonna shoot us with his salt gun," said Heather.

"We want to get some beer, and drink at the fort before Jenny Harrington's party," said Robert.

"How will we get it?" asked Jasper. "I got a plan," said Alex.

Pork Chop Hill was part of local folklore. Everyone knew someone who had been in the garage, maybe got close enough to open the fridge, but none of them ever scored any actual beer. They all decided tonight was the night. They were going to storm Pork Chop Hill, and succeed where all before them had failed.

Alex hoisted on his backpack. "Let's go."

Alex and the crew ran up to Old Man Pork Chop's single story home.

They hid behind some bushes.

The house sat on top of a steep grassy knoll. The garage and driveway carved into the hill underneath the home. He sat on his front porch in a rocking chair in all his glory. Dressed in hunting gear. Armed with an air rifle. A large wooden cross hanging on the front door behind him.

Alex saw the garage door opened. On nights like this, Pork Chop left the garage door opened. Welcoming all takers. They watched Pork Chop load salt crystals into the air rifle as he rocked in the chair.

They moved closer to the garage ducking behind a large pine tree where Pork Chop couldn't see them. Heather let out a sigh of relief. Alex took out the eggs and handed Robert the empty backpack.

"Go now." Alex said in a loud whisper.

Heather and Jasper ran up and down Pork Chop Hill screaming, "Hail Satan! Hail Satan!"

Old Man Pork Chop got up to fire salt at them. He missed both shots.

As the old man reloaded, Robert made a break for the garage via army crawl to avoid being seen.

Alex ran around the far side of the house.

In the garage, Robert took off the backpack and opened the fridge. It's filled with cans of Natural Ice beer. He looked over his shoulder and frantically began filling.

On the side yard, Alex kneeled down next to the house waiting for his moment.

In the front yard, Pork Chop finished reloading. Heather and Jasper ran around for another diversion. He raised the gun and took a shot. Jasper pushed Heather out of the way and got one on the butt cheek. He yelped in pain.

Heather came to his rescue. She pulled Jasper behind a bush. Pork Chop made his way to the driveway for the others.

Back in the garage, Robert heard Jasper yell and accidentally dropped a beer can. The can fell in slow motion, and hit the ground with a foamy metallic splatter.

Robert zipped up the bag. Threw it on his shoulder. Turned to run then met the business end of the air gun. Pork Chop pointed it directly at his face. He gives Robert a menacing look. As he put his finger on the trigger to shoot Robert in the face, Alex jumped out.

Alex hit Pork Chop with a barrage of eggs. The nasty old man slipped on the eggs. The gun misfired and shot out a window next door. Robert and Alex escaped. They ran as fast as they could. Heather and Jasper followed.

Alex, Robert, Heather and Jasper walked the tracks. A freight train came by. They got out of the way. As the train passed, they threw rocks at it.

Before heading to the fort, they made a pit stop at a limestone quarry at the edge of the woods. Jasper pulled out a little leather pouch and filled it with limestone dust.

"What's that for?" asked Alex.

"We may need it for another diversion," said Jasper. Alex agreed. "Good idea."

They got to the fort while it was still daylight. They made a fire in the old air conditioner jutting out from the side of the little shack.

Alex pulled a BB gun pistol from his backpack. "Guys, check this out." "What the hell is that for?" asked Heather.

"I got it from Joe's closet." "Get rid of it." she said.

"No, we may need it." Alex shoved it in his pants.

A voice from outside yelled. "Police! Come on out!"

The kids ran from the fort in a flash. Alex forgot his bag. They got far enough away to duck and see who yelled. Alex didn't think the raspy voice sounded like a cop, but you can't take any chances when you're 14 with a backpack full of beer.

They saw someone in shaggy clothes climb into the fort and come out with the backpack.

"It's Bob the Bum," said Robert. "Who?" asked Heather.

"He's a guy that used to play football with my dad, but became homeless after a bad acid trip."

"He drank acid?" asked Jasper.

"No, he put it on a piece of paper and ate it," said Robert. Heather didn't get it. "Why would anyone do that?"

"I don't know," said Robert.

"Guys, shut up," said Alex. "He's going to the crick."

Bob took the bag to the big stream. He sat down on the shore and cracked open one of their beers. He chugged it like a champ. Crushed the can on his head and tossed it aside. He began stripping off his clothes down to his underwear.

Alex removed the gun from his pants.

Heather stopped him. "What're you doing?" "I'm gonna shoot him in the pecker," said Alex.

From the creek, they hear what sounded like a fountain. Bob cracked another beer and took a dip in the water. They could see him spitting some out like a fountain. Bob stood up in the water. He was wearing pink and black tiger print briefs.

Heather voiced her disgust. "Ewe!"

Bob heard her. "Hey you over there. You got any coke?" "What's coke?"

asked Robert.

"Dude, you got that white powder," said Alex to Jasper.

"Our diversion." Jasper said to Alex. Jasper stood up holding the bag high. "Yeah, we got some coke."

On the creek bed, Jasper held out the sack like a peace offering. He looked back at his friends for support. He got none. Bob moved closer still in his underwear.

Robert and Heather inched closer to the backpack.

Alex moved to Jasper's side with the BB gun behind his back.

Bob reached for the sack. Jasper flinched, but handed it over. Bob shook some on his hand. He snorted it.

Silence fell over them. They stood frozen as did Bob until his face turned bright red.

Bob screamed a guttural, painful, insane scream.

Jasper screamed too. From behind them, Heather screamed. Robert slung on the backpack, and pulled Heather by the hand. They ran.

Bob screamed louder. His eyes a terrible color red. His brown teeth exposed. Jasper screamed again. Alex shot Bob in the pecker. When Bob fell to the ground Alex and Jasper made a break for it.

Alex and the crew strolled to the party at sundown. They took the long way to see the progress on Park Avenue.

On the rooftops of the row homes, teenage boys strung black sheets between the chimneys. Joe and Tyrone carried cases of Campbell's soup cans from a car. They see Gabe coming down an extension ladder from one of the rooftops. They gave quick bro hugs, and handed off the soup cans. Gabe took one of the cases and went back up.

Alex saw his brother. "Yo. You guys almost ready?"

"Yeah, but you better beat feet. I'm not getting in trouble if you get caught. Uncle Scott's back in town."

Alex looked concerned. Scott's a cool uncle, but he's known to be crazy. "Where is he?"

"Last I saw he was walking around the alleys earlier looking for a fight," said Joe.

"Is he staying for a while this time?" asked Alex.

"I know he's staying at his girl's place." Joe pointed to a row home just down the street. "His car's there, but he's out."

Jasper looked around for his brother. "Hey Joe, you seen Jason yet?" asked Jasper.

"Jason was up on the roof last time I saw. Him and Gabe hung those." Joe pointed to the black sheets.

"Guys, we gotta go," said Heather impatiently as she pulled at Alex's arm.

"You better go. Shit's about to get real lil' man," yelled Joe. "That's what we're afraid of." Heather responded.

Robert shifted the bag in a way that Joe heard the *clank* of the cans. "What's in the bag, Robert?"

Robert shook with fear. "Nothin."

Joe moved in closer. "Oh, I think there's something good in the bag."

Tyrone creeped up from behind. "Oh yeah. I think we hear the *clank clank* of some cans of beer in that bag of yours."

"No, you didn't," said Robert.

"Yes, we did." Joe and Tyrone ran after Robert.

Alex took the backpack from Robert to make him run faster. The crew ran to the alley behind Southern Avenue for safety. Alex heard Joe and Ty laughing from behind. Home free.

"Guys, let's hang out in my garage until the party starts," said Heather. "Come on." She led them further into the alley. She tried to open the garage door, but it's locked. Alex took off the backpack, and knelt behind her parent's car. The rest of the kids did the same. Alex took out a beer.

"What are you doing?" asked Heather. "Cracking a beer," said Alex.

"You're crazy. We're gonna get caught."

A deep voice boomed from the darkness of the alley. "You got that shit right."

Alex gasped. Uncle Scott found them. Scott yanked the beer from Alex's hand and took a long pull. The foam dripped down his chin. In the darkness, Scott looked like Stone Cold Steve Austin.

Alex grabbed the bag and tried to run. Scott reached out a meat hook like hand to stop him. "I don't think so," said Scott confidently.

Alex could feel Scott separating him from the backpack. Alex had no choice in the matter.

Scott held the bag in one hand and Alex in the other. "This bag belongs to me now." He put Alex down gently, and patted his head. "Run along now children."

Scott walked away chugging the beer.

"That's the second time we lost the beer tonight," said Robert as he kicks a stone.

Alex wanted to think of a plan, but he couldn't. "We'll get it back somehow."

Alex and his crew moped their way to Jenny's party.

***

Alex walked into Jenny's basement with Heather on his arm. Robert and Jasper trailed behind. "Firework" by Katy Perry blares from a pill shaped speaker on the snack table. It sat among a punch bowl, cups and another large bowl filled with folded paper.

They started mingling. Alex saw Heather talking to Jenny.

Jenny turned the music down. All the kids looked. "Guys, it's game time."

Jenny picked up the bowl of paper and held it in the air. "Whatever I pick out of this bowl is what we play first."

Jenny reached her hand in and unfolded a piece of paper. She read it with a smirk. "It's Seven Minutes in Heaven with Alex and Heather!"

Alex felt butterflies in his stomach. He wasn't ready for this. Alex was excited, but always so nervous around girls. Even if that girl was Heather, the girl he married back in August. They'd kissed a bunch and got to second base, but if Robert's right, then Alex was not ready for what could happen next.

Heather walked toward Alex. She took his hand and led him to the little bedroom that used to be the garage. The other kids "Oooh" and "Ahhh" on their way by.

Jasper stood in their way looking at them with an angry face. Alex felt the tension between the two of them when it came to Heather, but right now he chose to ignore it. Robert shoved Jasper out of the way to let them by.

Heather led Alex into the room and locked the door.

They laid down on the bed and started kissing slowly. Alex feels he didn't move fast enough for her. He also felt that if he touched her too much that she'd push his hand away. He tried not to worry. *Just enjoy the moment.* He told himself. Alex's hands started to move. She let him. They moved more. She let them. Alex put his hands in new places on Heather's body. Still OK. *This could be it.* Alex said to himself. This could be his lucky night. Alex felt

263

Heather readjust to let him go further. Alex was so nervous he could hardly contain his joy. He didn't know what to do. He wanted to know, but Heather was his first real girlfriend. His first love. He was so scared to do the wrong thing. He'd been so careful not to go too far until now. Alex lost track of how long they'd been in the dark room.

A crash happened outside the room. Back at the party, there's commotion. People yelling at each other. Jenny banged on the door. "Alex, you need to come out here."

Alex and Heather put themselves back together. Heather kissed Alex. "Too bad we didn't have more time."

Heather opened the door. Jenny stood there with punch on her shirt. She looked at Alex and pointed to the snack table. "You need to do something about your step-brother."

Alex walked into the basement to see what happened. One of the kids in Alex's class held Robert back. Alex looked at what used to be the snack table then noticed Jasper lying underneath it. The punch and snacks all over him.

"What happened?" asked Alex.

Robert pointed at Jasper. "He wants to steal Heather from you."

The kid holding Robert back smiled and talked to Alex. "Dude, your step-brother gave Jasper the Jim McMahon." Referencing a notorious hit on the quarterback during a 1991 Eagles game. Alex got it, but couldn't believe Robert did it. He took his brother outside to talk.

"Robert, why'd you do that?"

"I didn't want him talking about you like that?" "What did he say?"

"He called you a dork and said Heather's too good for you?" "So you threw him into the punch table?"

"He ball tapped me first." "Why'd he do that?"

"'Cause I called him a needle dick butt fuck, and Jenny laughed at him."

The door opened. Heather and Jasper came out to talk. "Robert, Jasper has something he wants to say."

She shoved him forward. "Sorry, I ball tapped you, Robert." "And to Alex." She tapped her foot waiting.

"Sorry I talked smack."

Alex slapped his hand. "It's cool, man."

Heather looked up at a kitchen window. "Hey, isn't that your Uncle Scott?"

"Yeah, it is," said Alex.

"Wonder if he stashed the beer in his car," said Robert. "Only one way to find out." Alex led the way.

Alex and crew find Scott's old Chevy Caprice on Park Avenue. They ducked behind a car across the street. Scott and his girlfriend watched out the front door to see if anyone was causing trouble. They lit up a joint and smoked together, somewhat distracted.

Jasper wanted to get Alex's trust back. "Let me and Robert check the car. You two stay here." Alex agreed.

Jasper and Robert don't see a backpack. They climbed in the car and shut the door.

Alex waved them down. "What are you doing?"

"Creating a diversion. The backpack's inside with him. I got this." Robert said from inside the car. He checked the visor. Keys fell in his lap. Robert started the car. Alex could see Jasper panicking from inside. Robert put the car in reverse and slammed into the car behind him. He put it in forward and hit the one in front.

Scott saw this from the window and made way for the door. Robert managed to get out of the spot and sped down the street taking Jasper along for the joyride.

Scott and his girl darted from the house chasing the car down the street. Alex ran to the house. He got inside and found the backpack in the living room. Four beers left. He ran back to the street where Heather waited.

They hid.

Alex saw a car come round the corner. It was a Cop. An Ambler squad car stopped in the middle of the block. Alex heard Gabe yell from the rooftop. "Now!"

From behind the black sheets on the roof, dozens of teenagers threw cans of Campbell's soup at the squad car. Alex could see the Cop duck inside the car. The windshield cracked. The barrage stopped long enough for the Cop to get out and take cover on the other side. From behind, Joe and Tyrone leapt from a bush to throw eggs at him. They missed. The Cop pulled his gun. Joe and Ty dropped the eggs. The Cop cuffed their wrists and shoved them in the car.

Alex could hear him call it in. "Officer Tim Logan calling in. I have two perps from Park Avenue in the back of my car. There's more on the rooftops."

Alex saw lights from the top of the street. Scott's Caprice sped toward the parked squad car. The Cop jumped out of the way for cover.

Robert crashed into the back of the car. The car door swung open. He and Alex locked eyes.

"Meet at the garage!" yelled Robert as he and Jasper got out and ran for the breezeway.

The Cop tried to get up to see who exited the car but instead finds Scott running directly at him. Alone. His girl must've fallen back.

Alex tugged on Heather's sleeve. They made their way behind the parked cars toward the breezeway to follow their friends.

Scott ran up and screaming at the top of his lungs. Flexing his muscles. Raging like a professional wrestler. Alex thought he looked like Cyclops from the X-men. So angry he could shoot laser beams from his eyeballs. The Cop confronted Scott.

He pulled out a Taser. "Lay down on the ground now!"

Scott looked in the back. He saw Joe and Tyrone. "Fuck you!" Scott punched the window out with one shot. The Cop Taser's Scott, who absorbed the shock. Feeling no pain, Scott tackled him. They tussle on the ground. Alex saw Joe and Ty wiggle from the broken car window and run away, still in cuffs.

Alex and Heather saw their opportunity to get away from Park Avenue.

It was dark and quiet in the old garage behind Alex's house. It was late night. Alex and Heather found Robert and Jasper unharmed. Robert got up to give him a hug. Alex showed him the backpack.

"We did it." Alex rubbed Robert's messy head.

Robert opened it. "Only four left? I took almost twenty from Pork Chop's beer fridge."

"Thieves drank 'em all," said Jasper. Heather reached in. "One for each of us."

Everyone held their beer. Alex made a toast. "To Mischief Night." They all clinked cans, popped them open and took a swill of the warm beers. Then promptly spit out every drop.

"Ewe!" said Heather. "That's nasty," added Jasper.

"Natural Ice sucks!" exclaimed Robert.

Alex tossed his aside. "Come on, guys. Let's do something else."

***

Alex and crew ran around Mattison Avenue far away from Park.

They tossed rolls of toilet paper back and forth. Alex sent one to the trees.

Jasper and Heather tossed some over porches.

Robert sprayed silly string all over parked cars.

They had a blast. For the first time all night, they were kids again. Having harmless, sober fun. It's exactly what they dreamed of all day. Absolute freedom. All a kid could ever hope for.

Chapter 46
Alex

Alex readies the bags for vacation. It's the week where his grandfather invites the whole family to the shore house. The same week every August. Julie will be home from working at the NICU soon. Around the same time the kids get back from their shift as Camp Counselors at the Ambler YMCA.

A TV plays in the background. *"A group of Missionaries went missing a few days ago in Cuba. The bodies recently found washing ashore in Miami. Local authorities have named…"*

Alex Junior had grown so much over the past 16 years. He'll be driving soon, and asked Alex for a Jeep Wrangler. Just like the one Alex had in college when he toured with the band. It wasn't much of a tour that summer, but Alex likes that his son thinks of it that way. Lizzy grew into a smart young lady. Much different than Alex had been at 14. Where he had been running the streets of Ambler, she chooses to play sports and study. Lacrosse is her game of choice. Alex would stand against the stone garage wall out back, and let her shoot at him as hard and fast as she could. After developing a killer instinct on the field, she had no problem scoring goals. The kid's a natural.

Alex places the bags by the front door. As he sets them down, he sees a strange old man walk on his porch. He waves to Alex.

Alex opens the door and steps out to talk. "Hello, can I help you?"

"I'm hoping you can," says the nice man with hot breath. "My name's Bob. I'm here on behalf of an old friend of yours, Gina. I believe the two of you went to Franklin Tech together."

"Wow. Yeah. I haven't heard from Gina in over 15 years."

"More like 17, OK." Bob smiles gently. "I have something from her that she wanted me to deliver to you in case of an emergency."

"Is she alright?"

"I'm not at liberty to say, but she wanted you to have this." Bob hands Alex the letter. He walks to the edge of Alex's porch and takes in a big breath of air. "Do I detect a tinge of something in the air today?" asks Bob.

Alex opens the envelope. Half listening. "Yeah, that's the sewage plant. It does that when the wind stops blowing on hot days…" Alex looks at the letter. Not understanding the situation.

Bob looks at him sympathetically. "Take care Alex Walker. Hopefully, we won't have to bump into each other like this again."

Alex looks up more confused than ever. "Sure, buddy. You too."

Alex goes back inside. He makes his way to the kitchen island where Julie pays the bills. He kicks a stool out and takes a seat. Alex holds the letter from Gina in both hands. Before reading, he looks around the room trying to make sense of his current situation. He can't, so he reads.

My Dear Alex,

If you're reading this, a series of unfortunate events has led my associate, Bob to your home to deliver this letter.

The last 17 years has been interesting to say the least. After we parted ways, I went down a dark path with someone I didn't love. I traveled that path in a fog of despair. I left you for him in an attempt to fill a void in my soul. One that could never be filled with booze or drugs, yet I tried over and over again to do so. After his death, fate had intervened in my life. I took on a job as a Missionary that led to an exciting career path, but as life would have it, that exciting career path led me to another dark place.

I tried for years to contact you to apologize for what I did. I'd give everything back to be in your arms again. Listening to No Doubt. Eating popcorn on my couch, and watching movies with you. All the parties, drugs, and booze in the world couldn't compare to the happiness I felt in those days with you. Unfortunately, I was too blind to see it.

I wish nothing, but the best for you, Julie and your children. Even though we never spoke over the years, I was never too far from loving you still. In reality, I never stopped. You and your family deserve all the happiness and good fortune you've earned, and you did that. No one else. I know you didn't like yourself much, Alex. I really hope you've changed that. If you haven't fixed that part of your heart, please do it now. Don't be like me. Don't wait for a stranger named Bob to deliver your last words to someone you loved. Someone you were too much of a coward to approach on your own. Tell everyone how much you love them and do it today. Do it for me. It's my dying wish.

There may currently be a quiet viewing being held in a concrete building somewhere in Virginia in my honor. At this viewing, there may be a tiny star carved into a wall that has no names. If this is happening, I will receive no recognition, and will not have a normal funeral. What will happen is that life will go on. People will still believe in good guys and bad guys, and the world will still spin, but I want you to know I tried to make it a better place. Each and every day after we parted ways, I understood the world a little better. I grew a little more, and I have you to thank for that. It was my sadness about leaving you that led me to create a better life. Not only for myself, for hundreds of people, maybe more, that I'll never meet.

So in my closing words, I say this to you Alex Walker, "We will not walk quietly into the night. We will not disappear without a fight." The single shred of happiness I've felt in my life. I owe to you. My Dudeman. My Moon Knight.

Love you always and forever,
~Gina